A PLU

RACE ACROSS THE SKY

Kerri Sherman

DEREK SHERMAN works in advertising as a writer and Creative Director. His work has received every major industry award, and been named among the best of the last twenty-five years by *Archive Magazine*. He is a cofounder of the Chicago Awesome Foundation, a charity dedicated to awarding micro-grants. He lives in Chicago with his wife and children. This is his first novel.

Race Across the Sky

A NOVEL

Derek Sherman

A PLUME BOOK

PLUME
Published by the Penguin Group
Penguin Group (USA) Inc., 375 Hudson Street,
New York, New York 10014, USA

USA | Canada | UK | Ireland | Australia
New Zealand | India | South Africa | China
Penguin Books Ltd, Registered Offices: 80 Strand, London WC2R 0RL, England
For more information about the Penguin Group visit penguin.com

First published by Plume, a member of Penguin Group (USA) Inc., 2013

REGISTERED TRADEMARK—MARCA REGISTRADA

LIBRARY OF CONGRESS CATALOGING-IN-PUBLICATION DATA
Sherman, Derek.
Race across the sky : a novel / Derek Sherman.
pages cm
ISBN 978-0-452-29906-1 (pbk.)
1. Brothers—Fiction. 2. Marathon running—Fiction. 3. Biotechnology—Experiments—Fiction. I. Title.
PS3619.H4647R33 2013
813'.6—dc23 2012045790

Printed in the United States of America
10 9 8 7 6 5 4 3 2 1

Set in ITC Galliard

PUBLISHER'S NOTE
This is a work of fiction. Names, characters, places, and incidents either are the product of the author's imagination or are used fictitiously, and any resemblance to actual persons, living or dead, businesses, companies, events, or locales is entirely coincidental.

For Noah and Sage. You are the inspiration for this book.
Each of you appeared and brought a part of this story with you.
Thank you both very much.

If we don't play God, who will?

—James Watson, after discovering DNA

PART ONE

Hymns for the Earth

1

They ran together across the trails toward Twin Lakes, so close on the narrow path that their slick shoulders touched.

June stayed just beside him, thin, tiny, her straw-colored hair tied back, her blue shirtsleeves rolled up, her arms damp. The feel of her skin kept him awake, alert, possibly even alive. Fourteen hours ago, Caleb Oberest had started running these trails outside Leadville, Colorado, at four in the morning. He still had not stopped.

The Leadville 100 ultramarathon course had taken him fifty miles along alternating patches of sage and gold forest, over open chestnut earth, and up twelve thousand feet of narrow, tawny trails skitting between the bluestem and switchgrass. He had run over Hope Pass into the small mountain town of Winfield, and now he was making his way back.

Two hundred other runners were scattered along the course behind him. Just a few hours earlier, there had been three times as many; Caleb knew they would thin down to half that before long. He was sixty-seven miles into the race, the point where bodies began to break apart, when runners collapsed along the trails, when the goal shifted from distance and time, to survival.

Caleb's tall forty-three-year-old body and narrow face had long since been depleted of all fat. His thinning brown hair dangled just below his ears. When he ran, a straight line could be traced from the top of his head to the balls of his feet. His arms pumped as pistons. His long, reedy legs leapt over roots and rocks. Only his eyes moved freely, drifting upward, sweeping the ground in front of him for stones and tree roots. They focused on nothing. Circles. Blurs.

Mack had instructed him to finish in the top ten. To accomplish this, Caleb would need to reach the finish banner in the old mining town of Leadville in under nineteen hours. Last year he had finished in twenty, placing thirteenth. The year before that, he had collapsed in agony on the eighty-first mile, two of his abdominal muscles torn and a small bone in his heel broken. But none of that mattered now. The outcome, Caleb knew, had nothing to do with the past, or the banking crisis, or the value of the dollar. It was dependent only on his own focus and desire. They called it the Race Across the Sky, but Caleb understood it was just the opposite, a race into himself.

The course markers led diagonally down the mountain along a trail filled with different sized stones. Caleb's left leg was a good eight inches above his right. It would be simple to tear a knee, or fracture a hip. In the distance the sky seemed to signal the end of day.

Beside him he felt June, heard her breathing, and her soft encouragements. Of course she didn't need to speak. Having her there was enough.

June was nowhere near as strong a runner. She was solid for seventy miles give or take, but after that her body broke down quickly. She had volunteered to pace him these last thirty miles. Caleb had not approved; it raised too bright a flag. Mack did not allow romantic relationships of any kind in the Happy Trails Running Club. They were, he taught, defocusing. During Caleb's ten years in the Happy Trails house, he had seen Mack expel many members who breached this protocol. And he had agreed completely.

Caleb had come to Happy Trails seeking pure isolation, focus on himself, and forward motion, and for eleven years he had lived in this exact state. He had never been afraid of mudslides, bears on the trails, having to make it nine more miles with a fractured ankle, or suffering weeks of pneumonia without antibiotics, even though all of these things had happened to him. But now he felt a desperate fear of losing something he could not bear to.

During these two months since June had moved in, Caleb had found himself watching for her in the house, in town, on the trails during their daily eight-hour run; it seemed to be out of his control. For a month now, he had been meeting her secretly in the fields around the mountains, and there they would consume each other with a veracity which overwhelmed him. If Mack had understood just how deep they had already gone, he would have enacted drastic measures. He would expel June from the house. And Caleb was no longer sure that he could continue without her. The thought of breathing this same air without her weakened him more than any seventy-degree ascent. The burn of his feelings had to be pushed deep inside, where they would be invisible to anyone else. And so to move now with June through these darkening trails was a bliss that overwhelmed the agonies ripping through his bones and lungs.

The two of them ran down into Twin Lakes. A few townspeople stood there watching, some clapping for them, and then the paved street led back into the wilderness. A copse of branches extended over the path ahead like witches' fingers, trying to pull them into the woods. Caleb raised his free hand over his eyes and broke through into an open field, which spread to the granite peaks of La Plata and Elbert ahead. He pulled away from June and ran free under the vast sky, lost in the raw energy of the world.

The physics of running one hundred miles was simple: for the first thirty miles, his body burned protein and glycogen. The protein he could restore with food at the aid stations that appeared every seven miles. Glycogen was another matter. When the body exhausts the liver's store, it assumes that whatever it is running from has either gone away or is about to kill it, and stops production. If pushed forward beyond this point, the body begins digesting itself. This had begun happening to Caleb seven hours ago.

His feet had swollen a half size; they pushed against the thin fabric of his running shoes. A tight knot of compressed heat had begun burning in the ball of his left foot. Ahead the sun dipped behind a distant peak, like a lamp being shut off, and the bruise-colored sky lowered behind the mountains. Caleb tensed. Nights were his weakness. He suffered hallucinations. Strange deliriums would descend; anything might happen.

The course turned toward a creek. By its bank he recognized Lynette Clemons, a music teacher who had been last year's women's champion.

"Nice job," she smiled. "Awesome day."

But Caleb did not speak during runs. For him, talking ruined the inner exploration that he had thought everyone did this for: the digging to the bottom, the scraping of the deepest nerves. Instead, he plunged into the creek. The cold pierced his body to his waist, took away his breath. He felt June's fingers brush his, slip away, and finally grasp his hand, a nearly symphonic energy flow between them, his depleted body recharging.

"Slow down," she told him. So he did.

They were nearing the next aid station. Inside these tents were coolers of food and drink, and a cluster of spouses, friends, and children of competitors, waiting nervously for their loved ones to limp inside like refugees. Caleb had no relatives here, but he had something demonstrably better: the Happy Trails Running Club.

Sixteen people who were his housemates, his partners, his team. Half of them were scattered somewhere behind him, running through the Rockies. Mack had installed the other six as pacers, waiting to run beside their housemates for twenty miles, and sacrifice their own opportunity to finish Leadville to urge them on.

On the far bank a blue tent fluttered silently. He glanced at June as he emerged from the creek, to be certain she was all right. As he did, his left foot scraped a jagged stone, and the hot ball inside it broke open. Caleb gasped. Everything spun madly. As he doubled over on the rocky ground, he felt June touch his back.

She slipped her thin arm under his shoulder and tried to

pull him toward the aid station. It did not seem like a workable solution. His body began to feel shockingly tired.

"Look," June pointed encouragingly.

Distantly he saw Rae and Kyle running out toward them from the tent. Rae was dark-skinned and stocky, her straight black hair pulled back in a tight and ever-present ponytail. She might have been of Pamlico or Sicilian descent, but Caleb had learned that her parents were prominent members of a western Long Island synagogue. She had been living in the Happy Trails house for two years when he had arrived.

June took a self-conscious step away and let Rae help him into the tent, where a twenty-eight-year-old former methamphetamine addict named Kyle stood with a kit bag. Caleb sat on the cold ground, shivering as he watched Kyle pull off his left shoe, roll his white sock down his ankle, and unwrap his Elastikon tape. Caleb chanced a look at his bare foot. His toes were permanently swollen into unrecognizable shapes, the nails black and violent. On the ball he saw a blister the size of an egg pulsing with his heartbeat.

Kyle held a razor blade between his fingers. With a grimace, he sliced the blister and pushed its sides together. Caleb cried out, his eyes rolled up to the dark sky. The stars there spun, he saw, like circus toys, pulling him into their glittering orbit, then dropping him with disregard back to the cold ground.

Kyle rubbed benzoin over the wound, wrapped his foot in fresh tape, and shook baby powder around the edges. He pushed new shoes, a half size larger, onto his feet and helped him stand.

Caleb pulled deep breaths as strands of wet brown hair

fell across his eyes. Rae handed him a cup of chicken broth, and the salt absorbed into his starving cells; the small pieces of soft carrot were gone before his tongue could taste them.

"Twenty-five more," Rae told him.

Twenty-five miles seemed impossible. An essential rhythm had been broken, was gone and could not be recaptured.

Rae turned to June. "I can pace him from here."

"I'm with him," June replied.

He hoped Rae had not caught the underlying meaning.

"Yeah? You feel good?"

"She's warm," Kyle agreed. "We can wait for Juan and Leigh. They'll both need a pace."

He leaned in and strapped a Petzl headlamp around Caleb's skull. Caleb felt its band snap tightly around his hair.

"You're awesome," Kyle nodded.

Rae looked at June. "Keep him slow, okay?"

Hobbling out of the tent, Caleb took in the situation. The neon course markers pointed a path toward Halfmoon, a steep ascent he knew well from previous years. He attempted a very slow jog. It was not too bad; June was next to him, whispering affirmations as they moved upward. Just then the sky gave up, and he was propelled into absolute darkness.

The circle of bright yellow light from the Petzl was all he could see. Even with June there, Caleb felt an isolation so immense he could not grasp it. His other senses heightened, he heard the air echoing through his lungs, animals scurrying, a metallic taste ran over his tongue. He pushed into a light run, but the course seemed against him now. At some point the orange course markers lifted off the ground and floated in the air, leaving tracers behind them. His teeth chattered violently in the mountain wind. Once he had chipped a bottom tooth on a night like this.

"Slow it down," June called from behind him.

But he couldn't. There was no way to get through the night but to try, ridiculously, to outrun it.

Some miles later the dirt trail under his feet became paved road. His bones took this poorly. The road had been closed to cars, but in the darkness the headlamps of the runners behind him appeared like headlights. He slowed to a fast walk, and June ran her hand along his thin shoulders.

"Smile with the sky," she whispered.

Caleb forced a smile onto his face. This was one of Mack's infamous techniques. Other runners joked uneasily about the Happy Trails Smile, but it created oxyendorphins, which helped push pain aside. Amazing, Caleb thought, how kinetic energy works in the world.

They approached the Fish Hatchery aid station. Under the fluttering nylon they slammed Powerade and some thick orange puree. A surprisingly large crowd had gathered here in the pitch of night, cheering anyone who made it by. He heard runners who had dropped out exchanging stories of what had broken them. What was it about night, he wondered, that compelled people to talk so much? He had prepared for agony; he had prepared for blisters and night terrors; he just had not prepared for so much jabbering.

Outside, the paved road returned again to dirt, signaling the climb up Sugarloaf. As he began to ascend inside his circle of yellow light, he remembered what he had done.

He had sent the letter.

It had been hidden beneath his mattress for a week. At

night, Caleb could feel the energy seeping up through the fibers of his futon. Just having written it, he understood, had altered him somewhat, rearranged the chemicals of his cells.

Before the start, during the distraction of the weigh-in, the crowd, and the darkness of three in the morning, Caleb had slipped briefly away, pulled the letter from his waistband, and dropped it casually into a Leadville mailbox.

Now he shivered. What events had he just set in motion? After eleven years of silence, how would Shane react? How much at risk had he just put himself of losing everything?

The idea of this blue envelope journeying to his brother carried him up the incline. He passed a runner who was clearly sleeping as he shuffled up the path. At Hagerman Pass, he felt strong and believed he could finish the final fifteen miles without walking. They passed the next aid station, but he kept running. Even though he knew June would stop to rest, he could not risk stopping. That was past him now.

In the dark the course corkscrewed downward; a vertiginous spiral appeared before him. He focused on his legs, one foot, then the other. He found the void. It seemed to be going well.

But at the turn of the trail, somewhere near ninety miles in, Caleb's legs suddenly convulsed, and before he understood what was happening he had stopped, pushing his hands into his swollen quads, willing the blood to reverse out of them, tears rolling from his eyes. He opened his mouth and began to vomit.

A tall runner caught up to him then, panting, slid around him, and continued down the course. How many more were ahead of him? Less than ten? Had he failed his promise to Mack? Time passed, he had no concept of how much. He stepped off the trail to urinate. What came out was brown and thick.

And then, next to him, he heard a different voice, softer, gentler.

"Blend with the air, Caley."

A bluebird's voice. June had not stopped back at the pass; she had been out here behind him this whole time. He had given up on her, but she had not on him. He stared up at her, amazed.

And the two of them began to run together though the dark terrain. Caleb wanted to hold her, but there was nothing left in him now except this putting of one foot in front of the other, this breathing in of air, the lifting of his legs.

The course wound down to the Tabor boat lake. The mist was stunning in the light of the half moon, swirling around their ankles, whispering toward the water. Just before eleven o'clock, they jogged on smooth pavement, passing parked cars, toward the distant lights of Leadville.

A few people stood in front of the old, solid houses, clapping. A few filmed them on phones and video cameras. A thin red neon tape, he saw, had already been broken and lay crumpled across the street. June stepped aside, applauding, and Caleb crossed under the gray finish banner, and it was done.

He fell into the arms of his housemates.

"What's my . . ." He panted, unable to force the words out. He shook his head roughly.

Hank Gutterson, a smaller, buzz-cut kid of military bearing, ruffled his hair.

"You're eighth," he laughed.

Someone pulled off his tank and handed him water. He grinned. It was incomparable, Caleb thought, being so complete. He sat on the curb, watching the next runners jog, stumble, and crawl across the line.

Juan finished nineteenth, Leigh twenty-sixth overall, eleventh among women. Alice, Kevin, and Makailah all placed in the top forty. As they had each of the previous fifteen years, the Happy Trails Running Club owned Leadville. Caleb pulled off his shoes and limped barefoot down the dark street to a parking lot. The license plates rose and waved like banners. They shouldn't be doing that, he knew. He needed fluids.

Mack was waiting for him by his dusty black Jeep, standing with his ankles crossed. The first time Caleb had ever seen him, at the Rocking Horse Tavern a decade ago, he had experienced this same sensation of running into a wall of solid energy. Mack was a small man. Black hair curled around his ears and tufts of black beard were spaced sporadically around his sunken cheeks. His face was a riverbed of wrinkles. With his tie-dye, he had the appearance of an aged roadie. His teeth, long stripped of enamel from decades of running these mountains, were the gray of tombstones. His eyes were a blue so brilliant they seemed not to belong to him at all.

"Ride with me, buddy."

Inside the Jeep, Caleb was overwhelmed by the scent of sweat and pine. The leather seat irritated his raw thighs as he pulled Band-Aids from his nipples and set them in the ashtray. His body spasmed violently. Mack handed him an old sweatshirt, and Caleb pulled the green hood tight around his head. For all of the rocks, creeks, ascents, dehydration, snakes, and hallucinations, the biggest danger he faced was right now. The total demolition of his endocrine system from the constant exertion, stress, and the chemicals in the sports drinks had left his body defenseless. Any inconsequential virus that happened to be wandering through the Colorado air would find its way in without resistance.

Mack spoke in an animated manner, waving his hands. He preferred to drive off-road, even when a highway presented itself, and so they bounced roughly between firs and black-eyed aspens, a blur of hieroglyphic eyes dancing around them.

"You know Anne Luchamp?" he asked in his nasal voice.

Caleb shook his head.

"She finished third in Women's. She'll join us next year. I didn't speak with her, but I felt her energy," Mack stated matter-of-factly. "Let's bring her to a party at the house."

Reading the waves of kinetic energy that propelled all living things was not a unique gift, but Mack possessed it as strongly as anyone Caleb had ever seen. It was how he healed them, helped them push past any barrier, physical or emotional. As a coach it made him, Caleb understood, a genius.

"I saw June pacing you there at the end," Mack turned, a wry grin across his small mouth. "She giving you some special training these days?"

Caleb tried to shake his head no, a trembling taking over his entire body.

Mack laughed and sang out, "'I bequeath myself to the dirt to grow from the grass I love.' You are bequeathed to the dirt, right Caley?"

Caleb nodded. Yes, he thought, he was bequeathed. This was the pledge he had made, all of those years ago.

When they passed Superior, Mack turned back onto the old dirt road. They drove for some time, and then he pushed the Jeep around a cluster of oaks, their long roots intermingled as the fingers of lovers, and a simple house made of planks and beams appeared in the distance. It lay just two hundred open yards from the base of South Boulder Peak. Safe, hidden from the toxic world, and plugged directly into the real one.

Mack shut the engine off and looked at him. "I got a surprise for you. It's crazy good."

"What?"

"It's a secret. I'm announcing it Sunday night. You're gonna love it. Let's get you iced."

He opened the door. Inside, a warm smell of root stew filled the open room. They climbed up creaking oak stairs to the second floor. In the bathroom was an old ceramic tub, which Mack filled with ice. Caleb felt a need to go to his room, sweep his hand under his futon on the floor, and determine if his memory of mailing the letter was a hallucination.

But Mack took his arm and led him into his bath. Ice water rose to his waist. Time revved forward violently, then stopped like a navy jet landing on a carrier, and a seizure rose through him all the way to his lungs. Caleb lost his breath and sank into the tub. Mack leaned over and held him under his arms. And then Caleb blinked, and shuddered gently, and smiled.

He had placed eighth at Leadville. At forty-three years old, after eleven years of work, he was ready to win a major ultramarathon. His next one would be the Hardrock 100, up and down thirteen peaks of the San Juan Mountains. His next months would be devoted to training for its dangers. He could have no distractions, nothing could threaten his focus.

Somewhere outside, he heard June's voice.

2

When Caleb's letter came, Shane was out selling drugs.

It was a stunning San Francisco afternoon. He could see the city behind the gleaming bay from his parking spot in Larkspur. Blue sparks fluttered between the shoreline trees like fairies, beckoning him someplace, he wasn't sure where, perhaps to drown.

Shane opened his trunk and peered down at the white cardboard boxes full of pills. Purple ones, blue ones, annular and elliptic. He balanced a stack on one knee, shut the trunk, and walked toward a flat, single-story building baking in the sun.

He carried samples of two new drugs: Epherex, for anxiety, was in high demand. Solistan, for otolyrangological infection, however, was a dismal failure. The drug was underperforming in its clinical trials, with scripts running 20 percent below estimates. His mandate from Saint Louis was to reverse this trend, this quarter.

There were four doctors in residence at Larkspur Internists. Three men and one woman; two Asian, two Caucasian. Pulling open the door, Shane went over his calculations. Male Caucasians were the most amenable, he had found, and female Asians were the toughest sell. It was telling that he had married one.

Inside, the air was accented with redwoods.

"How's the puppy, Anne?"

The receptionist's face lit up, pleased he had remembered. "Ate a box of Claritin last night. Have a seat, sweetheart, I'll get you in."

As Shane waited beside three patients to see the doctor, he studied the Solistan logo, which had been created at great expense. Some of Shane's high school friends had possessed a talent for band names; now he knew what they had done with their lives.

These names and logos were worth the cost, because they worked. Patients walked into practices asking for them. In fact, sometimes Orco would develop a drug just to fit a particularly sticky name. "Confilox" had tested so well with adolescents that the company had reformulated a failing antidepressant by one molecule and created a thirty-million-dollar-a-year brand. Drugs, names, sales: for years Shane had felt that this cycle was a thing of beauty.

Twenty minutes later, Shane followed a nurse down the hall. The air felt stuffy; germs, it seemed, might thrive. He passed examination rooms with color-coded charts on the doors. What was blue, versus red? Was his own chart colored in any specific code? Was Janelle's?

Shane possessed a round face; his eyes, the color of amber ale, were alive and welcoming. And yet their warmth was betrayed by the sly curve of his mouth, which produced an unintended air of superiority. A college girlfriend had suggested that this was simply the muscle makeup of his face, but from birth, an almost ethereal self-confidence had bloomed inside of Shane. He had never known a time when it had not been there, prodding him forth.

So it was really no surprise that life had led Shane right up to sales and introduced them with a knowing wink. After only a few years at Orco Pharmaceuticals, he had been handed the prized Bay Area territory as incentive to stay with them. He had spent the last decade driving through Marin County farmland like an Old West medicine man, stopping to display his potions. For years, he had felt content and unrepining.

But recently, his sense that all was right in the world had begun slipping. Frenzied mandates were coming from headquarters to grow scripts by 12 percent, an astonishing number. The sales reps he saw now seemed more desperate than the patients they passed in the waiting rooms. They had shifted to seamier tactics: spreading online falsities about competing medicines, hiring ghost writers to write glowing articles about ineffective drugs, and paying editors at esteemed medical journals to run them. This new breed handled their expense accounts like investment bankers, taking doctors on lavish trips. Orco raised prices accordingly, and the insurance companies did the same. This new cycle made Shane uneasy.

He found Doctor Felger at a spartan metal desk, his narrow back hunched, writing with a sharply turned left hand, the posture, Shane thought, of a schoolboy. Felger was a fifty-five-year-old Caucasian, right in the top spot in Shane's target, but he had never been easy to sell. When he looked up, his eyes were tired. Dots of black and gray stubble sprinkled his jaw in irregular patterns.

"What have you got?" he asked wearily.

"Solistan," Shane offered. "And Epherex."

"Leave the Epherex. Can't use the Solistan."

"I saw a patient out there who was holding her ears."

"Doesn't work."

"The Swedish Institute of Otolyrangological Studies said that—"

"The Swedish what?" the doctor looked up in angry disbelief.

Shane continued gently. "Doctor Felger, you write fewer scripts for Orco brands than any doctor at this practice. May I ask if there's a reason why?"

Felger's eyes filled with an expression of amazement. "How do you know that?"

Shane had purchased this data from a national chain drugstore data retailer. He smiled peaceably.

"That's very powerful information and I want to know where . . ."

"What could we do to up your participation level?"

Clenching his jaw, Felger muttered nearly silently, "We need a laptop."

Shane nodded. "Mac or PC?"

He placed his boxes of Solistan samples on the edge of the doctor's desk and walked out feeling unwell. Ahead he saw his dusty, ten-year-old Civic. It had become a joke among his friends; clearly he could have bought a new car anytime he wanted to. But there was something in Shane that clung stubbornly to the things he loved.

• • • • • • •

That afternoon, he went for a five-mile run through the Marina.

On his way home he had stopped at the corner grocery and carried back a collection of pink plastic bags filled with produce. Sautéing Chinese eggplant and garlic for Janelle, he still felt the sensation of soft earth against his falling feet.

"How's the camel's back?" she asked him as he brought their plates to the dining room table.

"Hanging by a ligament."

"The Russian Hill Starbucks," she told him, "is looking for baristas."

Over dinner they discussed his options. Pfizer and Bayer would be no different, he knew. He could take time off, she suggested. The baby weighed in on that with a sudden kick to Janelle's abdomen. She laughed loudly.

His wife was the most astonishing woman he had ever known. Her father Liu had been a mechanical engineer in Anhui when something fearful had sent him and his wife, Hua, onto a rat-filled ship over the endless ocean to restart life as American peasants. Liu had gone to work in a distant cousin's tofu plant, which he now managed. Liu and Hua had named their only child Janelle, because it sounded to them like an Americanized form of *Jinsong*—sturdy pine. And sturdy pine she proved to be. Janelle worked her way through the uncertain North Beach public school system to UCSF and joined the biotech giant Helixia just after their late-nineties surge.

Janelle possessed a beauty that could shift forms. She could exchange her sleek biotech persona for hiking shoes and a sleeping bag in the time it took to change shirts. Shane loved her as completely as he might have loved anyone. Time with her was his only real concern in life.

"We don't work like that at Helixia," Janelle said when he had explained his meeting with Dr. Felger.

"Because you guys are biotech."

"Because," she explained, pushing excess garlic away with her fork, "we're Helixia."

"Are there any more places like you?"

"Dennis knows about every pharma and biotech company here. He could tell you who the good guys are. You should see what he thinks."

Shane raised his eyes. "Will you run into him before maternity leave?"

"Sure, I can ask him. Or talk to him yourself." Janelle touched her belly and looked down frowning. "I don't think our boy's a garlic lover."

She stood up. Shane watched her move through their narrow hallway and open the front door. He felt the salt-swollen air pour in. Their narrow blue house was possessed of chocolate wood floors and rounded archways. They had kept it minimalist but were trying to brighten it for the baby. Janelle had found a cheerful cerulean for the nursery walls, which Shane had painted on a breezy Sunday. They had hung a copper wire mobile he had picked up in Berkeley above the empty crib, abstract shapes to lull anyone into slumber.

When Janelle came back in, she was staring at him.

"You got a letter."

He saw a blue envelope between her elegant fingers. Who sends letters, he wondered? Shane extended his hand and recognized the handwriting instantly: Caleb's impossibly small block letters.

His brother had recently touched this; something of his DNA remained on it. When it brushed against his fingers, Shane felt himself fighting a childlike impulse to store the envelope away unopened, to save it for later.

He felt Janelle watching him. Inside of her, their little boy was spiraling and twisting, testing out appendages, luxuriating in warm amniotic fluid. How was he to know that soon he would enter a world in which hundred-foot redwoods dappled against a buoyant blue sky, companies created drugs capable of fighting disease, and his uncle chose to live in an antiworld, running an endless marathon into himself?

Then he tore the envelope open. There was just one small sheet of paper. Handwritten, of course.

"Hello, Caleb," Shane muttered casually. "What's going on?"

He read aloud. "Dear Shane, I hope you're well. I need to talk to you about something important. Do you want to come out here for a weekend? You can write me at my job. Love to Janelle."

"Love to me," Janelle said merrily.

"And he's never even met you. You're that loveable."

"What job?" she asked.

The concept of Caleb working again filled him with hope. There were consultants in Boulder. Perhaps he had rejoined the world? Shane flipped the small envelope around.

"O'Neil's Copies," he whispered. He pushed his hand roughly through his short black hair. "Jesus."

"Go this weekend."

"This weekend?" He pointed at his letter. "He said *a* weekend."

"That's not what he means."

"The baby . . ."

"The baby will be here in two weeks. You should go now."

Janelle walked to the kitchen. Somewhere far away Shane

was aware of the sound of a refrigerator opening and closing. The whir of its motor, the hum of its light.

Ten years ago, Shane's older brother had unexpectedly quit his high-salaried consulting job and gone to live with a running club in a cabin near Boulder. No phones, no Internet. Neither he nor his parents had seen him since.

Over the years, Shane and Janelle would google him and find his name listed among the entrants of races through a hundred miles of wilderness. They read other ultrarunners' online musings about what went on in the Happy Trails house under a man called Mack's direction, which were profoundly disturbing. Occasionally, Shane would send a letter to Caleb care of Happy Trails. He was careful never to demean his lifestyle; instead, he wrote about their parents, Fred and Julie, who lived outside of Seattle in Issaquah. About meeting Janelle. Inviting him to their wedding, which Caleb had not attended, crushing them all.

These letters were never answered, but once or twice a year he would receive a blue envelope with a two-line, small print note. *Thanks for your letter. Western States was insane. Finished twenty-second.*

Ten years of this. Shane tossed the blue paper onto the coffee table.

"I'm not going to Boulder just because he asks," he announced to the room.

Janelle placed her hand against the back of his neck, calming him somewhat. He could feel the warmth from whoever it was inside of her, like a ghost trying to make its presence known.

After Janelle went to bed, Shane nursed a glass of pinot in the darkening house. In the stillness he could hear the beeps of plastic toys, Janelle running after a toddler, like ghosts from the future. He wondered how much he would miss this quiet. His thoughts turned again to his brother.

Running had been an Oberest family sacrament, a fact of how one lived, like brushing your teeth. Their father Fred had been a paunchy thirty-six-year-old lawyer when the jogging craze hit Seattle in 1975. He had been converted by a senior partner one Saturday morning along the road to Lake Washington. When he saw the effects of his new hobby upon his clarity of mind, he decided to pass this gift along to his children.

And so on weekend mornings, regardless of weather, Fred would stretch in his nylon red shorts and white headband, and guide Julie, Caleb, and Shane onto the misty Issaquah roads, where they would follow in his wake like Mrs. Mallard and her Ducklings.

Shane imagined them the way a passing motorist would have seen them. A thin middle-aged man running with his hands held limply in front of his chest in late-seventies style. His wife behind him, wearing a white terry-cloth headband. Behind her, a six-year-old boy keeping up as best as he could. And in front of them all, a tall, thin eleven-year-old, clear plastic running goggles strapped around his head with a thick black band, loping effortlessly like a palomino.

In a decade, Shane's letters had not provoked a single invitation to speak, let alone visit. Caleb had to know what reaching out like this meant. Didn't he? He sat there, wondering, until Janelle was asleep, and the wine was empty.

3

Caleb woke up coughing.

A thick yellow phlegm came up from his mouth as he blinked. His room was dark, the mattress on the other side of the floor was empty. It was his roommate Kevin Yu's morning to make breakfast. It was, he figured, around four in the morning.

Caleb took note of his body. Turning forty, he realized, had done something to his systems. For years, he had gone running the mornings after an ultramarathon. But for two days following Leadville he had been unable to do more than walk, and the expected after-race virus had hit his sinuses harder than usual. He'd lain in the house taking Mack's reiki healing and mugs of goldenseal tea. It was only this morning that he would finally force himself to jog up the mountain.

Caleb began a Lying Meditation. He visualized healing energy flowing into each organ of his body: liver, marrow, kidneys, heart. When he was finished, he moved on to his muscles. Bones. Blood. This took him over an hour. Afterward, he moved slowly downstairs and found Kevin in the kitchen, standing over a large Crock-Pot of multigrain. The recipe was balanced to contain 40 percent fat, 20 percent protein, 40 percent carbs, a proportion which Mack had determined encouraged the body's most efficient fuel consumption. They ate this every morning, and a root stew of similar composition at dusk, and no more.

"You're looking alive, Caley," Aviva yawned. She was tall and large-boned, covered in bright tattoos of ghosts and stars.

It's a good look," Caleb smiled. He filled a bowl, shuffled back to the main room, and sat on the floor next to an abandoned Monopoly game and a dozen empty beer bottles. He brushed brown hair away from his eyes. The rest of the Happy Trails Running Club emerged from upstairs and joined him. He looked around the big room for June but didn't see her; still he was sure he smelled her skin in the molecules of the air.

He felt a hand on his shoulder and glanced up.

"Coming?" Juan asked him.

Each member of Happy Trails worked a few days a week in nearby towns and handed their checks to Mack to cover their share of house expenses. Since these jobs had to accommodate long midday training runs and could not exceed three days per week, they tended to be of a minimum wage variety.

"Absolutely."

Aviva heard him and squeezed his shoulder admiringly as they joined Juan and Makailah outside on the porch.

Mack walked over to them, his beard parted by a wide and jubilant grin. "'Who has gone farthest? For I would go farther. And who has been happiest? O I think it is I.'" He took a step closer, raised his voice louder. "'And who possesses a perfect and enamour'd body? For I do not believe any one possesses a more perfect or enamour'd body than mine. And who has made hymns fit for the earth? For I am mad with devouring ecstasy to make joyous hymns for the whole earth.'"

Whitman was his favorite poet; he never seemed to tire of calling verses out to them. Makailah waved to him, Caleb nodded happily, and the four of them began their run up the mountain.

Under the pale sky Caleb's quads came alive. The road was a sixty-degree incline. In its early valley stretch it was unpaved; cars were less likely to pass them than canyon wrens. Tangerine butterflies fluttered between the aspens, their flares of orange threatening to set the trees aflame. Dragonflies came and disappeared like dreams. In their wake he felt part of something wondrous.

Soon after the dirt turned to pavement an SUV passed them loudly, full of a heavyset family on their way up to the city. A child seemed to stare at them from the rear window. Aviva laughed, waving madly at him.

She and Juan worked at Pedestrian Shoes, selling 150-dollar footwear to college kids who never dreamed that these weather-beaten clerks kneeling at their feet could execute feats of physical endurance beyond their wildest imaginings. Aviva had finished fifth in the 24 Hour Run Championship, running 240 miles around an oval track.

"You sure these shoes won't fall apart after a year? I run five miles a day," a lacrosse player would ask her haughtily.

"Pretty sure," Aviva would yawn.

They leveled off into Rocky Mountain National Park as the May sun broke over the Front Range and then jogged into the city. Caleb rarely saw more of Boulder than these downtown blocks, but he could discern the almost daily changes. The excavators like prehistoric predators prowling new avenues each month, the pale newly transplanted faces, wearing shiny running clothes and making overeager strides. The mountains almost visibly recoiled from them.

Aviva and Juan peeled off for Pedestrian, Makailah toward the tea shop where she worked as a barista, and Caleb slowed to a walk, letting the light sweat on his body disappear into the pine-accented air as he moved toward O'Neil's.

Caleb unlocked the door. O'Neil's possessed two old beige copiers beside the window for customer use. A few yards of old blue carpet led to a counter, behind which stood two more powerful laser printers, work space for cutting, mounting, and laminating, and a small office. The shop had been opened in the seventies by Ed O'Neil, who had fended off the onslaught of Kinko's and OfficeMaxes with a relatively successful campaign to support local small businesses. Ed was fascinated by Caleb's consulting days, and happy to have someone older than a sophomore in the store, even one who required a four-hour break in the middle of the day to run.

Caleb found his blue apron and waited patiently. These wasted hours under the fluorescent lights irritated him, but over the years he had learned to not stand in idle stasis, but constantly engage himself in slow movements. He powered up the machines, made sure their trays were stocked. He turned to a wall of small metal postboxes. The top row contained Ed's box for store mail. He retrieved the small key from a hook and checked to see if his brother had sent a response. He took its emptiness with a healthy detachment.

An hour passed, for which he was paid six dollars and fifty-five cents. It amused Caleb how much he had once been paid for an identical hour. Before moving to Boulder, he had been a consultant for InterFinancial, in Manhattan. It had been tedious work, and the company of his strip-club and vodka-obsessed colleagues had depressed him. His final project had been for the Phoenix Suns. He had lived in a Fairmont Hotel by the US Airways Center for three months and watched the season from a luxury box stocked with prime rib and beer. For this reason, his father Fred had considered the job glamorous. But studying contracts with food service companies and practice facilities in beige offices had left him exhausted. Afterward he had flown home to his Upper West Side apartment and bought a top-of-the-line Wolf stove, which he used only to make popcorn. Now Caleb stood in his blue apron, for a fiftieth of that salary. He felt far wealthier.

At noon a young college student relieved him, and he folded his faded blue apron considerately, and jogged toward the park. For four hours he covered its least-traveled trails, weaving through filberts and blanketflowers, thinking of nothing but the hundreds of scents in the air. When the sky grew violet he jogged back to O'Neil's to close up.

June walked in as dusk filled the front room. She wore a long green dress and sandals, and carried a plastic yellow bucket of cleaning supplies. Her face was thin and flushed, her dry hair like shoots of straw, her eyes enormous and blue. She possessed a mouth as small as a drop of rain. He knew she was not beautiful, but in his forty-three years, he had never felt this way upon seeing another human being.

"I'm done early," she announced.

She walked around the counter and touched him lightly. Her fingers slid in between his like the thighs of lovers. Breathlessly, Caleb opened the door to the small office that

Ed maintained in a back room. It was just a metal desk pushed against a wall, surrounded by stacks of boxed paper.

She fumbled with his apron and sat on the metal desk. As he kissed her the phone fell loudly from the table. She undid his belt and crossed her ankles behind his back. The hard edges of the desk chafed the front of his thighs.

These moments made him feel lost and weightless; afterward he had no idea how much time had passed. When she went to the bathroom, he felt a fissure inside which frightened him. He had moved to Boulder to immerse within himself, had lived this way successfully for ten years. And now, here he was, immersed in someone else.

Caleb powered down the machines, sprayed disinfectant over their buttons, turned off the lights. Then he held the door for June and locked it behind them. A warm breeze blew down from the range onto Broadway. Their sky was a sweet plum. Around them graduate school couples carried groceries, long-haired kids spun strange silver orbs for tips, young women sped by on bicycles.

They turned onto the Mall, where the streetlights glowed like the cheeks of excited children. A long-haired brunette with a hula hoop executed yoga poses in the midst of the open promenade. What could have been a father-son duo created Renaissance Faire music, and the spring tulips bloomed in a thousand shades. They roamed slowly through the warm glow coming from the redbrick streets.

"Did your brother write back?" June was trying her best to be offhand, but her squeezing fingers told him otherwise.

Any of their housemates could walk past, finished with their own jobs. Makailah's tea shop was just a block away, Kyle could be picking up supplies. Just one sighting of them holding hands would bring problems he was not prepared to handle.

Caleb let out a dry cough and shook his head and let her hand go.

• • • • • • •

"An announcement," Mack cried, "of earthshaking proportions."

The Happy Trails Running Club assembled on the wood floor of the large open room. Waves of heat and crackling cherrywood swept over Caleb from the fireplace.

Mack sat cross-legged on the floor. In the flickering flames the dark circles under his wrinkled eyes were accentuated; Caleb thought he could see each of his forty-five years in them. His blue irises seemed to dance with some inner light.

"Y'all ready for something?"

Caleb straightened. Was this what Mack had been talking about after Leadville? He sat in a circle between Aviva and Gigi, a new girl from Winter Park. On the other side of the circle, June was sitting between Hank and John, their oldest housemate, a close-cropped white-haired survivor of Vietnam-era excursions. John had finished the Badwater ultra five times. One hundred thirty-five miles through Death Valley, at temperatures exceeding 110 degrees. He told tales of his sneakers melting into the blacktop, and once leaving his body for nearly an hour. Caleb sensed June trying to look away from him, which, he felt, was wise.

"Ready!" Alice shouted, and the others laughed.

Mack nodded. "Okay. For fifteen years, we've owned the hardest ultras in the country. Yes?"

With wide smiles the group responded, "Yes!"

"We are the premier ultrarunning club in these United States. Even if the running magazines won't talk about us. And we'll continue to rock them all. But you know what? What's next for Happy Trails?"

Mack paused, letting his bright eyes roam the circle. An energy was building. Caleb saw it materializing like a ring around them.

"Because there is a next. There has to be. What happens here is too good to be hidden away by the running establishment motherfuckers. We can be a beacon for people seeking rescue from the sadness of the world. I want to have Happy Trails houses all over the country, in every state. Think what would happen, right?" His eyes beamed. "The more people live our way, the more kinetic energy will be created, and flow out into the world. And the better the world will become. But people can't join us if they don't hear about us. Several of you came here because of my book. But we need something bigger than a book to get the country's attention."

Mack took a swig from a white bottle of Beam; with a nod he passed it to Makailah.

"I've been working with Barry Strong out in California. You guys heard of Barry? He's Desert Masai. They do the Peru jungles."

A sense of excitement swept the circle. Barry's group was well known. They were cousins in endurance.

"Barry's been feeling the same way. We were talking about how we could create an event to get people's attention. We decided to make one, that combines endurance and distance. The killer blend."

Juan asked, "Isn't Western States that?"

"Western's a tough challenge for sure. But they've been running it forever and nobody outside of the ultra world gives a shit. We need something bigger. So Barry and me, we made a decision. We're relaunching the Yosemite Slam."

The impact of this hit them. They all stared at Mack, as the bottle moved around the circle. Aviva raised her hand. Mack nodded to her.

"But they shut that down," she said, confused.

"They did?" asked Ryan. "Why?"

Ryan had been with them only a year. He had been jailed twice in his early twenties for crushing oxycodone into powder, adding various forms of laxative powder, and selling it to high school football players outside of his local Walmart. A twelve-step counselor had introduced him to the runner's high, and two years later he'd won his first Fat Race. Mack had met him at the Rocky Raccoon in Vermont, where Ryan had been running unsupported, carrying thirty pounds of water and food in a backpack. Three months later, he had moved into the house.

"They shut it down," Rae explained softly, "after Steve Brzenski died there."

"Who's he?"

"He was a great runner."

"The Yosemite Slam was crazy dangerous," Hank picked up. "A hundred and ten through the park, in summer. The hardest climb came at the end, when everyone was exhausted. Steve was climbing near Taft when he fell. He broke his back."

Rae added, "The year before that, Pete Fresciente had a heart attack the day he finished. They found him in his motel room. That was two in a row, there was police involved, and the owners shut it down."

Mack spoke roughly. "I can't tell you why those people died. I can tell you they did not train with me."

He had everyone's attention.

"We are not just bringing back the most challenging physical event in the country, we are amplifying it. And the whole country is going to fucking watch it." He beamed. "I already talked with a gal at ESPN. She says the country is ready. Because it ain't no bullshit Iron Man, watching dudes jog down a *highway*.

"This is going to be like watching a war. Seventy-two straight hours on old mining trails, up twelve thousand feet and back a dozen times. In complete darkness, in brutal sun, over waterfalls, through mines, Half Dome, up El Capitan. Rescue can't even get to eighty percent of the course. Stunning shit to look at on a plasma screen. But the most stunning things will be you. People want to watch people who believe in themselves."

"ESPN?" Rae frowned.

"This event is going to be the spark for our whole movement. ESPN is the wind. People are going to watch this in bars, at home, at the gym."

"That'll bring out all the hacks," Rae suggested anxiously. "Clogging the trails, puking all over the place."

Mack shot her a riley look. "A hack golfer can buy expensive clubs and clog up a pro course. But no fancy sneakers can force you up El Capitan in your sixty-sixth hour. It'll make pretty amusing television to watch poseurs try. People can place bets on when they'll drop and beg for ambulances."

"I just don't get it. What's wrong with—"

"Go upstairs please."

Caleb watched Rae stand solemnly, heard her callused feet shuffle up the wood steps behind him.

Mack turned to the group. "We have a great world here, but I feel stasis. We run, we work, we travel, we enter events, and we kick their asses. But what's *forward*? I want kinetic energy in this group, not just in our individual bodies. A new event, the hardest event in the country, that's motion."

"Cool." Ryan raised his hand for a high five and got one from Makailah.

"We're going to spend the year training. And someone here"—he looked at Caleb—"is going to win."

Aviva put her hand on the small of Caleb's back and rubbed a gentle circle. The bottle of Beam made its way to him, and Caleb took a good pull, feeling its warmth slide into his belly. Across the circle, he tried to catch June's eye, but she was watching Mack.

"But before Yosemite, we have the Hardrock, and that's no Fat Race. Hands."

Aviva took Caleb's left palm, and Gigi took his right. Mack put a small pipe to his lips, lit a soft ball of chocolate brown hashish, took a hit, and passed it on. Its sweet thick scent blended with the cherrywood, and the house entered a dreamlike phase. Caleb exhaled deeply.

This morning, he had spoken with his brother for the first time in ten years. Shane's voice had sounded different than he'd remembered, but their conversation had been easy. They had agreed on this weekend for his visit. At first he had felt a deep relief, but now the guilt of what he wanted Shane to do bubbled through him, and he worried that Mack would see it in his soul.

But Mack was occupied, rubbing his hands together, collecting his energy, his voice quiet and sincere.

"We had some injuries this week. Leigh's ankle, Hank's neck." He closed his eyes. "'Smile O voluptuous cool-breath'd earth. Earth of the slumbering and liquid trees. Earth of the mountains misty-topt. Rich apple-blossom'd earth! Smile, for your lover comes.'"

The pipe reached Caleb, and he inhaled; the hashish encircled his head immediately. He felt the blaze of the fire, heard the crackling of the birch. He felt Gigi's small fingers hover near his back and a furnace emanate from her palms. Under his skin he felt a shudder, as her energy unblocked closed channels throughout his body. This heat spread to his foot and knee and sinuses, everywhere he had difficulty. He did the same for Aviva beside him, and she for Hank.

Happy Trails was made up of seventeen people, of different ages, backgrounds, parts of the country, but they were one single being now. When he healed Aviva he was healing June. It was, he thought, a type of prayer. Communion in its most literal sense. Mack believed that sexual energy creates a chemical enzyme called orgone, which he regarded as one of the body's most powerful forces. On Sunday evenings they created orgone in each other, and this in turn helped them heal.

Across the room he heard June's distinctive breaths. His stomach clenched. Do not look, Caleb told himself. Do not. But he did, and on her face he saw the look he loved. Her eyes squeezed shut, her mouth open, her arms raising beside her, hovering as though in a penitent prayer.

Mack lifted his hand, and they each stopped moving, holding it. Caleb felt a hot energy fill his lungs and pulse out into every limb. He felt his blockages burst open, dead zones spring to life; he felt swallowed whole.

Then Mack nodded, and they all shifted, and then like fission, waves of kinetic energy bounced through the house, out to the mountains and into the sky and back again, and he could feel June connected to him all the way across the circle, a part of him now, where she was supposed to be.

4

As Shane hit the freeway, rays of light bounded off the bay beside him.

This morning he had an informational interview with Dennis Adderberry, the Director of Commercial at Helixia, which Janelle had arranged the morning following the arrival of Caleb's letter. He had never met Dennis, but he had heard of him for many years. He had a reputation as genuine and honest, and Shane was flattered that he had made time for him.

But Shane knew he was not prepared. That short letter on blue paper had stolen his attention from everything important. When he had phoned the copy store listed on the return address, their conversation had been disappointing. After a silence, Shane had explained that their due date was next week and offered to come this Saturday. The whole exchange had been stilted, and Shane had hung up feeling disoriented and doleful.

Today, he swore he would focus on his own future. He was listening to sports radio, wearing his brown suit with a French blue shirt and his blue tinted wraparound running shades. His short black hair was gelled back. His mouth tasted of mint. He kept a watch out for the South San Francisco exit, and took it to Pinon Drive.

As always, he felt astonishment at Helixia's headquarters. Visitors to Orco Pharmaceutical's campus in Saint Louis drove a winding, tree-lined mile down Orco Boulevard, and parked by a reflecting pool in front of an imposing black glass headquarters. Where no one could miss it, an enormous sign listed directions to the gym, the steakhouse, the helipad.

Helixia's architecture conveyed the opposite message entirely. The headquarters of the third-largest biotechnology company in the country was a simple seventy-year-old brick warehouse. Two decades ago the company had constructed a separate two-story concrete building beside it for research and production labs, an addition as drab and unadorned as a Midwestern middle school. All the money here, the buildings communicated, went to research.

Shane stepped inside. Here he saw that Helixia was not without some unnecessary adornment: by the reception area stood a small corn plant.

"Well, hi, Ruth," he nodded to the elderly receptionist. He had known her for some years.

"Janelle just got in," she informed him.

"Actually, I'm here to see Dennis Adderberry." He signed in and smiled at her. "You have a great morning."

He rode an old freight elevator to the third floor, and walked down a long hallway to Dennis's office.

Dennis Adderberry was exceedingly tall. He seemed around forty years old, with striking silver hair offset by thick black Scottish eyebrows, over a boyish face. In place of the Orco

Director of Sales' blue suit and American flag pin, Dennis wore a loose yellow golf shirt and khakis. He smiled broadly.

"You're here," he said in a surprisingly deep baritone.

"Thank you for seeing me."

"Well, I know a little bit about you. First, sir, you have excellent taste in wives."

Shane grinned.

"Second, you have great relationships with doctors. I wish our team had more of that. You'd be surprised how many oncologists still aren't comfortable with what we do."

"They're not paid to be comfortable with it," Shane ventured. Why not throw his real feelings out there, he figured?

Dennis studied him, eyes sparkling. "We don't do that here, you know."

Shane sat down. "That's what I wanted to talk with you about. I've been in pharma sales my whole career. And maybe it's me getting older, but I feel like it's moved somewhere I don't really want to be."

"Where is it you're looking to be, Shane?"

"I want to rep drugs that help people survive disease, not de-stress before the golf course. I'd like to go to work for a boutique. Do you think my experience is transferable? Is there a path from Big Pharma sales to start-ups?"

Dennis thought for a moment. "Well, the cliché says a good salesman can sell cars one day and raincoats the next. But I don't believe that. I think you need to have passion for what you sell, feel and understand it as if you made it. We've hired quite a few pharma people. My feeling is they tend to think of our drugs as products. That's the way they were trained. But I don't think of them that way, I think of them as medicine. As lives."

Shane was nodding.

"So my question back to you Shane would be, your skills are transferable, but is your passion?"

"I already have passion for what your guys do."

"What do you know about biotech? I'd imagine being married to one of our best product managers, it's quite a lot."

"Not as much as I should. If I get a chance to interview somewhere, I'll tighten up."

"Give it a shot." Dennis's eyes sparkled.

"Okay. Well, the big idea of biomedicine, as I understand it anyway, is that all living things, plants, animals, fish, viruses, bacteria, insects, are all made of the same genes. And that these genes are interchangeable. Like Lego pieces. They will work the same way in any organism they are transferred to. So we can move a gene with a specific property from one organism to another."

Dennis was nodding encouragingly.

"For example, a major problem in cancer surgery is that surgeons leave microscopic particles of a tumor behind, which grow back. You guys took the enzyme from a firefly gene that causes its tail to glow and grafted it onto a chromosome in a human cancerous tumor. So that in surgery, every molecule of that tumor glows like a firefly."

"Two-hundred-million-dollar a year product, by the way."

"Congratulations. Orco made that much with a female Viagra that was ineffective."

Dennis smiled. "What do you think our biggest challenge with internists is?"

"They still think that biotech is a cutting-edge new science. When actually, the Romans used biotechnology. Any time you add yeast to make bread, or wine, you're transplanting bacteria. Beer is biotech."

"Beer is biotech. I'll have the T-shirts printed this weekend."

Shane shifted in his seat. "So, you know who runs each sales department. Who do you think might be a good fit for me?"

"I have an opening for a sales director."

Shane blinked.

"I realize we have more than ten employees just in our mail room," Dennis shook his head, his voice dropping as he considered this.

"That's not why I came to see you."

"I know. And I know we're the opposite of a boutique or a start-up. But"—Dennis raised a finger and narrowed his eyes—"we started that way, and many of the people here can remember those days. That ethos hasn't gone anywhere. And I do have a solid position open. I'm supposed to interview someone for it after work tonight."

"Don't you guys have a nepotism policy?"

"You don't graft firefly cells onto human genes if you're following every policy."

"What's the director lead?"

"Sorion."

Shane swallowed a wash of disappointment. Sorion was Helixia's marquee drug; the nanosecond it had been approved, in 1994, their stock had doubled. Its use had spread so quickly that conferences detailing its growth had to be rewritten quarterly. The time to be working on it, Shane felt, was fifteen years ago.

Dennis read his eyes. "It's a good place to learn our business. It's stable. You can make connections, get your footing.

And there's none of the frantic all-night panics of a Phase Three."

"I like all-night panics," Shane told him.

Dennis smiled, revealing surprisingly yellow teeth. "Oh, don't worry," he assured him, "you'll get them."

• • • • • • •

That evening, he and Janelle walked into a small Nob Hill steakhouse.

They were greeted by dim lighting and a somber jazz. The whole vibe seemed too down for Shane's mood, but it was too late for a change of plan. Doctor Wenceslas Chin and his wife Cynthia were waiting for them at the bar, and Wenceslas loved his steak. Shane felt lighter the instant he saw them.

Wenceslas was an internist at Greenbrae Medical Associates, a general practice catering to Marin's elite. He had a wide South Chinese face and behind his round eyeglasses lay happy eyes. He and Shane had become close friends these last years, played countless rounds of golf, and shared many bottles of Shane's beloved Washington State reds at medical conferences, on Orco. This dinner would be their last with the Saint Louis pharma picking up the check, without the accompaniment of an infant, their last before so many things promised to change.

"Oh my God," Cynthia laughed, hugging Janelle. "When are you due, today?"

"Next week."

Her eyes fell to Janelle's protruding belly. "Can I touch it?"

"Go crazy."

Watching Janelle lean forward stirred Shane. Nine months

of pregnancy had only made her more alluring to him. She wore a black and gold top over ashen maternity cigarette pants that expanded over her belly. Her black hair was parted down the middle, the steakhouse's soft light showcasing its maroon highlights. When he touched her arm and back, her skin seemed moist. Small black moles had begun to appear on her body, and a slight vertical line had developed from her navel southward, as if her seams were showing.

Plus, Janelle had a new way of looking at him, with swollen eyes, and a slightly upturned mouth, that made him feel something very deep that he could not quite identify. Shane took her hand as they walked to an oddly high table, which added to his mounting sense of silliness.

"Hey"—Wenceslas leaned across the table—"I got one of those checks."

Shane nodded. The Big Pharmas had begun sending unrequested checks for between ten and a hundred thousand dollars to doctors. Fine print explained that cashing them was the equivalent of signing a contract for exclusive prescriptions. The FDA, Shane felt, would come down very hard on these companies and doctors soon. Except that after a decade, they still hadn't.

"How much?"

"Thirty thousand. With a letter about being a valuable doctor at an important practice."

"You cash it?"

"I shredded the thing." Wenceslas looked horrified. "My patients expect me to write the best script available. If they knew I was pledged to one drug company?" He shook his head no.

But Shane shrugged. "One day doctors will put up signs like the ones about which insurance companies they accept. Except about which drug companies they work with. 'Greenbrae Medical Associates only prescribes drugs from Merck,' or something."

"Ah," Wenceslas nodded. "If we did that, they wouldn't need you. How much money would pharmas save with no reps?"

Shane considered this. The amount seemed too staggering to verbalize.

"They're about to get that money back anyway," Janelle grinned across the table.

Wenceslas stared at him. "Really? Where are you going?"

"Helixia."

A prolonged whistle escaped from Wenceslas's lips.

Cynthia asked, "Is that a different drug company?"

"It's a different category. It's biotech. Where Janelle works."

"What's the difference?"

Janelle explained, "Pharmaceutical companies create chemical compounds that are delivered into the body to cause a specific reaction. But the body reacts to these foreign chemicals in a myriad of ways, and you get side effects. If you have a stuffed nose, Sudafed unstuffs it. But it also makes your heart race and your mouth dry. Biotechnology treatments use natural proteins from the body, which it recognizes, and never fights. So only the intended reaction happens."

"Sounds amazing," Cynthia said happily. "Congratulations."

"We can play a celebratory round at Peacock this Sunday," suggested Wenceslas.

Shane raised his eyes. "Love to, but I'm going to Boulder this weekend."

"Last romantic getaway before the baby and the job?"

"I don't know about romantic. I'm going to see my brother."

"I didn't know you had a brother. You never mention him."

Shane drank more wine. "Don't I?"

"Boulder sounds fun," Cynthia told him.

"Oh, fun fun fun," Shane said. Janelle pressed his leg under the table.

She started to tell an amusing story about a lactation video she'd seen online. He tried to pay attention, but Caleb had hijacked his thoughts again. What would he find at this house in Boulder? Who would he see there, calling himself his brother?

As they rode in their taxi back toward the Marina, Janelle leaned against his shoulder. Outside, a neon blur of North Beach topless bars created sparks against the city sky.

"Have you told your parents you're going?" she asked softly.

He shook his head no. "Think I should?"

"They'll want to come with you."

"Let's not start a full-scale intervention. They can see Caleb when I get him home."

"Is that your plan? What if he just wants you to watch a race?"

"He's wasting his life."

"What if he's happy?"

Shane frowned out the window.

"Seek first to understand, baby."

"Seek first to kick his ass."

Janelle looked at him, concerned. "I know you take it

personally that he disappeared on you, but give him two minutes before you put him in a half nelson and throw him in the car. If you turn him off, you'll never hear from him again."

"Okay," Shane nodded, exhaling. "I'll give him nothing but love. But the guy that runs that place? Him not so much."

The taxi wound through the wharf toward the tiny house they had invested everything in. He realized that this might be the last time they would ever approach it as just the two of them, focused only on each other. He kissed Janelle's cheek and glanced out at the bright buoyant lights of Tiburon and Sausalito, and the curve into the cold Pacific beyond.

"I'm going to get him out of there," Shane stated quietly.

In the morning, he left for the airport.

............5

"Your bro's coming today?"

It was just before nine in the morning; Caleb had been running for four hours. Bumblebees nearly the size of eggs skittered through the gaillardias. A cluster of bluebirds burst over his head. Moving at a good speed, Caleb felt an ascension of joy that he supposed classical composers and Renaissance painters had touched. Running was art, he knew, and its masters were also capable of masterpieces.

As he galloped through the familiar trails, Caleb visualized the Hardrock 100 course that awaited him next month. He saw himself in its hundred miles through thirteen soaring peaks of the San Juan Mountains, its fields of wildflowers, its granite peaks covered with snowpack. He felt he was there. Running trails, he could imagine anything he wished with stunning clarity.

He was in the midst of this revelry when Mack jumped out from behind an especially bountiful white ash.

"Caley!"

Caleb stopped suddenly; immediately his body began to overheat.

Appearing unexpectedly at the end of a run to add more time was a favorite training technique of Mack's. He'd written about it in *You Can Run 100 Miles!* Ultramarathon courses are full of unpredictability. A sudden rainstorm might create a mudslide, an animal might carry off a course marker, a lateral muscle might tear. Unforeseen requirements to double the body's effort without notice were part of the sport and so, Mack taught, it should be part of the training. But today, instead of shouting his usual "add ten" Mack asked about his brother.

"What time's he showing up?"

Sweat poured from Caleb's chin. "I don't know. This morning."

Mack was grinning, fingers playing with his black beard. "We gotta make tonight *good* for him. I'm throwing a shindig."

Caleb squinted uncomfortably. "I think he just wants to spend some time with me."

Mack went on as if he had not heard him. "I'm getting two kegs of Fat Tire, two one-point-seven-fivers of Beam. I'm inviting some people from the Horse."

"Okay," Caleb gave in, "that'll be great."

"So, Shane," Mack asked jauntily, "friend or foe?"

Caleb hesitated. The truth was, he wasn't certain. Whatever attitude Shane was bringing was beyond him. As he stood breathing hard under the pines, a memory surged from the recesses of his brain. He had been fifteen, listening to *The Wall* in his room. Caleb had overheard a girl he admired talking about it before class, and he had dutifully sought it out at Mills Music. Shane, who must have been ten, had wandered in. The two of them had not spoken but sat listening to this strange, sad music. This had not succeeded in bringing him any closer to talking to the girl at school, but it had brought the brothers together for an afternoon.

"Friend," he answered. "He just wants to hang out."

Mack slapped his shoulder. "Add seven."

Without another word, Caleb pushed off into the underbrush.

From behind him he heard Mack shout his Whitman. "'Allons! The road is before us! It is safe—I have tried it. My own feet have tried it well. Be not detain'd!'"

And so Caleb burst over the earth, spine straight, arms like pistons, landing on the balls of his feet, in a state of constant forward motion. This was how the body built up its store of its key fuel, what Bergsonists called élan vital, what Mack called kinetic energy. Without forward motion, Caleb knew, the body sinks into stasis, depletes, decomposes daily. It was no coincidence that disease rates had exploded exactly as human culture sank into ergonomic chairs. He thought he might talk to Shane about this. He wanted his brother to understand his life, just a little, before he asked him.

He tried to recall if he and Shane had ever spoken about something this important. The five years between them had been too long a distance. He had been on the Washington State distance team while Shane was still in middle school and starting InterFinancial's training program in Manhattan while Shane was negotiating college applications. Caleb was aware of being watched from afar, like a runner cheered from the stands. Still, some bond remained between them, he could feel it, somewhere deep within his cells.

When he emerged into the open field behind the old house, he saw a strange car, rental-company purple, parked in front. Caleb sprinted the hundred yards to the back stairs, took them three at a time, and pushed opened the back door. Sweat dripping from his forehead, he went through the kitchen out into the expansive main room.

It was too much to absorb right away.

The two people he loved most in the world were sitting on the floor, knees up, talking as casually as if they had known each other for years. Behind them, Kevin, Leigh, and Alice bustled around with dustpan and broom. Seventies reggae played from the old plastic boom box on the floor, as the sun streamed through the dusty windows.

June's voice fluttered through the air and landed on him like a kiss.

"Caley, look. Your brother's here."

• • • • • • •

Shane looked different.

His round face, his bright eyes, his short black hair were unchanged. But a new thin line stretched across his forehead like the impression left by a Halloween mask. The skin under his eyes seemed to have taken on a slight shadow.

Shane stood up and Caleb hugged him; his body felt thick, like a good tree. But Caleb knew by the way he pulled away and stared that the feel of his own body had proven startling. Suddenly Caleb felt embarrassed, by his letter, his need, his body. He glanced nervously at June, but she did not seem to share his anxiousness; she was gazing at them both from the floor, her pale eyes wide and happy.

"How was your trip?" Caleb asked quietly.

"Easy."

In truth, Shane was feeling a little shaky. His drive from the Denver airport had taken him along a harrowing mountain road, with a sheer drop just a few yards to his right. Initially, the lack of a guardrail had exhilarated him. But suddenly a sense of consequence washed over him, of leaving his unborn son fatherless, and Janelle a single mother, and he had felt a sharp and vicious fear. He had slowed to a cautious thirty-five miles an hour. By the time Shane arrived at the old wood house, he understood that something had left him on that road that would not be so easy to get back.

When he found the isolated dirt driveway, the door had been opened by a thin woman with pale skin and an explosion of marigold freckles. Shane recognized the face of a hardcore athlete—a complete absence of body fat accentuated every muscle. Even her hair seemed poached, like a horse's mane. Her lips were thin, her mouth small, and her nose had a tiny, turned-up way that made him think of money. But her eyes were enormous and they seemed to live completely apart from the hard face that encircled them. They were the eyes, he thought, of a softer soul.

June had led Shane to the middle of the room and sat now on the wood floor with him. Through the windows he could see the bark of forest firs. People of all ages walked barefoot around them, sweeping the floor, leaving for and returning from runs. They came over and introduced themselves in a friendly manner that struck him as wholly genuine. One would never know, looking at them, what their bodies could accomplish.

And then Caleb had walked in from the back of the house. Of course, Shane thought, he would not come through the door that he expected.

Standing, Shane had to remind himself that this was his brother. Close up, his face was that of a much older man than he had seen in online photos of race winners. There were lines, his teeth had darkened, he seemed whittled down to his basic self. Bones and will.

Suddenly, June announced, “I see it.”

They both turned to her.

“You guys have the same mouths. That’s where you’re brothers.”

Shane blinked. Where they were brothers was in their shared fear of their father Fred playing endless Tony Bennett eight-tracks in the station wagon, in being guinea pigs for their mother’s sporadic attempts at starting a catering company, in their uncountable shared miles jogging as a family through the winding roads of Issaquah. Where they were brothers was in the fact that each of their molecules shared chemical proteins built from recombinant DNA that was 99.9 percent identical. It was a lot more, he wanted to tell her, than their mouths.

“So”—Shane spread his arms wide—“we’re having a baby.”

Caleb glanced at June, and then quickly touched Shane’s shoulder. “That’s awesome. Do you guys have a name?”

“Nicholas,” he confided, his voice lowering conspiratorially, as if someone might inform Janelle’s friends. “Nicholas Wei.”

“Way cool.” June clapped her hands.

Shane looked down sheepishly.

“Should we go for a hike?” Caleb asked him suddenly.

“Didn’t you just get in? You’re all sweaty.”

“Let’s get you changed.”

Shane followed his brother up a short flight of wood stairs. That he was this close was incredible to him. The days he had dreamed about some moment like this were too many to consider.

The second floor emitted a thick scent of wood and skin. They passed a series of closed doors, which looked to have been made recently. Rooms, he guessed, had been divided. Caleb led him to the room that he shared with Kevin Yu. It was not dissimilar to a college dorm: two futon mattresses lay on the floor, separated by only a few feet. Next to Caleb’s was a small closet, open and full of folded T-shirts and a neat row of beaten sneakers, each the multiple colors of running shoes. Who had established this design sensibility, Shane wondered, and why? Swirls and lines of different colors, what had they to do with moving through nature?

Under a window sat a boombox and a couple of blank CDs with handwritten labels. Shane squinted to read them; they appeared to be recordings of meditations. A stack of running magazines had been piled next to Kevin’s futon; each had clearly been read repeatedly. A small metal fan was plugged into a floor socket and spun uselessly.

“We can share this tonight,” Caleb offered, pointing to the mattress.

“Sure, cool.”

“We’re having a party. But we could go hear some music in town after?”

“Don’t you guys go to bed pretty early?”

"Usually around twelve. We get up at four."

"In the morning?"

"You're having a baby," Caleb smiled. "Get used to four hours' sleep."

Shane found running clothes in his bag. As he changed he was aware of Caleb watching him. He almost asked him then: what do you need that you can't explain in your seven-point handwriting? But Caleb wanted to hike, he guessed, because he wanted to speak privately.

Caleb was pointing. "Hey, that shirt."

Shane had brought an ancient Grateful Dead concert shirt he had purchased in Seattle in 1989. It had holes in both sides, was yellowed under the arms.

"I remember you screaming at Mom for putting that in the dryer."

Shane glanced down. "I guess you can tell you're getting old when your favorite shirts become workout shirts."

Walking downstairs he mentioned, "Hey, before we go, I need to eat something."

"We eat at five."

"Yeah, okay. But it's twelve. All I ate was a muffin at the airport."

"We don't have anything."

"You don't have anything?"

"You can do it," Caleb assured him, turning through the kitchen.

Shane acquiesced. In contrast to his bluster with Janelle, his goal was to play ball here, to accept Caleb's world, and keep all paths open. A sound he recognized caught his ear from down the hall, but he followed his brother out the back door.

At the far end of a crudely constructed deck, three wood

planks led down to an expanse of beautiful, pristine wild tall-grass, which opened to the base of South Boulder Peak. On the deck, an older man with a bare chest covered in white hair raised a hand. His head was shaved close, and he held the posture of a naval officer.

"Hey John, this is my brother."

"Welcome," John said amicably as they shook hands. John's grip was sure. "Enjoy round two," he exclaimed, patting Caleb's back.

"How far have you run today?" Shane asked as they crossed the field at a quick walk.

"Just six."

"Miles?"

Caleb shook his head. "Hours."

The heat hit Shane then, intense, energy-sapping. He felt trapped and vulnerable, without any cover or shade. Half a mile later they approached the beginning of some winding trails, ascending up into the trees. The start of the mountain.

"Mom's good?" Caleb asked him suddenly, as they started.

"She's all right. Considering."

"Considering what?"

"She hasn't seen her son in eleven years."

Caleb said nothing. Shane felt a need to stop the tension he felt mounting.

He tried to say something lighthearted, but the chemicals of food deprivation were sludging through his frontal lobes, mucking up the action. He found it difficult to formulate thoughts. They moved into the shaded trails in silence.

And suddenly his world shifted. The shuffle of their sneakers on the dirt seemed shatteringly loud, the breath in his lungs felt pure. The metallic aftertaste of his flight, the stress of his drive, his resentment at the thought of their mother's pain, dissipated, and a pleasing lassitude enveloped him. A good hike, Shane decided, might be the perfect thing in the world.

"So, who's that girl?"

"At the house? June."

"Is she your girlfriend?"

Caleb's stomach jumped, as somehow the smell of June's skin sailed out of the sky. "No. We don't do that here."

"Don't do what?"

"Have . . . girlfriends."

"Is that like a policy?"

Caleb stared at him. Shane took a breath. Handling Caleb felt like tense negotiations with the North Koreans; they might break off at any time.

"We had a no dating policy at InterFinancial too," Caleb added.

"Sure," Shane answered, "I can see how that would be tricky."

They turned deeper into the woods, walking uphill.

"But you've been here eleven years. Are you doing the abstinence thing?"

"No. Sexual energy is very powerful for healing. It overcomes blockages in the body."

"You guys use sex for *training*?"

Caleb looked at him carefully. "You shouldn't be out of breath yet."

In front of them the narrow trail rose dramatically. Blue flies spun around their heads, spittlebugs frothed on plant stems.

"How do you do these trails," Shane huffed, "running?"

"How do you not?"

"My body doesn't work like yours," Shane laughed.

"Sure it does. I don't have any body parts you don't."

"Yeah, well your body is in a little better shape for it."

"The body you've got is designed to run all day. It's how we hunted. What happened is, we got horses. Carriages. Cars. Evolution works in reverse too. But your body can do it if you want it to."

Shane stepped over a mossy rock and sweat cascaded down his back. "So what's the farthest you've ever gone?"

"I don't keep track. It's not about how far the runs are, it's about what happens during them. The farthest I've gone in an event is a hundred and two miles, at Western States. But I've gone running for days and I have no idea how many miles I went."

"I thought you race these ultramarathons? You sound pretty zen about it, but don't you try to win them?"

"Ultras are different. Those are competitive, and I absolutely want to win them."

"What's your next one?"

"It's called the Hardrock 100. It goes across thirteen mountain peaks, for a hundred miles. There are set distances and cutoff times you have to make or you're out. You have forty-eight hours to finish it. I'm hoping to get it done in twenty-three." He paused. "Don't look at me like that."

"I can't help it."

Sheepishly, Caleb shrugged. "I love it, Shane."

"What do you love about it?"

"When I'm running like that, pushing myself to win, it feels like what I should be doing. It's the most honest thing I've ever experienced."

"What do you mean by honest? Like you can't cheat?"

"I mean the ultras don't care what you look like, or what you believe, or what you do for a living. The only thing that matters is if you can control your body, and your mind. A banker won't beat a janitor unless he can do that. And every race, I experience the best moments of my life. Also the worst," he laughed.

They walked farther into the trails, and the insects began to find them. As mosquitoes covered his arms, and the air thickened, Shane found his good feelings turning sour.

"So at what point are you done?"

A look appeared across his brother's face, a noncomprehension that bordered on disdain.

"Done with what?"

"Seeing how far you can go?"

"Why would I ever be done?"

"Because you're giving up so much for this."

"What am I giving up?"

"Seeing your family, for one thing."

"Start-up founders, restaurant owners, lawyers trying to make partner, they all go months without seeing their families. But you wouldn't ask them when they're going to be done. We all give up things to pursue the things that matter to us."

"I'm giving up my last weekend with Janelle before the baby right now," Shane panted.

"Right. Because you want to see how far *you* can go."

"Go with what?"

"You want to see if you can do it," Caleb nodded.

"Do what?"

"Get me to leave here with you."

Shane stopped and put his hands on his knees. He took

a long breath, to give himself a moment, and because he needed it.

"Come on"—Caleb stared at him openly—"I'm ready for the speech."

"I don't have a fucking speech for you."

"Okay." Caleb turned and began walking up the mountain again, as easily as if these were his first steps of the morning.

Shane scrambled behind him. "I just don't see why you can't do what you love and stay connected with the world."

"I'm more connected to the world than I can ever explain to you." He gestured to the thin aspens around them, the trail, the grass. "We just define the world differently. I do what I love every day. Isn't that a great thing to you?"

He wiped sweat from his forehead, trying to keep up. "Sure, of course."

"To make this life possible, I need to be around people who live the same way. I need coaching, training partners, a specific routine. Mack provides these things for me, and he just asks that I agree to a few basic rules that aren't so different from the ones at any company."

Shane held his palms up. "Okay."

Caleb stepped off the trail into the brush. Their dad, Fred, had always taught them never to leave a trail, and so Shane hesitated. Then he ducked beneath the nettles after him, breathing in the moldy exhaled breath of the undergrowth. When he looked up, wary of stray branches, he saw that they had arrived at a small clearing.

"You meditate?" Caleb asked casually, hands on his hips.

"Janelle tried to teach me once. I started thinking about her boobs."

"Just count to two. Over and over."

"That's not going to make me think about boobs?" Shane grinned. He was aware of a certain manic ascent in his voice. He attributed it to his low blood sugar.

Caleb sank to the ground, crossed his legs, and stared ahead, his eyes defocusing. Shane watched him with some disbelief. Looking at the sunlight breaking through the chocolate branches, he felt an intense longing to speak with Janelle. He spent some time thinking about the baby, wondering how much it would change him.

"Hey." Somewhat louder, Shane said, "Hey, it's been like an hour."

Caleb remained in the same position. Then Shane turned his back on his brother and made his way through the dense brush toward where he thought the trail might be. Once he found it, getting back should be simple, he thought. But he would need to be careful; this weak, it would be easy to become lost.

The insects seemed to have tripled around him. Sweat streamed down Shane's neck; he felt in danger of passing out. Far off he could see a small pinprick of blue. A butterfly? Some runner's shirt? A branch scratched his cheek hard, startling him. A Clif Bar, he cursed. He might have been offered a goddamn Clif Bar. He placed his hands back on his hips and turned around, disoriented. He hurried his pace, afraid it might get dark.

The more exhausted he became, the angrier he felt. He still had no clue why Caleb had asked him here; he had assumed it was to leave the house, but now he was fairly sure it wasn't. A long time later he saw a clearing far below that looked familiar. Stumbling down the mountain base, he made out the wooden cabin in the distance. He experienced a fierce, visceral hatred for it.

His rental car was parked at its side; he could get in, eat a big steak in Boulder, drive to the airport, and be home in time to sleep beside Janelle, wrap his arm around her belly, and feel the kicking heels of whoever was inside waiting for them. But first he would raid their kitchen.

The trail widened into the field, and he walked the open half mile back to the house. Shane marched up the steps to the back door. In the kitchen, a short, dark woman with a long black braided ponytail stood over the sink. He stood in the doorway, streaming with sweat.

She smiled. "Hey, you're Caley's brother?"

He shook his head, breathing impossibly hard. "I'm really thirsty."

The woman stood on her toes, opened a cabinet, and took out a pint glass with the faded words ROCKING HORSE TAVERN printed on its side. She poured tap water and handed it to him. Shane chugged and refilled it three times.

"I'm Rae," she almost laughed.

"Anything to eat here, Rae? I'm starving."

"Orphans in Sudan are starving. You're hungry."

"Crackers? Banana?"

"'Fraid not. Supper's in an hour."

"How do you guys live?"

"How do you?" she smiled, amused.

Shane shrugged agreeably.

"Your brother's one of my favorite people. He's always so busy. I don't see him as much as I'd like to."

"Me neither." He hoped the resentment in his tone was apparent. "Where's the shower?"

"Upstairs, to your left."

Shane went weakly through the kitchen door. The main room of the house was enormous. People milled about with what seemed to him to be very clear purpose. He looked for June but didn't see her. On the stairs he had to grab both railings to steady himself.

"Caley take you out hiking?" a grinning young guy asked him.

Shane nodded.

"Don't let him brutalize you." The guy squatted beside him. "I'm Kevin Yu. Caleb's roommate."

They shook hands. Carefully, Shane asked, "How's he doing?"

"Great. He rocks, man." Kevin waved some people over. "Hey, meet Caleb's brother."

This drew a crowd. People gathered around the stairs, peppered him with questions. Fuck, Shane thought, my brother's a Beatle.

He went back down to the couch with them. Why not? No one else here seemed to care about showering, and he was cooling down with the house as the light faded out its windows. He listened to stories about his brother, insane races they had run, up mountains, through snowstorms and mudslides, on broken bones and under blazing sun. What concerned him was that none of these people seemed crazy. A couple of them had that weird gleam in the eye he had been expecting, like very committed Evangelicals, but nothing made him feel uncomfortable.

And suddenly everyone turned toward the front door.

A small man bounded into the house with the energy of a

Labrador. His black beard was patchy, as if it had been stunted in childhood. He wore a swirling blue and yellow tie-dye, damp with sweat. But mostly Shane noticed his eyes. They were made of a blue unlike any other he had seen before. As if they were filled with souls.

Shane smiled and said, "Hi, Mack."

6

"Hey," Mack cried gleefully, "the *brother*."

Shane considered him: he was much smaller and slighter than he had expected. With the ponytail, the ungroomed beard, he might be sitting at a bar in North Beach, complaining about gentrification. Instead, he ruled seventeen impossibly conditioned athletes with a glance, possessed a reputation for faith healing, and according to Internet reports, could outrun any of them on their daily eight-hour sojourns.

As Mack walked into the house, the others seemed to part to make way for him. Shane stood and shook his hand, and followed him toward the mantel, where two younger housemates were starting the evening's fire.

"So finally," Mack grinned. "What took you so long?"

Shane stared at him. Was that mischief in his tone? He decided to return to his policy of respect. "Thank you for having me. I'm glad to be here."

"No worries. What do you do for work, Shane?"

"I'm in sales. Just starting for a biotechnology company."

Mack's blue eyes intensified. "Biotechnology? Let me ask you, I read this thing about biology once. It said the single-cell organism is the most perfect form of life on this planet. If you lost all the weak parts of us, the parts that are vulnerable to attack, to disease, and stripped us to our purest being, that's what we would be. A virus. The amoeba isn't what life's evolving from, it's what life's evolving *to.* You ever heard that?"

"I haven't. It kind of makes sense though."

"Yeah?" Mack asked happily. "I thought so. Hey so, where's big bro at?"

"Meditating on the trail."

A warm bell sounded, and the sixteen present members of the Happy Trails Running Club appeared. They came from outside, upstairs, from places Shane had never noticed, and sat in front of the fireplace in a circle.

"So, we have a guest with us tonight," Mack announced to them. "Caleb's bro, Mister Shane."

Immediately two members of the circle shifted, making space. He sat down appreciatively.

"Hi, Shane," came a chorus of voices from around him. Pats on the back, nods and smiles from across the circle.

Shane came alive a little, unable to resist the vibe. In its cloistered, warm ritual it reminded him of visiting a friend's fraternity house. They had established their own patterns, which happens, he thought, whenever people live together.

Rae, whom he'd met in the kitchen, and a taut young man with a buzz-cut named Hank brought wooden bowls filled with something that smelled very strong. Shane took his with a grateful thank-you and inhaled its steam, marvelously happy for it. He guessed it would be the healthiest dinner he had eaten in a while.

The conversation revolved around who was running tomorrow, and who was working. A woman talked about a dying deer she'd seen in Rocky Mountain National Park. The bowl held a thick stew of vegetables and herbs. Shane devoured it. When he stood to get more, Kevin quickly touched his arm.

"One helping."

"Sorry, I didn't eat today."

"It's an engineered stew," Mack explained from across the circle, "for people who run thirty miles a day. You don't need any more."

"Cool," he said, sitting back down.

"Good deal."

When everyone finished, Shane spotted a bookshelf by a closed door near the stairs and went to it. It was filled with some well-thumbed books about meditation, vegan diets, reiki. And numerous copies of *You Can Run 100 Miles!*

Shane took a copy; his left knee cracked worrisomely as he shifted his weight. The back cover was a shot of a much younger Mack, smiling triumphantly against a mountain background, wearing yellow running shorts. His wrinkles were shallower, and his skin looked better. His eyes were just as mesmerizing. Under the photograph Shane read, "Ultrarunning is the sport for our times. Now Ultrarunning's premier trainer shares his methods for taking your body—and your life—past all limits."

He thumbed through the book with a grin.

"Prefer chick lit?" Mack asked jauntily from just behind him.

There was an awkward silence, not helped by Shane's near complete mental and physical depletion.

"It's amazing"—Shane's face spread into his most salesy smile—"what you do with people."

"Shit." Mack pushed a hand through his thick black hair. "It's amazing what *you* do. Selling biotechnology. Tell me, how does it work?"

"Basically, we help the body heal itself."

"How do you do that?"

"Instead of adding man-made chemicals, we use proteins that our bodies already make to cause a reaction it already knows how to. Just hasn't been doing."

Mack pointed excitedly, his finger barely missing Shane's chest. "See? That's exactly what *we* do. We help the body heal itself and do things it already knows how to, with a substance it already makes. You call it proteins. I call it kinetic energy. We believe in the same things."

"You think so?"

Mack raised his bearded chin. "You guys make a cure for the cold yet?"

"Nope." Shane replaced the book.

"We do. No one here's needed antibiotics for years."

"But our patients are free to leave and visit their families."

Mack locked eyes with him, nodding. So, here it was.

"Caleb has a job up in Boulder. If he wanted to leave, he'd hop a cab to the airport. He's living here because he wants to."

"He thinks he wants to. You have him running all day, sleeping four hours a night, eating twice a day. That's not a recipe for clear thinking."

Mack smiled, much more pleasantly than Shane would have supposed. "You think if Caleb was eating steak and sleeping in, he'd wake up and think, what am I doing, I want to be a consultant, and move back to New York City?"

Shane did not break eye contact; he felt like a fighter before the bell.

But Mack's face burst into a wild grin. "Come on, brother. He's happy. He's not sleep or food deprived, he's sleep and food *heightened*. His body is functioning in a near-perfect state, rid of the toxins of oversleeping, overeating, over-Tylenoling. You have to understand the compulsion of feeling this good. Of course he avoids anything that might try and pull him away. Once you get your body to this point, you don't stop. Trips home, different food, people telling you you're crazy, it's not the way to stay in the flow. It's great you're here. He needs you to be supportive."

"Oh, don't worry about that."

Mack looked as if he was trying to determine the extent of Shane's sarcasm. "It's great to meet you, Shane. I'll tap the keg in an hour." He opened a door beside the bookshelf, and shut it behind him.

Caleb means too much to these people, Shane realized, standing there. They would never let him out of here. He had found a home, of that there was no doubt. Whether it was a healthy home, that was the question. He looked through the back window out at the field. The older military man, John, and a large-boned woman with star tattoos stood on the grass in some kind of yogic pose, their arms raised toward heaven. Behind them the base of the mountain was cast in amethyst shadow.

And then he saw a slender silhouette walking calmly toward the house, thin amber hair slipping over his ears. And like healthy cells mutating into cancer, Shane's good feelings transformed into a thunderous resentment. He opened the back door, ran down the steps, and charged him. He felt he might be flying. When he met the yellow-shirted figure of his brother, bone thin and of sour smell, Shane shoved him with both hands.

"I've been waiting for you for hours."

Caleb looked surprised.

"You asked me to come here. You wrote to me."

"I was meditating. If I came to see you, I wouldn't be angry if you went to meditate."

"If you came to see me," Shane spat back sarcastically. "When exactly is that happening?" His voice rose into the bruised sky. "It's so incredibly *now*, isn't it Caleb? To do this extreme running lifestyle thing? In the fifties you'd have been riding trains and talking about individuality. In the sixties, you'd have moved to a commune. Every generation has its way to rebel against society. But it's all as conformist as working at any consulting company."

Caleb's voice came oddly even. "This isn't about conforming or not. I don't care what anyone else is doing."

"We know that, Caleb." Shane looked up to the thin branches. The summer mountain air was breathless around them. He felt so tired he could hardly believe he was still moving. He heard his words coming out of him too fast, as if whole sentences were simply syllables. "But you care about Mack. He tells you what to eat, how long you can sleep, and you do it. And you care about that girl, June."

Something in Caleb's face noticeably changed, and Shane straightened. It came to him now. The way Caleb had looked when he'd walked in and seen them talking. The way she'd looked back at him.

"Is that why you wrote to me? Because of June?"

Caleb paled. "I call her Bluebird."

"Because of her eyes."

Caleb's eyes swelled. It moved him beyond words, that Shane could see her that way.

And Shane watched the old Caleb materialize out of the blackness like a ghost. It was in the muscles around his mouth, the relaxing of his shoulders. He touched Caleb's shoulder. "What do you need? You want to get in the car? With her? Just tell me."

"I need to help her."

"With what?"

Caleb started to tremble, looking around at the aspens. "She can't breathe. Her lungs don't work. Her feet are all swollen."

"Okay. We'll take her to a doctor."

"I did that." Caleb looked up, as if pleading with the sky. "They did a blood test. There's something wrong with her genes. Mack is doing energy healing but I don't think it's working. This is . . ."

"This," Shane said respectfully, "is beyond him."

Caleb looked spectral. Shane had thought it was the physical stress he put on his body that had aged his brother so drastically, but now he saw there was more than that.

"You work with doctors," Caleb whispered. "You know about new drugs. Can you find out what we should do?"

"I . . ."

Caleb bent his forehead to his brother's. "I'll leave here to help her." He pulled back, blinking, as if shocked at having said these words out loud.

Shane stared at him, his mouth dry.

Caleb walked past him to the deck, opened the back door, and Shane followed him through the kitchen, into the main room, where some of the Happy Trails members sat by a fire drinking black beer. Together they ascended the creaking stairs.

At the landing, instead of going left for his room, Caleb turned right. At the very far end of the hall was a door. The old floors creaked underneath them as they moved toward it. Caleb hesitated, his face narrowed in concentration.

He reached for the doorknob, quietly turned it, pushed the door open. Shane took in a pale light. On the left side of the room he saw June, standing over something he recognized. She looked up, smiled shyly, waved him over. A sweet, familiar smell rose around him. He realized now that he'd caught traces of it in the air downstairs, that it had been there the whole time.

A wooden crib had been pushed against the left wall. Shane walked over slowly and peered down. Inside, a baby was sleeping. Wisps of reddish hair shimmered in the starlight through the window. She seemed very thin, and pale. She wore a yellow sleeper that was too big for her, her tiny milk white arm curved above her head as if performing an arabesque. She was, Shane guessed, maybe ten weeks old.

A sound came to him then. It stopped him. A sharp, high-pitched wheeze that pierced the air like a kettle, coming from the baby's breaths.

"This is Lily," Caleb smiled.

Shane gripped the crib's railing, watching, listening, confused.

Outside, a breeze tumbled down from the mountain, gaining speed as it headed for them, as if it intended to rattle the wooden cabin and everyone in it and strip them down to their basic cells.

PART TWO

Orphans

7

On Monday morning, Shane began his first day at Helixia.

He was greeted unexpectedly at the second-floor elevator by a short, Sicilian-looking brunette wearing oblong maroon glasses over a punchy nose.

"I'm Stacey," she told him. Shane started to shake her hand. Instead, she tossed him a baseball. "You're Janelle's husband?"

"It's amazing, I know."

As they walked down the hall she waved at a few people.

"Dennis says you were a star at Orco."

"That seems overstated."

"I can see why you left," Stacey frowned. "Any company where frat boys make two hundred grand a year has to be full of assholes."

He felt unsure how to respond. She dropped him at a cubicle with a wave.

"I'm on your team. There's a weekly sales review with Dennis in half an hour. I'll pick you up."

Shane stood in his empty cube, staring at a note from IT

about his computer. Leaves from a plant spiraled down the right side of the partition from the adjacent desk.

His flight home had been difficult. He had spent Saturday night watching the Happy Trails house fill with guests. Many of them looked like other runners; some were clearly locals there for free beer. He had drunk moderately, his eyes lifting frequently toward the second floor, where he knew the baby to be sleeping. Although Caleb had spoken of going up to Boulder to see a band, he had not had time alone with him again.

"I'll leave here to help her."

The words had burned through Shane's body as he drove back to Denver. During the flight he lost himself looking out at the Rockies. They seemed alive to him, rippling and flowing with some inner force. He could make out small roads along their slopes. He imagined the overwhelming awe of the first settlers who encountered them. Which of them had dared dream that they could scale these sharp, infinite peaks? What kind of person had laid down these roads? He thought of his brother.

By the time he had landed, his exhaustion had turned into a thick syrup behind his sinuses. Janelle greeted him with jasmine tea, and they sat on their old white sofa. She had put some Internet radio on, and sleepy ambient music soothed his head. Outside their bay window, a streetlight battled with the fog.

"Is it his baby?" Janelle asked right away.

Shane watched her; the intensity behind her eyes might, he thought, be the thing that made her most beautiful. "He says no."

"What's June like?"

"Kind of mousey. But she runs these ultramarathons, so how mousey can she be?"

Janelle placed his hand on top of her belly and pressed down, and he felt their baby push back. It filled him with something like magic.

"What are the others like? Super weird?"

"A little weird, for sure. But they're nice, you'd like them. There's twenty-year-olds, thirty-year-olds, forty-year-olds. One guy, John, is in his, like, late fifties. You know, they all work in local towns, or even up in Boulder like Caleb. They see a lot of regular people. They're not trapped in some compound." He nodded to himself, as if just realizing something. "They could leave there anytime they want to."

"They're brainwashed," Janelle pronounced, sipping her tea. "Four hours of sleep a night? Two meals a day? Eight hours of running a day? They're all exhausted, dependent physically and emotionally, on this Mack guy. He can give them some leash, they're not going anywhere."

"Just to play devil's advocate, it seems to work."

Janelle frowned. "How do you mean?"

"They kick ass in these ultramarathons."

"Well, I guess their lives are great then."

"This is good," Shane yawned, finishing his mug. "What did you put in it?"

"Tell me about the baby."

He leaned back into the sofa. "She has a genetic disorder. I searched it on my phone. It says there's no treatment. June brought her there so Mack could cure her, he's supposedly this healer? This whole thing is predicated on him being all-powerful. They all have stories about him healing their injuries and diseases"—Shane waved his arms—"with the laying on of his hands."

"Energy healing works," she informed him.

"If you're Chinese."

She shook her head at his ignorance.

"But it's not working for Lily. June and Caleb, they've lost faith in him. I need to find options. There has to be something in trials, don't you think? If not from Helixia, then from someone?"

"There are trials going on for almost everything," she agreed.

"I need to find one to get this baby into. One as far from Colorado as possible."

Janelle considered this. "Talk to Dineesh. He's our Director of Immunology. He'd know all the stuff that's not public yet."

"Cool," Shane replied, pressing his eyes with the flats of his hands.

While Janelle slept, he'd lain on his side, staring at her stomach. Her body was making calculations and divisions beyond his understanding. The big questions about their son had already been decided: would he have an instinct for trigonometry? A wide Asian nose? Would he shoot with his left? But other decisions were ongoing. Every day, billions of Nicholas's cells were splitting and dividing, agreeing on details without bothering to check with Shane.

And this was where things went wrong. Too much or too little of one protein in one cell, and their lives would all change forever. Written into the spiraling strands of Nicholas's genetic code were secrets they would only learn by watching.

Shane's knowledge of genetic prenatal disease, which he had picked up during his career selling these drugs, might have frightened him, but Shane felt no real fear for his unborn son. Things did not go wrong in his life. Only his brother had ever disturbed his confidence in the universe.

Stacey took him to his first meeting, where Dennis Adderberry greeted him warmly. He was introduced by conference call to his team of sales reps around the Northwest. They briefed him on the current state of the cancer drug Sorion. It was selling beautifully, though its chart seemed to have plateaued some years earlier. Dennis gave a cheery speech about the future. Afterward, Shane stayed behind to speak with him.

"The scientists who created this," he asked. "Do they still work here?"

"Most of them, sure."

"I'd love to talk with one of them. I like to have an idea of the thinking behind products, understand the passion they have for it. I use that when I sell to doctors."

Dennis's jet black eyebrows arched, and Shane sensed he had made an unorthodox request. "Well, you should talk to Prajuk Acharn. He led the team. I'm sure he'd tell you what you want to know, if you can get him to leave his lab."

So at lunch, Shane walked out into June's early breeze, across a brick walkway to the concrete, five-story Research and Laboratory building. It reminded him of a Lego piece: blunt, flat, unadorned, ready to be transplanted like a gene onto another building.

When its industrial door closed behind him, all signs of day disappeared. There were no windows, and no reception area. A small sign directed him to Protein Chemistry. He turned left, facing a long straight corridor, and noticed a pungent chemical scent dominating the air. Though the corridor was empty, he could feel the presence of scientist specters. He walked past narrow offices adorned with names from every culture imaginable, until he found the nameplate for Dr. Prajuk Acharn.

His knock pushed the door open, revealing a slight man behind a small desk. He seemed to be in his early sixties. He wore a white shirt and a brown tie too thick for these times. He possessed a narrow face on the edge of delicacy, and his straight black hair was combed harshly to the left, though it faced a counterinsurgency along its part. He was glancing between an old PC on the side of his desk and a larger Mac monitor in front of him. His neck, Shane thought, must ache at night.

"Excuse me? Doctor Acharn?"

The scientist looked up at him.

"I'm Shane Oberest. I'm the new Director of Commercial on Sorion."

An empty swivel chair sat just out of reach, but Shane didn't feel he should make a move for it just yet.

"I'm fairly sure I've never seen anyone from Commercial in this building, unless we're in a Phase Three." Doctor Acharn's voice was unexpectedly high-pitched, that particular nasal blend of Asia and California.

"Are you Korean?" Shane asked him impulsively.

"No, I'm from Khon Kaen."

"Really? I'd love to see the beaches."

"All American college students want to see the beaches. This thing has become some rite of passage."

"It used to be Jamaica," Shane told him.

"A huge loss for the Jamaicans," Prajuk replied dryly.

Shane smiled and took a tentative step inside his office. "So, I just started on Sorion." He placed a thick purple-bound deck onto his desk. "They gave me this."

"They want you to learn about a biologic from a PowerPoint deck?"

Shane grinned. The doctor's eyes brightened, and he knew he was in.

"I'd love to ask you a couple of questions really, really quick. Do you have a few minutes by any chance?"

"A few, sure."

"I'd like to understand more than the numbers. Can I ask you about its genesis? You guys were looking for a cure for prostate cancer?"

"Oh, no. Is that what that deck says?"

He sat in the chair, as Prajuk shook his head. "This thing, 'cure,' is what they say for investors. We are not looking for a cure for cancer."

Shane frowned. "You're not?"

"There is no such thing."

"If you don't believe in curing cancer, then what do you want patients to do?"

"Live with it." Prajuk leaned back into his chair.

"Live with it?"

"Why not? Your body already lives with cancer every day. Stop anyone on the street at any time and screen them, and you'll find some cancerous cells. So what? Your body absorbs them, most of the time. We place our bet on aiding the body's natural processes to absorb these mutations before they grow large enough to interfere with life. We do not bombard it with radiations and chemicals. Attack the body, and it will attack back. That is what kills people."

"Well, the tumors kill people."

But Prajuk shook his head no. "Most cancer patients don't die from cancer. They die from having their immune system and red blood cells obliterated by chemotherapy and radiation. They get pneumonia, infections; organ failure. With Sorion, we were not starting from a place of, how do we cure cancer? We were studying B and T cells, to understand how they function. Nothing in the body exists to do nothing."

"Except male nipples."

Doctor Acharn looked at him. A moment passed.

"What we noticed was that cancerous cells produce an enzyme that healthy cells do not. This thing, a telomere, is an enzyme which prevents a cell from dividing. So it keeps growing, until it interferes with the body's essential processes. If we could focus on inhibiting telomere production, we could stop this thing, tumors, from growing, without trying to kill them. Our idea is to keep this thing, tumors, at a size where the body can live with them. And manage cancer, the way you manage diabetes."

Shane blinked. "That's a pretty radical notion."

"To doctors, maybe. But not to the body. B cells already produce a monoclonal antibody that targets telomeres and inhibits them. That is what our team discovered. The challenge is, the body does not produce enough of it. So obviously, if we could isolate these telomeres' antibodies, if we could reproduce them in the lab"—he opened his arms—"then we could have a drug that targets only the cells which produce telomeres and leaves the healthy cells alone. With healthy cells alive and functioning, there are none of the side effects to current chemotherapy treatment. No pneumonia, no hair loss, no weakness, the immune system is left whole. Only the tumorous cells are targeted."

Shane shook his head. Coming from Orco, a company that sold chemotherapy drugs, and then more drugs to address their side effects, this was a revelation. "I think I'm getting this. It's enzyme profiling."

Doctor Acharn clapped his hands. This small gesture of joy seemed a complete breaking of his character. In his high-pitched voice he exclaimed, "Enzyme profiling. Yes. Definitely you are in Commercial for a reason."

"So, is that what Sorion is?"

"Yes. We cloned the gene that produces this antibody that attacks telomeres. We placed it on to an HIV virus, and introduced it back into the body. The virus carries the new cells through the body where . . ." He noticed the look on Shane's face. "This thing is a disabled form of HIV. We are not injecting cancer patients with live AIDS-causing organisms."

"Okay, that's good to hear."

"HIV is actually a wonderful vehicle for transporting genes through the body. What makes it so terrible to fight also makes it unstoppable in advancing good. Just because it is being used to destroy life does not mean it cannot be used to save it. Everything in nature is a tool, you know."

"I'm starting to understand that."

Doctor Acharn was watching him. "Now maybe you can help me understand something."

"Sure."

"This name 'Sorion'? This thing sounds like a whale. What has this word got to do with telomeres?"

Shane grinned. "That's actually in the PowerPoint."

He noticed several picture frames on the doctor's desk, but their backs were to him. He wondered what they displayed.

"You should write a book, Doctor."

"I'm reading one."

Shane understood; he was talking about the human body. "How long have you worked here, Doctor Acharn?"

"A long time. I was employee number five."

"Really? So you know Steven Poulos?"

"My mentor."

Helixia had been founded by Steven Poulos and Walter Pietrowski, known to the biotech community ever since as P&P, in 1979. Poulos had been a young researcher at Stanford when he isolated and cloned a protein that replicated red blood cells. His lab assistant had been Prajuk Acharn. When a twenty-eight-year-old venture capital banker named Walter Pietrowski heard about this on the Palo Alto party circuit, he tracked him down. Two months later, they started Helixia as a research boutique.

In 1980, Genentech completed the biggest IPO in history, and Wall Street went insane for any biotech, boutique or otherwise. Eighteen months later, Pietrowski took Helixia public; anyone who stayed a year past that date was in this to save lives. Prajuk was one of them.

Now his eyes darted to one of his monitors. Shane watched his forehead wrinkle and stood up.

"Thanks for your time, Doctor. I do have more questions, things I can work into my sell."

"These things, e-mail them to me."

Prajuk extended a hand over his desk. As Shane leaned in, his forearm brushed a framed photograph and almost knocked it over. His face hardening, Prajuk reached out quickly to straighten it.

. . . .

Helixia's speed and intensity made Orco look archaic.

Shane felt as if he was constantly catching up. Dennis needed him to run a major annual sales conference on Sorion, for which he was vastly unprepared. He spent hours each day introducing himself to oncology practices. Each time he began to type "alpha-one antitrypsin deficiency" into his computer or phone, his e-mail would sound, a text would come, someone would swing by his cubicle.

And as soon as his workday ended, Janelle would call him from the lobby to attend infant CPR class or to hit Babies "R" Us to pick up some last remaining item. Per Janelle's suggestion, he sent an e-mail to Doctor Dineesh Pawar asking for an appointment, but at the end of the week he had still not received a reply. On Thursday, he blocked off an hour in his calendar and drove to a nearby Peet's to begin some focused research into Lily's disease.

What he found saddened him. Lily's lungs were hyperinflated. It wasn't that they could not take a breath; it was that they could not exhale one. The air the baby inhaled became trapped inside of her, leaving only a sliver at the top for fresh oxygen. The remainder of her lungs were atrophying, unused, gray and shriveled; this produced the chronic wheeze and dry cough he had heard in her room. The condition was irreversible. It led to early onset emphysema, and an unhappy, short life. He quickly pushed the image out of his head, as if some form of transference could spread this disease to his own unmet baby.

For a decade he had wanted Caleb to leave Boulder, but felt selfish and childish each time he considered it. So his brother was living a different life than they all wanted him to, what was wrong with that? There had never been any concrete, objective reason to try to make him leave. Now, awful as it was, he had it. If he could find some test, some treatment, here.

It would take time, massive amounts of time, to research this condition, contact specialists, learn things that weren't to be found in online message boards and medical sites. In the car he punched his steering wheel. For a decade, Caleb had run beside strangers, knowing how much Shane would have given to have just thirty minutes with him. And after eleven years of total silence, Caleb had chosen this time, the busiest of Shane's life, to reemerge? Rounding the Embarcadero toward home, he resolved to devote the rest of his night to e-mailing this Doctor Pawar, and tomorrow morning to personally introducing himself to everyone in Immunology.

He opened the front door to find Janelle on their couch, beads of sweat making their way down the smooth skin of her temples.

"Get the car," she whispered.

Shane ran for her blue gym bag and helped her out to the Civic. Her body felt foreign and awkward, this body he had known for years. At the street she tightened her jaw.

"Are you uncomfortable, or is it real pain?"

"I'm having contractions. Don't be an asshole."

These words, reverberating into the bones of his fully formed son, hurt him in a new and profound way. Shane brought the seat belt carefully over her belly and drove slowly over the huge hill of Mason Street as Janelle gripped his wrist.

At the hospital, a butch nurse laid Janelle on a cold metal table and attached a fetal monitor. The nurse gave it an odd look, tore the paper from the twitching needle, and walked away without a word. More time passed than seemed necessary. Janelle expressed concern, but Shane inhaled easily; there was no problem, because in his life things did not go very wrong.

When the nurse returned, they were taken to a wide delivery room. An epidural was called for, and Shane ordered out of the room. He wandered to the lobby, looking out the window at its glimpse of the Pacific beyond. He called Fred and Julie, and Liu and Hua, whom he had to dissuade from coming immediately over. He considered finding the number of that copy store in Boulder, but he figured Caleb would ask for information about Lily's illness, and Shane had no answer for his failure to obtain any. Tomorrow, he promised himself. He made his way back into the warm room where Janelle lay smiling. A nurse was pointing toward a monitor.

"That green light," she explained, "is his heartbeat."

And Shane was lost in a green bouncing haze. It seemed to him to possess personality, playfulness, eagerness to see him.

"Ready to meet your little boy?"

It was happening so quickly; he would have liked some time to inhale. The doctor instructed him to take Janelle's leg. This he was unprepared for but he felt more connected now, touching his wife's body, feeling the energy burning from it, as she pushed. And some time soon after, he saw Nicholas's head appear facedown, covered in matted, thick black hair. He watched the doctor grasp his son's shoulders and turn his body clockwise, and then in one seamless, sudden burst, this whole being was propelled into his life as if there had never been a moment without him.

Shane looked to Janelle, her arms outstretched for the writhing baby, and he began to laugh, and every other thought he had in the world was swept out, out into the endless ocean.

2

"They're bike riders." Mack shook his head in disgust. "What the fuck is that?"

Beside him, Caleb smiled. They were driving a back stretch at dawn, under protection of full blue firs which lined the sides of the road like riot police. Last night they had been at the Rocking Horse Tavern, whose flat screens had been showing coverage of the Tour de France.

"They go up really steep mountains," Caleb offered helpfully, "for three weeks."

"On *bikes.* They only ride six hours a day. Surrounded by teammates to shield them from the wind. They have cooks. This shit gets you famous? Lance Armstrong is a national icon, but Scott Jurek works at a shoe store?"

"It's a global event."

"We should fly over there and run that whole course. The month before they ride it." Mack turned to him mischievously. "Might show people a thing or two."

"That would be fun."

Thursday night at the Rocking Horse was a Happy Trails

ritual. Friends from their jobs, intrigued running aficionados, and people who just enjoyed drinking with the freaks met them there. The gathering had turned into a standing party, a night for them all to get loose; things could become rowdy.

The first time that Caleb had attended a Rocking Horse Thursday, he had been confused by the Happy Trails runners' ability to put down so much alcohol. Pints of microbrew and shots of Beam flowed like air.

The bartender had explained, "These guys' metabolisms are insane. Their bodies process food so fast, the alcohol gives them a buzz, then evaporates from their systems. No matter how drunk they get, they're sober two hours later. They don't even get hung over."

But Caleb enjoyed Thursdays less than the rest of his housemates. Drinking had never interested him. More than a few of his housemates had been addicts of one sort or another though, and for them this ability to imbibe without consequence was a sort of superpower.

Mack forced the Jeep over a pile of igneous rock. "How many people you think started biking because of Lance Armstrong? That's how many people will start ultrarunning because of the Yosemite Slam. Once they see you."

"Is that what having the Yosemite race on TV is for?" Caleb asked carefully.

"We shall spark a holy fire. A network of Happy Trails groups, all around the country, thousands of people creating kinetic energy. Can you see what would happen? There would be enough healing energy in the air to close wounds instantaneously. Cancer would end. Emotional trauma would heal like skin. You would fill your lungs with air and be whole."

A jarring transition from the dirt road to concrete bespoke the entrance to Superior. There the endless sky was replaced with strung traffic lights and gray billboards for attorneys-at-law. Mack swerved suddenly into a short driveway, throwing Caleb against the side door.

"It's time to go mass, brother."

Caleb opened the door to a small, ancient storefront gym. Inside he encountered the musk of a century of sweat, walked past old weights, first-generation exercise bikes, ancient metal machines, red mats with exposed yellow padding, on which measureless sit-ups had been performed.

In the back by the lockers he took off his shirt, leaving on his small blue running shorts, socks, and an old pair of gray and blue sneakers. He took measure of his long thin torso in a mirror, as Mack unzipped a gym bag and started pulling out bottles and placing them inside the old sauna. He opened each of them; later Caleb's hands would be too wet to do it.

The sauna was the size of a large closet; it smelled of cedarwood and fungus. Caleb opened the door and stepped inside, heard its hiss and crackle as it fired up.

Mack raised a fist. "'Oh to struggle against great odds. To meet enemies undaunted. To be entirely alone with them. To find how much one can stand!'"

He nodded and closed the door, and Caleb began to jog in place.

Sweat filled his shoes within seconds. Each lift of his legs came with a deep intake of hot, oxygen-starved air, which scorched his lungs. His pores opened. His brain unleashed torrents of adrenaline, its pain receptors warned his body to stop.

Blend with the air. Blend with the air.

His discomfort grew into a sharp pain in his sides. His kidneys, he knew. Caleb found a spot on the cedar wall and stared at it. In his little spot, Caleb found the void. Here he experienced a sort of hyperspace; he registered discomfort, but distantly, the way a passenger inside a train registers landscape.

But the void held a tricky duality: awareness that he was inside of it made it disappear. And then he was thrust into his body's miseries. Mack had trained them to develop an unconscious muscle memory to block them from snapping out. This time the void carried him long enough that he did not notice finishing two water bottles as he pounded against the steaming cedar floor.

Mack tapped on the narrow Plexiglas window and held up four fingers; somehow, he was only a quarter of his way through. Abandoned in a searing agony, Caleb searched for that spot again but saw only a haze of heat. Sweat burned his eyes. Desperately his mind flailed for something to grab onto.

During a race, he would have goals that would accomplish this: the next aid station, the next climb. Now, there was only depletion, as his sneakers slipped in puddles of his own sweat. Here he was training for anguish.

Where was Shane? It had been three weeks, and there had been no word at all. He tried to recall his brother's exact words: Had he said he would help, had he promised? He could not remember.

Caleb grabbed for another bottle; the water was hot in his throat. He turned around to face the bench; there was a chance that its long slats of wood might take him on a hallucination for some length of time. But before he could slip into one, Caleb heard a tap on the glass door; Mack was holding three fingers now. He knew they signified some code, but he could not recall its meaning. His kidneys were swelling against his skin.

If not the wood, if not the void, if not a visualization, then memory might take him from his suffering. He thought of June's soft face, there, that felt right. He reached out a hand to feel her skin. Bluebird, he smiled. He tried to recall the first time he had seen her.

He had been on breakfast shift on a windy March morning, simmering the grains in the kitchen, when he had heard a rare knock upon the front door. The house was two miles' dirt drive from the nearest paved road, and visitors did not appear often. Rae had opened the front door to find a thin woman, her hair like wheat, her eyes wide and blue. She had asked for Mack. In her hands she gripped a dark blue plastic car seat, with a sleeping infant.

Mack had been out leading a group of twelve through the chilly trails. Rae invited her to sit with them and wait.

"So cute," Rae had exclaimed, staring at the baby. "What's her name?"

June had smiled shyly. "Lily."

"Lily. Beautiful."

"How old is she?" Leigh had walked over asking.

"She's three weeks."

Caleb had stood in the kitchen doorway, squeezing a dishtowel, watching in the way he had watched girls from a high school classroom. The thin woman met his eyes across the expanse of the room and smiled. The energy between them felt as real to him as a rope line.

"We drove from Taos to see Mister McConnell. I hope that's okay?"

John walked over and sat down. "Are you a runner?"

"Yes. I read his book." She looked extremely nervous.

"You want to run with us?"

"Oh, yeah, but . . . that's not why we came." She had hesitated, looking at them all. "I need healing. My daughter does. Do you hear?"

Caleb walked across the wide room, the scent of pines pouring in through the open windows, to the long old couch. Arriving he heard a sound like a mountain train coming with her every exhaled breath. That was when he noticed how small the baby seemed.

"Does she have pneumonia or something?" Leigh asked, her eyes narrowing.

June shook her head. "They thought it was asthma? But none of the medicine works. It just makes her heart race and race. They don't know what all it is."

"Doctors don't know much," John commiserated.

"But I was watching a cable show, and Mister McConnell was on. He was talking about how you build up this energy by running, and it heals you? And I thought, I run. I just thought, I think he can teach me how to help her."

"How far do you run?" Rae asked gently, prepared to explain.

"I've done fifty miles."

Leigh looked to Rae and raised her eyebrows.

"Where's her father?" she asked, glancing out the door at the small rental car.

"Not with us. Todd left me right before she was born," June explained plainly. "I got these mood swings . . . I guess I was kind of a beast."

"Asshole," Rae exhaled.

When Mack returned, he saw them and beamed beatifically; he had a way of smiling that brought a whole room to transcendence. Caleb had pulled himself away for a run in what was left of the mountain snow. Afterward, he looked for the woman and the baby.

"How long did they stay?" he asked Leigh as casually as he could.

"They're still here. They've been in Mack's room for a while."

Mack possessed the only private room, next to the bookcase. Walking inside his room he felt as if he had stepped into a warm bath. His sore body began to feel stronger. June and Mack lay on a soft white rug that Mack used for private reiki sessions. They looked up at him.

Caleb stared helplessly. And saw that the baby's pale body lay between them. Mack was holding his hands just above her chest, while June cradled her head. June was crying.

Mack looked up harshly. To come here without an invitation was unthought of.

Caleb was overcome by a desire to join them. "Can I help?"

"In the morning, you take June out. See what she can do."

"All right."

Like a servant taking his leave, he had backed out of the room. After he closed the door he stood in the hall, breathing, for a long time.

• • • • • • •

That first run with June was a morning that would replay itself, on other runs, at night, during his dreams.

He had led her toward the steep open road up to Boulder. Along the tapered trails he would have been forced to lead or follow single file, but here they moved side by side, as he wanted. The wide mountain road steepened, and he inhaled deeply, enjoying the burn through his legs.

"Wow, I feel like Superwoman or something," she had laughed. "This altitude's so much lower than Taos."

No one had told her that he did not speak during runs. It was so foreign to him that he had forgotten how to do it.

"This is actually the first run I've been on since Lily was born," June went on nervously. "I was crazy guilty about leaving her with someone when we left, but this feels good." She hesitated, glancing at him. "So, am I being judged by you?"

Caleb grinned. "I wouldn't know how to judge anybody. What happens is, you can't build enough kinetic energy to heal like we do if you aren't running around eight hours a day. People always try to join us, but that's the part they can't do. Usually we'd take you out on a group run to see and let the trail do the judging. But that's been embarrassing for people. It's better just one-on-one like this."

June laughed. "I'll tell you right now I can't run for eight hours."

"That's all right. I'm not wearing a watch or anything."

"It must be so nice, to have a house full of people who get you."

"It's perfect."

"Are you from Boulder?"

"Seattle."

"Seattle. So how did you hear about Happy Trails?"

He almost told her, but instead he simply described his

years in consulting, the depletion in his bones. June had listened, amazed. Other than the occasional customer at her bar, she had never met anyone who had earned what Caleb had, let alone who had walked away from it, to run.

"Where are you from?" he asked.

"I live in Taos, but I'm from Arizona. Outside Phoenix. Not a lot of anything, you know, kinetic, going on there. My parents were always in and out of work. My stepbrothers, they were big into crystal, Xanax, shooting guns. I started running to get away from it.

"I did some 5ks, then tens. Then I started to get super into it. At a 15k I met a woman, she was from Taos. She told me it was mystical. And that word stayed with me, *mystical*, for like a year. In my mind it meant that Taos had like unicorns and castles, you know?" she laughed.

Caleb listened as if her words were rare fabric brushing his cheek.

"After I saved enough for a good start, I drove there in my beater. You know what? I never ran into that woman, anywhere. And Taos is small."

"What did you do there?" he asked, so unused to this expulsion of breath while moving. But June had no concern or issues with talking and running.

"Let's see, I worked in a ski shop, a dying travel agency, I mean who uses travel agents anymore? I house sat. And then I started as a server at the Gorge. It's a bar, near the mountain. A year later I graduated to daytime bartending, and then I got some of the good après-ski shifts. Which is where I met Todd."

"He worked there?"

"When he wasn't working on mountain crews. He was super thin, with this beard, and this super-wiry energy. People like him. Being with him, it came with a whole circle of friends, and stuff to do, and I wasn't lonely anymore. I ran for a couple of hours every morning, in the open fields and trails. Todd, with his cigarettes and drinking, he was never encouraging. He came to the finish line when I did my first marathon, but that was it. Three years ago, I signed up for the Jemez Fifty, down in Los Alamos?"

"Did he come to that one?"

"Todd wouldn't even drive me. He said running fifty miles was crazy. But there was a bus of locals going, and the ride was actually so much more fun than I was expecting. People were singing and whatnot and being goofy. I finished way in the back, but I was totally excited that I made it. I rode back with my arms wrapped around strangers. At home, Todd was smoking his Newports, staring at the computer. I told him I finished, and he just mumbled something and left for the Gorge."

"Not everyone understands," Caleb offered.

June was silent for a spell. They turned up to the top of the road, where Rocky Mountain National Park sloped west. A titian sliver slipped into the sky, and they plunged straight into the trails.

"I got pregnant by accident. Todd, he told me to stop running. He was really worried about all the jostling. But having this life inside of me, it made me want to run more. I stayed away from rocky trails, but I kept going out every morning.

"'You're going to kill that baby,' he'd shout at me, finger in my face.

"And then in my third trimester, the snow and the tourists hit, and I got kind of super clingy with him. I kept waking him up at night, and calling him at work. And he said he needed to move out, just so he could sleep. But he never came back."

Caleb said nothing. The park was humid; mosquitoes swarmed. He wondered at how well she was running.

"Now, I wonder if Todd was right. Maybe all that running while I was pregnant, like, dislodged something? Or sent some adrenaline into me that did something to Lily?"

"I don't see how it could." He hesitated. "Did she always breathe like this?"

June nodded, "Oh yeah, since the first day. They sent me home from the hospital with this machine called a nebulizer, this stuff called prednisone. I had to force a plastic mask over her face. Her bones were so soft they didn't even seem finished, I thought each time they were going to break. I put this medicine into the machine. When I turned it on, it was so loud, and the mask filled with this mist, and she was scared, she flailed around. If she could have, she would have pulled it off. I felt like I was torturing her. And after it was done, her tiny heart would just be racing, I could actually see it pounding underneath her skin. After a week my manager at work called and said everyone wanted me to bring Lily in. But I stayed in the apartment, listening to her breathe. Twice a day, I sat with her in front of the TV, with this loud machine.

"One night I was looking for a kids' show to calm Lily while I put the nebulizer on her, and I stopped on a show with these two men talking on a couch. It said *Running Talk.* And that was when I saw him.

"He was wearing a purple T-shirt, and these orange Crocs, and he was talking about the miracle of kinetic energy. And I felt this explosion in my belly. Maybe my running caused Lily's problems? But maybe it could also heal them. I read all about you guys online. And I figured, Boulder isn't so far. So last week, I drove out of one bunch of mountains, and up into another."

For a few hours they ran single file, and he watched her thick hair slip in strands from its clip. At a switchback the trail widened and June pulled next to him.

"I think," she panted, "I'm done."

Caleb nodded and slowed to a walk.

"Did I do okay?"

"It's been four hours."

"It has?"

"You're in better shape than I was when I came here."

She touched him then, her damp, hot hands around his arm. For a moment he had believed she was going to kiss him. But he felt her fingers trembling, and her voice came an octave higher.

"Can Mack help my baby?"

"Yes, he can." He blinked. "We all can."

The look she gave him then, the way her eyes, almost too big for her, swelled, made him stumble. She was out of breath, and he wanted to breathe for her.

• • • • • • •

A week afterward, Mack had announced that June and Lily would be moving into the house.

Leigh and Makailah bought a crib in town, and played roots reggae from the boom box as they all assembled it. John moved into Hank and Juan's room, and they painted the empty one yellow, with a moon and stars on the east wall. Alice drew up a schedule of care for Lily, so that June could run every day. One day Makailah came back from Pedestrian with a purple Kelty hiking backpack, designed to carry babies on long hikes, for their group runs.

Every evening in his room, Mack performed energy healing on Lily. June laid her down on his mattress, and he would hover his palms over her lungs and heart. June could feel the inexplicable heat pulsing from them, but Caleb saw no change in her baby's breathing.

One morning, preparing to go up to O'Neil's, he watched Rae holding her and cringed at the sharp whine of her wheezing. From somewhere deep inside of him, a feeling arose. He barely recognized it.

All day he lived with it. Ringing up customers, pacing the store, filling his trays and cartridges, it gnawed at him. It was doubt.

When Mack had cured his recurrent sinus infections, he had been a part of that process, willing Mack's energy through his head. Energy healing seemed to him to be a two-way process. This baby could not participate.

In the morning, he found June by the kitchen and motioned toward the back deck. Outside the air was crisp, as if spring had reconsidered its advance.

"I think we should take Lily to a hospital."

June looked at him appreciatively. "Caley, I did that. Nothing they gave her worked."

"What did they tell you when you told them it wasn't helping?"

"They told me some stuff about testing her genes."

"Did you ever do that?"

"I came here," she explained.

"I think it's a good idea to do it." Caleb hesitated. "But let's not tell Mack just yet. Let's see what they say, and if they have something that works, we can talk with him about it then. Would you want to do that?"

"I'll do anything," she whispered.

At O'Neil's that day Caleb called Boulder Community Hospital and obtained the name of a pulmonary specialist. The nurse told him to have Lily's blood drawn at a local clinic and sent to their office, and an appointment would be scheduled. June accomplished this between cleaning apartments.

The following week, Caleb left the house for work, but instead met June and Lily in Rocky Mountain National Park, and they began walking toward the hospital. Above them bramblings flew in formation, a straggler coming in from the west.

"We're not really adding very much around here, are we?" June asked him.

"What do you mean? Everybody loves having you."

"I doubt it. A crying baby all night?"

"You make it nicer. And you're on the other side of the hall," he smiled.

June looked at him as if she might cry, and she took his hand. He glanced at Lily in her bright sarong, a smile spreading like an amoeba across her mouth. In a coffee shop window, Caleb saw a man in a banker's suit, drinking from an enormous cup, glowering at his phone. He was reminded of himself a decade ago and felt pleased at his progression.

They arrived at an office building adjacent to the community hospital. After a long wait, they were seen by a young doctor. He had missed a spot, Caleb noticed, when he'd shaved. He listened to Lily's tiny chest, while a nurse called up her blood work on an old PC.

"I can see why the steroids aren't doing anything," the doctor explained affably. "Okay. Your daughter was born with a genetic condition called alpha-one antitrypsin deficiency. We don't see this a whole lot. That explains why no one diagnosed it before."

"I don't understand," June frowned, glancing at Caleb.

Caleb watched the doctor try to smile gently. His eyes, however, held large quantities of concern. "The air is full of things that harm our lungs, okay? Bacteria, viruses. We inhale them with every breath. And we survive. Because our lungs release a substance that attacks these foreign bodies, called neutrophil elastase. It's like a pit bull, it attacks anything in its path."

Caleb was nodding, following. June gripped his fingers and he squeezed them. "But like a pit bull, it needs a leash to hold it back, or it will attack the good things too. Like healthy lung tissue. That leash is a protein that your liver produces, called alpha-one antitrypsin. It all works fine. But," he swallowed, his eyes moving to Caleb's and then to Lily's, "what the blood work is showing, is that Lily has a nonfunctioning gene."

"What does that mean?" June shook her head at Caleb. She was lost, frantic.

"The gene that instructs her liver to produce alpha-one antitrypsin is switched off. The reason the inhalers don't work, okay, is that they are anti-inflammatories. And your baby's lungs aren't inflamed. They're being attacked."

"When will it stop?" she shouted.

"It's not going to stop."

Tears slid down June's thin face.

"What *happens* to her?"

The doctor took a deep breath. "Most likely, she will develop emphysema. Probably within a year or two. There's some medicine for some of the symptoms, but there's nothing to really address the disease. I'm sorry. I'm going to call some friends of mine who specialize a little more in conditions like hers. We're going to figure this out, okay? Rosa will make an appointment for you to come back in two weeks."

On the street outside, June collapsed. It was all Caleb could do to catch her in his arms. He walked with these two girls, with the loose aim of walking to Dushanbe, a tea shop nearby. He was aware of some strange fracturing inside of him. It was time for his run, which he had not missed in ten years, but he had no thought of leaving them to begin it.

After an hour of herbal tea, June felt strong enough to go home. As they walked down South Boulder Peak, June had stopped and kissed him.

"I think I love you," she had told him quietly.

He had possessed no idea of how to respond. Caleb felt that there might be two of him now; one running alone along the trails, headed only into himself. And one running with June, toward some new life. It might go either way. He felt like a coin which someone had tossed in the air. He knew that whichever way he landed, there would be consequences he could not stand.

The sauna door opened. Caleb blinked, trying to remember where he was. Cold burst around him, and the image of her face under the noon sky fell drastically away, and Mack pulled him out of the sauna.

The old man who managed the gym was standing there. He shook his head.

"You guys some crazy fucks."

• • • • • • •

Mack dropped him at O'Neil's.

It was two in the afternoon, time for his second shift. A small college kid took off his blue apron and handed it to him.

"Do anything interesting with your morning?"

Caleb nodded and went to stock paper trays. When he was sure Mack had driven away, he found the store mailbox key. He had been sure Shane would have sent him the names of doctors by now, but again he found it empty.

His stomach tightened; it did not escape him that this must be how Shane had felt, all of these years, waiting for an answer to one of his long letters. Caleb worshipped silence and so had not seen its hurtful edge. He hadn't realized he had been causing so much pain.

He began his run back down the mountain. Along the curving isolated dirt road, he watched the house emerge from behind a cluster of pines, standing proud against the sun and wind and snow as if it believed in itself.

After dinner there was Beam and board games. Caleb hung around the landing until he was reasonably certain that he wouldn't be noticed, then moved quietly upstairs to June and Lily's room.

He could hear the baby coughing from the hall. Opening their door, he saw June on the floor, holding Lily in her arms, whispering to her. Her palm covered Lily's chest, moving in circles, but the cough kept coming, always followed by a sharp wheeze. She caught sight of him and her eyes seemed to clutch madly.

"Can you call Shane from work?" she whispered.

Caleb swallowed unsurely. He had asked Shane to visit, and for his help. He accepted his silence as meaning he was working on it. Meanwhile, there was help here. After all, Mack had cured Kevin Yu, who had arrived at Happy Trails with type 2 diabetes and not shown symptoms in years. And Caleb had his own experience of Mack's gift: he had suffered terrible sinus infections in New York, and now the only treatment he received was the heat shooting from Mack's hands hovering above his forehead. Mack had only been working with Lily for two months; perhaps invading bacteria and glucose levels were easier for him to normalize than genes.

"I'll get Mack," he offered.

"He'll want to know why you're in here."

"I don't care. She needs him."

"Wait," June said, "hold her head."

Caleb cradled Lily's head in his lap, and June shifted and moved her hands up from Lily's ankles, over her belly, toward her chest.

"This is what Mack does. You push the energy of her whole body up from her legs into her lungs. Okay? Now you do it from her head down."

Caleb ran his hands from Lily's smooth shoulders down to her heart, where he met June's hands, gripping her fingers. He was in communion with both of them. And he understood then that something in his heart had shifted. He had thought he wanted to help the baby out of love for June. But really, he saw, he was in love with Lily too. He held each of them in his heart equally. He willed all of his own body's strength and energy into this tiny little being, whose lungs he could feel under her skin scratching and searching for breath. He willed it so hard he began crying.

"I love you Lulu," he said softly into Lily's ear.

June looked at him. "Did you just call her Lulu?"

Caleb peered down into Lily's eyes, which sparkled in the fading light.

"He's your brother," June told him. "What's he doing?"

Caleb looked out the window to the white aspens and their hieroglyphic black eyes, which he knew were watching his every word.

3

Every day his face appeared different.

Sometimes he looked like an aged Shanghai bureaucrat, or a Florentine cherub, just like Janelle, nothing like Janelle. His face seemed to be a template formed by whichever spirits happened to be floating by.

He's completely pure, Shane thought, lying next to him in their bed. The air that passes through his body comes back into the world purified.

Then the thought of the air trapped and spoiling in Lily's lungs swept over him; he pushed it away as fast as he could.

Janelle's mother Hua arrived daily bearing fragrant Hunan lactation herbs, and Fred and Julie flew down the following weekend. Recently Fred had become adept at making sushi and spent Nicholas's nap time rolling maki, squinting through bifocals under arched white eyebrows, adding his personal touches. His lifelong focus had never left him, Shane saw; it was simply being deployed in new pursuits.

"Dad looks," Shane commented to Julie, "like Gepetto."

His mother laughed. Her chestnut hair was cut short, and

she wore a shapeless sweatshirt and high-waisted jeans. What force was it, Shane wondered, that commands women over sixty to take on the fashion of lesbians?

Watching them, he realized with some melancholy that he had never really known his parents, not the way they saw and defined themselves, at their peaks, vital, alive. He had no memories of Fred winning a case, of Julie on the eve of starting one of her ill-fated catering companies, laughing in the messy kitchen as she made Fred try obscure appetizers. He had no image of them arriving at a cocktail party together, young and magical, or of them standing over his crib, full of dreams, the way he and Janelle now did at Nicholas's. He knew them only as older people. He felt as if he had missed something significant.

And, he understood with a sharp stab in his belly, Nicholas would never know him or Janelle the way they were right now, which seemed to be the real them worth remembering.

After dinner, and several pointed glances from Janelle, Shane looked at his parents. "I saw Caleb."

Julie whispered, "Oh."

Fred shifted in his chair, lawyer's eyes narrowing. "How did that happen?"

"He wrote me a letter."

Janelle stood, opened a desk drawer, and retrieved it. He handed the blue paper to Julie, who stared at every word.

"I didn't tell you, because I wasn't sure what I'd see. So, it's a lot like we thought. He's living with sixteen or seventeen other people in a house, a big cabin really, in the middle of the woods. It's about half an hour from Boulder."

"The Manson Family Runners," Fred stated.

"But they're not like that. They're nice, kind of normal people. And, he's involved with someone."

"A woman?"

"Versus a man?"

"Versus himself."

"Ah."

"You met her?" Julie leaned forward, her elbows digging into her knees.

Shane nodded. "Her name is June."

"We got a letter from him a few months ago, but it didn't say anything about a girl? It just said he was fine," she said quickly, looking from Fred to Janelle to Shane as if they had an answer.

"How does he look?" Fred asked quietly.

"Good. He's really, really fit. He's working at a copy store."

"A copy store."

Julie asked, "Did he say anything about coming home?"

Shane did not reply.

Janelle added, "But he reached out. It's . . . fragile."

"Can we go see him?" Julie asked desperately.

Shane touched her arm. "I know it's hard, but I think you guys ought to wait. We need to let him lead."

Fred pursed his lips as if he had eaten something unpleasant. "You think I don't know you all blame me?"

Shane rushed a smile onto his face. "Nobody blames you for anything."

"Sure you do. I took him running all those years. I took you too, and you didn't end up in a cult."

"Caleb would tell you I did."

Fred stared at him, and he changed his tone of voice. "Look

Dad, it's not our lifestyle, but it seems to work for him. He's getting pretty known for these races."

"Events," Fred corrected in a bitter voice. "That's what he calls them."

"Do you follow him online? See how well he's doing?"

From the way Julie looked at Fred, he knew they did.

In bed that night Shane stared at a spiderweb that had appeared in the corner of the wall. Did he blame his father for Caleb's choices? No, he knew, of course not. He felt that he had learned only positive things from their ritual family runs. Goal setting. Discipline. How to see things in miles rather than in yards. Running had taught them all focus. And this focus had propelled Fred to senior partner at his firm, and fueled Caleb across finish lines so distant that Shane could not imagine them. Lying there, he wondered if this focus was coded deep in his genome, waiting to rise out of him, too.

• • • • • • •

Shane went back to work that Monday. Almost immediately, he felt different.

Walking through the halls, he noticed specific products that had not before caught his attention. Helixia's product line was like taking a course in incomprehensible human suffering. Dozens of types of cancers, Parkinson's, and to his dismay, rapid onset childhood disorders that had been rare during his youth but were now exploding.

Neurofibromatosis, up 45 percent in the last five years. Childhood leukemia, up 110 percent. Asthma. Cushing's disease. Marfan syndrome. All up by astounding percentages in the past decade.

Helixia's researchers possessed many theories as to why: the average American mother's breast milk contains fifty toxic chemical compounds not known a generation earlier, baby formulas which fail to fully develop the infant immune system, constant exposure to low-level radiation from cell phones and airplanes. Whatever their root causes, these diseases were each the subject of long decks, all of which contained a section entitled "Early Symptoms."

When Shane returned home each night, his eyes would wander to the slight widening of the base of Nicholas's head, a tiny red dot on his leg, all bullet points on those pages. At night he would listen to the bassinet next to their bed. Was Nicholas snoring? Did he have infant sleep apnea? Would his resulting moodiness be misdiagnosed as ADHD, and Nicholas end up lost in a swirl of psychotropic overmedication?

The universe was revealed to him as a forest at night, with spirits hiding behind the trunks of wicked trees. But Shane shook these off with relative ease. Environmental concerns could be mitigated: he and Janelle used no products with artificial scents of mountain breeze, cleaned using only the vinegar their grandmothers had used. It did not go unnoticed that neither of their grandmothers had died of cancer.

But there was nothing he could do to protect his boy from genetics. What happened there had been embedded deep in code, far beyond him.

That week, the annual sales conference for Sorion was to be held at the Union Square Sheraton. Shane was responsible for a presentation on the drug's past, current, and future, and the status of prescriptions in his region. Besides getting up to speed, simply learning Helixia's style of presentation took attention. He could feel his promise to Caleb drifting out to sea.

On Wednesday, sitting at his desk, he scanned the guest list. Investor Relations, Corporate, Physicians, Patients. He noticed someone missing.

"Hey, it's Shane Oberest," he said when Prajuk answered his phone. "What are you doing today?"

"I am working. Did you have some more questions about this thing?"

"Actually, I'd like to invite you to join us at the Sorion sales conference."

"You're kidding. Science is never invited to these things."

"Science is the Star. Says so right on my mouse pad."

He heard the doctor laugh.

"Come on, I'll drive you. You should see this."

After a pause, Prajuk's nearly falsetto voice returned. "This thing, when would we be back?"

And so on Thursday morning, Shane stood in the courtyard between the two Helixia buildings, watching an astonishing mix of people emerge from Research. South Asians, Africans, Nordic blonds. There seemed to be no cultural lock on the study of enzyme proteins. And here came Doctor Acharn, lighting a Parliament. He had a manner of smoking Shane had never before encountered: he gripped a lit cigarette in his fist an inch away from his lips and sucked loudly at his hand. It seemed an utterly foreign act.

"What do you want to listen to?" Shane asked, as they drove the blue Civic out of the lot.

"The Giants are playing."

Shane's radio was already preset to it. They hit the 101 to

the sounds of the second inning. Half an hour later, the unsightly Union Square Sheraton appeared, hovering over the low-end pornography shops. Shane and Prajuk made their way past tourists in college football sweatshirts toward a ballroom. The hotel's beaten carpeting and stained floral furniture had clearly been abused by conventioneers for generations.

In the hall, a group of older people congregated by the main ballroom. They seemed displaced, called to come, but unsure where they were supposed to be. They wore yellow cotton sweaters, tennis shoes, a specific look on their faces; even if Shane had not known what this conference was about, he might have guessed. There is a look in the faces of cancer survivors that causes them to stand apart from the earth.

Shane walked over with a friendly nod. "Are you Sorion patients?"

Each of them nodded.

"This man"—Shane gestured to Prajuk—"invented it."

A stocky woman in her sixties exclaimed, "Oh, my Lord."

She took a step forward and hugged Prajuk. Shane watched him accept uncomfortably.

An older man, with a head full of thick white hair and eyes that registered honor, stepped forward. This man, thought Shane, had served. His watery hazel eyes never left Prajuk's, and he clasped his shoulder as if there were some secret history between them.

A well-appointed woman, possibly his daughter, spoke softly. "He was wasting down to nothing. He had pneumonia, he couldn't walk. Then he started on your drug. Now you just look at him."

Shane asked, amazed, "Did it work right away?"

"Oh no," she shook her head. "When he first took it he got a bad fever. A hundred and four, the doctors wanted him off of it."

"That is a good sign," Prajuk nodded. "That is the cancer cells dying in the millions. The body just cannot process all of these dead cells at once."

She went on, "He still has his tumors, but they stopped growing. He plays golf. He does the yard."

The man finally spoke. "I know you saved my life."

And then overhead lights blinked, signaling the start of the conference. Shane presented an overview of Sorion's sales, projected growth. He ably charted Asia-Pacific projections and gracefully handed the stage to the finance team. Patients spoke, some of them moved to tears, then oncologists, and one medical school dean from San Diego. Afterward, the trade reporters began to drink at the hotel bar. At Orco, he thought, he would have laid down a corporate card and suggested some stories on his other drugs. Now, he just went to find Prajuk.

On the drive back, Shane watched the slight scientist look out at the orange electric buses.

"Thank you for inviting me. This thing, I am very . . ." he seemed to be searching for a word. "This mattered to me."

Shane smiled. "That's really, really good."

"We never see the patients."

"We'll do it again." As he hit the on-ramp, a thought occurred to him. "So, do you know anything about lung disease?"

"Lung cancer?"

"No, more inherited genetic diseases?"

Prajuk raised his eyes. "A bit."

"My brother knows a baby who has one called alpha-one antitrypsin deficiency." His mouth stumbled over the syllables. "It's pretty rare."

"I know it. How old is the baby?"

"About four months."

"In infants the prognosis is fairly poor. Is that what they told your brother?"

"That's right."

"Of course we've been quite involved with immune-system-sponsored lung disease for a long time."

"Helixia, you mean?"

"My team."

"You work on lung diseases?"

"We developed this thing Airifan."

Shane slowed behind a truck and looked at him. "You worked on Airifan?"

"This thing is going to save quite a lot of lives."

"It's out of trials, right?"

"It resides in a lovely limbo between FDA approval and Marketing. One is understaffed, and the other is busy designing golf shirts with the logo."

Shane took the hit with a grin and changed lanes.

"It must feel incredible," he said quietly, "to create something that saves people."

"Oh, definitely. Airifan will save many lives. It will also prevent other suffering. Current childhood asthma medication is steroids, and there are many concerns with steroids in children. Airifan has no steroids at all."

"What are projected sales?"

"Oh, you would need to ask the finance people but it's

blockbuster for sure. A billion a year, probably. But asthma is just a part of it. The real target is emphysema, which is fatal one hundred percent of the time. The technology we developed for Airifan is the key to a treatment. We believe it will be prescribed off-label for emphysema fairly quickly."

"My wife's grandfather died of emphysema."

"Big smoker?"

"He's Chinese."

"Ah," Prajuk said flatly.

Shane's eyebrows raised. "Children with alpha-one antitrypsin deficiency get emphysema."

"Definitely."

"So they're linked?"

Prajuk began slowly, as if deciding exactly what he wanted to say. "Drugs are like houses, Shane. They have many doors. We open each door to see where it leads, but we can't go wandering around. If a door leads to the room we intend to visit, say asthma, we go through it. If it does not, if it leads to a detour, we close it behind us. The question is always, which doors should we go through, and which should we shut?"

Shane nodded, picking up speed.

"Emphysema is a Helixia priority. A few years ago, Amgen put a treatment on the market, but it only worked for ten percent of patients. Anthony feels that Airifan may work for eighty percent. It took us six years in the lab to get there, and then another eight years of trials. Fourteen years. A hundred million dollars. In terms of my career, this is a huge project. We cannot afford any detours." Prajuk swallowed. "This thing, alpha-one antitrypsin deficiency, is a door we opened and closed some years ago."

"Closed?"

"The protein in Airifan affects alpha-one antitrypsin production in the liver. But we do not use it that way in the drug. Our goal was asthma and emphysema, two of the major diseases of our time. We could not step through a door into that room."

"What are you saying?"

"I'm saying, we have it."

Shane pulled over and stared at him. "You have what?"

"A protein that solves for alpha-one antitrypsin deficiency. We have it," Prajuk assured him. "We just left it behind a door."

4

In August, Caleb fell off of Engineer Mountain.

He was thirteen thousand feet up in the air, just underneath the belly of the clouds, seventy-one miles into the Hardrock 100.

The race had begun in the antediluvian mining town of Silverton, Colorado. It looped counterclockwise through Lake City, Ouray, Telluride, and back to Silverton, over thirteen peaks of the San Juans. Last year, his descents from the snowcapped summits had given him trouble. The trick was to slide down the snow on one hip, but the powder hid sharp rocks, and Caleb never managed the necessary abandon. He had finished twenty-seventh. All last winter, he had practiced proper glissades.

So at dawn Caleb stood in front of the Silverton high school along with 140 other runners, from their twenties to their sixties, staring ahead at the mountain range. A few hopped up and down to warm up in the mist; most conserved their energy. Just ahead of him he recognized Julien Chorier, Betsy Nye, a few other top-ten finishers from last year. He also spotted other runners whom he had witnessed sobbing and vomiting along the trails.

In his hand Caleb gripped lightweight trekking poles for the snow and ice. Across his shoulders he wore a small orange backpack filled with energy gel, sunblock, shades, and water. Everything else he would need lay in drop bags strategically placed inside the aid stations.

Mack had called them together in the dark, held their hands, and gave them some Whitman: "'Not I, nor anyone else, can travel this road for you. You must travel it by yourself. It is not far. It is within reach.'" He nodded, then burst into a wild grin. "'Each of us inevitable! Each of us limitless!'"

They had held each other, heads bent. A runner named Joel Zucker had died of a brain aneurysm on this course in 1999; Rae reminded them all to stay alert. When the gun sounded, Caleb sprinted through the narrow streets of Silverton, past *Runner's World* magazine photographers, cheering fans, and curious townsfolk. Behind him Kyle Meltzer, who had won more than a few ultras, shook his head at whoever was so foolish as to run off the start. But Caleb never walked the start of a race, he knew no other way than to gallop into the distance, as he had in Issaquah as a boy, until he had no choice but to slow.

A few miles into the mountains, Caleb plunged into Little Giant Basin. It was like running down the inside of a deep bowl of jade. Caleb found his rhythm, breathed deeply, and trotted across the lush green field and up the other side of the basin.

He was the first to the Arrastra stream. The smell of salmon filled the frigid water. It felt good to be shocked alive. When he emerged and began jogging up the trail in his wet shoes, and his calves awoke, Caleb felt as happy as he guessed was possible in the world.

He drank his water and ran past a cairn toward steep beige cliffs. He ascended up to the scree fields, rock crumbling beneath him; he might slip and shatter his legs with any step. Below, he saw the magnificence of Cunningham Gulch, its ribbons of white snow winding through dark brown granite.

The first aid station appeared on his left. A good crowd wearing Gore-Tex shells of various neons stood by the blue nylon tent, clapping for him. A few held video cameras, and there seemed to be lots of parents and children. It looked like a stranger's family reunion, and Caleb had the mind to run past it. But then Alice appeared, beckoning him inside.

"Nice race. But slow down," she told him, handing him a banana milkshake.

Caleb nodded, sat on a bench, and stared down at his wet Montrails. Alice rubbed sunscreen onto his reddening shoulders and refilled his water bottle.

"I'm pacing you this leg," she informed him.

He nodded.

"Meltzer," Alice gestured.

Caleb watched him approach. He was walking quickly, apparently taking in the glory of the day. He must have run and jogged to be here this quickly, but he did not seem to have broken a sweat yet. Caleb found a baseball hat in his pack, grabbed his poles, and ran out with Alice onto the trail toward Green Mountain. Leaving, he heard someone say something about sleet.

The course grew steeper, punishing his quads and calves. Butterflies brushed against his shoulders. Alice held him back as they ascended toward the white snowpack; anytime he began to move faster she touched his shoulder. Some miles later they were confronted by a herd of goats ambling across the path. Just to their left was a sheer four-hundred-foot drop, and on their right a granite wall. There was nowhere to go, Alice said, flattening her back nervously against the rock. Caleb plunged straight through the herd, causing a braying that echoed down into the valley.

As the trail rose, he concentrated on his heart rate. Monitoring his body took all of his attention, leaving none for such tangents as the contemplation of pain. Even as he starved, he felt his soul being fed. He took his first steps on snow.

And then the course shot steeply downward. At Maggie Gulch he ran through a summer field covered in orange wildflowers, while a microclimate of a snowstorm drifted just ten feet away. Alice handed him an electrolyte gel. His stomach clenched unhappily; he had the experience of these gels causing him trouble.

They reached the end of the first leg, two hours under the cutoff. Caleb checked in with race officials at the Sherman station. He had lost three pounds; seven was an automatic disqualification. Alice kissed his cheek, and Leigh, willowy and red-faced, walked over with climbing equipment and called to him as to a puppy, "Come on, Caley!"

Some miles later they moved into a grove of aspens, where black flies flew from the conifer and bit his neck. He watched Handies Peak materialize ahead of him.

Leigh whispered, "I dropped here last year."

He recalled it. A severe thunderstorm had swept in, crushing the trail to mud, pelting the climbers with hail. Luckily, he had been on his way to Telluride by then.

They stopped to pull crampons from their packs and over their shoes. He shook loose his trekking poles, and their points plunged through wet tufts of frozen grass and snowpack, scattering loose stones beneath him. He called a warning to Leigh behind him and pushed himself skyward. It was not his job to worry about her.

The ascent up to fourteen thousand feet took longer than he had anticipated. Below them the approaching runners seemed to be coming at him in one large pack. He began to visualize his old flowcharts from his days at InterFinancial, going over them as his legs pushed against the granite, lost in math and equations.

At the summit the air around him was as pure as newborn breath. Fluttering orange flags pointed them toward a narrow natural bridge, made of rock, covered in snow, which connected them to the south face of the next pass. The drop below them was astonishing. They crossed carefully, hovering eleven thousand feet in the air with no guardrail, suspended above the world.

On the other side, the trail dropped abruptly into boulder fields. Without thinking about it he executed a perfect glissade down the snow, ice lacerating his cheeks. Halfway down, he turned his head, saw Leigh just behind him, and Kyle Meltzer at the top.

At the next aid station, Kevin Yu was waiting for him with bigger shoes. This was good; his feet had swelled half a size. Where was June, he thought? She wasn't quite ready to run Hardrock, so he imagined Mack had told her to pace. He felt the need of her as the sky began to dim.

Caleb slammed a nauseating glucose polymer mix. He

considered his situation. His fifth mountain peak confronted him. He had been running nonstop for sixteen hours. He should be fine.

He followed Kevin up the incline ahead. Maybe June was meeting him in Telluride, and they would have time together until the dawn. He was visualizing this when he jammed a foot under a large purple rock. Nerve pain shot into his right knee like fire and he fell hard to the snowy ground.

Kevin caught up, panting. He kneeled and looked at Caleb's leg. His kneecap had shifted out of position; it bulged ugly and rocklike against his stretched skin. Kevin touched it and Caleb shut his eyes tight, the pain blinding. His poles slipped from his hands and rolled down twenty yards. Meltzer jogged ahead into the dusk. Caleb stared after him, sweat soaking through his shirt. He started shivering.

"They have medics at Grouse. Should we go back?"

Runners began passing, some nodded in empathy but most were too focused to notice. If Caleb were helped to move in any way, it would be a disqualification. Kevin looked to him, asking with his eyes if he should do it. Caleb nodded grimly.

And Kevin raised the flat of his hand and slammed it against Caleb's kneecap. Once. Twice. Caleb screamed. Red agony tore him asunder as if he had stepped on a third rail.

"Sorry," Kevin muttered, frowning.

He hit it again, harder this time, and the kneecap shifted back into place with an audible click.

This moment, right now, was the finish line. If he could not cross it, then no other banner mattered. Caleb knew enough to understand that the longer he sat here, the more his knee would swell and stiffen. It was either keep it loose, or end this. So he stood gently, hopped on his left leg, took a very long breath, visualizing kinetic energy flowing from the trees into his kneecap, and took a full step on his right leg. The pain was horrific. Somehow he did not collapse, and he tried another step. Eventually the pain would subside, he knew, but it might take miles.

Kevin stood beside him. "Engineer's gonna hurt, bro," he said seriously.

The sun fell behind the mountain, plunging them into a sudden and complete darkness. Kevin took two headlamps with Petzl lights and pulled them onto his head and Caleb's. Only the five yards of trail directly in front of him were visible in the circle of yellow light. Moving into it felt like the night swimming he had done in Issaquah. A primal fear pushed against a sense of deep trust and faith, a sense of the unknowable.

After some miles of ascent, the pain in his knee began to subside. Tomorrow it would be a very different story, he knew, but right now it was nearly numb. He looked below him. A wave of golden lights hovered below like Japanese lanterns. They were the headlamps of other runners weaving through the darkness. A beautiful sense of camaraderie overtook him.

Engineer became a pure climb, hand over hand, fingers tugging at rock and dirt. He was fully engaged, focused entirely on each step forward, and the pain in his body, his lungs, his legs, fell away.

"Hey," Kevin called, unable to match him.

But he moved faster, almost gliding. He was deep-diving into uncharted regions.

He was shocked, therefore, to see his brother sprint by in his ratty Grateful Dead Tacoma Dome '88 shirt.

"Hey," Shane called, grinning.

Caleb stopped, awed. "How did you get here?"

"I wanted to see what you love about this."

"And?"

"It sucks," Shane pronounced. "Everything hurts."

"Why haven't I heard from you?" He tried to catch his breath. "Why don't you help us?"

"I have an answer," Shane announced brightly. He seemed full of energy. "But you have to follow me." He waved and took off up the mountain.

When he understood there was no Shane, only darkness and his frail body, Caleb touched a solitude that shook him. He had been broken at Massanutten, where he had suffered hypothermia, and at the Wasatch 100 in Utah, when he had thought he might die of fever, but he had never felt this alone.

Miles below, the lights of Ouray blinked like buoys. A sudden explosion of lightning ripped across the sky, and rain pounded over him. He scrambled up in the dark, trying to reach the peak before the dirt turned to mud and began to slide. At the top he found solid earth, curving away from the sudden storm. Kevin was long behind him now.

He decided to catch up with Shane. He had more to ask him.

He must have slipped in the dirt. His exhausted body lurched helplessly left, and unable to right himself he skidded off the edge, frantically clutching at the sheer mountain rock and teasing tufts of green along the side, fingernails tearing along the granite.

He tumbled down the steep incline, his legs kicked madly looking for a way to stop, his fingers clutched at loose rock and air, and then, twenty feet down, he hit a protruding ledge of granite. He landed on his face, bloodying his mouth, and lay breathless. A foot to his left was a sheer plummet of thousands of feet.

Behind his closed eyes he felt like he was falling. Finally he opened them to the gray shelf and dared to look down. In the breaking light he could make out the corkscrew trail below, and antlike blurs of runners moving up the mountain.

Carefully Caleb turned, scraping his elbow, and lay on his back. Above, a sunrise broke in feverish hues. He could see the red sky, and shadows of people jogging past the point where he had slipped. He tried to call out to them, but an agoraphobic shiver overtook him, he feared yelling might shake his body over the narrow shelf, and so he lay silently, pulling deep breaths.

On the wind then he smelled June's skin. He heard her voice, whispering an affirmation. And then Lily came to him. Her laugh, her own sweet scent, were all around him, as clear as air. He had not noticed how deeply they had permeated him, how much he needed them both now, not only to run, but to even breathe.

....

Caleb had been in a restaurant.

His suit had been gray, conservative. His hair had been short. He had been pale, and a paunch had overtaken his belt. He had been nursing a breakfast of granola and coffee with two partners from InterFinancial and new clients from an

Ohio packaged meats company, at a financial district restaurant. Caleb had not been saying very much; he was the analytics guy. The sell was for his colleagues.

They were discussing the InterFinancial process when a roar of background noise rose from outside. Caleb turned and looked out the plate-glass window, and saw a woman in a white blouse running with her arms out in front of her face.

She was followed by other people, coming from the same southerly direction. An older man, his eyes wide, screaming. Three black women sprinting with their heads down. Caleb turned back to his table to comment, but by then there was something in the air that forced them all outside. He saw the enormous crowd running right at him, jumped backward, out of its rush. That was when he noticed the rolling panzers of black smoke behind them, coming fast.

Caleb started to run. Instinctively, he reverted to the quick long-legged run of his youth. People were convulsed, sobbing, pointing upward. Confused, Caleb followed their hands as they lifted to the firmament.

Caleb grasped how close he was to being swallowed by the chemical smoke pouring over them. He ran as hard as he could with the stricken crowd until it broke into pieces like an army in retreat. Near Mott he was swept into a platoon pushing relentlessly toward the water.

The Brooklyn Bridge loomed ahead. In the windows of the endless maroon housing projects, people pressed at the glass, gesturing madly. Caleb never turned around to look at the devastated skyline, at the collapsed people on the street, or the screaming engines headed toward the smoke, and in this he was nearly alone.

Crossing the bridge he became deeply aware of its swaying; he felt sure that it would collapse and he would plummet. On the other side sirens blazed, blue lights flashed, the policemen's faces were tilted to the sky.

On the other side, he stopped. He had not considered direction, or how far he was from home. He needed to get back to the West Side. He spied a subway stop and descended its dark steps, but the trains had been shut down, and he stood at the locked gate searching inside the blackness for something alive.

He reemerged onto the smoke-filled street and finally watched the chaos across the river. Around him those he had run with were embraced by their families, friends, and neighbors. Caleb stood alone in his filthy shirt, his sweat-strewn face turned toward the burning, closed city, and understood that, for a long time, he had been running the wrong way.

• • • • • • •

A week afterward, Caleb wandered into a bookstore.

His office was of course closed, and though he was meant to be working from his apartment, he felt a need to be near people. He flipped absently through books on ice, the Giants, Israel, looking for something to pull him into its world. Nothing engaged until, wandering through a dim aisle with a green plastic sign reading SPORTS, a cover photograph stopped him. On it, an elfin hippie looked to the camera with an expression of total, perfect confidence that reminded him of Shane.

The man wore an orange and blue tie-dyed T-shirt, and a scraggly black beard which highlighted eyes the clear blue of an infant's. He stood before the peak of a mountain. Across his chest, in proud yellow letters, read the words YOU CAN RUN 100 MILES!

Caleb took up a copy, sat down on the worn carpet, pulled his knees to his chest, and began to read.

"Kinetic Energy is the energy that we build when we move. This is the energy that our body uses to repair its cells, to heal itself. It is blood's sister. And yet we deprive ourselves of this vital force in fatal amounts.

"The faster you build up your stores of kinetic energy, the faster your body will revert to the perfect machine it was born to be. You will be able to heal without the use of toxic drugs. You will be able to live on four hours of sleep a night, extending your waking life by almost a third. You will live without exhaustion, without doubt, without illness. You will experience a life totally unlike the one you know now. And all you have to do is run."

Caleb flipped over the book. Its back cover showed another picture of the man, running up a mountain trail. Underneath it said: "John 'Mack' McConnell is the founder of the Happy Trails Running Club in Boulder, Colorado. Runners coached by McConnell have dominated ultramarathons for the last decade."

Caleb purchased the book and went back to his apartment feeling oddly awake. That evening, for the first time in a year, he went for a run through Riverside Park. Lactic acid seared his chest from the start; at three miles he sat down on a bench, chest heaving. All around him the world was in trauma, and yet for the last hour, he had been completely immersed in something else entirely, and not given it a thought.

When the airports opened, Caleb packed a small bag and

flew to Colorado. His flight had been a mess, the paranoia of airport security outmatched only by that of his fellow passengers.

After the tension at LaGuardia and Denver International, he felt the peace of Boulder immediately. The mountains seemed almost too present, and he walked with his eyes focused on the streets, until he acclimated to them.

Caleb checked into a Marriott on Canyon and went for a jog. He made it to Flagstaff and meandered slowly into the dirt trails. The sun was strong, bathing the woods in olive, ginger, and gold. He loved how these trails were as alive as Manhattan. Birds, lizards, runners, passed him in all directions. His lungs gave out after three miles in the unfamiliar thin air, and he stood with his hands pulling down on his shorts, watching the sun lower behind the Front Range.

The next morning he went without his coffee, walked to Fleet Feet, and asked one of the employees about the Happy Trails Running Club. The name seemed to inspire suspicion.

"I heard they all live together," a salesgirl nodded her head, tying his new Salomon trail running shoes.

A pockmarked kid told him, "They're all at the Rocking Horse on Thursdays."

All week, Caleb ran beneath the autumn sky. He taught himself Mack's running form as described in the book, landing lightly on the balls of his feet, never his heels, body straight, running on a treadmill by a mirror in the Marriott gym until he felt confident of his posture. He ate Boulder food, organic, less meat. The following Thursday, Caleb ran six miles in the deep woods. At dusk he emerged and went straight to the Rocking Horse Tavern.

His nose was running as he hesitated by a pile of free local newspapers in the doorway. Inside, twenty people in old T-shirts relaxed in a cluster amidst the damp thick pub smell, conversing noisily at round wood tables, cradling pints of dark beer.

He inhaled as he recognized John McConnell seated at a window table. Mack was digressing on his unique method of tying shoes; he had found some pattern to the laces that he swore added milliseconds to one's time. When he finished, Mack pounded a pint in two swallows and shot his eyes unexpectedly straight to Caleb.

"I read your book," Caleb blurted out. "I came here."

Mack smiled. For the first time, Caleb felt the pull of those eyes.

"You run, dude?" His voice was surprisingly nasal.

"I just did six."

"Miles?"

"Yes."

A pained pause followed. The other people at the table were looking at him.

"Come back when it's hours."

"I can't run six hours straight."

"Sure you can. Isn't that why you came here?"

Through the holidays Caleb ran seven days a week, base building, exercising ladders and cutdowns and pyramids. He practiced meditating, to direct kinetic energy deeper into his body. He e-mailed his resignation to his manager and signed a year lease near Centennial Park.

By then he had cut refined sugars and red meat from his diet. His musculature began to harden, while he lost fifteen pounds. His first runs through subzero temperatures made him gasp. In February Mack saw him on a frozen trail and complimented him on his progress. It was considered a long winter, but to Caleb it went by in a white blur.

That April Caleb returned to the Rocking Horse, and waited for Happy Trails to arrive. When Mack sat down, Caleb approached his table.

"Come out with us Friday," Mack offered as he lifted a shot glass.

"I can't do six hours yet."

"Let me tell you what you can do."

Caleb's first run with Happy Trails was ecstatic. As the sun rose he moved with fifteen other rigid-spined, piston-armed, wide-smiling runners. He could feel warmth emanating from their bodies, just as Mack's book had described. The runners in front of him kicked up last evening's rain, which fell around his eyes like an angel's tears. After five hours he bent over on a narrow trail, his hands on his knees, and threw up. Mack jogged over, and leaned down.

"Run."

Caleb shook his head, heaving. He tightened his eyes, shaking, acid burning through his chest. But somehow his legs started moving. Within a half mile his stomach cramped, and he stumbled, fire raging through his spasming body.

"Drop," Mack explained quietly, "and this is your last run with us."

Caleb stared wide-eyed at him, seeing that he meant it.

Suddenly Mack raised his hands and shouted, "'Now triumph! Transformation! Jubilate!'"

Caleb straightened. There followed the hardest minutes of his life. He deteriorated from a walk to a crawl. Mack stayed beside him the whole hour, repeating affirmations. When the stopwatch hit six hours, some of the others carried him, he had no idea how far, to their house.

He awoke on a mattress on a floor, to the sound of group chanting downstairs. When he appeared in the big room, they all stopped and clapped for him.

Afterward, Caleb was admitted into membership. He ran with Happy Trails several times a week. He discovered how to absorb the energy in the steam emitting from a buck in the woods, and from the friction of a warbler's wings against a branch.

By this time, it had become very difficult to speak with his family. When he called, Julie spoke to him as if he were a child suffering some shock. Fred wanted to find him a job in Seattle. Shane explained that he *understood* and wanted to come out and see him. Their disconnection from what he was experiencing frustrated him; they assumed he was in trauma, when really he was in transcendence.

That fall, Caleb ran his first ultramarathon, a fifty-mile Fat Race in Winter Park. When he finished in eleventh place, Mack hugged him, his breath steaming in the cold.

"'Henceforth I whimper no more, postpone no more, need nothing. Done with indoor complaints, libraries, querulous criticisms. Strong and content I travel the open road.'"

Caleb felt hot tears streaming down his face. Afterward, Mack gathered the house in a circle. They held hands, and quietly initiated Caleb into Sunday energy healing.

Once he moved into the house, he experienced total clarity about his life. He knew what was expected of him each day, and still each minute was filled with unpredictable pleasures.

Every two months he competed in hundred-mile ultrathons, moving gradually from placing sixtieth, to thirtieth, where he plateaued for some years, and then the twenties, and now, finally, the single digits.

Caleb kept his life this way for ten years, until the morning when he had been in the kitchen and heard a knock from the front door, and watched it open, revealing June and Lily.

After that, there was no such simplicity again.

• • • • • • •

Now, lying on this narrow shelf, inches away from an endless drop, the smell of Lily's skin washed over him like a rain. He thought of how he had accomplished nothing to help her, and he let loose a prolonged and agonized scream. A face appeared upside down far above him.

"Oh, Jesus!" a woman shouted.

Eventually someone arrived with a rope. Caleb pushed his pelvis up and tied it around his waist as instructed, held it even as it sliced into his fingers, as he was lifted from the berm, dangling in the perilous air, his feet kicking at the dirt and rock, multiple hands grabbing his shirt and pulling, and only when he felt the canyon trail beneath his back did he let go of the rope. A stretcher, oxygen, and blankets awaited him.

"We've been looking for you for an hour, buddy. Thought you fell through a cornice. Your pacer's been going crazy."

Caleb's voice, husky and broken, asked simply, "What's the cutoff?"

The Search and Rescue workers stared at him as if he had lost his bearings. But a watching race official understood.

"You're forty minutes over."

Caleb accepted water, thanked them, and started into his antelope strides back around the ridge of Engineer Mountain.

Behind him he heard the rescue workers shouting for him to come back. His lungs hiccuped brown sputum as he made his way down toward Telluride, where the sudden appearance of people and cars panicked him. He ran as quickly as he could through its streets, for the safety of the trails.

After miles of switchbacks he encountered a runner dry-heaving on the near bank of a river. The recent storm had flooded its banks; the water was far too high to run through. Caleb jogged west, his exhausted eyes searching for some way across. A mile upriver he dove in to swim. The current pulled him back east. It didn't matter; he was simply moving.

On the other side he found the course and began to see other entrants sitting wretchedly along the trail like refugees; one young guy lay on the ground sobbing. Caleb's sides began cramping, and his incoming breaths sounded like Lily's exhales. He guessed himself to be around eighty miles in.

At the Chapman Gulch aid station, Juan hugged him.

"Where you been man? Mack almost called out Search and Rescue."

"I had a problem."

"Man, you hear about John?"

"No."

"He lost it at ninety-nine."

It sometimes happened that a runner collapsed within sight of the finish. The mind has focused on this image for so long that as soon as it sees it, it assumes the goal has been met, and shuts off its systems.

Juan gave him an energy gel. He gagged on it, spitting blue fluid onto the ground. Then they ran to Porcupine Creek. Each mile took much longer now. The runners he passed now smelled like sulfur.

He could see Silverton far below him, its colorful small buildings in a crooked line, like dominoes placed by a toddler. He had run the equivalent of four marathons, up thirteen peaks. Six hours later than he had intended, Caleb stumbled into town and kissed the white-painted rock at the finish.

When he looked up, June was sprinting toward him.

..........5

"We call them orphans," Janelle explained as she took the exit to Target.

Shane had never encountered a woman who needed to drive as much as his wife. She could not bear a passenger seat. He had long since accepted this as his lot and sat semicontentedly watching the hills. August had brought storybook pink skies to the bay. Down a particularly steep hill the megastores appeared like coliseums.

"Orphans are conditions that are so rare, that producing drugs for them isn't feasible."

"Feasible?"

"Profitable."

"Ah," Shane nodded.

"Well," Janelle explained, switching lanes, "it takes as much money to launch a drug that helps ten million people as a drug that helps ten. Rounds of clinical trials all over the country, lawyers, dealing with the FDA. And if you get past the first round, you do it all over again, and then a second and a third time. It takes a decade, and half a billion dollars, to get a biotech drug approved. And, if you ever get as far as approval, there's Marketing, supply chain, educating doctors. And people wonder why the drugs are expensive."

She paused, pulled the car aggressively into a tight spot, and looked at him. "Helixia expects ninety-five percent of our attempts to fail. It's built into our share price. So our successful products need to pay for themselves and all of this research. If they don't, our share price plummets, we have less money for new research, less drugs get discovered."

Inside, they loaded up two carts full of diapers and wipes, and a makeup remover that Janelle favored. Nicholas hung snugly in his Baby Bjorn; Shane could smell the baby shampoo on his fine black hair.

In one aisle he spied a tired young mother speaking harshly to her fussy baby and tensed. Ever since Nicholas's birth, he felt a new responsibility toward infants. He hesitated there, unsure what he would say if she met his eyes. He caught up with Janelle in the paper towel section.

"Why not produce an orphan drug and charge whatever we have to not lose money? It might be crazy expensive, but we'd have it. And then in a few years, generics could come in cheaper."

Janelle frowned. "That would be four or five hundred thousand dollars a dose. Who pays for that? Insurance companies were set up to pay for eighty-dollar antibiotics, not six-figure biomedicines."

"There are families who would spend that in cash to cure their children."

Janelle patted his back as they walked slowly toward checkout. "So medicine for the super-rich only? There's a great idea."

"Well, 'only super-rich children live' is better to me than 'no children live.'"

"We're just at a place where producing biomedicines for a market this small isn't sustainable. And generics would lose money, so they wouldn't enter this market either. In fifty years things may be better. I know you want to help this baby, but Helixia isn't going to be the way. We need nipple pads."

While he unpacked their carts at the register, Janelle looked pensive. "Although. Have you heard of the Orphan Drug Act?"

"I haven't."

"In the early nineties this same problem you're hitting came to the attention of the government. They came up with a classic government solution. They created the Orphan Drug Act."

"What is that?"

"It allows companies to apply for grants to develop drugs for small populations. It gives them tax incentives and market exclusivity, which is a big deal. Now, this was in the days of a more progressive government."

"So could Helixia apply for a government grant to develop a drug for alpha-one antitrypsin deficiency?"

"We could. But we wouldn't."

Nicholas went full-on fussy as he loaded the trunk. Janelle whipped a pacifier from her pocket, and the boy was mollified.

"Why not?"

"Too much risk. The financial incentives are only worth anything if the drug is successful. Which, like I said, ninety-five percent of them aren't."

Janelle looked at him carefully. "Baby, you've only been here a month. Even if you'd been at Helixia for twenty years, you'd need a solid case that an orphan drug would pass trials before you could suggest it."

Confidently, slamming the trunk, he said, "I think I have one."

. . . .

As Janelle's last two weeks of maternity leave approached, Shane could feel a new stress working its way through her.

Hua had offered to take care of Nicholas, freeing them from a crazed nanny search. But Janelle seemed torn about going back to work. When Shane commented how lucky Nicholas was to be in the care of his grandmother, Janelle had turned unexpectedly harsh.

"My mother comes from a different country, a different way. I don't want her raising Nicholas."

"We're raising Nicholas, honey."

"A third of the time," Janelle had shot back suddenly.

That night, Shane awoke with a start; Nicholas was screaming. He shuffled down the short wood-floored hall in the darkness, and there was his new son, red-faced in his crib. Shane lifted his warm body and sat with him in a small blue rocking chair by the window. Stroking his fine black hair, Shane felt his tiny body shudder and relax against his chest. Where had he obtained the power to soothe just by touch? This must be what Mack taps into, he thought. The trick is, both the person being touched, and the person touching, have to have complete, doubtless faith in the procedure. Perhaps this was why Mack wasn't able to help Lily; she was too young to believe in him. A baby, he understood, only believes in her parents.

He thought sadly of June. What kind of anguish must she feel, listening to Lily's wheezing and coughing, unable to make it go away? A parent without power might be the saddest thing in this world.

He imagined being incapable of helping Nicholas, the pain and rage of it. He felt certain that he would do anything he had to, go anywhere, fight anyone, to save him. Nicholas and Lily began to blend into one. After all, he wondered, how were they different? Genes, spiraling strands of magic. Other than that, not at all. He was responsible for Nicholas's future, and so, he understood, for Lily's as well.

He prayed that the tiny red-blonde baby was sleeping well right now, and he held his son close. He wanted Nicholas to soak this power, this energy, this security into his skin, so that it infused him on some cellular level. And then, humming a berceuse, Shane laid him back in his crib, and Nicholas sank into whatever dreams await a six-week-old boy.

• • • • • • •

The following morning, Shane walked by Stacey's cubicle, cradling a paper cup of coffee. "Hey," he asked, "got a second?"

Stacey adjusted her red glasses. "What's up?"

"The Director of Immunology is Dineesh . . . ?"

"Dineesh Pawar."

"I sent him an e-mail request for a meeting, but I never heard back. Can you help me get in with him?" Shane smiled plaintively.

She cocked her Sicilian head. "Dennis mentioned you in a senior management meeting. Good feedback coming in."

"Thanks."

"I'll see his assistant tonight. I'll get you a slot, no worries."

The following day, Shane received notice that a meeting had been arranged in Dineesh's office. He found the Director of Immunology to be a surprisingly handsome man. Six feet tall, with a head full of slicked-back black hair, and perfect white teeth. He could have been, Shane felt, a Bollywood star. He wore a white shirt tucked into pleated black pants. A gold chain was visible inside his collar.

"Alpha-one antitrypsin deficiency," Dineesh considered, standing near his desk. His voice was quite deep. "Mutation of a gene on chromosome fourteen."

"I know a little girl who was born with it."

Dineesh nodded. "Pretty rare stuff. You'd have to address the mutated gene, wouldn't you?" Dineesh shook his head, looking at his BlackBerry. "A thousand fucking e-mails around here, you know?"

"If we had the beginning of a treatment, would we ever apply for an orphan grant?"

Dineesh's dark eyes snapped up, an amused expression on his face. "For infant-onset alpha-one antitrypsin deficiency? Very rare. Too rare for us, man."

As he walked around his desk looking at his phone, it was clear he had already moved on.

But Shane had not.

• • • • • • •

Caleb widened his eyes and made a funny face down to Lily.

She was surprisingly smiley for a baby who had slept so little. Something in the humid late August air was ratcheting up the tenor of her wheezing, and June had taken her into her bed at night out of fear.

Despite this interrupted sleep, she was growing, developing, in ways that astonished them all. Watching Lily became house sport; they applauded her, cheered for her, passed her from person to person, and she seemed to thrive with their attention. She would glance up at Alice, Rae, John, Juan, tighten her jaw, and a look of determination would sweep across her face, and she would pull herself panting across the wide wood floor.

"It's her personality," John told them, running a hand through his crew-cut white hair. "That's a determined girl."

Caleb never saw her unattended to. He supposed this was as good a way to be a child as any.

As September swept over the mountains, Caleb's teeth began aching. He was nearly forty-four and had not seen a dentist in eight years; he expected some decline in his dental health. But recently he had needed to keep his mouth closed against even the slightest breeze. Brushing his front teeth had become outrageous.

Caleb knocked on Mack's closed door.

"Yo," came a shout.

Caleb found him shirtless at a small and cluttered desk, facing a window that looked onto the pines across the road. Countless running magazines littered the floor. A bare futon with two crumpled blue sheets lay by the window. Tacked to the wall were maps of Yosemite National Park, in various sizes and details. On the far wall hung a white marker board with training, work, and chore schedules for each of them. Mack was online. Internet access was prohibited to all members, but he had possession of a battered Dell.

"Dude. Barry just sent me the course. It's wicked. It is the fucking devil."

Caleb took a tentative step closer and peered at the screen. "This is Yosemite?"

"I know spring feels like forever away, but it's only seven months." Mack looked at him with his dancing bright blue eyes. "You ever been there? Yosemite Park?"

"I never have."

"I went in college. Tripped and camped for days. It's so beautiful. Half Dome is from another universe. Whoever climbs it and wins this is going to feel like God." Mack clicked his mouse and the computer went dark. Then he swiveled on his chair and looked at him. In a very different voice he asked, "What's up?"

"My teeth hurt."

"Front or back?"

"Front."

"Enamel." He flicked his own teeth with a fingernail. "When you mouth-breathe during runs, the air dries out your enamel. All that friction thins it right down to the nerves. Surprised it hasn't happened to you before, dude."

Caleb felt a question emerging. Later he would wonder if it was a challenge. "Why don't you do some reiki?"

"As long as you're running mouth open? It's going to get worse. Better to do some visualizations on running with your mouth closed. After a month or two the enamel will recover."

Caleb swallowed. "I want to take Lily to a doctor."

Mack looked at him. "You do. Where?"

"I want to get her to New York or someplace."

"New York," Mack repeated.

"Maybe there's an expert. Maybe there's a new drug."

"You remember what happened to Hope?"

Caleb swallowed.

"She'd been with us three years when she got that tumor

in her titty. I was healing it, it was disappearing, but she kept on doubting me, kept on asking everyone if she should see a doctor. Doubt is as much of a cancer as a tumor. You remember what happened?"

Caleb nodded. Mack had driven Hope to Boulder Community Hospital and never went back for her.

"When I healed Kevin's diabetes, there were no experts or drugs. But it took half a year. Lily's problems are within her own body. It starts there. It stops there. These are serious problems and I need more than three months to rebalance her energy. Natural healing takes time. But, brother, I'm the reason Lily's still breathing."

"We know that."

Mack stared at him. "Look at you. Your focus is just fucking gone dude. You fell off Engineer. You're all"—Mack waved his hands in the air—"scattered. Now you want to take them to New York? Maybe you just want to go back there, and they're your excuse."

"No," Caleb stated nervously.

"Maybe that's what you need. To go back to your old life."

"I need to be here."

Mack leaned forward, his face inches from Caleb's. "Then detach yourself *right fucking now.*"

Caleb took a step backward.

Something wicked flashed in Mack's eyes. "Let me tell you something about history."

Caleb nodded unsurely.

"History is the study of small differences. When explorers discover a new tribe, on some remote island, you know what they find out? That the people with big ears hate the people with little ears. Fucking hate them. The big-eared people teach their children that the little-eared people eat their own babies. They go to war. There's generational violence over *ears*. Follow?"

"Sure."

"Ninety percent of all worldly strife is caused by small differences. And when you and June get this involved, you create a small difference with everyone else in the house."

"Are people upset?"

"People don't know yet. But relationships have"—Mack circled his hands—"reactions. If they succeed, other people feel they need one too. It's mimetic desire. If they fail, bad vibes invade our house. Look Caleb, if you feel the need for a one-on-one relationship, that's very cool. You can have that and still compete at a very high level. But not here.

"I like June. I love little Lily. But I don't care how good a runner you are. If you don't get it together, they're gone. I want you out training when June is in here. And in here when she's out." He nodded his head. "I sent Annabelle packing when she was winning in every Fat Race in Colorado, because she was spending time with that mustached motherfucker bartender. And June isn't winning any races."

Caleb's stomach clenched. If Mack expelled them, where would they go? He needed to keep them here, while he waited for Shane to tell them what to do. He would agree to anything for that.

Mack stared at him. "'But where is what I started for so long ago? And why is it yet unfound?'"

Cowed, Caleb turned for the door. Then, his hand on the knob, he turned and said boldly, "She's in her room. Lily is."

When Mack answered, his voice was gentle. "Okay, buddy. I'll do some work with her tonight."

Caleb opened the door, moved straight outside, onto the dirt road, through the field's fallen leaves, into the unfriendly sky, and began to run, out and out, and out, and out.

6

At midnight, Shane sat in his cubicle, dimly aware of the cleaning lady behind him.

He had decided to open an orphanage. A well-managed operation, with the goal of placing just one orphan: a drug for alpha-one antitrypsin deficiency.

Since his revelation in Nicholas's room, Shane had been overwhelmed by thoughts of Lily. Sometimes in the whine of the refrigerator he heard the wheeze of her breathing. When his foot hurt after a run, he thought of her swollen feet. It was impossible to conceive of continuing to live his life any longer without doing all he could to help her.

So all week he had stayed late, researching orphan grants. It had been days since he had seen Janelle or Nicholas at night; even Stacey left the office before him, casting him an arched eyebrow.

He had begun crafting a formal proposal suggesting Helixia apply for one. He filled it with numbers, charts, examples, projections, all based on profit models he had read online. Slowly he was piecing together a sober argument to conduct trials on Prajuk's drug, which would switch on the gene in the fourteenth chromosome that ordered the liver to begin production of alpha-one antitrypsin.

Orphan grants excited him. Cystic fibrosis and Tourette's syndrome were currently being treated with biologics which had been produced under the Orphan Drug Act. One of the most profound examples was Ceredase.

In 1984, scientists at Genzyme had discovered a treatment for Gaucher's disease. But the small number of people suffering from the condition, a few hundred thousand, gave Genzyme no financial justification to spend eight hundred million dollars producing it. Instead, the company had applied for an orphan grant. The National Institute of Health paid for small clinical trials, did very well, and now Ceredase was earning a billion dollars a year.

A billion, Shane whistled. And Genzyme had been granted market exclusivity for a decade.

Only a fraction as many alpha-one antitrypsin deficiency patients existed as Gaucher's, but his math still worked; they could assume some small profit. If they won a grant.

He had not realized how much he enjoyed putting together a report; it felt good to be so lost in work. That weekend, Shane printed his proposal and showed it to Janelle over a glass of cabernet.

"I think you make a good argument," she nodded.

"Thank you. So you'd product-manage this?"

"It doesn't matter what I'd do. The challenge is getting someone who matters to listen to you. You're a commercial specialist. I love you but that doesn't carry much weight with Science."

"I'll send it to Anthony Leone."

"Anthony won't read it."

Shane frowned, swirling his glass. Anthony Leone was Helixia's Director of Science, and one of the three senior executives. He was moderately sized, balding, and tended unfortunately toward floral ties. Anthony had made his millions decades ago but worked six days a week; his belief in the company was unshakeable and inspiring to all of them.

"Why not?"

"Because who are you? The scientist who discovered this drug should have his name on it and present it personally. You need creds."

"Prajuk won't do that."

Janelle shrugged. "You might be kind of fucked otherwise."

The following week, Shane sat nervously in his Sorion status meeting. A chart on the front page of their decks displayed its chemical compounds and genetic codes. Though he could not read it, Shane sensed its intrinsic majesty, similar to seeing a poem written in Mandarin.

Anthony was there, watching the team present an analysis of its generic competitors. Shane studied him surreptitiously. He seemed entirely focused, his hands rigid. He possessed the distant eyes of a mind on a different plane.

When the meeting adjourned, Anthony stood to leave. Dennis joined him by the conference room door. This was a study of biological opposites: tall, charismatic, silver-haired Dennis, and small, distant Anthony. Shane took a breath and walked toward them, clutching his carefully printed proposal.

"This is Shane Oberest," Dennis explained kindly. "Shane's lighting Sorion on fire."

"Hello," Anthony muttered, exuding the air of a professor late to his next class.

Shane brightened. "Doctor Leone, I was wondering if you'd have time to read something."

He was aware of Dennis looking at him and realized too late that he should have run this by him.

"What is this?" Anthony said, suddenly locking eyes with him.

"A proposal."

"Proposal? For what?"

"Actually, it's a proposal for us to apply for an orphan grant."

Dennis coughed; beneath his black eyebrows his eyes opened.

Shane pressed on. "There's a lung condition, a genetic mutation, called alpha-one antitrypsin deficiency . . ."

"It's a liver gene mutation," Anthony pronounced robotically.

"Right, liver. There's a high-potential cure using a protein we've already developed here."

Anthony shook his head firmly. "If a patient is alpha-one antitrypsin deficient, they'll develop emphysema. We're focusing on that."

"Would you mind maybe having somebody read it? I'd love to know if I made any sense," he said, extending the folder.

"We only pursue drugs for immature populations when there is potential for significant scientific breakthrough. You said we already isolated this protein?"

"Doctor Acharn did."

"So what is the potential for discovery?"

Dennis shot Shane a look. "Our motto is, Profitable Biotechnology. You should read your coffee mugs."

"I thought it was, Where Science Is the Star?"

Anthony stared hard at him. Angrily he said, "We're curing *cancer* here."

Shane felt his face flush.

"We're going to take our people off of diseases that kill tens of millions of people a year to put them on one that affects almost no one? With no hope of discovering anything new?"

"I guess it's called an orphan"—Shane smiled—"because it needs our help."

"It's called an orphan," Anthony replied, "because it is unwanted."

He took up his laptop bag, turned to Dennis, nodded sharply, "Okay," and left. Shane was aware of a ball forming behind his Adam's apple; his file stuck warmly in his hand.

Dennis's black eyebrows curled. "What the hell?"

"I know someone whose kid was born with this. I thought it would be respectful to have things thought through. I should have asked you how to handle it. That was bullshit. I'm sorry."

Dennis's face betrayed an almost parental frustration.

Shane left the conference room and walked down the hall. At the old elevator he turned. Dennis was still standing in the doorway; he had not taken his eyes off of him.

• • • • • • •

He sat across from Prajuk Acharn in a booth at a McDonald's near Pinon Drive.

Shane swallowed his lunch uneasily; it did not escape him that the biotechnology which made replacing proteins possible also provided the food in front of him. Outside a smeared window, a teenaged employee waged a futile battle against freeway grime with a window mop.

"So," Prajuk grinned. "Anthony told you to piss off."

"Right in front of Dennis too." He smiled. "Why are you laughing?"

"This thing is funny. Like watching someone walk into a door. Out of curiosity, what was this thing, your proposal, going to tell him?"

"A lot of it was a case study on Ceredase."

Prajuk chuckled. "This guy is top of his field in the world. He knows about Ceredase."

Shane frowned; the scent of grease and antiseptic became overwhelming. He pushed his tray away.

"Did he say anything at all?"

"He reminded me that we're here to cure cancer. Dennis talked about money."

Prajuk leaned back into the stained red leather booth. "Make no mistake, they are the same thing. P and P took the company public because they wanted money. To cure cancer. There is relentless pressure on everyone to beat these Goldman Sachs analysts' calls, because we want money to solve for cancer. If Poulos never figures out how to end cancer, I think he will consider his life a failure. Anthony too. And to do this thing takes a great deal of fucking money."

It was amusing, Shane thought, to hear him curse in his high voice.

"Look," he continued, moving his fingers over his fries, "we take money from hedge funds, and college endowment fund managers, and police department pensions, and soccer moms with an E-Trade account, to pay for all of this research. But these investors are not in our stock to cure cancer, or teach the body how to live with it. They are in it for profits. If our stock goes down? They will not care that we might only be a year or two away, they will sell. And we have to make appropriate cuts in research. And so Anthony Leone will not approve anything that threatens us with a loss. Unless"—he raised his finger—"it leads to something new. Which this does not. Why didn't you come to me?"

"I really thought he'd say yes."

"Even if he did, formal testing would take ten years. An infant with alpha-one antitrypsin deficiency," he reminded Shane flatly, "does not have ten years. Or even three."

"Clinical trials are fucking immoral," Shane spat. "At Orco, they tested a leukemia drug, okay? Everyone in the test was going blastic, but half the people got a placebo. The drug passed trials, Orco is making billions, half the test group was ignored. It's barbaric."

"Testing without controls is more barbaric. Imagine if the half they gave that drug to died instantly?" Prajuk was watching him curiously. "You have to think clinically, Shane. Phase One of a trial involves a hundred people. It exists to determine side effects. This is urgently important. Ninety-nine percent of drugs are proven unsafe right there. Without controlled Phase One testing, we risk killing millions of people later. Those people in that trial you mention understand their risk. They volunteer to participate to be part of finding a solution. One hundred voluntarily put themselves at risk to save millions. Those numbers are not barbaric, they are actually quite civilized."

"Thinking in numbers is immoral too."

"The dictatorship of numbers," Prajuk informed him, "is the process of history."

Shane shook the ice at the bottom of his cup. "I'm not going to stop. I'll go to other drug companies."

Prajuk smiled wistfully and wiped ketchup from his lower lip with the back of his hand.

"What about you? It's your discovery, your work, and it's just *sitting* there. Doesn't that bother the shit out of you?"

A knowing expression took over Prajuk's face. "I wanted to study computer science my whole life. But once I experienced biomedicine I was seduced completely. I left Khon Kaen when I was eighteen, to attend MIT. Afterward, I went for graduate work at UCLA. It was difficult. Even though LA was closer to Thailand, I felt much more homesickness there. I felt better at Stanford, where I did my postdoctoral work for Steven Poulos. We spent uncountable hours side by side in his lab, as he finessed his enzyme into Sorion. Which enabled the company to go public and hire hundreds and later thousands more people. All of this is in some way my work, Shane."

Shane watched the thin scientist, in his short-sleeved blue button-down shirt.

"Let's do it ourselves," Shane suggested.

Prajuk stopped moving.

"We'll come in weekends. We'll go back and find that door, and open it. No one will know."

"This is not a law firm. You cannot just come in on the weekend and use the company Xerox machines."

Shane's eyes smiled.

"There is not a drop of saline that is not accounted for. And this thing, the lab, there are people in it around the clock. But also, I discovered this protein in Helixia's employ. Any discoveries I make belong to them."

"But they don't use it."

"So because you're not using your car today, I can take it?"

"If a little girl was dying on the corner, you could goddamn take it. You'd be a criminal if you didn't."

Prajuk's eyes drifted down to his watch. "To manufacture a drug for the ten thousand people with alpha-one antitrypsin deficiency would cost ten million dollars and take half a decade, Shane. This is not something we can do after hours."

"What if I didn't want to help ten thousand people?"

Prajuk squinted, caught by surprise.

"What if I only wanted enough medicine for just one?" Shane looked across the table at this man he barely knew. He hesitated, breathless, and leaned forward onto the sticky Formica table. "What would that take?"

Prajuk crossed his small arms and stared out the window, at the haze of the industrial city. For a long time, only his little finger moved, unconsciously tapping on his tray.

In a much softer voice he answered, "Significantly less."

7

When Caleb came downstairs at five a.m., there were bottles everywhere.

The house reeked of beer. Large bottles of Belhaven lay like unfinished books on the floor. Two mostly empty big bottles of Beam stood by an open Monopoly set. The old boom box was still on, its green light fluttering like the heart monitor of a dying man.

Three light-bearded kids wearing T-shirts were asleep on the floor. Caleb recognized one as a regular from the Rocking Horse; the others he'd never seen before. He walked to the kitchen and was pleased to find it tidy. As Happy Trails did not stock food, there had been nothing for the party to raid. He carefully opened the glass containers of amaranth, faro, spelt, buckwheat, barley, blue cornmeal, and wheat germ, took a measuring spoon from the drawer, and began sifting them into a large cast iron pot filled with soy milk.

From upstairs came the creak of floorboards. John, he guessed. The older John became, the more his energy seemed to concentrate in these earliest of hours. Anyone who was assigned to prepare breakfast encountered John's help bringing out bowls, replacing the grains, wiping down the countertop.

Then a sudden sound surprised him. Just beside the front door, the door to Mack's room creaked open. Caleb stepped back into the shadows by the kitchen door. Rae, her hair loose from its familiar ponytail, closed the door behind her. Her full mouth was frowning, and her head hung limply from her shoulders. Her eyes seemed to be carrying black weights.

Caleb watched her move straight to the stairs and take them quickly.

•••••••

At noon, he left O'Neil's for his midday break and jogged steadily away from the shops.

Halloween themes had taken over the town. Orange and black banners hung from the streetlights advertising the upcoming parade, blocks of hay had been stacked along Broadway, and handmade posters for pumpkin coffees and beers hung in windows.

On Arapahoe he pivoted past the high school and took a quick turn down Nineteenth, a small street speckled with short trees and older single-story homes. By the doorway of a small apartment complex on Goss, he stopped and waited until June emerged, carrying her plastic bucket of supplies. She wore a soft turquoise fleece jacket and white running shoes, and when she saw him she skipped over the pavement and hugged him. They had arranged this assignation with a whispered word during the group run the day before. He kissed her, she left her bucket and jacket in the doorway, and they started jogging west. Beside him she felt tiny but steadfast.

Soon they were out executing a good pace toward Flagstaff. They seemed to be struggling messily with the process of synching footsteps and heartbeats. Eventually, through a subtle progression, they found a rhythm and moved into a vast meadow.

"So, I really need to talk to you."

Caleb glanced at her and nodded.

She hesitated. "I'm worried."

"About Lily? Look, we . . ."

"About you."

He was surprised to see the look in her eyes.

"You asked your brother for help, and it's been three months . . ."

"Three and a half," he mumbled.

"I haven't seen my family in six years. They've never even met Lily. But I know if I asked them for help, they would be there. If they blew me off? I'd be crushed. Caleb, are you crushed?"

He smiled, looking out at the gray road, and the rolling green and brown brush. "I disappeared from Shane's life a long time ago. Why should he jump just because I ask him to?"

"But he came out here, so we thought . . ."

"He must have seen something he didn't like."

"It's the way we live, or maybe Mack freaked him out. Or maybe me."

"I doubt that."

"I just, I wanted to tell you . . . I could see that he loves you."

Caleb felt that reach him with surprising force.

She touched his arm. "Ever since the Hardrock, I've been

realizing how vulnerable we are on these mountains. I don't want you to be distracted, by Shane, or us."

"I didn't fall at Hardrock because of you, or my brother," he lied. "I fell because the trail was muddy."

"Rae's been against Yosemite from the start. Maybe she's right?"

"She's right for herself. Not for me. I'm not going to fall again."

"What are your parents like?"

Caleb hesitated. He wanted to just pound the blacktop of Baseline until they reached Flagstaff; they were almost near the preserve, and he longed for quiet.

"My dad's a lawyer, very rational." For no reason he could fathom he added, "He has a mustache."

"Well, you need to be very rational to have a mustache," June offered brightly. "You have to trim it just right every day."

Caleb's laugh echoed through the hills. "He used to take me out running with him, when I was eight, nine. We went so far."

"You must have had some great talks."

"We never talked"—Caleb wiped his nose—"when we ran."

They were offered an opportunity to plunge into back-country along a single track trail. It was more humid, and insects swirled around them in spirals. He took her hand and dashed past buckeyes as thin as they were, their bark in undulating shades from milk chocolate to stout. A moose drank in a creek, steam pouring from its wide nostrils.

June gripped his hand and they ran faster, leaping over branches, lost in the world. When they were far from any path or tail, he pulled her into him and kissed her.

He had gone ten years without touching anyone alone.

Even after these months with June, the rawness of it felt alive. She reached for his shorts, and they fell onto the ground. She whispered into his ear.

"Please."

He looked down at her wide eyes. He supposed it was the most erotic word he could imagine.

Afterward he stared through the branches at the open sky. Regardless of whether he ever heard from Shane again, he understood that this life which he had built for a decade was finished now. There seemed to be no way back to its isolation and purity. Separating from it was going to be as traumatic, he knew, as anything he had ever experienced.

They followed along the black hardtop of Baseline back to the city and picked up June's things. After Caleb jogged back to O'Neil's, June walked through town, back to the park, and down toward the base of South Boulder Peak. A joyful peace settled inside her. The old wood house seemed to greet her from its clearing, the slabs of wood experienced and confident as grandparents. She retrieved her daughter from her housemates and took her out back into the field's fallen leaves.

"I love you. I love you," she kissed into Lily's hot neck, spinning her around. "I love our life."

June reveled in the distant music from the house, the singing juncos and pipits on the branches. Maybe it was a good thing that Shane had not gotten back to them. Secretly she felt relieved to not have to leave here; she didn't think she could ever live in any other place again.

Touching her forehead to Lily's, they both smiled spontaneously, as if they had been sharing the exact same thought.

.... 8

When his cell phone rang, Shane was feeding the baby. He reached across the kitchen counter and fumbled with it. His heart skipped when he heard Prajuk's high-pitched voice.

"I am in the Marina. Can you meet me?"

Shane went to tell Janelle, who was in the kitchen pumping milk. The breast pump, which Shane had anticipated with curiosity, had proven to be disconcerting; he preferred not to see it in action.

Janelle saw the look on his face and arched her eyebrows.

"Quick work thing," he explained.

"We're going to my parents' at ten."

"I just need an hour." His face brightened. "I'll take Nicholas."

The bounty of a morning alone lit Janelle's eyes like a hit of meth. Shane put together a balmy bottle and stuffed it, along with a pack of wipes and a diaper, into his shorts' pockets. Then he lifted the warm boy into a Baby Bjorn.

Outside, other parents, pushing awkward strollers, large coffees spilling from their cup holders, initiated an empathetic eye contact with him. But Shane's empathy lay with the babies. This is our time to be loved without inhibition, he wanted to tell them, and it does not last very long. Future spouses and children might love them, but would they kiss away saliva from their chins? Would they tell them in the gentlest of voices that they were perfect? Across the street he saw a heavyset, middle-aged man in a stained green sweater. Someone, Shane thought, had cradled him once, kissed his sleeping cheeks. We may be loved, but we are never loved this way again.

Beyond the green grounds of Fort Mason wisps of sails moored to the piers floated as seagulls in the sky. Ahead, a girls' soccer game was in effect. Ten shrieking eight-year-olds in white and pale blue uniforms, ten Chinese girls in yellow and red. The American parents held steel coffee mugs; the Chinese favored styrofoam. They sat, as always, on opposite ends of the field. Shane noticed Prajuk on an old bench, in running shorts and maroon Adidas, his thin legs extended, ankles crossed.

"You live around here?" Shane asked, sitting beside him.

"No. I run here on weekends sometimes. This is your little guy?"

"Nicholas."

Looking at the baby's face, Prajuk could see mostly Chinese features. Caucasian genes, he thought not for the first time, are the most easily overwhelmed in all of human history.

Prajuk saw every living being in terms of its genealogy. Genes, to him, were a diabolical puzzle in which one had to discover each piece, and was never shown the picture he was trying to complete. That his work led to the saving of lives was a good thing, but it was not what woke him up in the morning; the magic to Prajuk was the unveiling of life's blueprints, the piecing together of this puzzle. And so thinking about Shane's infant with alpha-one antitrypsin deficiency, Prajuk was moved less by the image of a baby struggling to breathe than by the notion of solving for another piece. Diseases were Easter eggs to him; he detested leaving one that he had spotted uncollected.

When Prajuk spoke, he stared straight ahead at the soccer game. "Do you know what a mast cell is, Shane?"

"I don't, no."

"Mast cells are like skunks in the lungs. Touch them, and they release a chemical spray that causes an acute inflammatory response. This thing is a good defense against viruses. But in asthmatics, IgE antibodies float around the bloodstream and bind to their mast cells, making them spray constantly. Like riding a skunk. The inflammatory response is constant. We give asthmatics steroids, which force the lungs to contract. They neuter the response, but they do nothing to stop the IgE antibodies from binding to the mast cells. So the body is initiating one action, and the steroids are fighting it. This is traumatic for the body, as you can imagine, like pressing on your gas pedal and brake pedal at the same time. The enzyme protein we found, this thing teaches the antibodies to stop attaching themselves to mast cells in the first place. This is why it will revolutionize asthma treatment."

Shane recalled something Janelle had explained to him years ago, while they were slightly stoned on hydroponic: the only solution to disease is to teach the body to heal itself, the way you teach a child to solve problems himself.

"That's Airifan," Shane guessed.

"Airifan would not help infants with alpha-one antitrypsin

deficiency, because their problem is not mast cells. But this enzyme also switches on the gene that instructs the liver to produce alpha-one antitrypsin. In a different formulation, however, it would reverse the problem. It is just a matter of producing it."

"What kind of a matter," Shane asked quietly, "is that?"

"I put this thing, this protein, in a vector. If you help me in the lab, I can come after work and maybe do a few runs a week. I can make two milligrams of a new formulation, a treatment, each run. This baby, she will need thirty to fifty milligrams to have enough for ninety years of life."

Shane was speechless. He waited tensely for Prajuk to go on.

"You understand this thing is a fireable offense. A career-ending offense."

"No one would know," Shane whispered.

"What about the baby's mother? And your brother? They could never tell anyone they have this drug."

"They won't. They're not the blogging type. I'll explain it all to them."

In front of them a pigtailed girl of Irish descent blocked a goal and a cheer rose from the sidelines.

"This thing cannot be done at work. You would need to find a lab."

"A lab. Sure."

"Purchase a Promega kit. Rent water baths, a centrifuge, an incubator. I will give you a list. I will come by with the vector. This will take your nights."

Shane glanced down at Nicholas. "That's okay."

"I would need a postdoc." Prajuk coughed and spit something phlegmy onto the grass. "Also, we will need to build a mouse."

"A mouse?"

"A knockout mouse. We knock one of its genes out through breeding, so it is nonfunctioning. And we use it for testing. This thing will take some time to deliver."

"How much time would all this take?"

"A month or two to set up. Three, four months, once we start."

Against his chest, Nicholas squirmed uncomfortably. Shane reached into his pocket for the bottle, which Nicholas was now somehow able to gasp with one small hand, like a hipster chugging a forty.

Prajuk turned and caught his eye intensely. "Can you live with this, Shane?"

"With saving this baby's life? Yes, absolutely."

"With not telling the parents of other very sick babies that you have a treatment for their disease?"

Shane caught his breath. He recognized this question immediately as the thing he had been ducking.

"Because this is the situation. There are ten thousand people with alpha-one antitrypsin deficiency. Many of them are also infants. But I can only produce enough treatment for this girl. There will be no mass production. If you think that you would post about this on some message board and start a frenzy in that community, then we cannot proceed."

Shane's chest constricted painfully, and he shifted.

"See, now you are in the position in which Anthony finds himself every day. Anthony must bypass a community of ten thousand people to try to save a million. You must bypass ten thousand people to try to save one."

"Uh-huh," Shane said.

"You and the baby's parents would also need to understand the risk of harm."

"I thought there are no side effects?"

"We do not have the time or money for ten years of trials. I am certain that it is safe, because this protein underwent intensive trials as part of the Airifan studies. But there is always an opportunity for surprise when it comes to the body. It is a small percentage, but the opportunity for toxicity exists."

"I'll talk to them about all of this."

"One last thing. If I participate in this, you can no longer think about applying for an orphan grant."

"Why?"

"A grant application makes this a matter of record, and I will not participate in it."

"That's how I was going to fund it."

"I assume you have lobbyists to speed up grant approval at the NIH? I hope you have a better plan than that."

Nervously Shane asked, "If I paid for it myself, how much would it cost?"

"Renting a lab, and the equipment? Ten, maybe fifteen thousand." He raised his eyes. "The mouse is more expensive."

"Start to finish."

"Maybe a hundred thousand dollars."

Shane felt fevered. In front of them a determined young Chinese girl kicked a soccer ball into the goal, and parents erupted on the sidelines. Above, the sky was as azure as God must have first planned it.

Shane squeezed his son's small hand. The saltwater swelled the air until he thought that it might burst.

9

Walking into work, Caleb ran into Ed O'Neil, struggling happily with an enormous roll of posters.

"The Gay and Lesbian Alliance ordered twenty oversized. I was printing 'til midnight." He added awkwardly, "They're pretty neat."

Caleb smiled in as friendly a manner as he knew.

For the next four hours, he paced around the store, making his constant small movements. At eleven, Enrique, the mailman, opened the front door. Enrique liked to brag that he was paid to get the best lower-body workout imaginable.

"I guess that seems pretty crazy to you, right?" he told Caleb, sorting bills into the open honeycombs. "Walking all around in the snow all day and liking it?"

Caleb wondered what Enrique would say about his night runs in total darkness and subzero wind.

"You got yourself a letter," Enrique said, handing him a white envelope.

Caleb hesitated. The envelope possessed a preprinted return address with an orange logo: Helixia. He abandoned Enrique and walked to the back office, shutting the door behind him. He was shaking. Four months of waiting. It bothered him, how much this meant to him.

> Hi Caleb,
>
> I have a present for Lily. I ordered it, but it's going to take some time to arrive. Would you all be able to come here to get it?
>
> Shane.

When a UC sophomore came to relieve him at noon, Caleb undertook a frantic sprint down the mountain to the house. At the slight curve of the road by the cluster of aspens, he came upon a small group of his housemates, huddled in a tight circle. The warm light fell on their suntanned skin so that they looked like warm stones in a fire.

Leigh, Juan, Alice, Makailah, and Kyle were listening intently to someone. Slowing down, he realized it was Rae. She stood so much smaller than the rest of them that it had been hard to see her. Her black hair was pulled into her usual tight ponytail, her arms folded. Caleb inched closer.

"It's too dangerous."

"It's all dangerous," Kyle was explaining dismissively.

"He's going to have aid stations," Makailah insisted.

"Look, he's not hiding it," Rae insisted. "Ask him."

"You're saying he wants us to get hurt?"

"He's planning to make this the most dangerous race in the country. They're *selling* it that way. The trails are totally isolated. No rescue Jeeps can get near them. They cancelled the original Yosemite because two runners died there, and they're bringing it back even more unsafe."

"But why would he put us at risk?" asked Alice plaintively. "You're not making any sense."

"It's not about us," Rae said, pushing a loose strand of Cherokee black hair from her forehead. "It's about television. He's not thinking clearly. Something's going wrong."

"You don't have to run it," Kyle told her.

"I'm not."

Caleb was stunned. Never had he heard dissension like this, in all his years here. When he shifted his weight, a tiny branch cracked beneath him. Kyle turned quickly, his marine instincts undulled by either the passage of time or his quitting of methamphetamine.

They turned as one and stared at him. He knew they all thought him to be closer to Mack than they were; he was, in their eyes, management.

"Hi, Caley," Leigh nodded gently.

"Why are you guys talking about this here?"

Kyle nodded at him. "You think Yosemite's too dangerous to run?"

Caleb shrugged unsurely, just wanting to get to June. He felt uncomfortable with how they all were watching him, all of them hungry for something. He understood now just how much Mack had riding on his Yosemite Slam. It was more than television coverage or the promise of more recruits. It was the trust of the Happy Trails Running Club.

"Every ultra is dangerous. Look what happened to me at Hardrock."

"Right," Kyle agreed.

"He just wants to get the sport seen. Like the Tour de France. He wants to open more houses. That's something he wants to do." Caleb witnessed a chipmunk sprinting through the thin bark of the trees. "He's been open about that."

"You're running it, right?" Leigh asked.

Caleb looked past them, toward the house. Through these trees, it looked vulnerable to him, sitting as it did in the shadow of the mountain. An avalanche, an electrical storm, might smother it. It depended on their nurturing, their priming, their care, more than he had realized.

"Of course."

He walked inside, up the stairs, and found June and Lily playing on the little oval rug in their room. June had hung bright yellow curtains with a blue moon over their window. Religious decorations were forbidden; Mack wanted no reminders of any faiths other than forward motion. But these he found acceptable. It is strange, Caleb noted, that the moon, moving tides, affecting behavior, a perfect circle, perhaps the most powerful proof of a guiding force in all experience, has no religious connotations at all, ignored by the symbologies of the world.

He showed June the letter. She read it, frowning, "I don't understand."

"He wrote it assuming Mack would see it."

"So it's code?"

He nodded.

"So, 'present,' that means medicine?"

"Yes."

"In San Francisco?" She stared at him questioningly. "How do we get there?"

Caleb shook his head. He was not in possession of a credit card, a driver's license, a cell phone, even a bank account. He supposed June still had these things.

"I guess Mack will buy us the plane tickets," June nodded happily.

"I don't think," Caleb said softly, "that he will."

She blinked, not following.

"He won't want us leaving here before Yosemite."

"But that's not for seven months."

Caleb nodded slowly.

"I have my license, I'll rent us a car. Mack always says we're free to leave."

"Yes. But not to come back."

She froze, understanding him now. "I need to come back here, Caley. This is where we live. I don't want to live any other way."

"Then we need to ask him the right way, so he'll help us."

"How do we do that?"

Caleb considered this. If he came through at Yosemite, if he won and delivered Mack into the pages of *Sports Illustrated*, then surely Mack would give them a month away from the house and welcome them back, if only to disprove certain media reports that Happy Trails was a cult.

But could Lily wait seven more months? Think it through, he told himself. Mack would never let him leave before Yosemite, but maybe he might let June and Lily go. After all, Caleb was his only chance to win. Didn't he need him happy and focused?

Possibly, Caleb understood, there was a deal to be made.

He looked down at Lily. Being near her created surges of emotions that he could not identify. There was no godliness in the trails which touched the depth and power of this.

"I love her," he whispered, as Lily's red and swollen feet kicked at the rug.

June kissed him; her breath was thin and sour. Caleb held these two girls, all the time listening for footsteps, for whispers of someone coming to catch them, and take away his perfect peace.

• • • • • • •

The broker was a frighteningly thin Latino man in his early twenties.

He wore a purple silk shirt and tight black jeans, and was the owner of a thin mustache that gave him the appearance, Shane thought, of a Guatemalan pimp. He walked Shane through a concrete building called Greenway Plaza as if it were an apartment complex on a beach. But it was not full of condominiums; the building was full of labs.

"Only thirty percent occupied. Quiet." He lifted a pointer finger to the air.

Shane assured him, "Quiet is good."

This was the second building he had been shown. It was difficult to see a functional difference between them, but Greenway Plaza had the advantage of being just ten minutes from Helixia, up Pinon Drive. Every floor held five labs, each the size of a grade school classroom. The labs came bare, just a long bench, two stainless steel sinks, a tall shelved cabinet. Specific equipment, materials, even chairs would need to be leased or purchased. Rent was three thousand dollars a month; Shane had been hoping for better.

"Will you be needing furniture?" the broker inquired with a smile. He must get a kickback, Shane realized.

"All taken care of."

"Okay, okay. So what are you going to be doing here? Just curious."

"Curing a disease."

"Oh," he nodded. "It's a perfect space for that."

Shane left in a sunlit daze. He had expected signing a lease to leave him excited and proud. Instead, he experienced a flood of buyer's remorse, which evolved into a previously unknown degree of terror.

Looking back at the building from his car, it occurred to him how many excited people rent labs just like this, each certain they possess a secret which will change the world. How long does it take for them to burn through their seed money and wind up handing these dull keys right back?

He desperately wanted to call Janelle and talk to her about what he had done. But he had made a decision that surprised him, which was to not tell her any of it.

It was the first and only secret in their marriage. At first he been shocked that it had even occurred to him, but he had understood quickly that this was his only option. Janelle had been with Helixia for eleven years. They had hired her with no experience and grown her into a well-compensated product manager. She was a tireless, loyal, and dedicated employee, and as soon as he told her, she would face an impossible decision: to say nothing, which would make her part of this and put her at the same risk as he and Prajuk of being fired and ruined. Or to tell her manager, which would mean she would betray him, Caleb, and this baby girl. It would not be love, he thought, to put her in this position. Also, he was reasonably certain she would take a management view of this endeavor.

Plus, Shane decided, there was no need to stress her out this early in the process, with so many pieces that could fall apart at any time.

Then there was the money. A hundred thousand dollars was a future-changing amount of money, and this was no investment. There was no chance of him recouping even a dollar. Even the three thousand dollars he had just signed over would astonish her. But, Shane felt, he had every right to spend it. During the decade before they had met, he had amassed six figures in savings. Janelle had told him while they were engaged that she was setting aside her own savings for her parents' care. How was this different? It was his money, from the same premarriage period, being used for his family's health. Morally, he felt in the clear. The difference of course was transparency, but he was certain that once Janelle knew everything, the question of whose money it was would be a minor discussion.

For these reasons, he had told his wife nothing as he researched labs, made appointments with this broker, accessed his entire Orco 401(k). But as he drove closer to home, he realized that there was yet another motivation to keep this to himself.

And that was that it lit up some primal part of his brain, in an unexpectedly profound way, to shoulder this burden alone.

One morning, after the drug was in Caleb's hands, he would take Janelle out to dinner and tell her everything that he had done. His tale would be complete, with no hanging threads, no stress. He would pour her a glass of wine and, as if unveiling a painting he'd been working on, tell her, "So this is what I did." And her eyes would widen. He very much looked forward to that.

He used his time waiting in doctor's offices with materials

about Sorion to peruse online catalogs and order equipment. He was startled to find that any biological fluid and technology was available for rental and delivered as easily as dinner.

Meanwhile, Prajuk began the process of finding a postdoctoral assistant. He placed calls to friends at Stanford and UCSF, describing a chance for a postdoc to work in a lab, doing hands-on gene splicing and cloning. Like all things associated with lab work, he informed Shane, this would take time.

That evening, lying on their bed, his feet brushing up against a board book about farm animals, Shane stroked Janelle's fine hair. The bedroom TV played meaninglessly in front of them. The baby was in his crib, trying to get himself down.

During Janelle's first weeks back at work, the interrupted sleep had not affected her adversely; in fact she had enjoyed waking every few hours to nurse. Maybe, Janelle had told him, sleep is like a glass of scotch, best enjoyed in sips. Her breasts, which she had been certain all her life were too small to ever nourish a baby, were producing enough milk to leave in sealed plastic bags for Hua to warm. Her mother would arrive at eight every morning in a huff of Shanghai provincialism, bringing herbs, reheating her sour cabbage soup. It all seemed perfect to Shane.

But tonight Janelle was torn. At work, she confessed, she suffered a sort of Nicholas withdrawal. Her office computer was split between spreadsheets and mothering websites, and she found it impossible to focus for more than an hour without calling home. Hua had a lifelong problem with phones and refused to answer unless she knew who it was, which caused Janelle no small amount of aggravation. And Shane was busier than she had ever seen him. He was not, she felt, present with her.

"Mom fed Nicholas bananas today," she informed him, sitting up.

"I know we haven't started baby food yet," Shane commiserated gently, "but it's not her fault. I saw a jar around here."

"Not baby food bananas," Janelle clarified. "*Actual* bananas."

"Doctor Hess doesn't want him to eat solids yet."

"I know. That's what I'm saying." She hesitated. "Should I stay home?"

"Oh," he said, nodding.

Janelle stared at him. And then, taking him by surprise, she leaned over and kissed him deeply. Her tongue sent a shiver down his back. Recently their lovemaking had begun to emerge from its tentative state and capture some of its pre-pregnancy tension. Its reappearance was like a sudden electric current, shocking them both.

In these dreamy moments afterward, strange memories came to him. With the birth of his son, a film seemed to have been lifted from his childhood. Specific images came rushing back to him as if they were boomerangs.

Last night their upstairs bathroom had dissolved into a lucid vision of his bathroom in Issaquah. He could see his childhood sink, its toothbrushes and plastic superhero cups, so clearly that he felt amazed it was not actually there. He suffered a pang of longing for that sink that astonished him.

In coffee shops, in waiting rooms, he was ambushed by visions of long-forgotten grade school and summer camp friends.

Having this baby, he thought, had done something to his mental processes. He was unsure if these visions were charming or dangerous. Fatherhood had connected him suddenly and without warning to both his past, and the future. It had made him an electric conduit where his memories and visions of Nicholas's life to come connected in an explosive current. He was expecting his first shipments at the lab, and responsibility of this secret second job began to build. To manage being a new father, his wife's emotions, his new job, and this, would require great control, confidence, and focus.

From his room, Nicholas began to cry.

10

On the first real snowfall of November, they realized Rae was gone.

Winter had come. At night, the temperature in the valley fell to single digits and did not warm up until late morning. Caleb awoke to half a dozen inches of fresh powder. He could only imagine the scene thousands of feet above, in Breckenridge and Vail; the cheers seemed to echo down the Front Range. The perfume of decaying autumn leaves drifted in through the windows; on the trails the sun against the snow created golds in hues he had no names for.

That afternoon, the Happy Trails Running Club meditated in a circle by the fireplace, their rows of wet shoes stacked neatly by the front door. Alice came slowly down the stairs. She stood there a moment, tears in her eyes, and announced that her roommate was gone.

“She just left?” Kevin Yu asked, shocked.

“I chased after her. I asked her what was up, but she just shook her head no. She was upset.”

“Was someone waiting for her?” John asked.

“She just started walking.” Alice told them, pushing tears

across her cheeks with the flat of her hand. "I don't know if she went to Superior, or up to the city, or where she went."

Mack walked in from his room and stood quietly against the bookcase, listening.

"Is she going back to Portland?" asked Leigh.

"She didn't say anything."

"Maybe she had a family issue. Like, her mom."

"She would have told me if her mom wasn't good."

"She's been acting strange," Kyle explained. His voice did not communicate empathy.

Aviva stared straight down at her feet, her brightly tattooed arms balanced on her knees. While Alice had been Rae's roommate, Aviva was her closest friend. She was clearly shaken.

"Let's go find her," John suggested, standing. He ran his hand along his crew-cut white hair, and waited. "We can check the motels around here. The bus station. She's probably still walking to Superior." There was some agreement here; people started to rise.

Then Mack dropped a book on the floor. It hit the ground with unexpected force.

"She didn't leave because she wanted to."

The room turned sharply to him.

"Who would leave here on their own?" Mack asked them, his nasal voice low and calm. He watched members of Happy Trails consider this. Caleb saw the muscle of Aviva's jaw tighten and release.

"Anyone hazard, you know, a guess?"

Kyle raised his hand.

Mack pointed a finger at him. "My boy."

"She was expelled?"

"Absolutely."

The room held its breath.

"Was it because she didn't want to run Yosemite?" Makailah asked.

"That's part of it. But that was a symptom. There was a root disease. She didn't like it here anymore."

"She loved it," Aviva muttered to herself.

"She was ill."

People sat straight, surprised.

"What's wrong with her?" June whispered.

Mack stepped closer to the circle. "Rae was infected with a virus. The virus of negativity. I asked her to participate in killing this virus, to use her kinetic energy against it, but she refused." He looked around the room, making eye contact with each one of them. "What I ask you guys to do matters. Every run, every private energy session, everything goes toward the collective kinetic energy of our house. We can't have one person refusing to participate. Creating stasis."

Caleb stole a glance at Lily, in June's arms. Rae had spent a lot of time with her, encouraging her to sit up, trying to get her to crawl, cradling her, singing to her. Lily would miss her, Caleb realized. To be loved is to never forget.

"When you feel negativity, like if someone at your job says something to you about us, or if you're injured for a time, when you're not sure what to think or what to do? Remember you always have the answer. What is it?"

"Run it out!" Kevin called.

"Run it out. Negativity comes from Taco Bells and flight delays, and its antidote is on the trails. When you're exposed to it, don't think, seek the trails. You always have a choice, to stop or to run. Rae stopped. What do we do?"

"Run!" they each shouted, the mood shifting.

"We'll have a healing session now, a healing of the emotional pain of losing a loved one. It's what we need."

Even Aviva nodded. Mack went to his room and emerged carrying a half-full bottle of Jim Beam and a small hash pipe. June took Lily upstairs and put her into her crib. John went to the fireplace and added a large amount of cherrywood, which popped like firecrackers in the flames. Caleb felt someone staring at him. When he dared to glance up, Mack caught his eye and winked.

Then he sat down in between Alice and Makailah, and they all began to chant.

....

On Thanksgiving, Mack allowed a tofurkey with root vegetables.

This rare deviation from their diet was accompanied by much local ale. The day began with the annual Thanksgiving Fat Race at Bear Peak. Two hundred locals showed up for the fifty-mile run through the snowpacked course. Caleb was a monster; he won by a full minute. Every member of Happy Trails finished in the top fifty, including, to Caleb's pleasure, June. Everyone was overjoyed, and they invited the other runners over to the house to continue the party. A blowout commenced. Mack held an increasingly drunken court, opening big bottles of Beam, dispensing new ideas for the perfect head position during descents. Mostly the guests wanted to hear about the Yosemite Slam.

"The most intense ultra ever run," he beamed.

"The ultra ultra," a girl who had placed eleventh suggested.

Mack laughed loudly. "The ultra ultra. That's cool. That's cool."

Caleb approached Mack when the last guests had left. "Can we talk for a second?" he began nervously.

It was eight o'clock, and Mack was tying his laces by the front door for an alcohol-infused sprint through the snow, one of his favorite things in the world. A new dusting of icicles grew against the windowpane like DNA, spiraling, precise.

Mack looked up. His eyes were alight, the wrinkles around them like rivers flowing in reverse. He looked then as if he might accomplish anything.

"You can come with me, brother."

Outside the cold greeted them harshly. The moon was buried behind a curtain of cloud. They took off as fast as their legs would carry them into the eight inches of new powder covering the field toward the base of the mountain, sinking with every step. Mack would not slow, Caleb knew. The idea was to run until exhaustion, to fill their bodies with blood and delirium.

Suddenly Caleb's right eye began bothering him; he felt a breathtaking and pure pain. Soon he could no longer blink. As they returned, wet with sweat and leaked toxins, sober and alive, Caleb stumbled against the side of the house.

Mack leaned closer. "Hey, that fucker's frostbitten."

He rubbed his palms together as if they were flints, breathing in deeply. He placed his palms an inch away from Caleb's face, and immediately Caleb felt a warmth caress his eye. Then it began to burn, as if a match were being held to his pupil. He pulled back.

Mack pushed his feverish hand closer to the white mucus of his eye, his face only inches from Caleb's. "So," Mack whispered, his breath full of Beam, "what do you want to talk to me about?"

Caleb stammered, "My brother wrote me."

"Yeah? What's Shane up to?"

Caleb tried to jerk away, but the back of his head pushed against the wood wall of the house. A gust of snow blew over them.

"He found medicine for Lily. If we get to San Francisco he can . . . oh," he buckled over, hands on his knees. Mack crouched down beside him, his palm still pressed to Caleb's frozen eye.

"Now, we spoke about this, Caley. I don't know how many times."

"He's got something for the baby. Can you get them to San Francisco? If I know they're there, I can . . . I can focus."

Caleb felt a crackle of fission inside his cornea, and Mack took his hand away, studied his eye. Above, Caleb saw the floating presence of a ferruginous hawk.

"Are you negotiating with me, Caley?"

"No."

"Kind of sounds like, if I say yes, you'll focus, and if I say no, you might not?"

"That's not what I mean." He felt confused. But as he blinked, his eye started to feel normal.

"Your energy is building up again. Look how fast you're healing. Most people would go to the hospital for something like that." Mack took a step back, looking into him. "You were so depleted, dude. But since I pulled you away from June and Lily, your training is astronomical. Everything I'm coaching you to do is working. After Yosemite you're going to be one of the elite athletes in our sport. And you're back obsessed with *them*?"

For the first time he could recall since he was a boy, Caleb felt tears running down his skin.

"Okay, Caleb. I'll bet you were a damn good consultant. Here's a counteroffer. I think if Lily and June are off with your brother, you'll be thinking about them even more than you are now. You'll be wanting to know what's going on, wanting to call them. And you will fail at Yosemite. So my offer is this: they stay here. You keep staying away from them. Think about nothing but the Slam. Win it. After that, if Lily's not one hundred percent better, I'm not getting it done. You take them out to San Francisco and focus on them. Take as much time as you need. And then come back, open arms. Okay?"

He took a shaky, deep breath. "Okay."

"In the meantime, nothing will happen to Lily under my care. She's starting to crawl and move, which means she's building up her stores of kinetic energy. Which I can build on." Mack wiped Caleb's tears with his thumb. "However. You just had your last day working in Boulder. You're on lockdown until Yosemite. For the next six months, I don't want you distracted by anything."

Caleb nodded.

"So we don't need to discuss this again?"

"No, Mack. I get it."

"Well, then. It's a deal."

Mack went past him, inside the house. When the door

opened, Caleb heard the joyful sounds of his housemates, laughing, dancing, turning up the reggae on the ancient black boom box. He stayed out in the starlit snow, his whole body shaking, a shaking that would not go away, not even after he went back inside, no matter how close to the fire he could get.

•••••••

On the Monday after Thanksgiving, Prajuk committed his first crime.

Sitting in his small office, he casually slipped a thumb drive into his computer, exported the Airifan section of his gene library, and dropped the drive into his pants pocket.

All afternoon he wondered how the rest of the world could not see it there, burning through the cotton. His hand slipped down into his pocket again and again, turning it over with his fingers like a nervous groom with a ring.

At seven, his shirt damp with sweat, he drove down the highway to Greenway Plaza and pulled into a five-story-tall concrete building. He lit a Parliament and smoked it in his strange manner, holding it in his fist and sucking at the air. Then he stepped onto the elevator for the first time. On the third floor he emerged into a dim corridor and opened a door to Lab 301.

He almost ran into a heavyset cable technician walking out. Broadband had been successfully installed. He glanced around the room. It was over-air-conditioned, and the sound of the giant ducts echoed through it. He could see that equipment was trickling in sporadically, and that Shane was not quite sure what to do with it all.

The incubator had arrived first. It was refrigerator-white, square, small. Water baths, gel apparatuses, shakers came next. Ice buckets. Bunsen burners. Lab gloves.

Shane had come straight from work to find them left in a pile by the locked door to Lab 301. He stacked them against the wall of the small room.

The Promega gene kit arrived two days later. A heavy box called a centrifuge, which looked to Shane like a miniature washing machine. He opened the top and peered down at the round hole. Some miracle might take place there. He worried about contamination and quickly shut it.

Metal stools came in next. Something called a flow hood, which Shane carried to a table and out of curiosity plugged in, revealing a purple light. He lost track of time in the windowless room, screwing the wheels onto three Aeron chairs long past Nicholas's bedtime. Prajuk saw him removing a water bath from a rental box and looking around for the proper place to put it.

"Here," he offered, taking it to the long metal working counter, "like this."

Shane grinned at him. Already he had found himself growing emotionally attached to this room, its unused double sinks, its off-white walls.

Prajuk slid the thumb drive into the rented Mac and exhaled shakily as his gene library appeared on its monitor. Then he surveyed the lab, his arms crossed.

"This is how it will work."

A sense of approaching motion hung in the air.

"This thing, alpha-one antitrypsin deficiency, is caused because the child was born with a gene switched off. We will isolate the protein that flips that switch on. Clone it. Grow it here. Make it therapeutic and inject it into the child. It will alter her DNA so that it instructs the gene to switch on. It's not complicated."

"Of course not."

"This thing will be taught in sixth-grade biology class by the time your son is six."

"My sixth-grade biology teacher was a hippie slide guitarist," Shane informed him.

"They let anyone teach in American schools, don't they?" Prajuk walked around the room, examining equipment. "Proteins march through our bodies like workers going into a city, flipping switches as they go. And the body responds. Many terrible diseases are simply workers flipping the wrong switch. Did the slide guitarist explain this to you?"

"I might have been dissecting a fetal pig that day."

"Apologies. We did not have the luxury of using pigs for children's experiments in my school."

"So, how do the genes know which switches to flip?"

"The brain follows simple instructions in our DNA. You would guess this recipe for human existence is quite complicated, with millions of different steps?"

"Sure."

"But there are only four."

Shane blinked.

"T, C, A, and G are the only four nucleotides in DNA. Depending on the pattern of these four letters, you can grow a fin, glow, you can process logic, you're a cat. And so on."

Shane leaned back, listening.

"In an alpha-one antitrypsin deficient patient, there is a random disruption of the pattern in the DNA. Fixing it is fairly simple. We splice out the extra nucleotide, restoring the pattern that was intended."

Shane cocked his head playfully. "Intended by who? Are you getting all Intelligent Design on me?"

"Ah," Prajuk nodded seriously, stopping to look him in the eye. "That a pattern is intended is obvious from the fact that we share ninety to ninety-nine percent of our DNA with every living creature, and that our genes are interchangeable with all of them."

Shane felt a desire to prod him. "Then changing someone's DNA means changing this pattern that was designed. Altering God's plan sounds, you know, concerning."

Prajuk looked frustrated. "Do you have an ethical concern over a surgeon repairing a toddler's cleft palate? Or removing a cancerous tumor? Or giving a feverish child some Tylenol?"

"Of course I don't," Shane grinned.

"You get pretty close to this thing, Christian Scientists, if you follow that path of thinking. When we fix faulty genetic code, we are not altering a plan, we are returning it to its Creator's intent."

Shane sat forward on the metal stool, his elbows pressing into his knees. His voice was hoarser, lower. "When I was a kid, I read about the Middle Ages, how people died from strep throat and ear infections. I thought, thank God I was born at the end of medicine, after all that's been taken care of. Then I understood that we're not at the end of medicine at all. We're in the Middle Ages."

"The Dark Ages," Prajuk told him. "We know almost nothing. Our treatments for just about every ailment are primitive. Two hundred years from now, people will be thinking how lucky they are not to have been born today. They'll think of antibiotics the way we think of leeches. And radiation the way we think of bloodletting. Which might be healthier for us." Prajuk looked around. "When is our mouse coming?"

"Charles River says March."

"That's good. This thing is looking possible, Shane." He nodded, seeming pleased. His high voice seemed brighter. "What are you doing with your holiday?"

Nicholas's first Christmas would involve a long, dumpling-filled day at Liu and Hua's, followed by an afternoon of watching football with Wenceslas and Cynthia. He could not wait to place a Santa hat on his head to the bewilderment of his five-month-old infant, to take those photos, to build those memories. To stand with Janelle and watch their sleeping infant and make love while Christmas music played. But Shane knew he would also feel an irresistible pull to drive back here and put more chairs together.

Leaving the lab, Prajuk explained this feeling to him. "I watched Poulos go through this. I know what you feel. You feel like an entrepreneur."

But Shane knew a few entrepreneurs and felt this was not an accurate description. Those guys were driven by visions of houses in Beaver Creek and fame. Shane had no financial future at stake, and the mandatory anonymity made sure no one would ever know his name. His surges of euphoria and terror did not feel to him like an entrepreneur's. They felt like he was losing his mind.

The next afternoon, as he sat in his cubicle writing last month's Sorion sales spreadsheets, Prajuk texted him to stop by the lab on his way home. It hadn't mattered; he would have gone anyway.

11

"Did you know," Mack asked her, "that Caleb offered me a deal?"

June rubbed her eyes. She had not slept well.

She had lain still and watched her baby awaken. Lily was thin, and small, but whenever she woke, Lily's face assumed a blend of wonder and confidence; try as she might, June could not recognize herself in it. She had recently grown a singular bottom tooth of astonishing bone white. But Caleb was right. Her breathing was no better.

She was beginning to crawl, but when she got more than a foot away her eyes would narrow with strain, her wheeze would grow higher pitched, and inevitably one of their housemates would snatch her up and place her where she had intended to go. And she was deprived of the opportunity to reach it herself. It would be like having someone lift you up at eighty miles and carry you to the finish line, June thought. It wasn't right.

Downstairs at breakfast, Ryan rolled Lily a balled white sock. A mischievous smile overtook her face, as she dragged herself forward, made it, squeezed the sock between small fingers, and brought it to her lips.

"Don't stress, it's clean. I only wore it three times."

June started laughing.

The door to Mack's room opened, and he walked out yawning. Mack was only five feet five, which always took her by surprise; whenever he came into a room, her first instinct was to look up, and she would have to adjust. This morning he wore a red Marlboro sweatshirt and black running shorts, his shaggy black beard bunched in varying directions. He walked over to Lily, a bemused smile on his face. He knelt by her, watching her play. Then he looked up, smiling.

"How's the day looking, Ms. June?"

"Great. I'm cleaning three apartments by Dushanbe. Do you want me to pick up anything?"

"Sencha would be great." Mack sat down beside Lily. "How is she?"

"It was a rough night actually."

Mack put his hand up the back of Lily's oversized yellow Goodwill shirt, flattened his palm on her back, and shut his eyes. "Teddy Roosevelt was born with severe asthma. Couldn't walk without wheezing. His father made him hike up hills for miles, and they didn't have trail shoes then either. He went from a sickly child to a bulked up motherfucker. The kinetic energy turned his body on. He was wrestling broncos and charging up hills before long." He paused, watching her. That was when he asked about the deal.

June squinted. "I don't know about any deal."

"I figured he had your approval?"

"Caleb didn't tell me anything like that."

"I'm going into town. Why don't you ride with me? We'll talk about it in the car."

• • • • • • •

The Jeep moved evenly through the snowpack. To her north, June watched Lone Eagle rise behind the sun. Somewhere out there, she knew, there were people moving along its trails.

"I'm going to Fadden's," Mack said. "You need anything for Lily? A rattle? One of those ladybugs?"

"Sure," June smiled. "She'd love that."

"She's getting so big," Mack said. "Our little girl."

"Our girl," June repeated softly.

"Hell of a family she has, right? Seventeen people?"

Mack slowed at the Oradell light, idling. Then he turned and looked at her with the full force of his visage. "Why would you ever want to take her away from them?"

June's mouth opened. But Mack was looking back at the road, driving slower now that they were in town. Outside she noticed the flannel jackets, wool hats, and beige work boots of the people who lived here. Many of them worked in Boulder or Denver, if they were lucky enough to be working at all.

"What do you mean?"

"Caleb says you want to leave here, because Shane has some *specialist* in San Francisco? Specialists," Mack muttered, "like they're special."

A cold shiver ran through her body.

"Let me tell you, doctors are employees of drug companies. They get them out of medical school when they're loaded with debt, and they sign them up for fucking life. To make their side money these doctors prescribe *infants* powerful psychotropic drugs, Prozac and Wellbutrin, sometimes three or four of them at a time. They tell their parents it's so they sleep through the night, cry less. And these dumbass parents are thrilled to give these drugs developed to treat schizophrenics to their babies. And then they're shocked to discover they have drug-addicted, psychotic teenagers on so many drugs it's impossible to ever get them back to baseline." Mack tapped his temple. "They don't follow the money, Junebug. These doctors sell out children for thousand-dollar kickbacks, and it's not rare either. And you trust these people with Lily?"

June began swallowing hard.

"You've been there before. When they gave her steroids that almost gave her a heart attack."

She shook her head. "But Caleb's brother . . ."

"Shane doesn't care about Lily. He cares about getting Caleb to leave here. Lily is his bait. And it's working. Caleb is all torn up, he doesn't know what to do." Mack took a breath, and squinted. "Do you ever worry about him?"

June flashed back to their run through Flagstaff, when out of nowhere Caleb had brought up missing his family. It had struck her as unlike him.

"Sometimes," she whispered.

"More and more, myself. Listen to what he offered me."

A fear fluttered through her now, a coldness upon her skin.

"He wants you and Lily go to Shane, while he stays here. He said he'll be more likely to win under those conditions." Mack slowed to let a yellow light turn red.

June's mind was racing, spinning. "He's just thinking about Lily."

"He needs to be thinking about Yosemite. Not his brother.

Not his parents. Not Lily. And not you. It's a dangerous race. If he's running it thinking about anything at all except his body, he's going to have another accident. And this time he won't land on a shelf."

June inhaled sharply, her eyes reddening.

"I mean, June, you must feel terrible. You came here because you were so worried about your daughter, and now, you're worried about Caleb. It's like everyone you care for gets to a place where they need worrying over. He was perfect until you met him, you know?"

She started crying as he held her eye.

"I want you to help me save him. And Lily. Because June, if you go to San Francisco, hand to God, he's not the only one who's going to die." Mack touched his chest. "Shane's drugs will kill Lily. I feel it. I *understand* it."

She stared at him as he pulled into Fadden's parking lot. The tears came fast now.

"You need to cut him off. You need to cauterize his infection." He grinned. "Be right back with one ladybug."

When he pushed the door open, the cold flooded over her, and she understood right there how it would never stop.

...........12

They began on the evening of December 27.

Prajuk was a blur, running what seemed to Shane to be a decathlon of chemistry, moving from the microscope to the centrifuge to the computer. Shane felt like a nurse, handing him parts and equipment when asked.

And he was following them fairly well. The 3-D images of twisting genetic code were still abstract and obtuse but lightening around the edges, starting to make more sense to him now. He found it fascinating to watch the manipulation of the basic blocks of life. Spinning them down, splicing them in new sequences. It was not science so much, he realized, as art.

Comprehending biology on this level, or at least comprehending the concepts behind it, made the whole world come alive for him. Eating a pear, he could feel its cells bursting against the roof of his mouth. Touching Janelle's skin, holding Nicholas naked against his chest, he could feel the movement of molecules, the energy of their friction. Their, dare he think it, kinetic energy.

On the second of January at eight o'clock in the evening,

he walked into Greenway Plaza Lab 301 and stopped, startled. A twentysomething kid was standing at the metal bench, destroying a green apple.

Shane extended his hand. "Shane Oberest. Can I help you?"

"Hey," the guy said, wiping his mouth with the back of his hand, "Jeff Healy."

"Jeff, how did you get in here?"

"I work here."

The kid reached into a pocket, produced a phone, and held it up. Shane squinted at an e-mail.

"I'm supposed to meet Doctor Prajuk Acharn?" he mispronounced both names.

Healy seemed in the lower five-feet range and looked to be a serious weightlifter. He was possessed of menacing eyes and acned cheeks and shoulders. Shane suspected him of steroid abuses.

Some awkward minutes later, Prajuk arrived in a short-sleeved white shirt and clapped his hands, grinning. It struck Shane that this was a different Prajuk than he had seen before. Upbeat, confident; he could envision him leading a team of bioresearchers.

"Shane, this is Jeff Healy. Our postdoc."

"We met."

"Do you know how to Atkins a gene?" he asked Healy, walking to the bench.

"No worries."

Shane stepped forward, wanting to stay included. "What's that mean?"

Prajuk lifted up the vector from the table. "The gene on the fourteenth chromosome, with the protein which produces alpha-one antitrypsin, is in this solution. A gene is full of carbohydrates and cellular matter, and we must strip these things away, to isolate the protein inside."

"Eliminate the carbs," Healy underscored.

"Oh, Atkins," Shane whistled. "I get it."

He watched closely as Prajuk held up the vector.

Healy cocked his head. "You look like you've never seen a human gene before."

Prajuk and Healy bent over the vector, chatting offhandedly. Shane felt as he had as a boy when Caleb and Fred went running ahead up the long road. He was a spectator; this was as close as he might get.

In the parking lot later, Prajuk held a Parliament an inch from his lips in his fist and inhaled loudly under the night sky.

"How much does he know?" Shane asked.

"He thinks this is a Helixia project, that we rent outside space for overflow."

"How much am I paying him?"

"Three hundred a week. Plus gas. I am very careful with company money, especially since the company is you."

"Much appreciated." Shane took a breath and pushed a hand through his hair. "So, when should I tell Caleb to bring the baby here?"

"Three months? Maybe four. It depends on our mouse."

"Four months feels like a long time."

"A minute can feel like a long time."

Shane nodded and stretched his back. He supposed that was as true as anything.

....

Isolating the protein took a week.

They had developed a rhythm. Shane arrived after work

with food from Thai Orchard. Healy, his headphones on, accepted it with a nod and remained bent over his solutions. Once, Shane glanced at his iPod and was surprised to see club music. It seemed to him that the relentless beats would be aggravating to someone patiently stripping molecules from strands of DNA. It seemed to require more of an ambient kind of deal. But though he maintained his Facebook account on a laptop at all times and stopped to text every few minutes, Healy kept up. Neither he nor Prajuk wore lab coats, Shane noticed. Other than their latex gloves, there was no sense of reverence; this was just work for them. Though to Shane it was a miracle.

One night over noodles, Healy showed him the process. He opened a flask. Inside was a liquid that looked to Shane like apple juice.

"It's media," Healy explained.

"What's media?"

"Just dead bacterial cells and sterile water. We place it in this shaker. Throw it in a plasmid. Spin it down in the centrifuge." He switched on the shaker.

"Like a margarita," Shane smiled.

"I wish. Over the next couple of days, when the culture grows turbid, we'll break the cells open, and wash out the purified protein." He gestured toward a collection of pink petri dishes. "Transect it onto an E. coli cell, where it will multiply."

"E. coli?" Shane asked, casting a worried glance at the petri dishes on the bench.

"Here's the secret of it all, bro. Everything bad has a good, and everything good has a bad. The gene that makes people dwarfs also makes them immune to mumps. You have to look at both sides. E. coli takes over your body and kills you horribly. But it also permits itself to be transferred peacefully into any organism as a carrier. Disabled E. coli is one of the bacteria we use most."

Shane shook his head in awe. For fifteen years he had been selling the products of pharmaceutical chemical labs, never appreciating the artistry of biotechnology.

"Got to piss." Healy stood up from the bench. "Don't let it eat your face while I'm gone."

During these weeks, Shane lived in a euphoric state. In the mornings, he looked out of their window at the bay sky and let himself feel part of the energy Caleb summoned in Boulder. He had spent his whole life watching his brother's back, a shadow of sweat spreading across his dark green T-shirt. In middle school he would step into new classrooms and wonder if Caleb had sat at this desk. He ran the high school track imagining Caleb's feet falling in the same lanes. Now, after all of this time, he felt finally connected with Caleb, through the simple act of breathing air. He wondered if it had always been this easy.

The sublimity of the lab was always with him. Like an adulterer, Shane invented after-hours meetings to explain his late arrivals home to Janelle. His heart battled itself: when he stayed there to work, he suffered an avalanche of guilt for not having seen Nicholas before he fell asleep. What kind of father was he? But on the nights he did go straight home, he felt a separation anxiety from the lab which he could not quite bear. During his drive back to the city he would experience wild swings of exuberance and depression, a simultaneous sense of oncoming glory and approaching catastrophe.

In mid-January, Shane opened his front door to find

Janelle sitting at their dining room table, waiting for him with a serious look. He sat down wondering if he carried a scent of the lab.

"I'm quitting," she told him.

Shane exhaled slowly, nodding.

As he listened to her, Shane attempted to fight off huge waves of terror. This was no time to give up her salary and benefits. He might be caught and fired by Helixia any day. He reminded himself that this was the woman he had pursued even while she was fully committed to an all-consuming job, had slowly won over during stolen camping weekends, and waited for on Sunday nights after her endless dinners with her parents just to catch a quick drink, for whom he had videotaped a tree she adored from her last apartment window, and projected it onto their wall. Now she wanted to stay in their home, to take care of their son. This, of course, should have been all that he wanted.

"Okay," he said, watching her face. "Whatever you need."

She was crying. "Okay."

"So, we're down to one paycheck," he reminded her. "And only my insurance."

"Don't fuck up at work." She kissed his cheek.

He knew he had to tell her. The burden of his secret now fell upon her too. This was the moment, before she executed her decision, while there was still time.

During a brief interior struggle, he realized how telling her now could come off as some kind of emotional blackmail, to guilt her into not quitting. She might resent him, and the whole project, for interceding now. So he let it pass. This weekend, he promised himself. But the weekend passed as well.

. . . .

The whir of the centrifuge was proof of their progression. He watched Healy graft their protein—for now it belonged to all of them, he felt—onto the E. coli viruses on the pink petri dishes, and Prajuk transfer this work into a small millimeter Eppendorf tube and place it into the freezer. Each run produced a thimble full of clear liquid, which might mean six months of life for Lily.

If it worked. Which they would only know when their genetically modified mouse arrived.

On a Tuesday toward the end of the month, Healy burst in fiddling frustratedly with his phone. "They can make these things do anything you want, but they can't make headphones that don't get tangled?"

He tossed it into his backpack and washed up in the stainless steel sink. Then he took a Clif bar from his pocket and walked over to have a look at the centrifuge.

"How long's it been doing that?"

Shane raised his eyebrows. He was alone in the room while Prajuk had gone out for food. "Doing what?"

"Making that"—he waved the protein bar in the air—"sound."

"I don't know." He listened. The whir did seem a little labored. "Is it bad?"

Healy grunted and moved over to the machine. He pressed its power button off and gingerly lifted its top.

"Oh fuck."

Shane stood up and peered over his shoulder.

Healy narrowed his eyes, lifting out something small and jagged. "Glass."

"Did a vial break?"

Ignoring him, Healy carefully examined the inside bin with his fingertips. "This thing," he whistled, "is fucked heinously."

Prajuk returned carrying three styrofoam containers of fried rice. His lips compressed and released like a young boy's fist as he examined the centrifuge.

"How long will it take to get a new one?"

Shane realized the question was addressed to him, the money man, the producer, the fixer. He blinked.

"Well, it took six weeks for this one to get here. Is there a repair shop?"

"A repair shop?" Healy shook his head. "We can ship it back to where you got it and wait for a replacement."

"We can't wait six weeks." Shane heard Lily's sharp breaths in the whir of the crippled motor. "Do they have some others at your school?"

"Centrifuges?" Healy laughed. "Sure, they leave them lying next to the Porsches."

Prajuk let out a phlegmy cough as he walked suddenly out of the lab. By the time Shane looked up, he was already out by the elevators.

Healy shrugged and nodded at the three containers of fried rice Prajuk had placed on the bench. "No thanks."

Healy stood and took them all.

13

Winter raged against the wooden planks of the house. At night the sound of it trying to get in through the walls, pushing, scratching, like wolves, kept Caleb awake on his mattress.

But for all its discomforts, the Happy Trails Running Club seemed in good temper; most of them loved winter. Running in the daily new powder was akin to running on sand. The extra effort strengthened their calves and lungs and hearts.

Caleb pulled on double layers of waterproof socks, fleece head gear, his Houdini shell, hat and goggles, and went downstairs to the back door to wait for everyone. Only June and Lily were missing. Caleb glanced around nervously. This was strange; morning was prime playing time for the baby. She adored crawling over seventeen prone bodies, everyone tickling her, holding socks, her favorite things, out to her. He turned to go look upstairs for them when Mack emerged from his room, his arms spread out triumphantly. He wore a small pine green hooded sweatshirt, his azure eyes beatific.

"ABC is covering the Yosemite Slam," he shouted, clapping

his hands. "They pulled it from ESPN, gave it to their big guns."

Everyone stopped and gazed at him. Caleb watched him with awe. He had set himself a goal, to establish Happy Trails as the premier ultrarunning organization in America, with a televised event. And he had accomplished this in under seven months.

"They'll have ten cameras stationed along the course." He spoke animatedly, rushing around the open main room like a dervish in a tie-dye. "Get this, they're going to fly a helicopter over the densest parts, to get aerial footage of everyone climbing Half Dome. Then they're going to edit it to four hours and air that on a Saturday in summer, and show the whole thing online."

Kyle, Juan, and John laughed and high-fived. Mack was smiling fully, his small arms literally shaking.

"You know what we need?" Alice asked loudly. "Team shirts!"

"Team goddamn shirts!"

"What color, Vive?" shouted Leigh.

Aviva smiled. Caleb had noticed a change in her mood since Rae had been expelled, a darkening sadness, but this seemed to draw her out.

"Pink?"

Makailah and Alice cheered, "Pink for everyone!"

Young Ryan called, "Screw that. Yellow and green, like Brazil. That shit's awesome."

"White," John added, "will keep us coolest."

"And match your hair," Makailah laughed.

John ran his hand over his crew cut head, nodding happily.

Mack raised his voice, "'Colorado men are we! From the

peaks gigantic, from the great sierras and the high plateaus! From the mine and from the gully, from the hunting trail we come, Pioneers! O pioneers!'"

They all shouted the last line excitedly. Caleb felt Aviva's eyes on him.

"What about you, Caley? What color should our shirts be?"

"It doesn't matter," Caleb told them, adjusting his goggles. "Let's just run."

....

Many times, when he was sure he could not be seen from another point in the cold, snowy woods, Caleb would break from the trail.

Then he would double back through the white firs, dodging the quicksand of powder and roots, until he reached a spot in the wilderness that he had marked with an old yellow sweatshirt.

There he would slide down the incline of the mountain, to a back road which wound in serpentine circles. He would run this west for ten miles. At the end he would reach a cluster of cheap houses, where the undocumented off-the-books workers lived. No stores, or town, just these twenty thinly constructed houses, and a low-budget playground.

It possessed an old chipped red seesaw, two infant and full-size swings on rusted chains, and a straight metal slide that burned skin in the summer sun and was covered in ice now. Behind them the red and brown houses popped against the white world.

This was his secret place, where he met June and Lily. When she had the good fortune to swing next to another baby, Lily would conjure a thin-lipped smile that lit her whole being. She would reach for them, emit sounds of such loveliness that he stopped feeling the icy winds and lost himself completely.

The first time Caleb had met them here, bathed in sweat and breathing loudly, a Mexican teenager had gone to get her boyfriend, a lithe kid with green prison tattoos along his shaved scalp. Since then, Caleb had slowed down to a walk a good mile before the playground, to try to appear normal.

He found June pushing Lily slowly on a creaky swing. The baby was dressed in a worn pink coat from Goodwill and a white fleece hat with ear flaps, both of which seemed too large for her. She was so thin, he saw, anything would look big. It was very cold, and they were alone. An empty playground, Caleb felt, is a sad thing.

When Lily saw him, she sang the syllables of his name: "Cay-cay."

Since Mack had ordered their separation, Caleb had spent less time holding her, stroking her cheek, inhaling her milky breath, and he worried that their bond might be thinning. Her hair was changing, its red evolving into a strawberry blonde, and growing longer. A cleft seemed to be retreating from her chin.

"Hey, Lulu," Caleb hollered, letting the vowels linger into silliness. She looked away demurely, and he laughed.

But June wasn't smiling. In her fleece and sky blue mittens she looked uncomfortable, her face was creased and distant. Now that he was standing still, the full chill of February hit him.

"I need to talk to you," she said quietly.

He smiled.

"I'm not doing it."

"Not doing what?"

"I'm not taking Lily to your brother."

Caleb's eyes darted to Lily nervously. "Why?"

"You know," June began in a new breezy voice like an over-rehearsed anchorwoman, "Shane's going to tell us about some chemical that he wants to put into her, how much of a miracle it is. But Buddhist monks live to be a hundred without ever taking any medicine."

Caleb smiled calmly. He understood now. "You talked to Mack about it."

She pushed a strand of hair away from her mouth with her gloved hand and frowned. "Even if Mack said he would buy us plane tickets today, I don't think it's right."

"What did he say to you?"

"He's worried about you."

"What else?"

Her voice got harsher. "He told me how these drug companies shoot people up with drugs they know nothing about, just to learn if there are horrible side effects. How they give babies drugs for adults just to make them be quiet."

He shook his head; she was even using Mack's inflections now.

"Mack's the one who can help her." She pointed to him. "He healed your knee. And Kevin's diabetes."

"But he's not helping her, Bluebird. She's the same as when you came here. It's been ten months."

"She's not getting worse. He's saving her every day." Her voice wavered and tears began slipping silently from her eyes.

"Is that what he's saying?"

"I'm so lucky Mack took us in. How many people show up here, and he turns them all down? But he accepted us. Without him, we'd be living in some studio apartment in Taos, I'd be working in the bar all day, with some day care watching Lily. I love you, Caley, but I didn't come here for you."

A sudden shortness of breath caused his chest to contract. Behind June, Lily's swing had slowed, and she sat still, waiting for them to notice. A sharp wind blew through the playground, rustling the ends of her reddish hair. All she had in this life was her mother, he understood that. All decisions were June's to make.

"If staying here is what you think's right for Lily, then that's what you do. It's simple. You're her mother."

June was watching him closely.

He met her soft eyes. "I love her."

June took a long breath. The sun shifted behind the smoke-white sky, and June lifted Lily out of the plastic swing. They carried her across the playground to a snow-covered slide. Caleb brushed it clean of ice and crouched at its bottom, waiting for Lily's laughing face. He felt, in this cold morning, like he imagined a family would. This could be enough, perhaps, to sustain him for some time.

When Lily grew tired, June loaded her back into Mack's Jeep, and Caleb kissed them each on their foreheads. Something hard and ruinous was forming in his stomach.

He turned and began his four-hour run, ten miles along the wintry road, a backcountry climb up the side of the snow-packed mountain, and another twenty miles through the ice-covered trails, back home.

PART THREE

Knockouts

7

"Good night, Doctor Acharn," Yasmine El-Fayed waved to Prajuk.

Yasmine was his youngest microbiologist, an expert splicer who had come to him from Amgen. Usually, Prajuk made time to talk with her, wanting to keep tabs on the mood in the lab. Tonight he barely heard her.

When the door closed behind Yasmine, Prajuk glanced around the empty room. In stark contrast to the small room Shane had rented, Helixia's labs were immense and immaculate. Stainless steel benches, sparkling glass beakers and vials, temperature controlled, and videotaped with three cameras at all times. The leftover molecules of chemicals, media, and the people who had been standing together all day in the room, along with the occasional mouse, were dissipated by an eight-million-dollar air-filtration system. The work done here continued even after the human beings departed, as the bacterium, the spores, the virus cells, reproduced, multiplied, spread in their petri dishes.

It was ten at night. Down the long corridor doors opened and closed. Prajuk composed himself and produced a beige key card from his shirt pocket. At the far end of the corridor, he pressed it and his forefinger against a plastic rectangle, which read his fingerprint and card code, emitted a clicking sound, and popped the storage-room door open.

Swallowing nervously, Prajuk went inside. A small desk, normally occupied by a short Honduran kid with a perpetually runny nose, sat empty, and Prajuk walked into the stockroom unhindered. Petri dishes stood in circular towers like stacked coffee-cup lids. Cardboard boxes full of test tubes, microscope filters and lenses, latex gloves, 3M masks, lots of stuff from 3M actually, were shelved to overflow. Prajuk moved past them to the heavy equipment. On one side of the wall were two top-loading centrifuges.

They were squat boxes, like small washing machines, the size of a desktop computer. Prajuk considered them for a few seconds, judging their weight. On Sunday he had done something to his lower back while jogging past the Marina Safeway. He exercised a deep squat, as they had taught him in the Khon Kaen gymnasium of his youth, placed his hands on the side of a centrifuge, slid them under, and lifted.

Carefully Prajuk carried the centrifuge to the door and glanced again at the desk. Should he leave a note? Sign for it somehow? He determined that his need for a centrifuge was impossible to justify; better to hope it would not be missed. He pushed the door open with his foot and started down the long, quiet hall, perspiring noticeably.

Prajuk decided to take the stairs; there was little chance that he would run into anybody there. He stumbled with the heavy instrument for a flight and set it down, promising himself a cigarette upon completion. Then he lifted it again and finally pushed through the heavy door into the lobby of the

Research building. Here was where he might be required to provide some explanation. But he met only the evening security guard, who said nothing as Prajuk set the centrifuge down and scanned his card. The benefits, Prajuk swallowed, of long-term employment.

Outside, he had difficulty spotting his car. A deep chill blew off the ocean. Why had he not worn his coat? His fingers began to burn. Soon they would numb, he thought, and he would drop the damn thing and break his foot. He was running out of bicep strength, and his lower back was protesting in a way it was now impossible to ignore. Sweat poured between his shoulder blades. In his pocket was his car key, with its red panic button, and Prajuk would have stopped to depress it but for the attention it would turn on him. Finally he spotted the white Volvo he had driven for almost a year a few rows away. He had just about reached it when he heard a voice.

"Doctor Acharn?"

Prajuk turned around and did not see, as he had briefly visualized, three armed Thais in black turtlenecks aiming assault weapons.

It was Jon Benatti, the Assistant Director of Science, and Anthony Leone's deputy.

Benatti approved budgets for equipment, raises, and new hires, though not the hires themselves, which was Anthony's province. Benatti's thin blond hair was combed over a balding patch, accentuating an elongated face and jaw. Prajuk set the big beige box down on the pavement, and to his horror its top popped open.

"Good to see you," Benatti smiled affably. He glanced down at the centrifuge.

Prajuk nodded, sweating. "Yes."

"How's Emerion going?"

"Oh quite well," Prajuk explained brightly. "This thing, it always goes slowly but we hope to be in Phase One this quarter."

"Taking your work home with you?"

It might be best, he felt, to act as if he did this every night. "What do you hear about Roche?" he asked Benatti casually. Rumors were flying that a joint research project with the European giant might be extended. Some rumors went as far as an approaching takeover bid.

Benatti gave him a poker face. "Over my head. Have you asked Anthony?"

"This thing is exactly what I tell people." Prajuk tried to smile.

Benatti touched his shoulder quickly and lightly in that odd American way; there was always a need in Americans, Prajuk noted, to show both sides. Many new arrivals from foreign lands sought his advice as to working in the States. When Americans smile and touch you, he answered, beware.

"Need some help getting that in your car?"

"It's the only exercise I'll get today," Prajuk said, popping the trunk.

He grunted as he placed the centrifuge gingerly beside his dry cleaning and a quilt-wrapped painting of a beach. Benatti kept staring at it. He clearly wanted to ask more, but Prajuk kept moving.

"See you," he said, shutting the trunk. He rubbed his shoulders to communicate his discomfort in the cold as he walked to the driver's door, hoping even Jon Benatti would realize it rude to keep him longer. He got in, fired the engine, and eased out of the lot. He spent a long time watching his rearview mirror, where Benatti stared after him. Then he drove to Greenway Plaza.

"What's wrong with you?" Healy asked him when he walked in.

Prajuk placed his car keys on the bench. His shirt was wet, his mouth dry.

"There is a centrifuge in the trunk. White Volvo."

Healy nodded and grabbed the keys. When he was gone, Prajuk sat down on a stool and placed his head between his hands.

• • • • • • •

Janelle left Helixia for good on the final Friday of January.

Her team threw her a nice party in the lunchroom, with boutique cupcakes and sparkling wine. Shane had attended and brought flowers. Her manager pulled her aside and reminded her that she could come back anytime. They all understood that this was not out of the realm of possibility. Janelle had been working since the sixth grade; they all sensed the potential for a serious reversal.

Driving her home, the car packed with office photographs and CDs, she seemed relieved, but Shane felt a nearly overwhelming anxiety. Everything had changed now; it was all his responsibility. And Prajuk was stealing centrifuges.

Shane promised to be home by eight every night to help out with Nicholas; twice he made it. But Janelle was not used to being housebound, and taking the baby to classes and museums did not satisfy her need to be out among people. He sensed the tension building weeks before she did.

Just before Valentine's Day, Shane sped back from the airport after a sales trip to Portland. It was nine o'clock at night. He had drunk an airport coffee too late, and now he was jittery. He parked poorly on Bay Street, opened the front door, and almost collided with Janelle, who was dressed in a sleek gray sweater and dark jeans. Her lips had been painted a matte red, her eyes brushed with blue, and she looked flawless to him. He started to put his arms around her waist.

Janelle pulled back, frowning. "Don't. I'm late," she said, car keys in her hand. "I've been waiting for you. Nicholas has some stuff in his nose. Use the aspirator."

"Aspirator? Where are you going?"

"I'm meeting Shia for a drink. I need to get out of this house."

"Okay, well, give me a minute? I just need to change clothes and . . ."

"I've been on all day."

"What have I been, off?" Shane stood in the doorway flustered.

"I know what you did today. You had a decent lunch with some doctors while you talked about Sorion. You had a beer on the airplane. You can handle a baby."

"You have no idea what I'm doing," he told her heatedly, the caffeine pushing his heart rate. He walked into their house, where Nicholas was indeed crying from his crib.

Janelle followed him, her heels clicking on the wood floors. "What does that mean?"

"Nothing, just go. Have fun."

"What do I have no idea about?"

He knew from her tone of voice that he had triggered a process which would not end quickly. Or particularly well.

"We can talk later," he tried anyway, starting for the stairs. Nicholas seemed to have stopped shrieking, but his own head was throbbing.

"We talk now."

"I'm tired."

"You've been working late constantly for months. What are you doing that I don't know about, Shane?"

He sat down on the bottom stair, gazing up at her. And then he told her everything.

He started with Prajuk explaining his team's discovery. He told her about Prajuk's interest in his idea to produce just enough of a drug for one person. About renting the lab, and how it worked there. But he was defensive and wired, and he ruined it. He had so wanted to tell her about this softly, proudly, when the drug was finished, when it was all beautiful. Instead, Janelle stood in their living room, her mouth falling open, while he rambled.

"You idiot," she whispered.

In all of his life with her, Shane had never seen this expression on her face.

"What?"

"You can't do this to us."

"Do this?" He cocked his head. "What's 'this'?"

"They'll throw you in jail."

"Who will throw me in jail, honey?"

She was shaking in the movements of an adagio. "Anthony Leone. Steven Poulos. Walter Pietrowski will have you renditioned to a fucking Syrian prison."

"They'll never know about this."

"Oh, Jesus. Jesus."

He stood up, spoke with a passion he felt emanating from

somewhere deep. "Imagine if Nicholas couldn't breathe. And someone saw a way to save him? Okay? Can you imagine that? What would you expect that person to do?"

"Please," Janelle said in a deeply mocking tone; immediately it became the worst thing she had ever said to him.

"If I didn't pursue this, what would that make me?"

"A father and a husband. Which you won't be in prison."

"Prison for what?"

"For theft," she whispered harshly enough that he felt her breath upon his cheek. "Of physical and intellectual property. For making a drug without any license. I can just see you, holed up in some lab like a high school kid making meth, thinking you're not going to get caught." Her mouth wrinkled in disgust.

"It's not as wrong as selling an antidepressant that I know doesn't work to every pediatrician in Mill Valley. And I did that for years."

"That was *legal*."

"Look," Shane nodded. "We're the only ones who know about it. Me and Prajuk. None of us are tweeting about it. There is no threat to us."

"Until Caleb's girlfriend, who you don't even *know*, posts it on her Facebook page."

"She doesn't seem like she updates hers very often," he replied with sarcasm.

Janelle stared at him. "It only takes one."

He punched his thigh in frustration, "I *asked* Dineesh. I asked Anthony. I wrote a request for a grant application. I did everything the right way. They said no. I'm going to help this little girl, Janelle. I am going," he repeated slowly, "to help her."

"Shane," she whispered to herself.

"So I did it myself. And I'm proud of it, actually. Anyway," he exhaled, "we're almost done."

"How can you be almost done? The approvals will take six or seven years." She stared at him. "Oh *God*, Shane."

There was nothing to say at this point, he recognized.

"You're not filing this with FDA?"

"This protein has already gone through testing as part of the Airifan trials. It was approved."

"In *babies*?"

He swallowed.

"Airifan was tested on children with asthma. Not newborns. You could kill her. This baby. You could kill her."

Shane spoke in a lower voice. "If this was Nicky, and we could cure him, you'd be driving me to that lab every night at a hundred miles an hour."

She hesitated then. From upstairs, Nicholas wailed again. Shane seized the opportunity to get off of the staircase. Upstairs, Nicholas was asleep; he'd been having a nightmare. Shane bent over him, stroked his black hair. At what age, he wondered, does the world become so imposing that fear manifests in dreams? He had hoped it would be later than six months.

He returned downstairs to Janelle, who was curled on the couch, crying.

"Bad dream," he explained.

She looked up at him. "Make it better."

2

All February, Caleb trained in the snow.

The mountains had received enough snow to turn the trails sallow. The expanse of pure white powder came up to his knees, his hips, sometimes his chest. It acted as resistance, like training in water. He welcomed it, choosing paths where he saw no footprints except a mule deer's, or the slithering impression of a milk snake.

Running across the snowpack was risky; danger lay in its blinding white. In the thick roots that hid underneath it like pythons. In the sharp rocks camouflaged in gentle sparkles. In the fearsome cold that could disorient as the beauty of the sunlit snow beckoned him farther and farther away from the roads.

Up in Boulder, people ran their daily five miles equipped with thermal gloves, expensive microfiber jackets, iPhones tucked into specially designed zippered pouches. Caleb disappeared into the backcountry wearing only his light Houdini pants and jacket, plastic goggles, an old fleece hat. In the shade, bitter wind blew shards of ice across his lips. Even under the sun the cold bore its way into his bones. But avoidance of pain was never Caleb's intent. Only avoidance of suffering.

Over the past decade he had successfully extracted any emotional confusion from his life. Jobs, career, family, the expectations of the world, were all like forgotten high school friends. But now, like a patient in remission who with horror senses his symptoms returning, Caleb felt a range of sharp emotions rising up; emotions he thought he had put aside forever.

He ached for June. He ached for her like he had for the heartbreaks of his youth. He ached for her with a desperation that pulled him back from every forward step. He ached for her in a way that affected his posture, his breathing, his heart rate, his clarity of mind upon these icy paths. Even while he slept, he ached. He dreamt of his first months with her, his hours in the fields and the back room at O'Neil's, and awoke in an agony that no strained quadriceps could touch.

Instead of floating in the void, he was constantly thinking of her, where she might be, whom she could be with, and therefore also unbearably conscious of the ripping in his sinews, the lactic acid burning his muscles, the white flame in his lungs, the cold torturing the exposed skin of his face.

And yet he could not stop.

His need was like a living being running beside him, jeering his attempts to return to his previous state. He could smell its funk. He heard its breathing in his room at night, and behind the trees on the trails. No matter how he begged, it would not leave him alone. And so he suffered, day and night, in a way far worse than any cold or ruined ligament.

The only cure for his suffering seemed to be agony. Caleb found that when he pushed his body far past its boundaries, its stress could reach a point where it commanded all of his attention. And freed him. And so even when his subconscious demanded he had to turn back, he kept going, into a place where

June and Lily could not reach him, where every step required all of his focus, where agony overwhelmed all thought. At times, lost in the snow and ice pack, he even succeeded in forgetting them for an hour.

He understood Mack's warnings now. Why hadn't he listened? Emotions do destroy the runner's focus. But he had a chance now, to go back to that time before they came, to again run without distraction. He had this opportunity, which June had given him by destroying his heart and leaving him alone. He could seize this opportunity, turn his suffering into anger, use it to train. And possibly survive this.

But still, the more he imagined the baby's soft skin, and June's body against his, and the way their eyes softened to him, the more he welcomed this suffering. It was worth it, he knew, because underneath this pain was promise. The promise that he would see her today. The promise that she might change her mind. And maybe he could not hold her. And maybe he could not tell her that he loved her. And maybe he could not get Lily to Shane. But he could still see them, feel their energy around him through the house. And as long as that promise existed, suffering or not, he felt hope. It was when the pain was gone, he understood, that he'd know his hope was gone too.

The following day, Mack drove him through a driving snowfall to the snow-covered Boulder High School football field. From the back of the Jeep, he jerked a rudimentary red wood sled onto the white ground. A sharp wind rippled across the flat field, shifting the snow in a way that reminded him of icing being spread over a cake.

Mack brushed flakes from his beard and loaded the sled with round black weights. Then he knelt and tied them to the sled with thick twine. Caleb placed the sled's ropes over his shoulders, and Mack tied them in anglers' loops.

"Pick you up later. Pioneer. O pioneer."

Caleb turned, squinted into the icy wind, and began to run hard. He made tight turns through untrampled powder, traversing the field with the weighted sled tied behind him.

At one point, a truck pulled into the lot. Inside were a father and son. They stayed in the cab, staring at him, for a long time. He pulled the sled across the snowy field, trying to ignore them. Finally a dog yelped from their back seat and they drove away.

Caleb returned to the house fevered and blue. The creases around his eyes looked as if they had been deepened with forks. In their room, Kevin was lying on his mattress reading *Runner's World*. His black hair had been recently buzz cut, and he looked to Caleb like a kid waiting for lights out. Caleb opened their shared closet and found his cold-weather running pants. He sat and pulled them on.

Kevin looked up. "Headed out?"

"Night run."

"You're going kind of hard, man."

Caleb inhaled sharply through his nose, a reflex he'd picked up somewhere in childhood. People at InterFinancial had done scathing impressions of it.

"Nights are where I'm weak."

"Yosemite is still three months away. You've got to slow down." Kevin dropped his voice. "Steve Brzenski died there."

"I don't plan," Caleb said as he pulled on his cold-weather shirt, "on having that experience."

............3

The mouse was four inches from nose to tail.

He had been hand-delivered in a wooden crate, on a Tuesday near the end of February. No one had answered the door at Lab 301, so the courier had called the number he'd been given, and Shane's cell rang in the middle of a team videoconference. He had been hoping to motivate his Southern California reps, who seemed to him to be suffering some kind of overconfidence. He hesitated at the number and ducked out to take the call.

"Can you wait?" he asked the courier.

"Nope, I sure can't."

"Can you leave it there by the door?

"Without a signature, I'll need to send it back."

"Back? It's alive." He could feel the courier's shrug. "Look, wait ten minutes for me?"

Apologetically Shane excused himself, garnering looks from the reps on the monitor, and jogged to the parking lot. It was exceptionally sunny, late February at its San Francisco brightest, and he had left his sunglasses on his desk. Squinting against the sun he felt vulnerable. He texted Prajuk.

M arrived. What do I do with it?

By the time he signed for his cargo, he had an answer. He unlocked the door and stepped into the cool swath of chemical air. Along the bench, rows of pink petri dishes were now covered in clustered tiny black balls of bacteria, like BBs. They looked like cancer. He recoiled from them.

Shane opened the crate gently. Beneath some padding he felt a small metal cage. He lifted it out and held it in the air for a moment. Inside stood a mouse. Their eyes met.

Its fur was the yellowed white of a lily. It was neither a cute plump mouse, nor a skinny rodent; rather it was something much more like life. It aroused neither his empathy nor his disgust; no particular emotion at all came to him as he watched its pink pupils.

"Hey, little mouse," Shane said, setting it down.

It walked in circles inside its cage like a dazed soldier.

He followed Prajuk's texted instructions, placed water and pellets of food inside, cleaned out the droppings, placed it on the bench, and shut the shades against the sun. Then he raced back to Helixia. When he reached the conference room, his meeting had ended.

"Sorry," he shrugged to Stacey, who was leaving. "My kid."

That evening Shane skipped the lab and lay on the living room floor, teaching Nicholas to crawl. He loved being eye to eye with him, and breath to breath. His baby's black eyes flickered to the mouse's pink ones, and Shane blinked. Janelle came downstairs, her hands wet from cleaning up a bath, and pondered him.

"Want to get a sitter tomorrow?" She frowned. "Or are you working late?"

This bothered him deeply. Referring to the lab as "working late" implied that he had undertaken some new minor assignment at work, and not the greatest venture of his life. Now that she knew everything, he expected more support. It was not forthcoming.

"Not sure yet," he answered, keeping his eyes on Nicholas's face, which smiled at him with utter love. "My boy," Shane whispered to him, "one day we will take a fishing trip."

Thinking the better of it, he added, "Yeah sure, let's get a sitter."

The following night, he stopped by Lab 301 intending to check in on the mouse. Healy burst upon him, holding an energy bar, grinning crazily.

"Congratulations."

Shane moved into the room, his belly buzzing.

Healy gestured to the cage, his mouth full of dried oats. "He's moving pretty slow. There a wheeze coming from his chest. I can tell you right now his oxygen's abnormal."

"Maybe he's just tired from his trip. I don't think they flew him First."

Healy slipped on a latex glove, opened the cage door, and lifted the mouse by the root of its rubbery tail. The mouse twitched as if touched by spirits.

"I always wondered," Shane asked. "Does that hurt them?"

"If he's hurting, he'll let you know."

Healy carried it over to a metal lab table.

"See if there's any hillbilly music on my laptop," Healy laughed.

"Sorry?"

"Because you're looking at one West Virginian hillbilly mouse."

"They shipped it from Boston."

As Healy took the mouse's measurements, he explained, "This guy is double inbred. His parents are brother and sister. And each set of grandparents are brother and sister too. If he were human, he'd be qualified to work at the DMV."

Shane shook his head.

"The guys at Charles River spliced his grandmother's DNA. They knocked out the gene that makes alpha-one antitrypsin."

"Knocked it out?"

"They added the code sequence to his grandmother's DNA. Shutting down the gene. Knocking it out. Injected that DNA into her embryonic stem cells. There are two copies of every gene, right? So when she had babies, all of them carried one of these reengineered genes, and then one normal one. That only gave her a fifty-percent chance of passing the altered gene down, so they bred two of her babies together. These guys' offspring carried two copies of the knocked-out gene. Guaranteeing that this guy has himself one badass case of alpha-one antitrypsin deficiency. You are the father of an inbred, but alpha-one antitrypsin–deficient mouse."

"That's how they do it? Breeding?"

"Incest is best. Put your mouse to the test."

Healy took a hypodermic and pushed it into the mouse's neck. The mouse squealed, jerking and spasming.

"Now," Healy yawned, "he's hurting."

He deposited the blood into a small vial. Gripping the mouse's tail, he lifted the top of a Buxco box. Which wasn't really a box, Shane saw, but a clear cylinder with a tube protruding from its side. When he'd ordered it, he'd wondered what it was for. Prajuk had positioned it in a place of respect, on the back bench, where it would not be accidentally swept off the table by an errant pizza box.

"It looks like Habitrail solitary confinement," Shane suggested.

"It looks like a mouse bong," Healy added.

That was true enough. Shane peered into the bottom of the glass cylinder. The mouse had a couple of inches of room on either side. A small protruding tube at the top let air in and out. Healy measured the pressure coming from it, noting it with squinted-eyed intensity in a small black notebook.

"His lungs are definitely hyperinflated," Healy said, pointing. "Not a lot of air coming out of there."

After a few more measurements, Healy returned the mouse to its cage, where it had room, but no desire to explore. Its door closed with a light metallic clang.

"We'll know for sure when the blood comes back from the lab."

Shane looked nervously at this mouse. He felt responsible for it; he had ordered its existence. Requested that its grandmother's DNA be spliced, its embryonic genes altered, its parents inbred, leaving it with the same wheezing and desperate gasps as Lily. He had fucked this mouse up.

Shane sat in one of the black chairs that he had put together back in December and stared at the twitching thing in its cage. Prajuk would inject it with his drug, and God willing, the faulty gene would switch on like Christmas lights and begin producing alpha-one antitrypsin, the enzyme which would hold the neural elastase back from attacking the healthy lung tissue.

Or, it would cause a toxic reaction, forcing the mouse's liver to shut down, and he would die of organ failure.

Or it would do nothing, and the mouse's labored breathing would continue until the lung damage was irreversible and he developed emphysema and died one morning not far from now.

Playing with DNA, injecting a laboratory-spun protein into a baby; this mouse's arrival had made it real. Shane considered this with increasing unease. Jesus had been nailed to a cross for less presumption than this.

Although Jesus had not waited seven years and three rounds of trials to be given green lights by a government body to cure the leper. In the end, he decided, He would have the last word on all of this anyway.

Shane rubbed his forehead. He had also ordered Nicholas's existence, he reminded himself, and he realized he could still get home in time to see him before he fell asleep. And that was when he remembered the sitter.

Fuck, he thought, pressing the elevator button a thousand times. What time was it? He took out his phone. Nine. Walking to the car he called Janelle, who informed him coldly that she was going to bed. He could still fix this, Shane hoped. He called her favorite pasta place, ordered what she loved. Driving, he could still smell the pungent sour rodent scent on himself, which was strange; he was certain he had not touched the mouse.

It occurred to him that the mouse might be attempting to communicate something: I am part of you now. Remember me, and what I have been through. Shane blinked. He had been caught up in the narcotic thrill of seeing if he could do this, but after tonight, he understood, he could not feign naïveté. Whatever happened, he would always know that he had possessed the opportunity to stop it.

Inside the house he tripped over a rubber ball.

"Shit!" he shouted with surprising vehemence.

He righted himself and looked around. The house was strangely silent. Shane set down the food and walked upstairs calling, "Janelle?"

It was ten o'clock. He passed the bed with his sleeping wife, ran the shower, and pressed his head hard against the tile. He stayed there for a long time. For years, he had spent his days driving leisurely between doctors' practices, taking a lunch-time run, taking Janelle out at night to see her favorite DJs. Now he could not seem to imagine doing any of those things.

He experienced an intense need to hold his son; had he spent more time with the lab than with him? It was unlikely, but that he even had to consider this made him feel ill. Child psychologists, he was painfully aware, stressed the urgency of the bond created in these first six months. He imagined Nicholas confessing to a college girlfriend that he had never felt close to his dad.

He went to Nicholas's room, bursting with the scents of baby lotion, fresh crib sheets, the baby's natural smell, and inhaled the goodness of those molecules into his body. He lifted the sleeping boy and sat with him on the rocking chair, swaying gently, and met his deep brown eyes as they opened. We fight wars over where the soul goes after death, he thought, but we never discuss where it lives before birth. For surely Nicholas had not been created by him and Janelle; as-suming this seemed the height of arrogance. This boy arrived from someplace else and seemed to have brought with him a knowingness. If only he might connect with it. What, Shane wondered, are you trying to tell me?

He thought again of Lily. A question taunted him: which would be harder to live with? Completing this drug, delivering it to Caleb, and finding out that it had harmed her? Or shutting the lab down right now, removing this insane risk to all of them, and finding out later that she had died from lung damage?

The struggle to answer this question should have kept him awake all night. He should have turned it over and over, sweating through his sheets, pacing the living room. And yet in the peace of Nicholas's room, in the lulling softness of this perfumed air, the terrible ache behind his eyes started to seep away.

And he knew exactly what he would do.

• • • • • • •

"Afternoon there, Caley," Hank called.

Caleb broke through the bare branches and into the flat expanse of snow behind the house. Approaching the steps, he saw Hank, squat and crew-cut, Kyle, young and steaming with energy, Alice, lithe and double-jointed, on the back deck, their breath like billow clouds against the beams.

Then he saw June.

Caleb stopped, and sniffed hard. They had not exchanged a word since the day she had told him she would not leave Happy Trails; this was the closest he had been to her in weeks. He felt her presence as if she were turned all the way up, shooting toward him on jets of air.

Nervously, June stretched her arms upward, affecting a

stretch. Her sweatshirt lifted, revealing the parchment skin of her belly. Caleb could not take his eyes from it.

"How is it out there?" Kyle asked him.

"Good."

"How's that feel?" Hank gestured to his backpack.

The perilous isolation in Yosemite necessitated wearing heavier packs than normal, filled with more water and clothing. Mack had begun requiring everyone in Happy Trails to train with them.

"Not so bad." With the back of his hand he wiped snow from under his eyes. "You get used to it."

Hank turned to June. "Are you going to practice with one?"

As June nodded, straw-colored hair flew into her eyes. "Sure."

"It's your first hundred-mile ultra?" Kyle asked her, squinting. "It's not the one to start with."

"If I drop, I'll work a station."

"If you can get to one."

"Leave her alone." Alice shook her head, smiling. "She'll be cool."

Kyle exhaled. "Okay, we're gone."

Caleb opened the back door and kicked off his wet shoes. Inside he found it difficult to slow his heart down. He went to the sink for some water and was on his third glass when he felt her behind him.

"Hey," June whispered.

He turned around, locked onto her enormous eyes.

"Makailah's watching Lily upstairs. Do you want . . ."

"You're running Yosemite?" Caleb asked her quietly.

She nodded.

"Why?"

"This is the Happy Trails race. We're all doing it together, right?"

"You can't risk . . ." He stopped himself. Running an ultramarathon and risk were, of course, inseparable. "Just be really careful."

She cocked her head at a dramatic angle. "Everyone's saying you're training too hard."

"Everyone"—he smiled—"doesn't know everything."

"So, what did Shane say?"

"Shane?"

"When you told him?"

Caleb looked down at his shoes. He felt weighted down and besotted.

"Oh, Caley. You never told him we're not coming?"

"I haven't had a chance. I don't work at O'Neil's anymore."

"You need to find a phone somewhere and call him. He thinks we're coming."

She hesitated. Was there something in her eyes, he wondered? Was this a struggle for her? He looked for something that might tell him it was.

"Lily's really missing you. She wakes up saying 'cay-cay.' Do you think you can play with her while I'm out?"

"Of course."

"That would be really great."

Caleb washed his glass in the sink, set it on a rag. When he had watched her jog down the wood steps and across the snowy field to catch up with everyone, he turned and pushed through the swinging door for the main house.

"Hey," Makailah grinned when he walked into June and Lily's room.

Lily turned her head to him right away, made a high-pitched and happy sound. A drop of saliva spilled down her chin when she reached out for him.

He sat on the rug, and joined Makailah in rolling a ball back and forth.

After a time Makailah yawned. "Mind if I go to the bathroom?"

"I have her."

"Yeah? Okay," she waved to the baby. "See you soon, sweetie."

Alone with Lily he wrapped her in his arms, buried his nose into the soft skin behind her neck, and held her, swaying her gently back and forth, listening to her scratched short breaths. He wondered if he had ever missed anyone so badly in all his life.

He was watching her fall asleep when some noise from downstairs snapped him out of his thoughts. Knowing it was probably Mack, he went downstairs to check.

"Ah!" Mack was shouting, "some help from the constabulary!"

Just behind him, two wide and well-muscled men carried a pony keg each into the house. On Juan's direction they walked across the large room and placed them by the fireplace. Music switched on from the boom box. As he descended the stairs Caleb saw at least twenty people standing around, red cups of beer in hand.

"Caley!" Mack called, waving him over. "Meet Superior's finest."

Caleb was introduced to the police officers, both off duty. He wondered how Mack had befriended them.

One of them was looking at him strangely, his head cocked. "You really run a hundred miles?"

"Not every day," Caleb smiled. He was feeling off-balance. Something of Lily remained in his arms.

At this point, Caleb would normally have excused himself. But the pain of having lost Lily and June erupted out of him now. He looked instinctively to the front door, considering plunging into the dark roads. Then someone handed him a red plastic cup; right, he thought, there was another cure for agony, and it was all around him.

He drained the cup, and helped himself to another.

Alice touched his shoulder, concerned. He shook his head, smiling to her.

Then he reached for the whiskey and shut his eyes tight as he tilted the bottle back.

4

The offices of Zouali and Rice were filled with the kind of light only San Francisco might bestow upon lawyers. Floor to ceiling windows looked down at the foot traffic on Geary Street. The downtown office buildings built on the hill seemed to open their arms. This was all visible from the reception area; however, the office of Brad Whitmore, who was not yet a partner, was small and bereft of sun.

Brad seemed to Shane to be around thirty years old, a bit too lean, with a sharply jutting Adam's apple. A desperate pile of thinning blond hair lay on his head. His long face bespoke a Northeastern lineage. He came recommended by friends of Janelle's.

Shane and Prajuk sat in difficult chairs, facing the lawyer's desk. Prajuk had needed to be dragged here; this was a step beyond what he had agreed to do. But Shane had persuaded him that he could answer questions, clarify, use the proper terminology, that Shane never could hope to. So Prajuk had come but he did not want his name on any document of any kind and seemed convinced that someone would surely force him to sign one. A line of perspiration ran down his brown temple.

Brad was looking at both of them, with an excited look on his thin lips. "So this protein you're using. Tell me exactly where it came from."

"My team and I studied, isolated, and cloned it while we were working on a new drug," Prajuk answered tersely, in his high-pitched voice.

"You first isolated it at Helixia," Brad repeated, scribbling this information down. "Is it patented by them then?"

"Yes," Prajuk nodded, shifting his weight. "I removed this gene straight from the vector and I took it to our lab. I understand that we are violating their patent."

Brad Whitmore shook his head. "No, I don't see it that way."

Prajuk glanced at Shane as if to suggest that they should ask someone more experienced.

Shane leaned forward. "How do you see it?"

"You guys are using this protein in a drug for"—he glanced down at his notes and seemed to suffer a hard time reading them—"alpha-one antitrypsin deficiency. But at Helixia, the protein was used to treat asthma?"

"Yes."

"How different are these two drugs?"

Prajuk replied, "Very different. They cause different reactions in the body."

"Do you think Helixia also patented it as intended for use for alpha-one antitrypsin deficiency?"

"No, most definitely they are not interested in using it for this purpose."

"How do you know?"

Shane cut in, "I asked them. Several times."

"Okay." Brad folded his hands. "You can claim a new composition of matter. See, it's like music. You can't copy someone else's melody and claim it as your song, right? But you can change just a note of it, and technically it's a new composition. This happens all the time, it's how commercial music houses work. And then also, you can patent musical notes in a specific sequence, but you can't patent a G note. That belongs to everybody.

"American genetics patent law works the same way. You can patent a gene or protein you've discovered in the specific composition of the drug you're patenting. But you can't patent the gene itself. That's everybody's property. A gene"—he smiled, unfolding his fingers—"is a musical note."

"Ah," Shane nodded.

"If you use this patented gene in a drug with a different composition, no matter how slightly different, then well, you're good."

Shane shot him a sideways glance.

"That is your opinion?" Prajuk asked nervously, "or this thing, it is legal fact, definitely?"

"Fact."

Shane smiled, thinking it was very possible that he loved Brad Whitmore. He started to stand. The cost of the attorney's hourly advice was out of the scope of his hundred-thousand-dollar investment, which had already been spent. These were bills he could not pay.

"And," Brad said, looking to him, "there's a whole other play here." He swung around on his chair, produced an impossibly thick pine green book, began turning pages. Shane heard the subtle click of a clock that he had not noticed before was there.

"Could you argue that a Helixia shareholder is being

deprived of proper value by the revenue you guys will be taking from them with your drug?"

"What revenue?" Shane asked.

"In their eyes, think of greedy little eyes now, are you stealing something of significant market value from them?"

"Absolutely not. They would lose hundreds of millions on our drug, they said so themselves, all the way up the ladder. That's why they said no to producing it, or even applying for an NIH orphan grant. Our drug will do no financial harm to Helixia, believe me."

"Because . . ." Brad read to himself, moving his lips, and then looked sharply up at them. "A company's patent is limited in cases where the benefit to the public outweighs the harm to the inventor."

He snapped the large book shut and gave them a proud smile. "There's miles of precedent for this, guys. If I spent a day in a research library I'd find a brief's worth. In fact, a new use for a known protein is fully patentable. You guys can patent this usage, your, you know, drug, yourselves. You could sell it to some big pharmaceutical firm. I'll draw a patent application up for you."

Prajuk shook his head. "No. There is definitely to be no record of what we are doing. This was our agreement."

Brad held both hands up. "No application. Now, let me be clear. What you're doing is legal. But they will fire you for this."

"You just said we're doing nothing illegal."

"They can fire you for bringing the wrong Munchkins to Doughnut Day. California is a Right to Work state. Your jobs are not secure. If they find out you took this vector from their lab, you're both gone. But they can't sue you. Well, they probably would, but they can't win. Just know that the law is on your side."

"They would send waves of lawyers and appeals until they bankrupted us," Prajuk said.

Brad looked away from them. "Yes, well," he nodded. "They could do that."

Outside Prajuk smoked a cigarette, sucking deeply from his compressed fist, held an inch from his lips. Shane slapped his back.

"I should not be gone this long," Prajuk told him tensely.

"Okay."

"This whole project is taking significantly more of my time than I had anticipated."

"We're almost done though, right? Should I call my brother?"

Prajuk nodded. "You should tell him to make arrangements."

Shane looked quizzically at him. "What is it?"

"I have to tell you something."

"What's up?"

"Jon Benatti came by," Prajuk whispered, his breath full of smoke. "He never comes to my office."

Shane smiled, trying to relay a gentle calm.

"He was very curious. How are things going? How is Airifan doing in clinicals? There are people he should ask about this thing, but I am not part of that. Is everything okay? This thing, Benatti, he is very concerned with me."

"To know you is to love you, Prajuk."

As they climbed into the car and began driving back to work, Shane continued. "You work on the most important projects here. You've worked with Steven Poulos. There are rumors about Roche buying us. He doesn't want to lose you to Amgen or somewhere."

"Yes, maybe. But this little man Benatti," Prajuk nodded. "He is quite a fucker."

"He doesn't know anything," Shane assured him, forcing his best sales confidence up through his eyes.

"He saw me with the centrifuge. He may have run inventory. I told you, if I had even a suspicion of this, I would stop immediately."

Shane felt a surge of panic.

"Healy is sufficient for you from this point."

"No, he's not."

They finished the drive in silence. Half an hour later he pulled into the Helixia lot.

"Hey, Shane," a woman's voice called.

He glanced quickly behind him and saw Stacey waving to him from the lobby doors, where she was opening an umbrella. He felt as if he were caught in the middle of some parking lot drug deal. Which in a way, he supposed, he was.

It was true, their absences were starting to be noticed. Their minds were elsewhere. People might be able to sense that there was something between them worth looking closer into. He patted Prajuk's skinny shoulder, and the smell of nicotine encircled him like a child's affection.

Above them rain began to fall. Funny, Shane thought, glancing up. There hadn't been a cloud in the sky.

· · · · · · ·

The mouse's blood came back positive for alpha-one antitrypsin deficiency.

Shane was elated. This was terrific news, it meant that they had a living creature on which to test Prajuk's drug. Shane read the e-mail from Prajuk on his phone and virtually danced in circles in the elevator.

They met at Greenway Plaza after work. Healy brought a paper bag containing three forty-ounce bottles of his favorite malt liquor. They were opened; ceremonial foam bubbled forth.

"To Thailand," Shane toasted.

"Are you guys going on vacation?" asked Healy.

He pointed at the mouse. "Thailand!"

"You named the mouse?"

"Definitely," Prajuk grinned.

"We don't name the mice, man. That's not right. Seriously. You don't want to bond with the thing."

Shane laughed, taking a great pull of the liquor.

Healy frowned. He lifted his bottle, then hesitated. "Why Thailand?"

"In honor of Doctor Acharn."

"Mot kiao," Prajuk toasted.

Shane raised his bottle, watching the scientist. The news of the mouse had proven strong enough to overcome his desire to stop. But gray half-moons had formed under his eyes. The smell of his hard-inhaled Parliaments preceded him into the lab. Shane thought a week in Phuket would do him wonders. Before he could suggest it, Prajuk gestured to Healy.

"You want to do it?"

The stout and ripped postdoc shook his acne-marked head no. "You go for it."

With a grimace, Prajuk opened the small cage, lifted Thailand by the tail, and handed him to Healy. Then he removed a syringe from a metal drawer. He took up a vial of opaque liquid and inserted it into the top.

"What's that?" asked Shane, feeling he was missing something of vital importance.

"This is your drug," Healy told him.

"Holy shit. For real?"

Healy nodded. Prajuk held the syringe up to the fluorescent light. His small eyes focused intensely as he tapped it. The wheezing mouse, seeming to sense something coming, thrust wildly in Healy's hand. Prajuk injected its flank with the fluid containing his isolated protein, which, mixed with media and transplanted into a bacterial E. coli cell, altered the instructions in his DNA.

Shane stood slack-jawed. He half expected the mouse to convulse and die right then. Healy placed Thailand back into his cage, and swept out some pellets of shit while he was at it. He went to the double sink, washed his hands, and refreshed the water bottle from which Thailand could drink as he either began a new life, or ended this one.

Shane watched Prajuk, looking for some sense of reverence. But if the scientist felt the presence of a momentous act, he kept his awe well hidden. Cold distance, Shane realized, was the order of the lab.

And then, to his surprise, Prajuk took his malt liquor and drank it dry.

............5

"There are two ways we can do this," Doctor Frank said carefully.

Caleb sat on the edge of a long metal table and glanced around the tiny clinic. The room carried the scent of cough drops; the walls held paintings of birds.

The old doctor lifted one of Caleb's battered feet. Caleb noticed him shake his head at this willful mangling of the human form.

"First way is, we put you to sleep. Other way"—he coughed—"is we don't."

The old doctor had run this two-room clinic in Arvada for decades. He employed an overweight middle-aged nurse named Sue, who sometimes smelled of alcohol. He was the only doctor Mack trusted with procedures of this sort, which energy healing did not affect.

"How long until I can run?"

"Depends on how your body heals. It's usually three weeks." He hesitated. "With you guys, I'd say one."

Caleb sighed.

"Are we doing all of them?"

"Please."

Sue entered the room, smiling cheerily. "Hello, Mister Oberest!"

Doctor Frank explained, "When we put you out, there's always some risk. And you'll be groggy for a day."

"I don't want to be put out."

"Well, I can use a local, but it won't be comfortable. The shots hurt. You won't feel pain when we do it, but it can be kind of, disconcerting."

"I'm fine."

Sue opened a metal drawer, and her hand emerged holding an alarmingly long hypodermic, glistening in the sunlight. Caleb lay down on the table. He noticed a long line of water damage running across the ceiling.

He felt Sue take hold of his right heel and balance it in her palm. Then he felt a sharp plunging into the tender skin just under the nail of his little toe. The pain was of a dental quality, sublime and unbearable. A burn flooded into his mangled toe, and Caleb cried out.

Sue said, "Sorry, honey. It'll get numb in a second."

She proved correct. The pain quieted almost instantly. He felt her take up his second toe. Blend with the air, he whispered to himself. He tried to force on his Happy Trails smile, but when the needle slipped deeply under his toenail, he jolted and ground his teeth.

"I think we should put him out," Sue said to Doctor Frank.

Caleb shook his head. "No risks."

The third toe was no better. He gripped the metal table

so hard that his fingertips went red and numb. As the needle went under his big toe he gasped so audibly that Doctor Frank looked down at him and stopped. Their eyes met. When he could, Caleb nodded for him to continue.

But as with all pain, the second it diminished, so did its memory. With all ten toes numb, he felt relaxed, and breathed deeply. Doctor Frank bent over Caleb's feet. The instrument at hand, Caleb saw from his prone position, was a jagged chrome tool shaped like the beak of an eagle.

Sue held a small tray aloft filled with plenty of gauze and a small plastic bowl. Caleb shut his eyes. A vision of the stunning sublimity of Yosemite Valley spread out before him; amazing things would happen to him there, experiences beyond contemplation. It would challenge him, and he would challenge it; he had the sense that there would be some finality either way. He placed himself in the middle of its fields, near wildflowers and waterfalls. But an odd tugging at his feet interrupted his meditation.

He opened his eyes and saw Doctor Frank's gloved hand twisting sharply in an unnatural circular motion. Caleb could feel a strange gravitational pull as the web of tendons holding his toenails to his skin began to tear.

Some of the nails came off easily, a sudden muscular twist, and then the sound of it falling into the tray. Others proved more difficult. He heard the doctor's tired breath after a third attack on the stubborn second toe of his left foot. His body screamed that this was not right, that he should do something.

When Doctor Frank was finished, Caleb risked a glance downward. His feet were both covered in thick black blood. Sue was bent over them with a needle and thread.

"Seven of these need stitches. All of them need to be taped for a week."

Caleb let his head drop back against the table.

"When the anesthetic wears off, maybe two hours, it's going to hurt. You won't want anything near your feet. No socks, blankets, or even sheets. Take some turmeric for the swelling. If that doesn't work take ibuprofen, or you won't run for a month."

Caleb's eyes widened.

"I know you guys don't like antibiotics. Sue's going to give you a tube of ointment, it's holistic. For swelling and pain and cleaning. But if you see any green fluid through the bandage, then you get this filled and take it for ten days. She'll make you an appointment to get the stitches out next week."

Caleb nodded, reaching for the prescription that he knew Mack would toss away. Sue helped him into open-toed sandals and slowly eased him onto his feet.

"Don't walk, just glide," she cautioned him. "Like you're skating."

Outside, Kevin Yu was waiting in an old T-shirt and sunglasses.

"I got you, dude," he said, slipping a surprisingly strong arm under Caleb's shoulders. He glimpsed Caleb's red feet, swelling madly at each end. They looked as though someone had held them over fire. The two of them shuffled slowly over to Mack's Jeep, and Kevin eased him into the passenger seat.

"You're shaking, Caley."

Caleb leaned his head back. By the time they drove over the dirt driveway, and Mack opened the front door smiling, his feet looked no stranger to him than they had the day before.

• • • • • • •

June saw Mack across the street, in the doorway of Pedestrian Shoes.

Spring seemed to have announced its intentions. The mid-March mornings were cold but full of promise. A clarity had developed in the light.

She wore a long sundress in a floral print, a head scarf, and old sneakers Alice had given her. She held a yellow bucket of cleaning supplies in her hand and carried Lily in her purple Kelty Kids backpack. June was on her way back from her day's second apartment; she had cleaned it for two hours while Lily napped in a queen-size bed. The African-American student who lived there had arrived home early. She had stared at Lily, and then back to June, as June had scrambled to leave.

Lily was wide awake now, excited to be out in the fresh air after a morning of cleaning fluids and rousted dust. She loved the energy of the street. The colors, people, and music never failed to elicit squeaks and excited arm-waving. From her perch just above June's head, she looked out at the world like a welcoming beacon. Students on the sidewalks sometimes reached for her fingers. Mother and daughter stood on the mall and focused their large pale eyes on John McConnell.

He was stepping onto the Mall with the March sun in his face, carrying six green boxes of sneakers stacked in his thin arms. The Yosemite Slam, just eight weeks away, was the sole focus of his life. He had stopped the house parties, Thursdays at the Rocking Horse, even accompanying the house on their daily runs. These final weeks required group focus, and no outsiders, he explained. Everyone had gotten into it.

From across the street, June noticed that he looked older. The crevices running from the sides of his eyes to the corners of his small mouth seemed deeper, his legs bony in their blue running shorts, covered with tufts of black hair; even his beard seemed coarser. Maybe it was just the strong sunlight.

June watched him fumble with the Jeep's back door and toss the boxes inside, many of which fell open and emptied onto the seats. When he walked back inside the store, June stayed where she was, letting people walk around her. A moment later Mack reappeared carrying another stack of boxes. From above her, Lily let loose a squeal of recognition, as if she were sighting land.

Mack heard it and looked suddenly across the street. He focused on them for a moment; then he waved. He placed his boxes in the Jeep, walked across the Mall, and reached up to the purple backpack for Lily's soft hand.

"How's the day?" he asked June, smiling at the baby.

"I cleaned two places. One of them gave me a five-dollar tip. She said to buy something for Lily."

"Cool beans."

"I have it here for you." She patted her pocket.

"See those shoes?" Mack gestured back at Pedestrian. "Montrail just released the new line. Their bottoms are just solid. Incredible. The guys gave us a good deal. So, everyone gets a present for Yosemite. Hey, Michael Jordan wore a new pair of Nikes every game, why not you guys? The Michael Jordans of running." He winked at her.

She smiled. "I'm more of a bench player."

"You've been nailing fifties all year. I know you can take a hundred, Junebug. It will be great for you." He looked up at Lily. "And the trip will be real good for our special lady here."

June started hopefully. "You think so?"

"For sure. Different air. Less dry. New input."

"Because it's been harder this week. The winter was hard for her breathing, but the spring, I'm worried about the pollen and . . ." she waved her arms around, unsure what to say.

Mack nodded sympathetically. "Some local honey will help. I'll pick us up some."

They stepped aside to let some skateboarders explode past. There was a space afterward in which June could hear her heart pounding.

"She gets better when she works with you," she explained, "but then it comes back."

"Well, my energy levels have been low." Mack became agitated. "I know that. I've been pouring everything into logistics, insurance, permits, press. It's hard not being out there in California, doing this from our house. I'm talking with running blogs and magazines and the ABC folks, right? But Barry Strong's guys are meeting with the park people, local police, hospital reps in person. I should be out there. I mean, I'm needed."

"We need you too," June smiled, wanting to soothe him.

"And it's sapping me. I'm only running four hours a day. I'm fighting mental stress. When I work with Lily at night, I have less kinetic energy to give to her. I need to get my energy up." He looked at her. "Swing by my room with her this afternoon. Bring me some green tea, yeah?" He looked up, smiling, the rivers around his mouth and nose deepening into oceans. "See you later, little Lily!"

She thought for a second that Mack would offer her a ride down to the house, but he drove off. So she stopped at

Dushanbe and spent some of her cleaning cash on a pound of sencha and chamomile-lavender blend. While the barista measured the bags, June stared at the muffins and scones behind the glass. It had been a year since she had eaten anything like them, and she felt hungry in a way she had not in months. Her desire for one of them was dizzying. But she swallowed it back. The kinetic energy her body produced on the trails this morning would be wasted trying to process the sugars and additives, and not be available to help Lily during the reiki treatment Mack seemed to have promised. It did not seem worth Lily's health to sample a scone.

She sang a little made-up tune as she walked with her daughter down Arapahoe into the darkening valley.

"I'm going to give you an amazing life," she promised in song. "We're getting you better. We're getting you better."

At the house, June changed Lily's diaper, kissed her soft belly, and brought her to Mack's closed door. She knocked.

Mack's nasal voice called out, "What?"

"It's June and Lily. And tea."

"Come on in."

Inside, a thick musk washed over her. The window in here should be thrown open, she thought. Mack sat on his futon mattress, on the floor.

"Hey, princess," he waved to Lily.

June set her down, and immediately she began a fast crawl to him, eyes wide, clear drool hanging from her smiling mouth. By the time she reached him, of course, she was out of breath and coughing, her tiny chest heaving.

Mack's eyes drooped, and his voice was lower than usual. "She'll be walking soon, you know."

"Oh God, I hope."

Mack stared intensely at her. "I think she should start on the program when she does."

"The program?"

"Multigrain in the morning, as much walking as she can do on those red feet, root stew at five."

"What about her milk?"

"No dairy, of course. We're not meant to process cow lactose, that's barbaric bullshit leftover from the times of leeches. No naps, no stasis. That's what's wrong, that's why she hasn't been able to build her own kinetic energy yet. She needs movement. Her body needs to work like ours. When she's six, she'll be running marathons. Right, little Lily?"

Almost on cue, the short and sharp inhales of Lily's breathing became audible. "When she gets excited, it gets louder," June explained.

"She's excited because she understands what I'm saying to you."

"Of course, Mack."

Mack drank his tea and lifted Lily onto his mattress. She seemed to anticipate the great healing heat that came from him and lay right on her back to meet it. Spreading his left hand out, his palm hovering an inch over the gentle skin of her chest, shutting his eyes, he began to fix her. When June held her daughter's hand, she could feel the hot energy shooting through her as she was entrained.

"Now you," Mack instructed her.

So June rubbed her palms together and held each over Lily's abdomen, her fingertips grazing Mack's. She closed her eyes to focus on willing her energy into her baby. And yet June felt uneasy. Limiting Lily to just two meals a day and no naps? Of course she would try it, she would try anything for her daughter. But it felt wrong. She glanced at Mack awkwardly; the smell of him was so raw.

As usual, Lily had fallen asleep under his touch. Her wheezing was still pronounced as she was unable to breathe deeply even in sleep. A cloud shifted and sent the room into shadow, and then Mack broke out of his meditation and looked directly into June.

"Come here."

June moved beside him, keeping her hands above Lily's chest. Mack touched the back of her neck, and she felt a shocking heat burn through her skin. Then he lay on his back, keeping his hand on the back of her neck, pushing her head downwards.

"Wait," she whispered, "what?"

"I told you, my energy is low."

"Sure, but I don't understand?"

"See June, what we're doing here, what you're asking? It *depletes* me. She's taking all my energy. I need you to give me more. It's something," Mack told her, "all the women here help with."

She recalled seeing Leigh, Rae, even Aviva, leaving or entering Mack's room at all hours of the day. No, she thought, this couldn't be why.

Mack pulled down his running shorts. His matted hair continued down his belly and below. June looked at the prone body of her infant daughter sleeping peacefully beside him.

Mack paused, staring straight into her. "You can start slowly."

June looked away. "Let me just move Lily."

June slid her hands underneath her daughter's warm, beautiful body, lifted her off the mattress, and carried her to a yoga mat by the window. As she laid her down, she stroked her sleeping, open hand, those small and perfect fingers.

She felt the exquisite smoothness of her skin slip away as she stood and went to him.

6

Shane picked up the phone to call Caleb at his copy store.

A nervousness that he had not felt in years swept through him as the phone rang. He felt as if he were calling his high school crush. A young man's voice answered. "O'Neil's Copies."

"Hi, is, um, Caleb Oberest there?"

A pause. "Caleb doesn't work here anymore."

"He doesn't?"

"Not in, I don't know, like three months."

Shane's stomach clenched. "Do you know how I can reach him?"

"Don't, sorry."

"Wait, does he come in for messages?"

"Not that I know of."

"I'd like to leave one. His brother. Tell him to call his brother."

"Okay. Have a nice day."

Fucking college kids, Shane exhaled. He stared at the pads of his cubicle wall. Meant for thumbtacks, he supposed, but similarly good for bashing a copy store clerk's head into.

This explained why Caleb hadn't responded to his letter about a present for Lily. Vague as it had been, Shane had expected some reply. There was no phone at the Happy Trails house. Where did June work, he wondered? Had she told him? If so, he could not recall. He stood, waved good night to Stacey, and walked slowly to his car.

This week, Dennis had sat him down to discuss adding a Phase Two Alzheimer's drug to his workload. Two hospital oncology departments in Oregon that had not had time for him suddenly asked him to make presentations on Sorion. Nicholas was starting to teethe, waking at night in fits of fury. He was overloading.

On Pinon Drive he saw Prajuk's white Volvo signaling out of a Taco Bell. He seemed to be manipulating a burrito in his car as he drove. Shane laughed; he liked this man very much.

The night had deepened; stars swept in from the ocean. Riding the elevator up with Prajuk, Shane felt a low rush of nicotine as if he were smoking by osmosis.

"We'll see how Thailand is doing. This thing," Prajuk explained, "should be generating some response by now."

"And if it isn't?"

"Then the dosage may be wrong. I will administer more, and we will wait another week."

"How many times would you do that before you figure it's not working at all?"

"Three, maybe four."

"And after that?"

They stepped out on the third floor and walked past the other closed doors, some with muffled voices coming from inside. What were they stressing, Shane wondered? How close were they to their dreams, or to failure?

"After that, we have to ask questions. How many months do we have to test a range of compositions and dosages? How many more mice will this thing need? How much more money can you obtain to build them? How much time is there before the baby's lungs atrophy?"

"I'm not a fan of those questions."

"Don't worry, please. Definitely we are not ready to ask them yet."

Prajuk walked to the deep stainless steel sink to wash his hands. Shane moved to the cage and looked at Thailand. Prajuk did not seem, he thought, to have developed any emotional attachment to this creature. He must have unleashed impossible cruelties upon generations of mice by now, given them tumors, asthma, open sores, blindness, diabetes, heart attacks, strokes, worse. But Shane could not help smiling at the tiny thing as Prajuk lifted him by the tail and brought him over to the Buxco box.

Once inside, Thailand adjusted to his claustrophobic glass. Only this time, Shane was watching a totally different animal. Instead of curling up, the mouse was up on its back two legs, attempting to climb out.

"Jesus, look at the guy."

Prajuk squinted at the levels meter. "He is processing significantly more air. Looks like eighty-five percent. Versus thirty percent when he arrived here."

"Oh, man. Oh shit. It works?"

"Watch his movements."

"I am. That's normal?"

"This thing is how a healthy mouse behaves."

They weighed and measured him. Thailand had been carefully constructed to have the same disease as Lily, the same train whistle wheeze, the same swollen feet, the same inability to exhale. Only now, he did not have any of those things.

"We need to send his blood out to measure liver and kidney function," Prajuk explained.

"How long will it take to get results?"

"Two or three days. While we wait, Healy and I will humanize the drug."

Shane felt his lungs pushing against his chest, as if the alpha-one antitrypsin deficiency had somehow been passed into him. Remembering Janelle's worry, he asked, "Lily weighs a lot more than a mouse. And she's growing. How do you know the right dosage?"

"This thing is not like Tylenol. It is not a question of dosage, it is a question of efficacy. The drug carries the protein into her genes, instructs it to switch on. Will her body respond? With this type of treatment, we give a dose periodically to keep the process in forward motion."

"Forward motion," Shane muttered. "I'm familiar with that concept."

"Trust me, this thing will be the correct dosage for the baby."

"You're giving this to a baby?"

Shane turned around. When had Healy come in? He stood there with his head cocked, his short, cut arms plunging into his pockets, staring at them.

"Of course not," Prajuk insisted, stumbling noticeably.

Right now, Shane knew, Healy was trying to re-create the conversation he had just heard. Everything would depend on his and Prajuk's reactions. If they communicated no emotion, then Healy might let himself dismiss these words. Anything else, and he would come for their jugulars; it seemed to be in his DNA.

"You said the exact dosage for the *baby*."

"A baby mouse," Shane began. "In case we need to try again."

"Listen," Prajuk tried, "Thailand is breathing at eighty-five percent normal. He has no wheezing."

But Healy's face did not change. "Who else at Helixia is working on this?"

"Just focus on what we're paying you to do."

"I'm taking a piss," Shane laughed, hoping to end the conversation.

He walked toward the door. Healy took a step forward at the same time and gave Shane a small but significant shoulder shove backward.

Shane yelled, "Hey, man, what's that?"

Healy walked to the Buxco on the back shelf and peered down at its instruments. He said quietly, "I want to speak to someone else who works on this."

Shane went to the bathroom down the hallway. Opening the door, he felt a light tap on his shoulder and turned around.

"Did Healy push you just then?" Prajuk asked, his fingers fidgeting.

"Yeah, he did. The little fucker."

"Tonight will be his final day with us," Prajuk said in a low voice.

"What if he tells the professor who recommended him what he heard?"

"Tom Sangee? He tells my good friend Tom that he

overheard us say something about a baby? Tom won't even call me. And definitely I liked your answer."

Shane glanced back down the dim hallway. "He didn't buy it."

"I will tell him he is no longer required here."

"Isn't he, though? Required here?"

"I can accomplish the rest with you. You've learned enough. He is a good postdoc, but he is an asshole."

"Little bit of a Napoleon complex, you think?"

"Oh, definitely. But these issues exist in many bioresearchers, you know."

"Why is that?"

"Because they are in touch with the mechanisms of our existence. Because they are playing with the raw materials of God."

"It must make you feel very powerful."

Prajuk looked at Shane. "No. That's the reason, you see." He smiled.

"Nothing makes you feel less powerful than manipulating life."

.... 7

"Happy Trails!" Mack called out loudly, and everyone laughed.

Outside the house it was pitch dark, four in the morning, and the stars shown madly, laughing like fairies in the woods. Each of them gathered in a wide circle outside for a standing hug, wrapping their arms around each other, heads down.

"'For we cannot tarry here! We must march my darlings, we must bear the brunt of danger. We the youthful sinewy races, all the rest on us depend. Pioneers! O pioneers!'"

Everyone clapped and hollered, and they climbed into the vans. Mack had rented three of them for the drive. They were decades old, their transmission and brakes shot long ago. The vinyl seats leaked foam, the floors covered with cigarette burns from another era. One of them carried the faint stink of vomit.

June carried Lily and her plastic car seat. The purple hiking backpack was stuffed full of clothes and diapers. She handed it to Kyle as they settled in the last row of a maroon van. She patted Lily's hand, and the whole van sang songs as the Happy Trails Running Club began their three-van caravan through the mountains, down to the desert, and into the forest, to Yosemite.

She had seen this same road a year before, only she had been coming the other way, from Taos. Since then, Lily had grown from infancy into a tiny person; her body no longer bore any similarity to her former self. And neither, June thought, did her own. The group diet and the running had transformed her into some abstract version of herself, lithe and pure. She wondered if Todd would recognize either of them if they walked into the Gorge.

As morning heightened they slipped into the red earth of Utah, its numinous red arches rising in the distance. She wondered who had planned this dull highway that shunned and avoided them. If instead they had plotted paths that wound close to the scenic beauty of this country, maybe more people might emerge from their cars and walk among the natural healing energy of the world. Instead, they suffered a system of flat straight roads that encouraged stasis. It felt as if the highways had been designed by the army, when they should have been designed by artists.

The baby seemed to enjoy the scenery blurring past her window. She held a book of animal pictures, turned its pages with what to June seemed great thoughtfulness, and slept. As the sky turned violet, they parked on the side of the highway and took a long run in the desert dusk. Leigh had come down with a cold and offered to stay in the van with Lily. Mack had purchased a cheap cell phone to stay in constant contact with Barry Strong and all of the arrangements in Yosemite. He was on the phone when June took off with everyone else into the open land. The dirt and clay felt warm against her feet. She felt as if she could run forever.

When Caleb ran unexpectedly beside her, June politely acknowledged him with a nod, knowing he would not speak. But to her great surprise, he did. He spoke, looking out at the beautiful sky, until some of the others slowed down and got too close. And then Caleb dashed ahead.

She stared after him and did not speak to him again.

Back at the vans, Leigh was giving Lily a bottle.

"I loved the company," she'd laughed when she handed Lily back into June's slick arms.

"Fresh diaper," June noticed approvingly.

"Damn right," Leigh high-fived her.

They ate root stew, which John had packed in containers and heated on hot plates on the shoulder of this road, watching stars part the evening. They joined hands and meditated together, building on their new kinetic energy. Then they climbed back in for the night's drive through the desert.

Three days later, the three old vans finally groaned to a halt outside the Big Oak Flat entrance to Yosemite National Park. They were staying four to a room at an old damp lodge just inside the park. Many of the other entrants were also staying here, and handwritten signs for pre-race meetings had been taped all over the lobby.

June stood with a fussy Lily in the lobby, trying to calm herself down as well. She was about to run one hundred miles into its old trails, with no safety net, save an occasional aid station, ending with a mammoth climb up Half Dome. She was confronted with the reality of her commitment. It was much more than she had ever done. She bent her head and prayed that she was ready.

The sky was the color of late lilacs; black tops of soaring oaks brushed its belly. June noticed Caleb standing outside, staring in the same direction. A force seemed to be pulling them from somewhere deep inside its trees. She was hoping to finish, but he was expecting to win.

It would be Caleb's energy against Yosemite's, she understood. Either the two would merge on the old trails and explode together to glory, or they would battle each other until one of them claimed victory.

Tomorrow, she knew, he would run into this wilderness until he arrived at its end, or his own.

....

"We have a problem."

Shane stopped on the street. His hand tightened around his phone. He had been undertaking a long-needed Saturday walk with his son. A bonding stroll. He had been regaling him with the world, placing his ten-month-old hands onto the bark of trees, pointing to seagulls and sails by the bay.

"What happened?"

"We need to talk in person. I can be at the Peet's near you in fifteen minutes."

Shane hung up and pushed the stroller quickly back home.

"Be back in a bit," he kissed Janelle.

"What's a bit?" she called after him, frustrated.

Running through the damp air, Shane felt as if his heart had been injected with thick sap. Something was wrong with Thailand. The mouse had undergone some failure of its renal glands. His chance to save Lily, and to bring Caleb home, was gone.

Inside the coffee shop the music was horrifyingly up-tempo; its optimism grated on Shane's nerves. He wished he had suggested a bar. He sat in a hard chair. Beside him a woman produced a shrill vibrato laugh after every sentence she finished.

Finally, after half an hour, a bell over the door twinkled, and Prajuk hesitated in the threshold. Worry seemed to contaminate his face. Shane watched him inhale one last mad pull from the Parliament an inch from his face. He lifted a hand, and Prajuk came over, reeking of smoke.

"What killed him?"

Prajuk narrowed his eyes, confused. Then he nodded slowly. "This thing, it works. I told you that it would."

Shane dropped his head. The flutter of a billion stars. When he looked back up, Prajuk was still staring at him. "The mouse is fine, Shane. We, on the other hand, are not."

"What happened?"

"Our Mister Healy."

"Healy?"

"He called Anthony Leone."

"He did what?" he shouted.

The two women at the next table turned to them. Shane took a hard breath through his nose.

"He left a voice mail for Anthony. Which Anthony forwarded to me. In this thing he says that he has been working for Prajuk Acharn and Shane Oberest in a lab away from the office. On a biologic which we told him is a Helixia project. He has asked to speak with the head of this project."

Shane let his head fall against his forearms. "Fuck. Fuck."

"And then he told him that he is concerned because we are planning to give this drug to a baby."

"What did you say to him?"

"Nothing. I just received this thing, this voice mail, on my e-mail. Clearly Anthony expects an answer however." Prajuk glanced around, as if the café were full of biotechnology spies, which, for all Shane knew, it probably was.

"I told you," Shane said softly, "if anyone at Helixia found out anything, you're out. You were never part of it. There are no records. I'm taking full ownership of it all. I'm sorry it came to this." He pushed his hands through his black hair as he thought out loud. "I can probably tell Anthony that I used your name to get Healy to work for me, but that you never had any part in it, and Healy's exaggerating or lying or something. I'll think about it."

The scientist stared at him.

"Look," Shane reminded him, "we talked to Brad Whitmore. We're not breaking a law."

"Laws and reputations are separate things."

Shane's amber eyes lit up. "Or, tell Anthony that you turned Healy down for an internship. He's making this all up."

"How would he know your name?"

Shane's head began to hurt. Outside a soft rain had arrived. The drizzle it left on the windows was, he saw, almost unbearably beautiful.

Shane reached across the table and patted his arm. "Stop smoking."

"I like smoking."

"Everyone likes smoking. But everyone quits."

"You never even started, not even once?"

"I never did."

"Because you are a runner."

Shane saw Fred and Caleb, far ahead of him on a winding morning road, in synch in the dampness of the ocean air. No, he thought. That was something he was not.

8

On the eve of the Yosemite Slam, they attended a pre-race briefing out in the park.

Whatever Mack had expected in terms of numbers, Caleb thought, this had to be bigger than he had ever hoped for. Whether it was the Internet, or Mack's efforts at press, there were at least six hundred runners here. This was the kind of number Western States drew. Mack had really done this. It was, Caleb thought, something of a miracle.

The Happy Trails Running Club assembled at the front of a clearing by the Big Oak Flat entrance to Yosemite. Walking among the crowd, Kevin and Alice commented that some new force was present, tangible. They all felt it. Caleb was not sure if it was positive or threatening. Perhaps it was coming from the presence of the camera crews, the trucks, the rumors of this event's difficulty. Perhaps from some other source.

All day, the lines had grown for medical check-ins. All the entrants were weighed, their pulses taken, and given waivers to sign forgoing their rights to sue for any reason. Caleb came in at 173 pounds, up three from the Hardrock. He was given number 24.

As the sun slipped behind Glacier Point, a broad man in his fifties wearing a tan cowboy hat turned on a beige megaphone. Beside him stood Mack, his face hosting a long-toothed grin.

Kevin tapped Caleb's shoulder. "Barry Strong."

Mack and Barry were nodding, looking out at the assembled entrants, at the camera marked ABC SPORTS, behind which stood a young man wearing headphones. The sun was falling rapidly, bathing the field in violet shadow.

Mack pointed to a young woman talking on a phone and gave a questioning shrug. She returned a thumbs-up. Barry adjusted his hat and began to address the crowd.

"Welcome to the Yosemite Slam!" he shouted into his megaphone.

Cheers went up and lasted a good two minutes. The producer flashed another thumbs-up at Mack. It seemed things were going well.

"I want you to take a good last look at yourselves. Okay? Because whoever you are tonight, you'll be somebody else from now on."

More whooping and clapping. Barry handed the megaphone to Mack, who waved it manically. His voice sounded tinny and distorted through its plastic.

"As you can see, ABC is taping this event. You will see some cameras on the course, at positions we can get a cameraman to. Don't let them distract you."

He looked around. An awkward stoppage of communication ensued. Eventually Barry took the megaphone back. He paced as he spoke.

"Okay, folks. Rule One. No bitching. I understand that a few newbies may be in attendance. So let me explain: you volunteered. We don't want to hear it."

Still more cheering echoed across the field.

"Rule Two. Do not underestimate this terrain. These are old mining trails. We did our best to mark them. But animals may have run off with them. If you think you've left the course, turn around. Going off trail here can be fatal for about twelve dozen reasons."

Caleb turned around. Was June here? He thought he might have seen her standing by John, obscured by his height.

"Yosemite has mountain lions. Grizzlies. Both have killed hikers in this park this year. They will attack a brightly dressed human running through their territory. We planned the course away from them, but we're not perfect listeners, and neither are they."

Barry shuffled the papers in his hand, and the megaphone gave a shocking shriek of feedback.

"Okay, injury. We can get minimal supplies to the aid stations on mules. But rescue Jeeps and ATVs will not be able to reach you on about two-thirds of this course. Helivacs are not an option. You get hurt, you find your way to the closest aid station. We can get you out of the park from any of them, though it may be on an animal.

"Rule Three. Do not push. This is not the event to test your limits on. Walk. Rest. If you're thinking about dropping, drop. If it is determined at an aid station that it is in your best interest, you will be pulled."

Barry Strong waited, narrowing his eyes, and looked at Mack with an expression of polite invitation to add a thought. Mack took the megaphone again but could not seem to think of anything to say.

"We have dinner in the camping area by the Ranger Station," Barry concluded. "Please come by."

The crowd rippled with excitement as they turned and dispersed. Caleb caught whispers of rumors, about the course, about the weather, about the news crews. The Happy Trails Running Club did not attend the pasta buffet. To the amazement of the other runners, they collected at the lodge bar, drinking beer and laughing until ten in the evening.

In the room he shared with Kevin, Hank, and Juan, Caleb carefully checked his drop bags, which had been packed with lightweight clothing for night and bad weather, shoes in increasing sizes, energy gels, water. As darkness fell, he would slip close to sleep, but halt there, touching vivid, mad visions. Finally he slept. At four, Kevin nudged him awake. He put benzoin on his feet, pausing to touch the oddly smooth skin where his toenails had been. He rubbed Vaseline on his body and partook of twenty minutes of lying meditation.

In the lobby he saw Lily and June, speaking with a middle-aged woman. Mack had arranged for Lily to stay with the lodge's owners. She was sitting up in a Pack 'n Play behind the front desk when Caleb last saw her. He thought June looked nervous; certainly leaving Lily here for two or three days would do that. He hoped it would not distract her on the course.

He opened the door and emerged into a chilly mist. Caleb wore red shorts, white and green striped Montrails, a yellow tank top. The seventeen members of the Happy Trails Running Club and their coach stood together in front of the lodge. Mack greeted them with great solemnity. This time, rather than shout his Whitman with joy, he spoke softly, slowly, with a rich resonance in his voice and an honesty in his eyes.

"'O secret of the earth and sky. O winding creeks and rivers! Of you O woods and fields! Of you strong mountains of my land! O clouds! O rain and snows! O day and night, passage to you! I in perfect health begin, hoping to cease not till death. Underfoot the divine soil, overhead the sun.'"

He nodded solemnly to each of them in turn.

Then he turned and they began to jog up a snaking service road to the opening of Big Oak Flat Road. A yellow banner strung between branches of black oak signified the start. The swelling crowd mingled there uneasily. Each had numbers written on their foreheads and shirts with black marker. A white ABC Sports van with a satellite on its roof was parked in the campgrounds lot. A reporter for the Outdoor Network stood by her own van, speaking into a camera. Light fog filtered through the trees, simultaneously enticing and foreboding.

The buzz of anxious runners swarmed over the field like mosquitoes, irritating Caleb considerably. Why can't they listen to the energy all around them, he wondered?

"I've been working all winter for this," a wiry woman said to Caleb, laughing, "and now I don't want to do it."

Caleb did not respond. Around him he heard the names of leading ultrarunners. The other name he heard everywhere was Steve Brzenski, whose death from a broken back had ended this event years ago.

Caleb inhaled hard, and jumped up and down. It did not matter whether it rained. It did not matter which elite runners were here. It did not matter whether someone had died. Caleb was not running against rain or Scott Jurek or the park. He was running into himself. He stood still, arms dangling at his sides. Later, Kevin Yu would say that the absence of his usual focus was obvious. But that morning, everyone had been concerned with his own race.

Barry Strong began speaking through his bullhorn, but it was hard to care about anything he said. In the sky a pink wave appeared like the wake of oncoming jets, revealing the distant peak of El Capitan rubbing against the belly of the sky.

He did not hear the gunshot. He just felt the crowd surge tentatively into the forest. Caleb shouldered past other runners, wove in and out until he was out front on the hard-packed dirt of Big Oak Flat Road. He should not be running this fast, he understood, but he had to get himself some space.

As Caleb disappeared into the park, Scott Jurek gestured at him, shaking his head. Someone else said that they would pass him heaving over a rock by Crane Creek.

Caleb, of course, never heard them.

• • • • • • •

At ten o'clock that morning, Shane dismantled his lab.

His golf shirt stuck to his back like a desperate lover as he bent over the open cardboard boxes, which lay everywhere, tops flapping like hungry birds.

He had told himself he had no time for melancholy. He double-checked each box to make certain the right equipment was returned to the right company. Microscopes and Bunsen burners, beakers, corks, the stuff he had ignored in middle school, now forever symbols of his life's greatest risk.

He dumped the large bottles of media into the double sinks. The petri dishes full of multiplying black miracle spores he tossed into the garbage can. He did discover an emotional attachment to the chairs he had assembled in December and decided to leave them for whoever was renting the lab next.

But the gloves and droppers, the big computers, the cables, went into cardboard boxes, which he assembled one by one with packing tape and an X-ACTO knife. He stacked the boxes outside in the hall by all the other closed doors, like a freshman expelled from college. UPS was supposed to be picking it all up in an hour.

Except for the cooler. Fifty milligrams of Prajuk's humanized drug in small glass vials rested contentedly in a styrofoam nest inside, chilling at a perfect 51.7 degrees.

"It's seventy degrees outside," Prajuk had explained, his voice high and slow. "The solution must be kept cold. You cannot be stuck in traffic."

Shane agreed, feeling extremely off-balance. "I'll blast the AC."

He rode the freight elevator down, carrying the cooler in his arms. It was more difficult than he had anticipated. Heavy, awkward, slippery, it was difficult to maintain a proper grip. He was breathing hard and felt unwell. The six months of worry and stress, that someone at Helixia would find out about the lab, of ignoring Janelle and Nicholas, of underperformance at work, over if what they were doing here would work, and Caleb not returning his calls, had all been far too much. It had launched an attack upon his systems. His sinuses throbbed, and he felt the stirrings of fever.

He desperately wanted to wipe the sweat dripping down his forehead as he stepped out into the bright day. Trying to get a better handle on the styrofoam, he blinked into the parking lot sun ricocheting off a dozen windshields.

Who was that, he squinted, leaning on his car?

"Hey," Shane said as he approached.

A thin man with short blond hair was watching him, affecting friendliness. "You're Shane Oberest?"

Shane's fingers squeezed the cooler.

"Can you get off my car?"

The thin man pushed himself off the Civic and walked right up to him, violating norms, Shane thought, of personal space.

"What are you doing up there, guy?"

In this sun he couldn't quite see the man's expression, but his voice was tinged with acid.

"Excuse me," Shane said, pushing past him.

The man grabbed his shoulder, and Shane whirled around, his fingers slipping down the cooler. Sunlight careened off the myriad of car mirrors, creating the effect of being inside of a moving marble.

"Do you know who I am?" the man asked.

"I have no idea."

"Jon Benatti. From Helixia."

The name struck Shane as somewhat important.

"I'm Deputy Director of Science. You're in a lot of trouble, boss."

"You want to let go of me now."

Benatti considered him and then took his hand away, and pointed at the building behind him. "You've got stolen property up there."

"What are you talking about?"

Benatti's voice rose. "You took a protein from our gene library. One of our centrifuges. God knows what else. Whatever's in that box belongs to Helixia."

Shane stared at him in disbelief. “It’s medicine for a baby.”

“Give it to me.”

There was no choice at all. He shouldered Benatti hard, knocking him backward, and started for the passenger door. He balanced the cooler on his left knee, found his keys in his pocket, and pressed his keypad. He slipped the fingers of his right hand out from underneath the cooler to lift the trunk.

He felt the contact just after he registered the rush of wind, and the peculiar energy of a human being in full motion. The ugly feel of Benatti’s bony body against him. The horror of the cooler slipping out of his hand, falling onto the parking lot blacktop, the styrofoam top flying off.

The sickening sound of the vials spilling onto the ground, the cracking of glass, and the sudden spilling of liquid.

9

The trail wove through the forest like fine brown thread. Caleb scanned the ground for rocks, loose roots, the occasional yellow lizard, anything that might trip him. Small bright birds darted out of the foliage, and red-tailed hawks floated above as if covering the race for ABC.

His stride was metronomic. His feet hit the earth lightly on their balls, regardless of whether he was leaping over a rock, or hit an unexpected dip in the ground. His breathing was perfect, his spine straight as pipe. A great confidence enveloped him; he had reached the point in his run where the cells of the body bind with those of the trees.

The first aid station came at Tuolumne Grove. A gray-haired official yawned in a chair behind a fold-up table. Plastic bowls of M&M's, energy gels, and bananas sat on the table; a cooler lay underneath. Hank was waiting for him beside the table. Hank was a huge live-music guy, always grabbing people for a run up to Catacombs, one of the happier and most helpful of the house. Caleb always blew by the first aid station, he knew, so he had prepared himself to start running as soon as he saw him cantering close. But surprisingly, Caleb stopped at the tent, grabbed a bottle of Powerade, and sat in a folding chair.

Other runners ran by for a bottle of water and back to the course; some didn't stop at all.

Hank took a tentative step toward him, his hand held out, as if about to touch a wound, when suddenly Caleb snapped his brown and earthy eyes open. He took the time to pour a salt packet into his sports drink. Then he stood and nodded, and they ran back onto the trail.

Hank ran out in front. He knew his role was to slow Caleb down, keep him from burning out. But Caleb never challenged him. In fact, turning around at one point, Hank had seen Caleb almost fifty yards behind him.

The course corkscrewed into a series of stunning ascents along narrow mining trails that had been closed for half a century. A yard to Caleb's left, the cliff dropped straight down to a canyon. On his right rose a solid wall of large pink-sheened granite rippling with blue veins. Rae had been right, of course; injury here would be fatal.

Eventually, they wound down into a canyon. With utter amazement, Hank watched Caleb run this stretch with his eyes fluttering closed.

Then he screamed.

Caleb whipped his head around. Hank was leaning against an oak, clutching his ankle, looking at the bottom of his sneaker.

"What?"

"Fucking acorn," he said in a calmer voice, sweat pouring from his crew-cut head. "Let's just go."

Later, Hank told Mack that he had been surprised by his ability to keep up with Caleb. They hit Jacob's Furnace just before noon, a shelf of exposed dark rock seven thousand feet in the air, under the burning midday sun. Caleb drained the last bottle of water in his pack and walked across the shelf trail. A wide stream circled below, taunting him with cool water to dive into. After a brutal hour he discovered himself at the top of a breathtaking gorge. Happily he watched hawks flying underneath him.

"Beautiful, right?" Hank smiled. "What a course."

Alice was waiting to replace Hank at the next aid station. She handed Caleb a banana, and took off with him into the afternoon. The course flags marked a path down to a fast-moving stream. White caps gurgled where its water met the rocks. No rope line had been fixed; this was either a major oversight by Barry and Mack, or their first hint of just how dangerous this race would become.

Alice looked around. "No good," she muttered.

Caleb waded into the water; immediately its force shoved him downstream. This was the answer. Rather than expend energy fighting the current, he let it push him like commuters exiting a subway as he walked, and crossed on a sharp diagonal, reaching the opposite bank two hundred yards downstream.

Alice followed him, but by the time she made it across, he was already disappearing into the distance, his long legs loping over the slippery gray rocks. Alice tried to pace him, but she was small, with stout legs, and when Caleb leapt like a palomino over a fallen stump, it was difficult for her to match him. Five miles in, she fell forever behind.

The light in the park turned a godly green. Prisms shone through the pine. Night, Caleb saw, was coming. At the Antibes aid station there was no one from Happy Trails waiting to meet him. Caleb found his drop bag, retaped his feet, put on a GoLite shell, fresh sneakers, and clipped a black rubber flashlight to his waist. He drank two cups of chicken broth, filled his water bottle, and left by himself.

Somewhere near Tamarack Flat, Caleb understood he had left the course. His eyes tried to adjust, but it was such a perfect blackness that he could not see the roots, rocks, or the steepness of the inclines. He stopped, enraptured by the woods around him. Above he saw a crescent moon among an initial gathering of stars. The world ahead felt like black water; Caleb imagined he could push his arms through it and swim upward, break the surface, and arrive somewhere entirely new.

In his peripheral vision he could make out pale purple silhouettes of sequoias, like pillars holding up Heaven. He stuck out a hand and stroked one; a tree that had stood here since Plato. In each of these trees, millions of insects were birthed, lived, mated, died, none aware that he was off of his trail, off his course. He felt he had it made it somewhere he had always guessed existed. He might wander in any direction, encounter any magic.

Caleb swept his flashlight around him, trying to find the small blue glow sticks that marked the course. He caught only the bizarre depths of nature, no less mysterious than space. In the distance—he hoped it was the distance—he heard the howl of something doglike.

And then, at last, his flashlight revealed a cluster of five blue glow sticks, removed from the trail and grouped together with definite intent. He closed his eyes thankfully.

When he opened them again, June was standing in front of him.

The moonlight bathed her face in alabaster. Caleb kissed her, stroked the back of her head.

"Okay," he whispered, and they turned into the backcountry.

PART FOUR

Ultrathon

1

Caleb and June wove through an impossible density of forest.

Between the redwoods, oaks, and underbrush, no moonlight availed itself to them. He found June's fingers in the dark and squeezed them. It was necessary to take her hand here, to protect her, and himself. It had been so long since he had touched her. A well of emotion rose through him and nearly burst. But he did not have time to nurture it.

Pine needles scratched their eyes, thorns scraped their thighs. As dangerous as it was to run blindly through the night, Caleb knew they had to hold off on using his flashlight until they were farther away from the aid tent and the hundred runners making their agonized way through the darkness. No one could see any beam of light bounding away from the course.

They were headed toward a parallel trail that Caleb had seen on one of Mack's blown-up maps. It was a popular hiking trail tourists strode with digital cameras and bottles of purified water. This wide, smooth trail would take them along easier ground and merge with a wider path back to Big Oak

Flat. Search and Rescue would never think to look for them here, and any tourists who might remember them would be sleeping now. They had until the park opened in the morning to get out. Which, Caleb estimated, gave them around eight hours. This was significantly less time than it had taken him to reach this point, but the trail would be significantly faster than the insane demands of the course.

But now, in the backcountry, they were in acute danger, intruders upon the natural order. There were cliffs. There was water. There were animals.

During the drive from Boulder, when Mack had stayed behind in Elko, Caleb had run beside her.

"June," he had started. "Can you listen to me?"

When she had turned to him, tears were forming in her eyes.

She had told him what had happened inside of Mack's room. Caleb had suspected this for years.

"He said he wants Lily to start early. If he wants her to start running marathons when she's six, what will he want her to do when she's thirteen? Do what all these other women do? I don't like how he's *seeing* her."

"We can get to Shane," he'd whispered, "from Yosemite."

At the weigh-in, while Mack worked the crowd and the press, he had seen her standing near John. On the way back to the lodge, he had been able to whisper a plan.

As Mack had instructed, June would run the first leg. Feigning injury, she would volunteer to work the isolated Antibes aid station, where Caleb guessed he would be when darkness fell. He planned to arrive there alone, rested. While she waited, she would gather blue course markers and cluster them at the first small clearing off the trail she could find.

Walk half a mile into the woods. And then she would listen for his footsteps in the forest.

Somewhere after midnight, the trail dipped drastically, and he knew they could not dare to run blind any longer. He switched on the flashlight clipped to his waist, let go of her hand, and they began moving faster.

By this time, Caleb knew, he would have failed to check into the next aid station. Word would be out that he was lost or hurt at night. With communications so poor, Mack might not hear of it for an hour. Then Mack and Barry Strong would begin frantically plotting to keep this from ABC's reporters. Or, he considered, seeing drama for the cameras, perhaps plot to involve them. Either way, Yosemite Search and Rescue would not begin operations until first light of dawn. And then, they would be searching for one man, hurt, confused. They would have heard the story of him falling off of Engineer Mountain, of training too long and hard, and look for him to be in a similar situation. They would have no idea to look for a couple running confidently the other way, along the easy trail out of the park.

But when Mack learned that June and Lily were also missing, he would understand it all, and his fury would be boundless.

He heard a noise, something heavy and deep. A bear, was his first thought. June froze mid run and looked to him. He unclipped the flashlight and waved it in circles above his head and shouted a roar of his own. They heard another sound, clearly alive, but moving away from them. After some time they started jogging again through the trees.

Finally, they broke through the dense woods and met a

dirt road. This was the trail he had found on the map. At least he hoped it was. Otherwise they might go off in the wrong direction, daylight would come, the park staff would be alerted to find them, and it would all end badly.

In the thin light of the stars Caleb could see a hand-painted, arrow-shaped sign pointing toward famous vistas. June fished through her pocket for some energy gels, which they swallowed as the widening trail made a grand turn, revealing a waterfall. He was lost in its churning aural symphony when they heard the engine.

He pulled June off the path into the dark forest. Headlights appeared fifty yards in front of him. The park rangers had the authority to hold them; he supposed they could be forceful.

Squatting in the wood he could feel his body slowing down dangerously, and he knew June's must be too. A green Jeep approached slowly. As with a bear, it seemed wise not to look it in the eye. When it finally passed, he retched. He had finished his water hours ago, his kidneys could fail any time. It was one thing to run an ultra, where every aid station held the promise of pacers and sustenance. It was another to run like this unaided.

They moved wordlessly along the dark trail under the clouds and the moon. Only the sounds of their breaths, deep and steady. Only the sounds of their soles against the dirt. Only the sounds of nearby animals and insects. Only the sounds of the real world, far from man. For hours Caleb moved through this sweet path, in a light sweat, June in perfect rhythm beside him.

Some hours later the trail hardened to pavement. The sky ahead threatened to lighten. June touched his arm and pointed to a sign. In the sliver of moonlight, he saw they were at the lodge.

"Stay here," she whispered.

Caleb found a grove of laurels on the far side of the road and slid to the ground; his palms grazed fallen acorns. He had a vivid dream about an old client. Then he snapped his eyes open in fear; how long had he been out? He was about to go inside when he saw June emerge from the old lodge with Lily perched atop her shoulders in their purple hiking backpack. When they met on the wide paved road June handed him a bottle of water, and he chugged it dry.

"What did you tell the woman watching her?" he whispered, wiping his chin.

"That I wanted my baby. She was half asleep anyway."

"We better hurry." He reached for the purple pack's thick black padded straps. "I'll take her."

June knelt, and Caleb slid the backpack onto his shoulders. He snapped the plastic harness around his waist, tugged it good and tight. Lily's arms and legs dangled freely above and behind him. He could feel them moving. He shifted his stance, adjusting to its weight. He guessed the pack, with the baby, was around twenty-eight pounds. He had run with heavier packs, but there was no anticipating this living weight, which moved and shifted and pulled playfully at the tops of his ears.

June had also brought a small yellow nylon backpack filled with minimal clothing, things for Lily, and cash that Mack had given her to buy baby food during the drive from Boulder. She slipped it over her shoulders, and they turned onto Big Oak Flat Road.

It was a race now, he thought. Either the sun would come

and reveal them like prisoners in a searchlight, or they would get to town, where no one would distinguish them from any other backpacking family. From there they would call Shane to come get them. They passed RVs and campers, heard the first stirrings of morning, and slowed to a fast walk, lest they attract any attention. A mile farther, Caleb spotted the entrance to the park. A booth stood beside the road. A ranger sat inside, ready to begin collecting fees and handing out maps. And the sky turned pink.

Already cars waited in a short line to get inside, engines idling, spewing exhaust into the trees. Caleb swallowed. It had been six or eight hours since they had disappeared from the race. He supposed word could be out among every park employee.

They waited awkwardly while Caleb tried to think. An SUV drove up, its window began to lower, and the ranger stuck his hand out for money.

Caleb took June's wrist and led her around the other side of the booth. Nobody called after them.

They walked onto the blacktop of what a sign told them was Evergreen Road. They picked up their pace, surrounded by the mountains and the sky. Caleb reached up and behind him, and squeezed one of Lily's ankles. She tapped the top of his head. The day broke open.

• • • • • • •

Evergreen Road curved like an undecided thought.

They jogged along its shoulder, staying clear of a sudden and endless drop on their right. Caleb guessed it was sixty degrees out here, perfect weather for a run. Lily was strapped comfortably into her padded Kelty, wearing a warm fleece hoodie, her beautiful blond-red head supported by a built-in neck rest. She seemed as comfortable as could be, even more, he thought, than in the car seat in the van.

Cars, RVs, buses, motorcycles, SUVs, all sped past across the road from them toward Yosemite. They stopped after a while to take Lily from her pack, stretch her legs, change her. Some hands waved from passing cars, and Caleb and June waved back, friendly, smiling, nothing wrong here.

They passed an ancient gas station, and a mile farther, the first shops of a town. Evergreen turned into a main street. It must, he thought, be called Groveland, for Caleb saw its name everywhere: Groveland Sweet Shoppe, Groveland Souvenirs, the same Ansel Adams posters in every window. On their left, small triangular ranch buildings stood like good neighbors, home to car-insurance and realtor offices. One of them held the Groveland Mini-Mart.

June helped him slide off the Kelty pack. She lifted Lily out and hugged her madly. The baby seemed in good spirits.

"I'll get food," June offered.

Down the street Caleb spotted a pale yellow building with white painted balconies, like something out of New Orleans. An old-world sign hung in front: THE GROVELAND HOTEL.

Caleb gestured, panting. "I'll tell Shane we're here."

He was feeling better, he considered, than he had any right to. Though his neck felt stiff, his shoulders and knees had handled the backpack nicely. He could wait here for hours, no problem. Certainly Mack would not expect to discover them in the lobby of a hotel.

Inside an elderly man stood behind a long front desk.

Caleb tried to smile patiently. "Excuse me? Where are your pay phones?"

The old man looked at him quizzically. Whether it was because of his appearance, or smell, or the oddness of the question, Caleb could see he had done something unwise.

"Ain't had a pay phone in years. Don't you got a phone?"

"I lost my cell," Caleb tried. "Do you have a phone I can use?"

The man exhaled and handed him a black cordless phone from under the desk. Caleb swallowed and dialed information.

"San Francisco. Shane Oberest," he responded to the automated question.

After a moment, a human voice clicked on. "I have one Shane Oberest in San Francisco, California. On one hundred twenty-two Bay Street?"

"That's great."

"I'll connect you now."

Caleb gripped the phone tight, heard its distant ringing. He pictured Shane walking across a room, his own baby in his arms. He might need time to get to his phone. A woman's voice answered, but it too had been recorded: "You've reached Shane, Janelle, and Nicholas. Please leave us a message."

Caleb shut his eyes tight. He had not anticipated this.

In an even voice he explained, "Hi. It's Caleb. I'm with June and Lily. We're in Yosemite, in a town called Groveland. At the Groveland Hotel. I'm wondering if you can get us. I'll call you back in a bit. Thanks." After a beat he added, "Love you."

Hanging up, he smiled at the man. "Thanks."

Caleb walked back out into the warming morning, rubbing his temples. He saw June on a bench in the sun, poking through a white plastic bag. Sitting beside her, he kissed Lily, who was chewing a banana, and tore into a burrito and Powerade.

June frowned. "I forgot napkins. I'll be right back."

She handed him Lily, a plastic spoon, a cup of applesauce, and walked back to the Mini-Mart. She took the two steps, pulled open the wood door, made her way to the register. She was smiling, prepared to shrug and explain her reappearance to the clerk, but someone else was already there. A thin middle-aged park ranger, with short black hair under her tan hat, leaned against the counter.

". . . having this crazy race. Up the old trails, all around the park. We're so pissed off about it I can't tell you. They said people was gonna get hurt, lost, we're going to be in and out trying to find them."

"What was a baby doing there?"

June took a step back, into the aisle. Panic spread throughout her body like an anaphylactic reaction.

The ranger was shaking her head sadly, "I guess it was part of this weird group. This guy who's in charge of them came to the main station and notified Emilio. Emilio said he was saying that two of his people have a sick little baby, and that they left the race to go to San Francisco or something. He was really concerned. They just took off with no money or food with this sick baby. Can you believe people?"

"Sick, how kind of sick?"

"Emilio said the guy just said that she isn't being taken care of right, and these two people aren't in their proper minds, and that we should find them right away. So we're all looking for them now. And that's on top of twenty of these idiots being took to the hospital. A bunch got lost in there, got a couple of broken ankles. Puking all over themselves. Now I got to drive around by the bus stop looking for this loony family. I tell you I'll be back here this evening for some of that wine."

June walked quickly back outside, down Main Street, to the bench.

"Oh God, Caley," she whispered into his ear as she bent over him.

Caleb listened to her, still as stone.

"He *told* them that," she almost shrieked when she had finished.

He looked at her. A ranger, a police officer, would see their dusty hair, dirty faces, the scratches along their forearms from the backcountry branches, the pallor of Lily's skin. Things might not progress well from there.

Caleb calmly stood up and unzipped June's yellow backpack. He found sunscreen and gently rubbed it into Lily's soft face and throat and neck and shoulders. Circles of dirt appeared over her cheeks; it must have been his fingers. He took out a soft white sun hat and tied it under her chin.

"Did you hear me?"

He fit Lily snugly into the purple pack and slipped it back over his shoulders, adjusted his weight, and snapped the belt around his waist. He blinked into the sun.

Then he started to run.

.... 2

Shane stood in their narrow kitchen, sweat running down his forearms, and began removing the contents of their open refrigerator.

He looked at the eggs, leftover pho, bacon, and milk at his feet, trying to judge which of them possessed some intrinsic right to stay.

"What are you doing?"

Janelle surprised him; he nearly jumped. He'd thought she was out for the afternoon with Nicholas. He turned to face her. She wore a thin black raincoat for the May drizzle, house keys still grasped in her right hand, Nicholas napping in his plastic bucket seat behind her.

"Close the front door?" he asked her quickly.

"Shane . . ."

"If the doorbell rings, don't answer it." He blinked rapidly. "Or the phone."

Janelle stepped closer, looking at the food on the floor, its condensation pooled on the tile like the blood of a mass murder. She arched her eyebrows questioningly. Shane steeled himself and pointed to the styrofoam cooler propping the refrigerator door open.

"It's the medicine."

Janelle hesitated, processing. Then she stepped backward. "Oh, Jesus."

"It's not body parts, for God's sake."

"You really did it." She repeated to herself quietly. "You really did it."

"I just need to hold this here for a few days."

"Hold it here? You sound like a coke dealer." She came closer, peering at the cooler. "Why can't I answer our phone?"

"Because," he offered helplessly.

"You want to elaborate?"

"Because Helixia found out. They know everything. They sent some asshole, he tried to take it."

Janelle's eyes narrowed furiously. He was fairly certain he had never seen this look in them before. "Who?"

"Jon Benatti? He knocked the cooler out of my hands. Some of the vials broke."

"They what?"

"I just need time to find a medical storage facility for what's left. These have to stay at fifty-one degrees until then. I found the temperature control on the fridge." He pointed, nodding. "It's inside the door."

And then, as if some biblical demon had suddenly abandoned her, Janelle pulled off her black raincoat, let it fall, and knelt beside the cooler. She pulled off its styrofoam top with a squeak. The vials emitted a smell like contact lens fluid. She ran her hands along a row of vials.

"They're cracked," she agreed.

Shane joined her on his knees and pushed the glass aside.

"The layers underneath look okay. But there might be some microscopic cracks. I don't know."

Janelle opened a cabinet above the sink and found a large glass mixing bowl. She began wiping each vial with a tissue, and inspecting it, holding the tissue to the light. If it was dry, she wrapped that vial carefully and placed it delicately into the bowl.

He joined her. They worked together quietly, checking the small vials with red stoppers and transferring the surviving ones from the cooler into the bowl. For the first time in months, Shane felt the sense of entwinement, and when his hand grazed hers she allowed him to linger.

"Twenty-one," Janelle counted, when the cooler was empty.

"I got twenty-two."

"Trust me, it's twenty-one." She wiped her forehead with the back of her hand. "How many did you guys make?"

"Forty."

In a gentler voice, she asked, "How many do you need?"

"If it works? She'll need two shots a year."

"So, there's enough to last until she's forty-three."

"That's not enough."

"No," she agreed, "it isn't."

"The world," Shane told her, "will have to get on it by then."

From the living room Nicholas broke into a full cry, and they each tensed.

"I told you something like this was going to happen," she whispered.

"You did."

"You did it anyway."

"Look, I just have to get this to Caleb. Then it's all over."

"How are you doing that?"

Shane shook his head in frustration. "I can't reach him."

"Why not?"

"He stopped working at that store, and he's not answering any letters. I think I should drive it to Boulder, explain to him how to store it."

"Jon Benatti?" she shook her head. "I can't believe that little douchebag."

"I almost put him through a windshield."

"Calm down. You're shaking."

Shane sat in a kitchen chair and pushed his hand through his hair. "You can't ever see things coming."

"It's all right."

Shane sighed deeply. He had never, he realized, felt this exhausted.

"I'll get Nicholas," Janelle said quietly, and left the room.

He heard her speaking gently to the baby, carrying him upstairs, singing sweetly into his ear. Shane took deep breaths, trying to find the comfort his son was feeling just hearing her voice. It was not, he saw, forthcoming.

....

The souvenir shops faded away, leaving only sugar pines along the sides of the road.

The road took a stunning sweep into the Sierras, during which Caleb almost forgot to count his breaths, or to recite his affirmations, almost forgot about the weight of Lily on his shoulders. He was lost in the curves and turns, the undulating ascents and descents over sheer granite, the mountain wall on his left and the rolling green mountain fields below him on his right. The energy he took from them was real and wonderful. It was so different from the blankness of the void. Running out here was like being plugged directly into the inner workings of it all. He felt alive and untethered to the earth.

Every so often a car would pass them from the other direction, headed toward Yosemite. So far only a handful had passed on their side. Each made June grab his arm and squeeze, for they knew no drivers were expecting to encounter them on the narrow shoulder. They could be hit or run off the road ridiculously easily. But at least none were police cars. They should hit the next town soon, Caleb thought, and then June could rest and he could try Shane again.

Some miles later the land flattened out and the green hills turned into hay-colored marsh. The geography out here was so new to him; he supposed he had never seen anything like it. The highway was sun-bleached, faded and forgotten. They found themselves in an almost lunar landscape of bare red clay, spotted with occasional green shrubs as if a bored road worker had lazily tossed them there. The light, undulating road reminded him of sound waves.

In the middle of this, June gripped his wrist hard.

He looked to her.

"I need to stop."

He could feel Lily in the backpack above him, playing with the ends of his hair. "No, breathe with the air."

"I don't think I can go anymore."

"You have to. Let go. Smile at the sky."

A halting hour passed. They moved in perfect solitude. But June began limping noticeably, holding her side. Caleb could see the energy dripping out of her and onto the gray road. They slowed to a walk, and he took her hand.

"You can do it," he told her. "We can't be far."

And then a noise gathered from the distance. It reminded him of something, a thing he had heard before, a rumble of sound, increasing, accelerating. And suddenly their mountain road was cut off by an explosion of eighteen wheelers coughing black spray, speeding SUVs, small cars whipping past them, blurs of color, deafening sound, a horrid thickening of the air. Lily burst out crying. Caleb stopped, his chest heaving, body dripping sweat, staring unbelievingly as they faced the onslaught of Interstate 120. It shot across their quiet road on a brutal and unforgiving diagonal, cutting them off.

There was no way across.

June bent over, panting. Above him, the baby was unhappy.

Caleb exercised a deep squat, and June took her from the backpack and sat down on the last patch of gray earth with her. She stroked Lily's head as she rummaged through her yellow pack. Caleb watched the thunder of the interstate, hands on his hips. He turned as June found a jar of baby-food peas and popped it open. Bugs emerged abruptly from everywhere. The smell was so thick that he became nauseated.

"The shortest distance to the next town has to be along the shoulder."

June shook her head, feeding Lily, who was quiet now. "We can't be on the shoulder of that thing. Everyone driving by will see us. They're going to think our car broke down and call the police for help. We're not even a town away."

Caleb worked through what would certainly happen: the police would find that they matched exactly the description of the couple being searched for in Yosemite, unfit parents who had wandered off from a strange group from Colorado without proper food or clothing. Lily would be turned over to Protective Services, examined by an overworked local doctor who wouldn't stop to think about genetic malfunctions. They would place her in foster care. Who knows how long they would keep her? He saw what Mack had done by telling the rangers about their lives. The simple truth was enough to punish them in the harshest possible manner.

"Hold on." In his voice he detected a scratch of panic. "I'll run up the highway, find a phone, and call Shane. You stay here with Lily and rest. I'll be fine. By myself I look like a guy taking a jog."

"You don't look anything like that," she informed him.

Caleb squinted into the noxious haze. To the right of the interstate there were dense woods. Caleb stepped closer, saw something there. A few yards into them, a narrow path had been beaten by road workers and littered with candy-bar wrappers, cigarette butts, soda cans. It was separated from the interstate by a thin curtain of brush and trees.

A semi exploded past, and its sound sent Lily into tears.

"Take her with you," June told him as the baby cried loudly.

"What?"

"I'm not keeping her out here in the open, where police could see us, in this heat. With these trucks. She needs milk and shade."

June began pulling the rest of the money, the blue fleece pullover Lily had worn at night in the van, a bottle, diapers, a stained white sun hat out of her yellow pack, and began shoving them into the big Kelty.

Caleb was still confused. "What about you?"

"I need time to rest. I'll be fine."

June's breaths shook her whole body. She changed the baby, kissed her ten times, and buckled her back into the backpack.

Caleb stretched his back, lifted the backpack, and nodded. "We'll be back for you in an hour."

"Don't come back."

Caleb stared at her.

"I'll hitch there. Don't bring my baby back to this place."

"I'm not leaving you here in the *woods*." His frustration was mounting. His body was slowing down, and once it crashed there would be no restarting it.

"Just go to the first exit you see," June cried. "Go to the first place to get food. Call Shane. I'll meet you there."

"No, we could get confused."

"You can't miss the first place at the first exit. Sit in a window booth. Let her sleep. I'll see you in there."

Caleb looked around helplessly, staring at the speeding trucks in front of him, the trees to his right, the hot sky above, as if beseeching them for answers. From above him Lily started crying again.

"Take my daughter out of here."

Caleb shook his head no.

"*Go!*" June shouted at him.

And without another word, he started into the woods.

............3

In the lobby no security guards pounced on him.

Riding the elevator Monday morning, Shane suffered visions of the entire Commercial Department turning to watch him walk through the hall like a high school kid caught with contraband. But then he blinked and saw Stacey tossing him her baseball as if nothing had happened. During that short ride, Shane seemed to exist in a world where a dozen different realities existed simultaneously; all he had to do was pick the one he liked most.

He got off on the executive floor and started down to Dennis's office. Dennis's assistant Danielle saw him approaching, she picked up her headset and called someone, her voice intentionally muffled, her brown eyes darting to him as he arrived. For his part, Shane stood with his hands clasped behind his back, studying a bright painting of a horse on the brick wall.

Some minutes later, Tonya Jackson, a large woman from Human Resources in a bright purple suit, and a slight young man who was clearly of the legal profession, walked into

Dennis's office. The door closed behind them. Some minutes passed. Shane spent them considering all the places he might take Nicholas this spring: a Giants game, music in the park. It would be great fun, he thought, to be a real dad, present. Then Danielle nodded for him to go inside.

As Shane entered the office he recalled his interview, just less than a year earlier. As before, Dennis sat, his torso towering above his desk, the gray hair over the young face, the Scottish black brows, his blue eyes as warm as ever.

He greeted him in his deep baritone. "Shane."

"Hi, Dennis," Shane replied breezily, returning the kind vibe.

Dennis sighed. "I'm really miserably disappointed."

"I'm right there with you."

"Can you please explain this to me? What were you guys doing?"

"I was doing some pro bono work after hours. It didn't affect my work here in any way."

"You asked me. You asked Dineesh. You even asked Anthony. And we all told you no."

"You told me not to apply for an orphan grant. And I didn't. What I do on my own time should not be a company concern. It doesn't impact the company in any way."

Dennis sat straight, his eyebrows arching. "You took a patented protein from our lab and cloned it. That's not acting as a private citizen, that's theft." He took an audible breath. "Unless, is that postdoc exaggerating?"

"Depends," Shane said, "on what he's saying."

Dennis rumbled, "He's a prick."

"We can agree on that."

"Jon brought him in to talk. And as soon as he was finished telling us about you and Prajuk Acharn, do you know what he did?"

"What?"

"He asked for a job."

Shane smiled. "Really? He did that?"

Dennis shook his head in disbelief, and for a moment they almost shared a laugh. The moment passed. "Jon told him we don't have any postdoc positions available. And the kid said then he wouldn't give an affidavit about what you guys were doing." Dennis rubbed a large hand through his thick gray hair. "Do you know why?"

"I don't."

"Because he doesn't want to hurt his *reputation.* He says no one will hire a postdoc they can't trust."

"Smart kid."

Dennis's eyes darted to the others, who sat together on a tan couch behind Shane like spectators at a ball game.

Tonya spoke.

"Did you and Doctor Prajuk Acharn isolate, clone, and humanize a therapeutic IgE antibody patented by Helixia?"

"I'm fired, right?" Shane asked Dennis.

"You were fired Friday."

Shane nodded. "I did some of those things. But I worked alone. I asked Doctor Acharn a bunch of questions, tricked him kind of. He didn't know what I was doing. As for the antibody, I can assure you that no protein created at this company was used for the purpose for which it has been patented."

He watched Dennis's dark eyebrows arch curiously at that.

From behind him the lawyer interjected angrily, "You

removed a vector with patented material from our premises and copied it."

"I broke no law."

"You broke corporate policy."

"That," Shane agreed, "may be a different matter."

Dennis leaned forward, watching him intently. "Your postdoc said you're giving what you made to a baby?"

"He's all 'roided out. It's messing with his brain."

"You mentioned a baby to me, and to Anthony. A baby you knew."

A security guard appeared in the doorway.

"Hey, Jose," Shane nodded to him.

"Shane," he replied uncomfortably.

"What about Prajuk?" Shane asked them.

Tonya Jackson took that one. "Doctor Acharn is one of our most important scientists, and a trusted colleague of Steven Poulos."

A cool stream of relief flooded his chest. He turned back to Dennis. "I really loved working here. I think you guys are geniuses."

"It sounds like you've seen counsel. Whoever you saw, make sure you get even better."

Tanya stood and handed him a manila folder full of documents and began to speak about the immediate termination of all benefits. When she finished, Jose followed him out of the room.

"Sorry, but I got to escort you straight out the building."

"Sure." Shane headed down to the lobby. Standing by the elevator, he smiled. "I've got a picture of my family on my desk."

"I'll get it to you, man."

Shane shook Jose's hand and walked into the cool day. He got into his car and without a second's pause drove out of the lot, past the McDonald's where Prajuk had first told him about closed and open doors, the Thai Orchid, where he had snuck quick dinners with Janelle before they were married. He took the short road to Greenway Plaza, stopped in the lot he had grown to love, and called her. He realized with a sharp pain deep in his side that he had just obliterated any chance she had of ever going back to her job.

She picked up frantically. "Why haven't you answered your phone?"

"I had it off during my . . ." It hit him then. "What happened to Nicholas?"

"Caleb's here."

He sat up straight, as some force lurched from the ground and slammed into his body.

"Put him on."

"Not here in the house. He's up in Yosemite."

"Yosemite Park?" Shane squeezed his eyes closed, trying to orient himself.

"He wants you to get him. He's at a hotel. The Groveland Hotel."

"You spoke to him?"

Janelle took an audible breath; in it Shane could feel her attempt to stay calm. "No, he left a message. He's with that woman, and her baby."

Shane's head spun, his arm felt numb, things in front of him seemed to slow drastically.

"I called the number but whoever answered didn't know who he was."

"When he calls back, give him my cell. I'm on my way there. I love you."

He screeched out of the lot, and took the 101 as fast as the old car would handle. How long was it to Yosemite? He had friends who'd gone up for camping weekends, and it seemed to him that they had said it was three or four hours. He would be fighting daytime traffic, trucks, and tolls to the East Bay. Then it should open up.

But at the Bay Bridge he slowed to a crawl, alternately gunning the engine and braking. It was afternoon, he clenched his jaw; no one should be going anywhere. Who were all of these people, not to be in their offices and homes?

Shane punched his steering wheel as the car stood still on the Bay Bridge, hovering vulnerably over the waving water.

• • • • • • •

In the woods the humidity jumped; he feared ticks and small snakes, tripping over tree roots, and branches that might scratch Lily's face.

He kept only a thin curtain of trees and brush between him and the highway, so that he was always just a few steps away. It would be a horrible thing to be lost in these mountains.

He walked quickly on this slight path for over an hour. At a certain point, he acclimated to the humidity and realized that the air felt fresh and full of pine. And he began to enjoy himself. The plants and leaves slipped off their coats, revealing a single, vibrating, golden energy. Caleb felt the forest rooting for them.

He reached up and back, and held Lily's dangling hand, as

he made his way along the workmen's trail. Later the ground sloped abruptly, and he met the concrete barrier of a curving off-ramp. A truck took it slowly, and Caleb peered over it. Below, he saw a cluster of gas stations, fast-food signs, and cars. He guessed they had gone four or five miles.

"Okay, Lulu," he said cheerfully, "let's get you some milk."

A steep decline like this was worrisome with his tired quads. If he slipped he would fall with her face unprotected. Caleb moved deliberately. At the bottom of the ramp, he found himself suddenly amidst the world. The first place with food, he repeated to himself. He passed two gas stations next to each other on the left side of the street. Did those count? No, she had meant a place you could sit. Across the street, he saw a small truck stop diner.

He stopped outside of it, on a concrete parking area. He slid off the pack, balanced it carefully on its three poles, and lifted Lily out. He kissed her strawberry hair, stuck to her sweating forehead.

"Let's go," he told her.

Inside the diner the intensity of the air conditioning, the smell of the grease, the sudden noise, launched his body into a kind of shock. Caleb moved uncertainly to the back counter and sat Lily on it, and himself on a stool in front of her, as sweat poured from his body onto the floor.

"Can I have a glass of milk, and some water, please?"

A middle-aged waitress nodded without looking up.

"And do you have a phone?"

She shook her head no. "There's one at the Mobil."

The waitress set a tall, chipped red plastic glass of cold milk onto the counter with a crack that made Caleb snap his head up. Caleb poured it into Lily's bottle and placed it into her wide, grasping hands. His senses heightened to the point of abstraction: colors lifted from the truckers' plaid shirts, swirled in the air. Outside the window, a nuclear bomb irradiated the county; it took him a moment to appreciate this as the noon sun. He slammed a full glass of metallic tap water, reached over the counter to a small metal pitcher, refilled it, and drank it down again.

"What can we get you?" the waitress asked, looking at him and Lily more closely.

"Bananas. Pancakes. Applesauce," he said, hoping June had given him enough money to pay for it. "Do you have a bathroom?"

"Over there."

He carried Lily to a plastic changing station and checked her diaper. It was wet. This was good, it meant she was still somewhat hydrated. Changing her, she batted at him like a kitten, her eyes playful, her lips happy. June was right, it would be madness to take her back into the woods. All that mattered was getting her to San Francisco, and whatever treatment Shane had waiting for her. June could hitch or walk here when she was ready. In the meantime he would get Shane going.

When the food came he held Lily on his lap, fed her, and ate while she played a game of pushing pink packets of sugar around the sticky countertop. Then he filled her bottle with cold milk and rummaged through the backpack for the cash which June had shoved into it. He found a bunch of crumpled tens, twenties, and singles, paid, and took a glass of icewater with him to the door to find that pay phone.

Outside, country and hip-hop played in tandem from the idling trucks. The sun blasted his eyes. His head hurt, he had eaten too much sugar too quickly, had too much rest. He stood staring at the trucks, black exhaust, loud diesel engines, pickups, neon signs, fast-food smells, gas stations, insanity—he felt it all pressing in on him. It was not safe here, he realized, among this plowed and destroyed earth. His eyes madly sought the trees. But they were far away, across the busy street, up in the hills. He felt that his body was about to collapse. Then, without an ice bath, he would go into shock. What would happen to the baby? There was no way that he could wait here for hours for June or Shane. His plan, he saw, was fatally flawed.

What was he supposed to do? The carbohydrates and potassium shook his systems, his liver needed to know whether to produce more glycogen, his body needed to know if he was running or stopping? He was sixty or so miles into this run, just warming up. And he had learned one thing, one thing with absolute certainty during his life: when in doubt, the answer was always to run.

Behind the gas station, Caleb noticed a narrow road leading away from the noise of trucks and people. It seemed to run parallel to the choked highway. He hesitated, confused at the progression of his thoughts. June would understand, he knew, as soon as she saw they were not at the diner, that he had needed to keep moving. A shaking began at the bottom of his tailbone and wormed up his spine. Here was the moment, move or fall. Here was the pivotal decision. Sit and wait for them, and possibly the police, to find him here? Or continue forward?

He doused Lily's sun hat with water from the red glass and tied it under her throat. He found the sunscreen and applied it liberally onto her skin. With a kiss he buckled her in.

"You all right, Lulu?" he called up as he pulled on the Kelty. He was rewarded with a playful tap upon his sunburned head.

Caleb started across the four-lane street, holding his hand up to slow approaching vehicles. He walked along the side of the gas station and began to jog the small brown road. Ahead he saw tanned hills dotted with Holsteins. He made cow sounds; Lily giggled and tried, he thought, to copy him. The movement was magic; his energy was back. Things, it seemed, were in their proper motion. Twisting rust-colored manzanitas splayed at his ankles as he pushed into a jog. He reached behind and tugged on her small ankle. What was Lily experiencing up there? It must feel like flying; he supposed it must be wonderful.

Caleb began to tell her fairy tales. Whatever he could remember of Little Red Riding Hood, Hansel and Gretel. But some these were frightening stories and not good for being so close to the woods.

Soon Lily fell asleep, he could tell by the way her weight slumped against his shoulders. Some hours later, the single-lane road widened, and traffic grew heavier. To his west he saw the outskirts of what looked to be a small city, and passed a blue sign. It read OAKDALE, 14 MILES.

The sky was turning violet, the weather was finally cooling. He felt they both needed to eat, and he wanted to change and hold her. He wondered if he looked normal enough to walk into a store.

Caleb slowed to a walk, let his breathing normalize, the sweat dry on his skin, and turned toward town. Sensing some change, Lily awoke crying. He felt her tiny arms pound the sides of the pack.

"Lulu," he called to her cheerily, "good evening to you."

In a convenience store parking lot he stopped. Removing her from the backpack Caleb noticed an annular patch of sunburn on her smooth shoulder; he must have missed it when applying sunblock. He kissed her damp hair and carried her inside in his arms.

He purchased cans of protein shake and pasta, baby food, a plastic tube of aloe. There were, he saw, a few big hills left. Outside he blinked into the emerging streetlights and saw a taupe Holiday Inn a few blocks away, lit brightly against the blackening sky. A bench had been placed under plastic palms and an orange heat lamp. A bellhop in a tan uniform watched them walk across the street.

"Waiting for my wife," Caleb explained, sitting on the bench.

He did not, he realized, look like a man waiting for his wife. He looked like a man who had been running for thirty-six hours. But Lily prohibited the bellhop's more obvious conclusions, and he looked away.

Caleb pulled off her shorts and diaper, fumbled through the back pocket of the Kelty for wipes, and cleaned her. He put on her blue fleece, fed her, and rubbed aloe along her sunburn.

"Cay Cay," she smiled, her one tooth protruding from her lower gum like some optimistic flag.

He held her wheezing chest to his. "We're going to get you better," he whispered into her perfect ear.

Caleb emptied packets of salt into the protein shakes and killed them in one long sip each. Then he took stock of his position. Possibly he should go inside this hotel and call

Shane, but the same issues he faced at that diner would assault him here. His running was going well, and anyway he was too tired to speak clearly. He laid Lily on the bench, her head on his lap under the heat lamp, leaned back against the wood, and dropped into a dense sleep.

Sometime later someone shook his shoulder.

"My man."

Caleb sat straight up, blinking. His mouth was dry. A Latino guy with a shaved head and strong breath was glaring at him.

"You been here like two *hours.*"

"She's sleeping," Caleb whispered, forcing his eyes open. His neck was stiff.

"What room you in?"

He blinked rapidly. What was his story again?

"If you ain't a guest here you got to move on, bro."

The man walked back inside. Caleb could see him talking to an older man with an earpiece. A cold panic shot through him.

Lily was sound asleep. It was the middle of the night, and red lights blinked in pitch blackness. A black Jeep squealed alongside them. Its doors were thrown open, and Kyle and Juan jumped out. They grabbed his arms, pulled them inside. Mack turned from the driver's seat, screaming.

Caleb almost fell off of the bench, and the shock snapped him out of this hallucination. He blinked, breathing hard. They must be out here looking for him, he realized. Gently he slipped Lily's sleeping body back into the Kelty pack, rolled up a T-shirt and placed it behind her neck for support, lifted the thirty-odd pounds over his shoulders, and clicked the plastic belt shut. Feeling a sour panic, he turned off of the main avenue onto a small street filled with aluminum houses. He read a street sign in the starlight and saw that by an act of karma he was on Yosemite Avenue.

The power nap had worked magic though; he felt recharged and able. If he had stayed in the Yosemite Slam, he would be scaling El Capitan now, he thought. It seemed a comparatively easy thing to run across these gentle dark hills, following the shadow of the distant interstate, beneath the silence of the stars.

But what about Lily? He considered the generations of babies who had survived hard passages into America. Who had been packed for months among tubercular émigrés on suffocating Irish ships. Who had been carried across the Sonoran Desert under raging heat. Who had been baked alive on Cuban rafts, laid among blankets crawling with boll weevils. Who had been frozen in open wagons, kept below deck on rancid boats, on their way to America.

These babies survived, grew strong, and all of them had made it without the benefit of a specially designed child backpack. Lily might get uncomfortable, and if so he would stop and help her. But she was would be fine.

As the weight of the pack pressed warmly into his shoulders, he could feel her slowly blending into him. Which was no hallucination, he understood.

Because, in fact, she was.

4

June sat on a small patch of land by the freeway.

She practiced a sitting meditation. Hearing Mack's voice guide her through each organ and muscle of her body made her feel sick so she replaced it with her own. She began feeling better. The pain in her side was subsiding. After a few hours, she considered the six-lane interstate in front of her.

Caleb would have arrived at the next exit by now. He would have taken care of Lily, found food, and then borrowed someone's cell and called his brother. They were waiting patiently in some Burger King booth for her, she imagined. That Caleb had stumbled, had fallen ill, had broken some limb or punctured some organ, did not occur to her. Lily was in the best arms in this world. June felt an unsustainable urge to get to them, and the more she envisioned Lily, the more insistent this need became.

She stood, tried taking a step toward the speeding cars, and extended her arm for a ride.

A small white truck slowed; she did not appreciate the appearance of its driver and shook him off. She kept walking, afraid to try to run. Her hand, she realized, was pressed against her side in anticipation of more pain. Perhaps a kidney was infected; if so, it would not take any more stress. And then an old blue Explorer paused and its passenger window lowered.

An older woman with long gray hair called to her. "Hey. You all right?"

The first time June answered her throat was too dry and no sound came out. She gathered herself and tried again. "Car's broke."

"Come on in here."

June drew a long breath and pulled the door open. She noticed a steel coffee mug in her cup holder. Her radio was tuned to slick country music of the sort Todd liked. It felt safe, she thought, in here. As June sat down she watched the woman pull back abruptly. Her smell, June understood.

"Are you hurt, honey?"

"No. Just, you know, really tired."

The smell of coffee, leather, the bounce of the wheels, she feared she might vomit. A vivid vision of Arizona overcame her, her brothers shooting targets in the desert, surprisingly sharp and defined.

"You sure about that?"

June smiled. "Our car had trouble. I just need to get to the next exit."

The woman nodded and drove forward. She signaled at the first offramp. June saw two gas stations, and a small truckers' diner. Some rigs were parked outside. She gazed at its concrete step, as if she recognized something there.

"My family's waiting for me inside," June told her, pointing to the diner.

The woman's face broke open with relief. "Oh, great."

"Thank you for the ride. You're awesome," June smiled, stepping out slowly.

When the car drove away, June hesitated. She wanted to take a minute to calm down, to appear strong, to get herself together before Lily saw her. But she ran to the door as fast as she could, pulled it open, and burst inside.

• • • • • • •

Janelle heard the phone from the baby's room. She had been replacing the soft lightbulb in the little blue lamp on the dresser. The noon light dappled the copper mobile above her. She had purchased it in Berkeley on a happy Saturday in her first trimester, and it always filled her with the joy of those giddy and expectant months.

"Is Shane there?" a woman asked in a painfully soft voice. "Shane Oberest?"

"This is his wife," Janelle stated, her voice rising as if asking a question. Over the phone she could hear murmurs of voices and distant music.

The woman asked urgently, "How is Lily?"

Janelle frowned. "June?"

"Yes. How are they?"

Janelle took a long breath, steadying herself against the dresser. She could feel this woman's anxiety across the ether. "So Shane's on his way to get you guys," she explained, her hands raising up to calm her.

"They're not *with* him?"

"June, I'm sorry. With him?"

"Lily and Caleb, aren't they with Shane? Driving?"

"Caleb left a message that you're at the Groveland Hotel?"

"No," June sobbed. "No. That was before."

All of Janelle's years as a manager flooded back through her body, and she turned very serious. Her voice dropped a full octave. "Where are you? Ask someone exactly where you are."

After some mumbled conversation, June answered with an address. Janelle went downstairs to the computer and checked.

"That's between Groveland and Oakdale. It's okay, it's right on Shane's way. He's almost there. It'll just be an hour or so." She paused. "But Caleb and your baby? You don't know where they are?"

"Oh, God." Janelle heard her say to herself. "They're still running."

• • • • • • •

Dawn unveiled a painting, pinks and grays, oranges and whites, masterly mist over brown tallgrass. It seemed a thing of glory. Far in the distance he squinted and made out a red barn. If ever there was such a place as America, Caleb thought, it was here.

Caleb was jogging through farmland. He stepped off of the curving road into a field of wild rye and brome. It was almost certainly owned by the occupants of the barn, who he hoped were still asleep. He knelt, slipped off the pack, and gently lifted Lily out into his arms. She was just waking up, and her warmth cheered his heart. But each breath she inhaled released the high-pitched scratch of metal upon glass. After all this time it still unnerved him.

He spread her arms and attempted some rudimentary reiki in the damp grass. Afterward he rubbed her swollen feet. Then he nuzzled against her until she laughed.

His own feet had swollen as well, and rubbed disconcertingly against the filthy fabric of his sneakers. The sides of them were raw. He would need to wash them soon, he saw; infection seemed imminent.

But he was proud of his night run; he had managed his hallucinations well, ignored roads that lifted without warning into the sky. He felt like he had finished another leg of a race. It was time to take a moment. He found a bruised banana in the pack and peeled it for Lily. She grabbed it in both her tiny hands, and he watched her enjoy it on the grassland.

By a fence he saw a hose. He took a risk and turned it on and cleaned his feet. Then he doused his shirt and washed Lily gently with it, dabbing at her peach and pink cheeks. He filled both of their bottles, and then they rejoined the country road.

In every ultramarathon he had ever run, he had enjoyed the benefit of pacers and stocked aid stations; it seemed an entirely different thing to be running unsupported. But of course he wasn't unsupported, he realized. He had this beautiful little girl.

He had thought that he had been carrying her to safety, but in fact, he understood, the opposite was true. It was Lily's fingertips brushing the back of his neck, her tugging of his ears, her energy seeping into his shoulders, that was propelling them onward. She was the fuel for it all.

The sun swelled against the sky. He scanned the countryside. Clouds, he saw, might not be forthcoming. In the increasing heat, wild mood swings descended on him. For miles he felt nearly superhuman, and then suddenly it would all crash down upon him, and he would slow to a pained walk and begin to cry. He ran like this, swinging from confidence to terror, under a fiery sun which lit the world with hues of orange in the millions and beyond.

Caleb stopped, hands on his hips, when he saw the animal.

At first he thought it was a wolverine. It was the size of a small dog, possessed of a long cracked snout over thin black lips and sharp teeth. Desperate coal eyes, mangy charcoal fur missing patches in clusters that looked torn out. A smell reached him, thick and hot and wrong.

The animal blocked their path. Stared right at them. Frozen there, Caleb thought that his own unwashed stench must make him seem like an equal, to be fought and eaten. Above him he sensed Lily stiffen. He raised his hands up to make himself appear bigger. But doing this exposed his chest and throat and he felt this was not wise. Then the animal lunged.

And he recognized Potter.

Oh, Caleb began to cry, where have you been?

Potter, the Oberest family dog, had been brought home from a shelter by Julie on the occasion of her fortieth birthday, but almost instantly she had become Caleb's. Coming back from a run with his father through the misty Issaquah roads, Caleb would emit some pheromone that bade the dog straight to him. Potter had slept on his bed, greeted him at the school bus, followed him around the small house, arousing Shane's jealousy in the bargain. Caleb had last seen her on a winter morning during eleventh grade when, after school, Julie had picked Caleb up in their station wagon, tears in her eyes.

"Lulu," he cried, "Lulu, look! It's Potter!"

Potter jumped up and put her paws onto Caleb's belly, then abruptly darted playfully off into the tallgrass. Caleb ran after her at a full sprint, as Lily grabbed his hair, shrieking with joy.

Finally the dog trotted beside him, slowing him down. And Caleb understood: Potter was pacing him. Ecstatic, Caleb began to tell Lily stories. How much Potter loved the snow, about the time she chased Shane's school bus halfway into town. In the far distance, he could see a mammoth parking lot and a Walmart against the brown hills.

He glanced down to Potter, who wagged her tail, flattened her ears, and pulled away from what turned out to be the outskirts of La Jolla. He followed his dog across the field to a lushness of Monterey and Foxtail pines. Coyote brush. Tarweed. White-throated sparrows. Goldfinches. The swirling world.

• • • • • • •

As Shane drove he searched for an isolated figure on the shoulder of the highway, wearing a tall purple backpack.

He couldn't conceive of what Janelle had told him. Caleb would be crazy to run here with a baby. The heat and exhaust from the blacktop would choke them. A sudden swerve from one of these SUVs would run them down. Was he crazy? This seemed to be the major question of his past ten years.

According to his GPS, the diner June was waiting in should be a straight line from his current position, maybe two more hours. But in the real world, this ridiculous highway curved and swung, west, then north, madness. All the while the Sierras rose on the horizon, gray and otherworldly.

Discomfort and anxiety pressed upon him. His phone

could ring at any second. Janelle, police, hospitals might be on the other end, with news he could not bear. All his life he had known only self-confidence, like his father, like his brother. Try as he might, he no longer felt confident of anything at all.

Just after seven in the evening he pulled onto the gravel by a truck stop diner just northeast of Oakdale. Shane saw her right away, sitting in a front booth. She wore a filthy tank top, and black running shorts. Her face was skin stretched over bone, her hair knotted and wild. Dust streaked her cheeks. He remembered her large eyes, so blue they were nearly white.

"Hi," he smiled, sliding into the booth opposite her.

A dirty plate and an empty plastic water glass sat in front of her. He could smell her from across the table.

"I had to eat," she explained softly, embarrassed, "but I don't have money."

"Don't worry, I got it. Do you want anything else?"

"Can we just go?"

"Sure."

He ordered a large takeaway coffee. It came in a styrofoam cup, as in the pre-Starbucks days. Ahead the sky was dark and limitless; he felt as if he had traveled light years. When June got into the car, he offered her mints from his glove compartment and lowered the windows.

"So, how did you get separated?" he asked, starting the engine.

June shook her head. "I just couldn't run anymore."

"He didn't wait for you?"

"He probably did, for a while. But he must have had to move. Once you start shutting down, you can't stop it. He knows his body. He probably just started toward the next town."

"You don't think he hitched a ride?"

"Caleb?" she smiled. "He's not asking anybody for a ride."

Shane found his phone and dialed 911. As it rang he realized he had never called it before; he wasn't sure what to expect.

"What's your emergency?" a deep-voiced Latina woman asked.

"My brother is lost."

"How old is the child, sir?"

"No, he's not a child. He's forty-three."

"Sir?"

"He has," Shane explained, "a baby with him."

June grabbed his hand, shaking her head wildly.

"No," she said frantically, her breath raw, "you can't call them."

He pulled his arm away, narrowing his eyes.

"How long has your brother been missing?"

This, Shane felt, was a good question.

"Around six hours."

"You'll need to contact your local police when it's been twenty-four hours."

"Hold on, I'm sorry." He kept his eyes on June, she kept shaking her head no. "Okay, I'll do that. Thank you, Officer."

Hanging up, he looked quizzically at her.

"We have to avoid the police," she told him, loud and exasperated.

"Why," he asked, stunned, "would we do that? They'll help us find them. They have cars, radios."

June explained what she had heard at the store, what Mack had told the rangers, what Caleb had explained would happen to Lily should the police take them in. Shane looked at her. It did not seem like a preposterous fear.

They would see Caleb after thirty-six hours of running, and Lily, pale and undersized and wheezing. They would find out that they were not father and daughter. They would listen to Caleb explain that he was running to San Francisco. And they would call in Child and Family Services without a second thought.

"Okay, so you think he's in the next rest area?"

"Well, either that or he kept going."

"Kept going? To where?"

"You."

"To my house?" Shane asked incredulously.

She nodded yes.

His frustration overflowed. "Caleb's not a superhero, okay? He can't run two hundred miles with a baby."

"Yes he can," she explained. "This is what he does."

"But things go wrong in these ultramarathons, don't they? Everyone who starts plans on finishing, but sometimes they don't."

"Please," she whispered, "he has my daughter."

Shane looked out the dark window, shaking his head. "I didn't see them on the highway."

"He wouldn't be on a highway."

"That's the shortest route."

"He'd be where he feels safe."

"Where is that?"

"In the mountains."

"Well, we're not going to drive through there," Shane gestured at the wilderness frustratedly.

"On the small roads," June nodded. "That's where they are."

Shane left the diner lot and pulled onto a smaller road that seemed to run parallel to the highway. This seemed to be what Caleb would have done. He moved slowly, thinking how senseless it was to imagine that they would just stumble upon them.

For the next hours they scoured the pitch-black road. Two hours turned to three, four. He found his way back to the highway and drove to another strip of fast food for coffee, but it was his fear that kept him awake. Next to him June's eyes strained, finding hope in every shadow, seizing it with an audible intake of breath, and then dropping it in pain.

They spoke very little; somehow the silence felt necessary. But somewhere near Stockton he felt a desperate need to connect, to stay awake if nothing else.

"So what's it like?" he asked her.

"What?" she replied, the exhaustion leaking from her voice.

"To run like this?"

An unexpected blissful expression took over her eyes. "It's beautiful."

"But you put yourself through all this pain?"

"Pain's not a problem. I mean, physical pain." She looked out her side window, speaking to herself. "The other kind of pain hurts more."

"What kind?"

"Being a mom."

Shane nodded.

"No one ever tells you how much it's going to hurt. They make it seem so perfect in those books," she said, her voice rising. "But when I'm listening to her try to breathe, watching her just try so hard to crawl, and laugh, and she smiles anyway? I've never respected anyone like that. She looks at me wheezing and I can't make her better. I'd rather run a thousand miles. I'd rather run Yosemite and break my back than go through one more second of not being able to help her." She turned her head from side to side in the manner, he thought, of an injured bird.

"I have a son," Shane reminded her by way of commiseration.

"Is he healthy?"

Shane put a hand on her shoulder. It felt to him like bone, and he pulled away. Embarrassed, he stared ahead at the amethyst sky, looking for shapes on the shoulders that might be his brother and her baby.

5

Light rain slipped from a crimson sun.

Caleb pushed himself across a road. Russet-colored cows speckled the hillsides, but none seemed to notice them. The rain refreshed him, though he worried the road would become slippery. He felt it ascending, felt his quads begin to burn. He noted with great relief that he needed to pee.

He stopped by a tree and pulled aside his begrimed shorts. The pain that came next made him shriek. An explosion of fire in his back and sides. What was this, he cried? He glanced down and saw that his urine was nearly solid. Chunks of matter pushed from him. He fell to his knees, swaying, Lily hovering in the pack above him. His kidneys were not functioning, he understood. If he did not drink water now, then his bladder would become infected. And this time there would not be Mack to heal him.

He opened his mouth desperately to drink in the light rain; in the distance a cluster of gray clouds promised more. But as he moved forward, he saw that these were not clouds at all, but mountains. He stared at the distant range in awe; with a shudder, he understood that he would have to run through them.

"Should we drop?" he whispered to Lily.

In seeming response, she slapped the top of his head.

More cars started to pass them along the road. A sign informed him that they were approaching a small city called Dublin. There would be motels there, he realized. He could call Shane, bathe them both in a cool tub, lay Lily out on a bed for a proper sleep. But fever awaited him there, he knew; his body would shut down completely, and he might not awaken for days. There was nothing but to keep going.

The light rain kept steady. As he ran, one of Mack's passages of Whitman came to him. He had always liked it, and so he recited it, but whether aloud or to himself he did not know.

"'Over the white and brown buckwheat, over the dusky green of the rye. Scaling mountains, pulling myself cautiously up, holding on by low scragged limbs. Carrying the crescent child. Storming, enjoying, planning, loving, cautioning, appearing and disappearing, I tread day and night such roads.'"

He whispered it again, and again, catching on the line about carrying the child, until the words lost meaning and only their sounds were left. He reached the final gas station before the mountains just before sunset. Pulling open its door, every smell was accentuated; the fake bread inside its plastic, the chemical Hefty bags, the detergents and the overripe fruit, overwhelmed him. A heavy-bellied man in a stained pine green golf shirt behind a counter stared over his glasses at him, his mouth opening.

By the microwave Caleb crouched down and used the sharp edge of a can opener to slice the outer sides of his sneakers. Immediately his swollen feet spilled out, a tremendous release.

He chugged a Powerade in the aisle, but his body responded too rapidly to the salt and corn syrup; his head spun, he went hypoglycemic. He rummaged through his backpack, trying to determine how much money he had left, but it all went blurry in his hands. It was difficult to grip any thought firmly in his mind now, other than his finish line, 122 Bay Street, San Francisco.

The man was watching him as if encountering something unholy.

"What you doing with that baby, man?"

"Please," Caleb rasped, dropping canned ravioli, milk, doughnuts, a pear, and two brownish bananas onto the counter.

"They's a shelter up on Conway." The man raised his eyes to Lily. Looking away, he said angrily, "You ain't need these doughnuts, man."

Then he swept his forearm over the rest of the goods, pushing them into a thin black plastic bag, and slid it across the counter to him, along with the money.

Caleb tried to thank him, backing out of his store to a bench. Outside he balanced the Kelty on its metal tripod legs, and sat Lily on his lap. He handed the pear to Lily by its stem, his fingers far too disgusting to touch it, and she held it and nibbled happily. When she was done, he ate its last bites, and turned and vomited it all onto the pavement.

Caleb glanced down at his infected shoulders. They bubbled wiht green pus where the pack's straps pressed into the skin. He saw what was left of his squalid sneakers. A nasty rash, scarlet blotches with white pinpricks, encircled Lily's upper legs like red ants. It would not be safe, he thought, to venture into any human contact from this point onward. When they had eaten, he changed Lily, deposited their waste into a trash can, and carried her across the street, into the trees. It would be wise to stay here in the shade. As he kissed Lily's cool forehead, his eyes were drawn up to the dusk sky. Soon the stars would come. They saw the whole field of play. They knew if Mack was still in Yosemite, or getting nearer to them, or back in Boulder, if there were police around them, if June was all right, if he was going in the right direction. Standing against an oak, he looked down. Kinetic energy was pouring from his body in long, golden lines. Dripping from his chakras, his forehead, the center of his chest, his groin, all over the ground.

When he looked up again, it was pitch night.

• • • • • • •

Shane woke to dirty sunlight.

It poured through the smeared windows of the room, filled with grease and dust. He rubbed his pounding temples.

On a single bed across from him, June lay face down. For a moment he thought she might be dead. She had not disturbed a single sheet. He forced himself to watch, and to his relief he saw her back rising and falling.

He went to the bathroom to wash out his mouth and use the shower. He returned feeling not much refreshed and shook June's shoulder. She sat up grimacing and touched her side. Her straw hair had gone crazy.

"Do you want some Advil?"

She shook her head. "I haven't taken anything toxic in a year."

"Some toxicity," he suggested, "may be necessary for survival in this world."

At a gas station, Shane stepped away from her and phoned Janelle. She answered on the first ring.

"I've called every shelter, hospital, and motel in between here and Yosemite," she told him, sounding exhausted. "They're not there."

"Caleb will call the house again."

"I've got the phone in my hand everywhere I go."

"Jesus," he yawned. "I slept for shit."

"Come home," she told him. "You're too tired to drive."

"I'm not," he lied.

"You'll get into an accident."

"I've been stopping to rest. I have to keep looking."

There was a long pause. "I know," Janelle told him.

The day seemed to promise haze. They drove silently near Modesto, its outlying farmland, straining their eyes for anything in the far distance resembling a human being.

"Can I ask you something personal?"

"Sure," June answered, "of course."

"What Caleb's doing, it seems like something you would only do for, you know."

He left his words dangling, but June did not respond.

"Is she his? Lily?"

June's face slipped gently into a smile, and she looked off wistfully into the distance. "I wish she was. I really do. He would be a great father. No, her dad is a bartender in Taos. He's not interested in her. But if you asked Lily who her dad is, she'd say Caley. When I came to Happy Trails, she was three weeks old, and he just took care of her from the first second."

"I've never seen Caleb take care of other people."

June watched him. She could see how much Caleb had grown to mean in his life, through his absence from it.

"How old is your son?"

Shane smiled. "Ten and a half months."

"Lily's almost fourteen. They can be friends."

He thought about this as he drove. This image of Caleb

living down the block, his adopted daughter and Nicholas growing up together as cousins, the family eating together every Sunday. It was a dream, he considered, realized by a nightmare.

"This kinetic energy?" he asked quietly.

"What about it?"

"Are Lily and Caleb giving it off right now?"

"Sure."

He gestured toward the windshield. "Can you focus on them? Like, pick it up?"

June frowned and shook her head. "That's what I've been trying, all this time. Every second." Her voice broke. "I can't *feel* them."

"It's okay," he replied quickly, sensing his question had pushed her someplace he did not want her to go. "Every car he sees has a cell phone, and he can stop any one of them."

She turned to him, nodding assuredly. "He's not stopping anyone. We're just on the wrong road."

Shane connected with her confidence. No matter how irrational, it gave him a certain degree of comfort. He noticed a sub shop across the street.

"Hungry?" he asked. "We're not going to find any perfectly balanced stew or anything. But you need to find something you can eat."

He took her inside and ordered for them both. He ate a sandwich and June picked at a salad, and they walked back toward the car. He stared at his Civic, which had accompanied him along his journey up the ladder at Orco, throughout the northern swath of the state, to thousands of medical practices, conferences, sales conventions.

If only, he prayed, it would only get him to his brother.

6

Bracketed by lights, the dark highway ascended straight up the mountain like a runway.

It possessed a wide shoulder; clearly it had been constructed to allow drivers some room to correct before plummeting to their deaths. This would provide them a little safe space, so long as a sleepy trucker did not run them off the edge.

"Okay. Lulu," he shouted, "lift off."

And he started up the steep incline under the flutter of a billion stars.

In the darkness 4x4s exploded past them like fireflies, small quick cars like lightning bugs. A large truck groaned by; from below them it had sounded like a wounded wolf. Caleb pushed a smile onto his face and forced himself upward. His quads and calves were engorged with blood to nearly twice their normal size. When he stopped and removed the backpack and reached for Lily, she pushed him away. She had never done anything like this before. He stood confused in the total blackness. Then he understood: it was his smell. It must be a baby's instinct to squirm away from a failing body.

His pain reached some new peak. Immediately he recognized it as different from any he had known before; he possessed no idea what to make of it.

As he moved forward, each step was its own war. His skin was so raw that the barest movement of his shorts and shirt felt like sandpaper. His shoulders bled where the straps tightened. His dry eyes ached from running against the air for three days. Everything from his feet to the tip of his nose was torn asunder. He felt frighteningly cold. Possibly his body had stopped producing rhodopsin; if that was the case, he thought, then he would soon go blind.

He felt as if he were being punished. But, he wondered, for what? For forcing himself off of his proper path, his father's voice explained. Fred appeared then beside him, it was just as it had been in those Issaquah days of his childhood. Only this time, he spoke.

"You have made a life that was not yours."

Caleb nodded. He understood. It was the truth, he knew. If he had never seen Mack's book, if he had just stayed in New York and continued with his life like most everybody else had, then certainly he would not be in the midst of this outrageous torture. Fred agreed.

Instead, he would have attended the 2001 InterFinancial Holiday Party at the Whitney Museum. There he would have been introduced to a colleague's roommate, Dania, a brunette psychology student. He would have felt an instant spark as their fingers brushed by the bar. A year later, he would have given up his apartment with the untouched Wolf stove and moved into her one-bedroom. And the following Christmas, at a Vermont inn filled with firelight, he would have proposed.

Shane and his new girlfriend Janelle would have been in their wedding. As the city recovered, and his bonuses exploded, Caleb would have bought a house in New Jersey. And they would have had two girls, with his thin brown hair and long, loping legs.

As he ran, these images pummeled him. No, he agreed, tear ducts swelling, he should not be running up this mountain in the dark; he should be in that warm house with his wife and their daughters. Look how happy they were, how they filled him each evening with awe. Oh God, he sobbed, what had he given up?

A new pain electrified him. It came from no muscle or joint, but it was worse than any he had ever known. It came from very deep inside and burned him as if his nerves were being set aflame. But he had been taught to never succumb to agony, to confront it, and so Caleb forced himself back to that peaceful house. He studied himself.

He had gained some weight. His body full of antibiotics for his recurring sinus infections. He watched himself put on some expensive but rarely used sneakers and begin to jog through the planned curves of his town. Three pathetic miles later, he was bent over, his lungs burning with lactic acid, tugging at his shorts. He felt that something had gone wrong, that some crucial thing had gone unnoticed, but he would never understand what it was. And he burst into tears, that would not stop, no matter how long he stayed hunched over on the street.

And watching this vision of himself, Caleb broke through the wall. With a rush of joy, he knew that had he stayed in this life that Fred had meant him to live, he would have died never understanding the source of his suffering. It would have been not the tearing of his tendons but of his being which would have tormented him to his last hours.

The road he was on right now was the correct one for him, he cried. After all, he had chosen wisely. The stars seemed to have receded while he was lost in this dream, and when he focused on the road again, he realized that his legs were no longer straining upward, but pushing against the blacktop as he moved downhill. In the distance he saw the dark shadows of a flatter plain.

He pulled off the backpack, lifted Lily out, and examined her as best he could in the darkness. Her diaper was damp, and she allowed him to stretch her legs and hold her, thank God. But it was time to end this.

Caleb settled the pack back onto the ruin of his shoulders; he began bleeding there directly. He clipped the waist belt shut and began walking down the final stretch of the mountain range, as the sky dialed back to a light gray of granite.

He saw houses then, emerging from the shadows. Small, close together, nestled in a valley. He could smell the ocean in the air.

And he understood that he was staring at the beginning of Oakland.

• • • • • • •

Shane awoke in agony.

His lower back ached. His neck had stiffened discomfortingly. He was in a terrible bed, in a roadside motel. He had trouble getting up to go to the bathroom, and something had begun to pulse above his right eye.

He went to the hallway outside the room and spoke with Janelle. When he returned, he stood in the doorway and stared at June.

"I need," he said quietly, "to stop for a while."

June seemed to look smaller, sitting up in her bed, pulling its thin bedspread against her chest. "Okay, sure. Of course." She hesitated, looking down at the same stained shirt she had been wearing for three days. "You want to stay here and rest while I look?"

"I need to go home."

"Home," she repeated.

"Food, a change of clothes, refuel. Caleb will call there. It's the best place for us to be."

June's face seemed to freeze. He watched her walk to the bathroom and shut the thin plastic door, heard the shower start. He closed his eyes, exhaling loudly. There was no right answer, that was the thing. Outside in the dusty morning sun the sight of his car filled him with dread. What he needed, he thought, were those beads that cab drivers sit on.

"I can drive," June told him.

He looked at her. Standing in a damp towel she seemed frailer than he had yet seen.

He smiled. "I got it. No worries."

He started down the same side roads, but they both understood that he was driving west. After two hours of silent motion, Shane saw his city rising up from the bay. The first mariners had built the initial houses by the docks, and the next wave had built theirs on top of those. The following settlers had wanted to live here so badly that they built even farther up the hills, creating this magic sweep of houses piled on houses like schoolchildren in a class picture.

Rain came as they crawled over the Bay Bridge. His wipers squeaked sadly against the glass, but they did not seem to cleanse anything. He drove around the Embarcadero into the Marina, parked on the corner of Bay, and led June up the front steps of their narrow blue house. Janelle was waiting in the doorway with some rice noodles and jasmine tea.

As she hugged June tightly, Shane watched her face. He could see she was repulsed by June's smell, and the feel of her body, and yet he watched her pull this woman in even closer.

"I've got clothes for you, honey, and a bath."

A flood of emotion washed over June's face. Janelle led her up to their bedroom, sat her on their bed, and stroked her hair.

"You guys are so nice," June told her in a voice like parchment.

Her voice sounded, Janelle thought, as if she had fractured both of her legs.

"Are you in pain?"

She nodded.

"Where?"

June began shaking wildly. Her teeth were chattering. Her eyes filled with tears. "I want my daughter."

Janelle watched helplessly. If she had lost Nicholas, she knew, she would have cracked much sooner than this. Outside the fog pushed past their front windows like a family of ghosts.

Shane and June slept through the afternoon. Janelle phoned her long list of local hospitals again, but none had seen Caleb and Lily. When Shane woke, she decided firmly, police were going to be called. She had given Caleb two days, and it sickened her that they had not enacted a full-force and professional search by now. She had picked up her phone to do this herself but hesitated. She felt the need of June's support; there were repercussions that she had not had the right to set off without warning. In the meantime, she took Nicholas for a walk down to Fort Mason, inhaling the damp air, until she felt ready to return home to whatever would happen next.

When Nicholas was asleep she sat on the couch, listening to the still sounds of the house. She must have fallen asleep somewhere around one. When she opened her eyes, Shane was sitting next to her, staring at the bay window. She smelled coffee, and him, and wrapped her arms around his neck.

"What time is it?" she asked.

Shane checked his phone. "Five." He leaned in and kissed her cheek. "I love you."

They stayed like that, arms around each other. When Nicholas cried, Shane was stunned to learn that a full hour had passed.

"I got him," he said, kissing her forehead.

Upstairs Shane glanced at their bedroom door. It was still shut. He changed the baby and brought him down to Janelle.

"I'll go get some muffins on the corner. Then I'm going to head back out."

"By yourself?"

"This is the first time June's slept more than four hours in a year. And when she wakes up, you can get out and do some stuff with Nicholas today instead of sitting by the house phone waiting for Caleb to call."

Janelle swallowed. "Listen, I almost called the police."

Shane nodded.

"It's time, for sure."

"Okay, I'll call now."

"I'll do it from the car."

"Take some water with you, some . . ."

They heard footsteps on the stairs and turned around. June was standing on the bottom step, thin and spectral, looking confused. He saw her lip tremble.

"I'm coming."

"I think . . ." And then Shane noticed a shadow upon their step.

Frowning, he set his coffee down and walked to the door, and opened it, and his brother fell into his arms.

............7

For a moment Shane felt himself sinking. A dull roar filled his ears like a swimmer being pulled underwater. Then he emerged, his head clear of the sea, and he realized that the baby was in the pack on his brother's shoulders.

He held Caleb with all of his might. His smell was unfathomable. His legs spasmed as if alive apart from him. June ran over, screaming, reaching upward for Lily.

The baby was crying loudly and pushed her arms out to her, her face bright red. June unbuckled her, pulled her out, and Caleb slipped down to the floor.

Shane was frozen. His wife was waiting for him to move, but it was stomach turning, the way Caleb's muscles were shaking inside his body. June knelt beside him, kissing his cheeks, Lily in her arms.

"Get them in the car," Janelle said.

But June clasped Lily to her chest, shaking her head.

"We're going to the ER."

"They'll take her."

"No one's going to take her away."

Shane caught his wife's eye. It was not, he shook his head subtly, out of the realm of possibility.

June explained, "Caley needs an ice bath. He needs one right now."

Janelle said clearly, "We'll take two cars."

Shane moved quickly. He took Caleb and Nicholas, and Janelle drove June and Lily. They moved up the steep hill of Van Ness. In the mirror, he saw Caleb's eyes closed. This did not seem good.

"Hey," he called.

His brother's brown eyes fluttered. His body shook immeasurably. Shane met Nicholas's happy eyes in the rearview mirror.

"Your uncle," Shane told him, "is out of his fucking mind."

At the hospital he was blindsided by melancholy; he had last visited here the day of Nicholas's birth, perhaps the happiest day of his life. He carried Caleb to the emergency room as Janelle took Nicholas, June, and Lily to the Children's Hospital across the street.

Inside, they sat in the crowded waiting area between a large Chinese family and an old ponytailed man who stank of something he placed as gin. Janelle texted a constant feed of updates: her mother was coming to take Nicholas home. Lily was being registered.

"Ice bath," Caleb repeated.

"Please be okay," Shane muttered. "Please don't go anywhere." This was the finest hospital in San Francisco, Shane told himself. There was no need to feel any panic. Still, he returned to the triage nurse, and explained Caleb's request.

"We have a gunshot victim," the nurse told him flatly.

Over the next hour, Caleb seemed to worsen. His muscles

stiffened and his breathing grew shallow. Finally, he was admitted to a bed. It was a small space, separated by stained green curtains from its neighbor, filled with clusters of wires, machines, the smell of pain and antiseptic. A new nurse brought in a thin faded hospital gown.

"Everything off. Tie this in the back."

Shane removed Caleb's disgusting rags. Underneath was a hell of welts around his waist from the pack's belt, sunburns along his arms and ribs, blisters and open sores all over his shoulders. He looked as if he had been tortured. Shane pulled off his shorts and saw Caleb's thighs, swollen and grotesque. Then he moved to his feet.

Shane jumped back.

They were all wrong. Gnarled, discolored, toes facing the wrong directions, absent of nails. The skin was black and scarlet. They were not even identifiable as feet. They were inhuman. He retched.

"Ice," Caleb slurred through cracked lips.

Shane sat him onto the bed and began to pull the gown around him. Jesus, he kept thinking, this body. What it was capable of. What it had been through.

"Hey, Caleb"—he tried to smile—"what do the losers of these races look like?"

The short nurse attached a heart monitor to his chest and began inserting IV lines into his forearms. When the needle touched his skin Caleb sat up and attempted to push himself off of the bed.

The nurse shot Shane a look of concern. "Please have him stop fighting."

"He needs an ice bath."

The nurse frowned. "He doesn't have a fever."

"That will stop his muscles from . . . look." He gestured to the convulsions in Caleb's body.

"You can ask the doctor," she informed him, opening and loudly closing the curtain behind her. After some time, a small physician swept them aside. He struck Shane as tired; in his eyes were long shifts of service.

"I'm Doctor Ong."

He began a cursory examination, pressing into Caleb's abdomen, listening to his chest.

"What happened here?"

"He ran an ultramarathon. Two hundred miles."

"Ice bath. Reiki," Caleb whispered weakly.

"We don't do reiki here. This is emergency medicine."

"He runs these all the time," Shane suggested. "He always does this ice bath."

"You can do that at home." Doctor Ong spoke seriously to Caleb. "Your heart rate's over one-forty. You're dehydrated. It's putting a strain on all of your organs. I'm going to order a CT and some blood work to check your heart, kidney, and liver function."

Caleb shook his head back and forth. He looked to Shane like an animal under threat. "No radiation."

Doctor Ong turned to Shane with a sudden force. "He needs to let us do our job."

"He will."

Abruptly, he left.

"Let them check you out," Shane said.

"I want to go home."

"What's one CAT scan, to make sure you're okay?"

"I have the right to leave here."

The nurse returned shortly, carrying a pill.

Shane squinted at it. "What's that?"

"It's to calm him down. Doctor Ong wants him to have it. I can put it into his IV," she whispered.

"It's up to him."

Caleb turned his head away. He's pushed his body like this for a decade, Shane thought. He knows what to do. But then he gazed at his brother's body and thought, maybe he has no idea.

He sat on a stained chair and attempted the conjuring of memories which might bind Caleb to him. Fred's Mariners obsession, the duck wallpaper in their kitchen, the time Potter ran into the woods for two days. When he mentioned Potter, Caleb smiled.

Then his phone rang, and Janelle's voice, one of his favorite sounds on this earth, came to him in the cramped room.

"How is Caleb?"

"He's a mess. But they're taking care of him. How's Lily?"

Janelle sighed. "She's lying on a cot with an IV in her. It's so hard to watch. She keeps saying 'cay cay.' June says that's Caleb."

"What are the doctors saying?"

"So, one doctor said babies are resilient, she's a little sunburned and a little sore, but she doesn't need to be admitted. They were going to let us go. But a few minutes ago, this other younger doctor came in. She's acting like we left Lily outside and went to a bar for a weekend. Her eyes," Janelle reported, "hold large quantities of anger."

"What's her deal?"

Janelle's voice was shaky. "She wants to know how she got

this dehydrated. I said my brother-in-law got lost on a hike, I didn't tell them it was a three-day run. June was right, they'd have called DCFS before I finished the sentence. She wants to do tests, but I don't see how they have anything to do with being dehydrated."

"What tests?"

"She's paging an eye doctor."

"Maybe she thinks her eyes got hurt in all that sun?"

"They want to x-ray her whole body."

Shane swallowed. "They what?" From over the phone, he heard Lily cry.

"What's wrong?"

Shane touch Caleb's shoulder. "You really took care of her. She's fine."

Caleb's eyes lightened.

"She's just pissed off." Janelle paused. "She's awesome."

Doctor Ong opened the curtain, accompanied by an unshaven resident and a thick-muscled Latino orderly.

"So, we're going to take him for his scans."

Caleb shook his head again. And then he swung his long legs over the side of the bed onto the linoleum floor. The resident gasped.

The orderly stepped forward, and Shane moved to block him; there was a second when violence seemed possible. Doctor Ong's expression communicated an exasperation that Shane felt deeply sorry for.

"If you refuse treatment, we are not responsible for the result, do you understand?"

"Yes," Caleb replied weakly, holding out his IV. "Please take this out."

"I'll need you to sign a document to that effect."

"Hey," Shane said softly to him, "you need to stay here."

"I'll sign."

"Well then," the doctor said to no one in particular, "discharge him."

"Hey, no," Shane said again.

"I know what to do," Caleb told him gently. "Trust me."

Slowly, the nurse bent to Caleb's arm and pulled out the plastic tubing of his IV line. No, Shane shook his head. He stepped outside to find Doctor Ong, the nurse, a hospital administrator, someone to stop this. Caleb dressed in what was left of his soiled clothes and limped out of the room. Moving past other green curtains, which hid other patients, he felt an obscene negative energy overtake him. He walked slowly back to the waiting area, his limbs shaking. Soon he would get his bath, more fluids, sleep. He decided it would be much better to wait for Shane outside, in the fresh air, under the healing sun.

He stepped through the hospital doors into the world. Caleb had never been in San Francisco before; immediately he could feel the sea-level oxygen, as rich as cream. The texture of this air, damp and rough with salt, surprised him. It was so different from the mountains. Behind light clouds a golden sun was beating, he could feel it soaking into his skin. He felt sanguine and alive. He was here. He had made it.

Running alongside the Arthur Breed Freeway, from the end of the mountain range into Oakland, had been a fever dream; he was still unsure what had been real and what was delirium. Drunk with hypoglycemia, he had woven nearly into the street. And then the Bay Bridge had risen like the hull of a battleship to a man in the water, offering rescue. Caleb had limped up its bike ramp and onto the swaying steel. At its summit, he had stared out over the water at San Francisco. A hill there possessed a beacon which appeared as if it had been placed there for them. He had started walking across the bike lane, suspended over the boats of the bay. Suddenly he had smelled black chemical smoke, heard police sirens, screaming. He froze, reaching up to take Lily's dangling feet. But then he had nodded, understanding; that had been another bridge, a different day. Now he was not running into chaos, but into safety.

In ultramarathons, Caleb was well aware, it was not uncommon to see runners collapsed within sight of the finish line. The agony on those runners' faces was one of the most horrible sights on earth.

And so Caleb had determined from the start never to visualize San Francisco as his finish line. He had focused only on an imaginary house called 122 Bay Street. And in the end, the moment he had seen that number on Shane's door, his mind had assumed victory and his body had ceased to function.

Yet now he felt kinetic energy surging through his exhausted legs. A warm sun caressed his shoulders, this rich air filled his chest, his blood returned oxygen to his starving cells. And the IV fluids had done quite a bit of good, he realized. Caleb felt a smile spreading over his face. Not one he forced on, not a Happy Trails smile, but a natural, primal joy with roots deep inside of him. In the distance he noticed a patch of blue water. The bay, he thought. He crossed the street, read a street sign for Ocean Beach. Oh, he whispered.

Caleb had not stood on sand nor seen the ocean in twelve

years. After all this time in the mountains, it would be wise, he knew, to feel the bottom of the continent.

As he walked downhill toward the beach, he missed the weight of Lily against his shoulders. He felt a melancholy, which was alleviated when he considered how soon he would see her. He believed he loved her as much as it was possible in the world.

Caleb walked slowly down to the waves. He felt the power of their energy immediately. As he stepped on the rocky sand, he could feel it washing his body clean. Now his pain was different; it was not a tearing, but a rejoining, of his tissues, of his cells. Even the cool salt air against his raw skin didn't hurt. All of that was behind him. He was connecting with something completely different now.

And then, instinctively, because it knew no other way, his body lurched forward, and he began to run. He broke Mack's rigid form. His spine was not straight, he landed on his heels, his face was turned up to the sun. He was looking out at the magnificent endless ocean, and, he laughed, his breath actually was blending with the air, he really was smiling with the sky. These were no longer just words, but facts.

As he moved he could feel the world melding with his molecules, there was no division between them any longer, no space at all, and so when he fell, and was distantly aware of the sand scratching against his knees, the saltwater filling his mouth, even while his body thrashed, he was still running.

8

He thought he might never stop sobbing. If it weren't for Janelle, he might never have left the hospital.

Shane moved through hours and days, met with whomever they had to meet, arranged for transport and accounting, worked with Fred over the phone on details. A mist followed them up to Washington. Staring out the airplane window holding Nicholas's small hand, Shane traced its long winding trail along the coastline. At the airport he introduced June and Lily to Fred and Julie, but they were all too overwhelmed to make much of an effort. All weekend, Fred maintained a stoicism that Shane believed could be punctured by a passing breeze. His mother, Julie, sat on the sofa, or on her bed, staring at nothing, and it made his heart break. No matter how many times he put his arm around her, tried to get her to speak, she gave only the most minimal response.

June held Lily at all times. She did not sleep. He could hear her at night, pacing downstairs. A house of zombies, Shane saw. That was what he had brought back from San Francisco.

June made a quiet plea for the scattering of his ashes along the trails that he had loved, but Shane shook his head.

"That's not going to happen."

"It's what he wants," she insisted.

"I know. But my mother wants him near her."

"He should be in Boulder, looking at the mountains."

"They think Boulder killed him."

June looked as if she had been slapped. "Boulder saved him. He told me, so many times."

"I know what killed him."

The service was small; Caleb had not stayed in touch with anyone here, and so Fred and Julie's friends had made up the majority of the guests. They stayed in Issaquah for three days, during which June fielded repetitive questions about Caleb's recent life. Fred and Julie eventually believed her when she explained that Caleb had been happy. If you could have seen him, she told them. But that had been the wrong thing to say.

And then, exhausted and with Nicholas showing symptoms of a cold, they flew back home.

The following morning, with no job to go to, Shane sat on the white couch. He was supposed to be watching the babies play on the rug, but his thoughts were far away. He had told June that he knew what killed Caleb. And it was true. It had been him.

By dangling a drug for Lily like bait, compelling him across mountains and heat, he had forced him to run himself to death.

And for what? Over time, Mack's healing might have begun working on Lily. Once she was old enough to raise her own kinetic energy levels, her body might have corrected itself. And she would have been raised in the Happy Trails Running Club.

She would have begun eating and running like them as soon as she was able. The people in that house might be exhausted, brainwashed into a cult of personality around Mack, might never be senior partners in a law firm, but they never worried about layoffs or what was in their food or what their houses were worth. They knew extreme physical pain, but they were taught to beat it. They were fulfilled and secure. They bathed in a boundless energy, enjoyed a connection to this world that Shane could barely conceive. Was this really something to take a child away from?

And if his drug worked? Then Lily would grow into some version of an American girl. She would not be taught to overcome suffering, but to indulge it. She would ignore the shimmering grass on her way to school, focused instead on what a classmate had posted online. She would exchange the power of kinetic energy for the stasis of car seats and couches. Walking along a street she would stare down at her phone, not ahead at the sky.

Had he helped her, or hurt her, by bringing her here, and taking away a man who loved her? What was the truth of that?

He heard Lily's wheezing from the floor, watched the stretching and reaching of her upper body for every breath. The idea of sitting on the vials in the refrigerator was beginning to derange him.

It took some hassle with the Greenbrae Medical Associates nurse to get Wenceslas to the phone. He was with a patient, his nurse explained. Finally he got on, sounding concerned. After some prodding, he agreed to stop by on his way home. Shane hung up, but did not move. The day passed slowly. There were some e-mails from Brad Whitmore recommending a labor attorney, but he did not act on them.

Shane ordered a dinner that he thought June might eat, vegetarian rolls, brown rice, tofu. He had been wrong; she would not touch any of it except the rice. At seven, the buzzer rang, and he opened the door to Wenceslas Chin.

"Hey, guys." Wenceslas's voice was a blend of lightheartedness and concern. "What's going on?"

He stood stout in his black suit and round glasses, a folded umbrella between his palms. Janelle handed him a peppery Shiraz and led him to the white sofa. As Shane told him everything, his face grew pale.

"He ran here from Yosemite?"

"Two hundred miles."

Janelle added, "Somehow he kept Lily safe the whole time."

"Who's Lily?"

"He had," Shane explained softly, "a baby with him."

Shane led him to the kitchen, where June was feeding the children. Nicholas sat in his high chair, Lily in the spare. Wenceslas looked at the strawberry blonde girl as she happily held a plastic cup.

"That wheeze, that's what you mean?"

Shane nodded.

Janelle spoke. "At the hospital they made us see an eye doctor. And they x-rayed her whole body."

"They were looking for abuse. In many abused babies, retinal hematomas are present. When they're shaken, or hit, damage is sustained behind the eye. The x-rays are to look for previous fractures."

"They didn't find anything."

"Why would they?" June asked her, shocked.

Wenceslas gestured to Shane, and they stepped out of the room. "Tell me about this drug."

Shane answered his science questions as best as he could. He tried to recall its precise enzymes, described the thrill of being allowed to look through the microscope at raw genetic matter, the building blocks of all. Wenceslas listened to him with a professional impassivity, but a clearly growing excitement soon revealed itself.

"You did what?" he asked several times.

When Shane was done, Wenceslas stared at him for a full minute.

"So it's in your refrigerator now?"

"Want to see it?"

Shane went back to the kitchen, opened the refrigerator door, and returned with one of the small vials. Wenceslas held it up to the lamp, as if attempting to divine its calibrations. He shut his eyes for a moment. Then he looked seriously at Shane.

"I can't let you give this to this baby."

Shane froze. "Sorry?"

"If you're really planning to administer this, I have to call Social Services."

"Oh, Wen. Don't."

"I don't have any idea what's in here."

"It's been tested. I told you. It might not work, but it won't hurt her. It's safe."

"They say Tylenol is safe, and it kills babies all the time."

Shane panicked. “Let me call Doctor Acharn. Let me just get him on the phone with you. I told him you’re coming. He knew you’d have concerns. He can answer your questions. Okay?”

He had his phone in his hand a second later.

“Prajuk, okay. It’s me.” Shane started. “My friend Doctor Chin is here. We’re about to . . . can you please talk to him?”

He handed the phone to Wenceslas. While he took the call, Shane considered the lab, the lawyers, the hospital, the FDA, Helixia. The forces at play here were too large to fight.

Thirty minutes later, Wenceslas walked inside and sat down beside him.

“So?” Shane asked him pleadingly.

“So, I told Doctor Acharn that I would read the research on the Airifan trials. That’s the most that I can do, Shane. He’s going to send me everything he has on this protein and what you did with your mouse. I was going to ask you to give the vials to me, but he feels they need to be temperature stable right now.” His eyes found Shane’s, and in them Shane could read different decisions being played out. “Promise you’ll wait until I go over this stuff. Promise me, Shane.”

“I promise.”

Janelle took Shane’s glass, swirled the wine roughly and drank.

“What do you think about this?” Wenceslas asked her.

“I think it needs FDA approval.”

To Shane’s surprise, Wenceslas cocked his head. “Why?”

She narrowed her eyes, confused.

“Unapproved medicines are given to children all the time.”

"No, they're not."

"I'm sure you know a few. Bear bile. Monkey claw?" He gave Janelle a knowing glance. "Chinatown doctors prescribe this stuff every day."

"That's different. Those have been proven over centuries."

"I saw echinacea in your kitchen. Echinacea is unapproved by the FDA. More than a few physicians think it causes liver damage. But it's on the shelf at every drug store, and in infant drops, by the way."

"Those are herbs. They're natural."

"Our drug," Shane informed them enthusiastically, "is natural."

"Natural herbs are as powerful as pharmaceuticals," Wenceslas added. "Anyway, it's not FDA approval I'm concerned with. There are thousands of drugs just like Shane's that are available without FDA approval."

"Where do you buy them, back alleys?" Janelle asked.

"Walgreens."

She stared at Wenceslas in disbelief. "They sell unapproved drugs at major pharmacies?"

"Every day."

"Where's the FDA in this?"

"Look, unapproved drugs are like illegal aliens. Does the government know about them? Sure. But there's way too many to stop them all. Some of them work well. And some approved drugs are killers. That's what I'm concerned about here. Knowing this will be safe. Safe and approved are two entirely different things."

"Read the Airifan research," Shane begged him.

Wenceslas stood. "You guys have been through a lot.

Please rest. I'll go over everything Doctor Acharn shares with me. I'm so sorry about your brother."

Janelle walked with him out to his car. Outside it was dark, and frigid. She couldn't help but imagine Lily and Caleb running in weather like this.

"How is he doing?" Wenceslas asked her.

"Not good."

"Yeah, he doesn't look good."

"He spent his life trying to get close to his brother, he would have done anything. This is so fucking rotten, Wen."

"Don't let him give that baby this medicine."

"Oh," Janelle agreed, "don't worry about that."

Over the next day Shane seemed to withdraw completely. He even turned down an invitation from Prajuk for a Chinatown lunch. Janelle knew Shane was not used to depending on other people's permission to move forward. This had served him well in his youth; now it threatened to undo him.

He waited a week. On Friday, he called Wenceslas and attempted to communicate his agony.

"I'm at the point," Shane informed him, "where I'm going to give her the shot and let you call the cops."

"Okay. I'll come by tomorrow morning. We'll talk then."

Somehow he made it through the day. In the morning, Shane went downstairs, made coffee, and sat stubbornly by the front door. Around ten, when Janelle and June were taking the babies for a walk, Wenceslas knocked on the door. He wore stiff dark jeans and a blue sweater, and thicker eyeglasses than was his wont.

"Come have a coffee," Shane told him.

They sat at the small wooden kitchen table, among chewed-up sippy cups, a parenting magazine, and a set of enormous plastic teething keys, while Shane prepared a press.

"So, I've spoken with Doctor Acharn three times," Wenceslas began. "He said he asked you to lunch?"

Shane said nothing.

"I've read the Airifan trials. They ran them on asthmatic children as young as six months old. In twelve- to twenty-four-month olds, there was a one point three percent incidence of liver damage. I have to say those are much better odds than a one-year-old child with alpha-one antitrypsin deficiency has."

Shane watched him blankly. "So you're going to call DCFS? The police? Just wondering who I can expect at my door? Because I'm giving her this medicine. I listen to her breathing all day and all night. I know why Caleb was desperate."

Wenceslas removed his glasses and rubbed his eyes with the backs of his hands. "I understand why you pursued this, Shane. I'm satisfied, with conditions."

Shane sat forward. "What conditions?"

"I need to be here when she gets it. I need to monitor Lily daily for a week. I'm not a pediatrician. Once we see if this is working, we'll need to find someone sympathetic."

"Of course. Thank you, Wen."

"I can be here the rest of today."

"Today?"

"In fact," Wenceslas cocked his head, "now would be good."

"But June and Janelle are out with . . ."

"You never hesitated this much pushing that Epherex shit on me."

Shane pursed his lips, went to the refrigerator, and

returned with a small opaque glass vial. Inside of it was Lily's life, he thought, or nothing at all.

When they returned from their walk, Janelle put Nicholas upstairs, and June set Lily on the rug among the toys. She joined them around the dark dining room table. The room's cream walls seemed to promise tenderness. There was only complete silence, save for the wheeze coming from Lily. June was the only one who had no idea what was about to happen.

"It's time," Shane told her evenly, "to talk about why you all went through all of this." He placed the small vial on the table. "This is a drug that a very famous biochemist developed for alpha-one antitrypsin deficiency."

Wenceslas told her. "I've looked at their data, I've spoken with experts in your daughter's condition. And I agree this is a treatment worth trying. I'm here to monitor everything."

June was nodding. "Mack said it would be toxic."

"It's not a pharmaceutical drug," Shane explained. "It's natural. It comes from the body. There's nothing artificial in here. It may not work, okay? It may not. But it's not toxic."

He leaned in closer. "But something could still happen. Lily could have some kind of allergic response. We've never tested this exact drug on a baby. Her liver could react in some unforeseen way to the protein, and liver damage is not reversible. We estimate a one point eight percent chance of a problem."

June had gone paler than he had ever seen her. She stared at the vial between his thumb and ring finger. "The doctor told me she only has a small chance of living past three years old," she nodded, almost to herself.

"That is the current statistic," Wenceslas agreed quietly. He passed her the vial, and she handled it nervously.

"How long does it take to work?"

"We don't know," Shane told her. "A week, a year? It took around a day in our mouse."

"Can I see the mouse?"

"Sure. You guys should have it, actually."

"If something happens to the mouse, we'll know to call you."

"His name is Thailand."

"Tell me what happens if . . ." June trailed off, looked down at Lily and hugged her close. Her voice broke a bit. "If something goes wrong."

"We'll get her right to the ER," Wenceslas answered. "I'll bring the rest of the vials, and we'll tell them everything."

"Can they just give the drug to her there, in the ER?"

Wenceslas shook his head and gave her a small, resigned smile. "We can't walk into a hospital with a vial of a home-made biotechnology drug developed in an unlicensed lab and ask them to help us inject it into a child. Should we stop?"

"And do what?" June gestured to her daughter. "She's dying. She's dying."

Wenceslas nodded. "I think she is."

"Caleb knew it. That's why he needed to bring her to you. He gave everything for this."

Shane laid his open hand onto the table. "Caleb can't be the reason you do this." He squinted, looking as deeply into her eyes as he could. "This can't be a memorial to him. It has to be because you believe it's right for Lily. You're her mom. It's your call. Not ours. Not his."

Shane turned to Janelle. He knew she was struggling, wanting to tell them all not to do it. But by the set of her jaw, he saw that she would defer, as they all would, to June.

Shane went to the bathroom and returned with a paper

bag. He placed a box of alcohol wipes and an Elmo Band-Aid onto the coffee table. Janelle and Wenceslas watched as he arranged them like sacrament. Outside a family ran laughing past their bay window.

Shane held out a packaged syringe to June. "Do you know how to use one of these?"

"I sure don't."

Wenceslas explained, "Better learn now. If this works, you'll need to do this every six months. You clean the side of her belly with rubbing alcohol. Let it dry. Pinch her fat between your fingers, three inches from her belly button. Very easy. Push the needle in straight. And press. When you remove it, push the plunger and it will click shut. I'll write Shane a prescription for the syringes."

June lifted Lily onto the table, facing her. She raised her yellow play shirt and touched her warm, thin stomach. June looked shaky. She's not going to make it, Shane saw.

"I love you, baby girl," June whispered into her ear.

Lily seemed to sense something then and squirmed away. June opened the wipe. The antiseptic smell reminded Shane of imminent pain. And then she took up the syringe, pushed it into the top of the vial, and pulled the plunger up, sucking in the opaque liquid of Prajuk's genius.

Her hand hovered over her baby. Tears began to roll along her cheeks. Nobody moved.

Janelle whispered. "This is enough for now."

And June pushed it through.

Lily frowned, and then tears burst from her betrayed eyes, and she howled. June withdrew the needle, laid it on the table beside the discarded wipe, and it was done.

Instantly a trembling began in Shane's fingers. It moved up his arms, as if he were suffering the physical reaction they all half-expected in Lily. He moved his hands to his lap so that no one would see. Wenceslas was looking at him. Then Janelle. He could not control it as it moved to his shoulders. Oh, Jesus, he screamed inside his head, what had he just done? He stood and walked into the kitchen.

Janelle followed him. "What?" she asked angrily.

He could not reply. He stared out the back window onto the alley. It took everything he had to remain upright.

"You can't," she frowned, "be thinking this *now*."

Shane shook his head back and forth.

"If you had any doubt, you should never have let her do it."

"I don't," he replied far too weakly.

Fed up, Janelle went back to the living room. He could hear them talking with voices reserved for waiting rooms. A hot flush burrowed its way into his temples. His chest tightened. He grabbed the countertop, squeezed, pulled deep breaths. It was not enough. A cool tingling shot down his left arm.

He waited to hear the screaming from the other room when the bruising of Lily's soft stomach appeared, and turned a wretched black. When her eyes began to yellow. When her body began to convulse.

Shane searched out some neutral object, the toaster, the window. Anything to focus on. It was no good; every nerve in his world tensed. Taking breaths became harder. He thought he might pass out.

The window of time Prajuk had set for a toxic reaction was twenty-four hours after injection. Shane could not fathom surviving this amount of time. Twenty-three and a half hours? How would he get through the next two seconds? The knowledge that Caleb had walked into his house and never come back, and that the same thing could happen to this baby and that it was too late to do anything at all about it enveloped and demolished him.

Sweating, he went upstairs and took Nicholas from his crib. The boy was asleep, and hot against him. Shane sat in the rocking chair and was looking at him, searching for Caleb in the bones of his face, when June came in.

"I'm wondering," she said quietly, "if we could stay here for a while."

Shane blinked.

"I mean, we could go back to Taos. Her dad's there, we know people there. Or maybe Arizona, maybe my parents can help me with her. But for now, just for a few weeks, I want her to be near Doctor Chin. And you guys." She hesitated. "Is that okay?"

He shuddered and looked up at her. "Of course. How is she?"

"A little feverish. Fussy."

"If it doesn't work, I'm sorry."

"You don't need to be."

"I'm sorry even if it does." He started searching around the room, his voice breaking, and June took his hand. "If I hadn't done this, if I hadn't . . ."

"Look, Shane, if you hadn't done this, Caleb would have learned about some doctor in New York, or Miami, and he would have taken her to them. He would have run there too."

She reached down and stroked Nicholas's fine black hair.

Softly she said, "Sometimes when I'm watching Lily play?

I feel like I'm not really there. I see how alive she is apart from me, without me, and I can feel myself slipping away. I can see her moving forward on her own. Sometimes I wonder if I died some time ago, and I'm observing her. If I'm a ghost." She looked up to Shane. "Is that kind of strange?"

"Maybe that's a little strange."

"You don't feel that way with your son?"

"No. I feel connected to him every second."

"Okay, well, keep it a secret."

Shane became quiet. Because he had his own secret. It might be time to tell it.

Everyone believed that he had the idea to help Lily. That he had persuaded Prajuk, emptied his savings, rented the lab, and produced this drug due to some notion of his own.

But actually, none of it had been his idea.

When Shane had returned from Boulder, he knew, he had been overwhelmed by the impending birth of his son, the start of his new job, and he had not done very much for Lily at all. Forget charging off to rent any private labs; he had not so much as found a specialist. Left to himself, he would have told Caleb that there was nothing in test for this condition, sent him some printouts from the Web, and focused on his new family.

And he would not have heard from Caleb again.

But instead, Nicholas had arrived. Nicholas had come and opened his sticky newborn eyes, and he had understood fragility and holiness.

Nicholas had shown him what to do. And kept him on his course. Producing this drug had not been the finest act of Shane's life; it had been the first of Nicholas's.

He stood and smiled at June, and they went downstairs. Beneath his feet the old house creaked with a future history.

Things would happen in this hall, in these rooms, which would define the rest of his life.

As soon as he walked back into the living room he felt something different in the air and froze. The energy had changed completely. Wenceslas and Janelle were staring at him, mouths open. He fought an urge to turn and run. He shot his eyes down to the floor.

Lily was sitting up, her head bent over one of Nicholas's foam blocks, clasping it between her hands. There was no sound save the passing of cars in the dusk.

There was no other sound in the room at all.

Somewhere over the Pacific a breeze shifted, waves hurried forth, and the smell of fresh water washed over the world.

Author's Note

Alpha-one antitrypsin deficiency is a real genetic condition. The descriptions of its symptoms, treatment, and mechanisms in this novel are neither expert nor entirely accurate. I have needed to simplify the disease both for readers and out of my own very finite grasp of it. Any errors here are mine entirely.

The Alpha-1 Association is a wonderful group of people dedicated to helping the newly diagnosed, advocating for patients, and fundraising for research. Please go to their website to learn more: www.alpha1.org.

Acknowledgments

Thank you, Rachel Vogel. You rock. As an agent, reader, and editor. You made this all happen, and made it all better. I'll never forget the moment I got your e-mail about this manuscript.

Thank you, Denise Roy, for being so collaborative, enthusiastic, and encouraging. And for being so patient with me. I appreciate everything you've done, including things I don't even know about. Thank you for taking a chance on my work. And for all you did to improve it.

Thanks to Kate Napolitano, Phil Budnick, John Fagan, Liz Keenan, Katie Hurley, Ashley Pattison McClay, and Catherine Hayden at Penguin, for all of your work on the publication of this book.

Thank you to the Backspace Conference, and everyone I met during that weekend. I will always remember the enthusiasm and momentum it gave me.

Thanks to the Metra Union Pacific Line for creating Quiet Cars.

Thank you to the doctors, nurses, and staff at Northwestern Memorial Hospital.

Thanks to all of my work partners and creative directors, who taught me to take critique and revise, skills that made this book possible.

Thank you, Brian Eno, Harold Budd, Explosions in the Sky, Bon Iver, Radiohead, Steve Reich, and Boards of Canada—this book was written to your work.

Thanks to Pete Figel, who first told me about the world of running cults, and to an assistant Brand Manager at Genentech, who first explained to me how biotechnology companies make decisions.

I am indebted to these books: *Building Biotechnology* by Yali Friedman, *From Alchemy to IPO* by Cynthia Robbins-Roth, and *Running Through the Wall* by Neal Jamison. Anyone interested in the subjects in this novel should check these out.

Thanks to all of the early readers, any of whom could have stopped this book in its tracks by informing me they hated it: Joel Jacobson, who suggested the changes that made the story work. Matt and Susan Skelly. Leah Fietsam. Catherine Driscoll, Julie Stevenson, Robin McAfee, Briana Danielson, and the rest of the Lake Forest and Boston book clubs who sacrificed a good erotic vampire book to read an unpublished manuscript.

To Madeleine and Alan Ferris, for their constant support.

To my dad, Ron, who would have loved this. My sister Samantha for her love. To Bronia, Jack, Sylvia, and Harry.

To Greg Ferris, the bravest, boldest man on earth. You know something about ultramarathons and medicine.

To my mom, Wendy, an incredible role model, who instilled a love of reading and writing into me. Thank you for encouraging me from the day I was born.

And to Kerri, my beautiful and talented wife. Thank you for giving me all of those hours to go work on this. And for giving me the greatest answer of my life. Which was, of course, yes.